SACRIFICED TO THE SEA LORD

LORDS OF ATLANTIS

STARLA NIGHT

❋ Created with Vellum

SPECIAL THANKS

to Kara Lockharte, Rosalie Redd, and Anne Brentwood for
diving in. You are amazing.

CHAPTER ONE

Elyssa snuck into the auditorium through an unguarded side door.

Clothes racks hid her entrance. Production assistants chatted into headsets as they crossed the dim, scratched wooden floor. Beyond them, purple velvet curtains showed sneak peeks to moving TV cameras, blinding stage lights, and a flurry of gorgeous women in stunning ball gowns.

She was firmly backstage at the Van Cartier Cosmetics Mermaid Queen Selection Pageant.

Hooray!

Elyssa let out a sigh as the door eased closed behind her. She didn't know the auditorium well because she wasn't exactly a Van Cartier Cosmetics superstar. Her daily work was filing and making phone calls in Human Resources. Occasionally, she passed out fliers and conducted internship interviews at college recruitment fairs.

Approximately three months ago, she adventurously invested her entire savings into an ex-employee's expedition to retrieve Sea Opals, a mystical gem with healing properties. The expedition had turned up not only Sea Opals but also the shocking revelation of merman societies that cultivated the gems.

The all-male warriors normally traded the gems to women they called "brides" on secret, sacred islands. The brides became mermaids, lived under the ocean to bear a son, and then returned to the surface alone. In modern times, rising ocean levels and mainland conveniences had emptied the sacred islands and left the mermen with dangerously dwindling populations.

Despite the mounting pressure, most mermen tried to pretend the reveal hadn't happened. Openly hanging out with humans went against a thousand years of secrecy and rules. The mermen and their cities remained hidden on the bottom of the ocean.

If the leader of that first expedition, Lucy, hadn't married and started living with her merman husband Torun in Newport, Oregon, skeptics might have dismissed the whole thing as a hoax.

One city finally answered Van Cartier Cosmetics' underwater broadcasts. Today, after talks and negotiations, five mermen from the city excitingly named "Atlantis" had come to Van Cartier Cosmetics. Their king, Kadir, was here to select a woman to transform into his mermaid queen.

Elyssa had been disinvited from attending by her aunt, CEO Chastity Angel.

Unfair as it was, Elyssa understood. She was kind of, maybe, sort-of accident-prone, and mermen were offended by casual touch. They would only touch the woman who was their bride. Lucy's husband Torun was extremely careful whenever he was in public, although he'd relaxed quite a bit since their first meeting. The newly risen king of Atlantis probably wouldn't be so well acclimated. Elyssa craved to meet more mermen, but the last thing she wanted to do was fall on top of one and cause an inter-species incident.

She had been resigned to staying home until yesterday at midnight, when Elyssa's cousin, vice president Aya, had begged Elyssa to come.

"I need you. It's critical," Aya said over the phone. Her voice was scratchy from the sleepless nights and hours she'd put into the pageant. "My mother can't know about this. You're the only one I can trust."

Elyssa's heart shot into her throat. "Me?"

"You." Aya spoke the words Elyssa longed to hear. "This is something only you can do."

The mermen would be in the audience, Aya promised. Elyssa couldn't possibly cause any incidents. And only Elyssa could do the secret thing Aya needed.

Well, Elyssa wanted to help more than anything. This was the first official merman-human meeting, and hopefully, it wouldn't be the last. Someday, when their races were fully integrated and visiting Atlantis was as easy as flying to France, she planned to petition the mer to let her visit.

She took a few steps toward the stage.

Was Aya still posing in the shimmering red gown Elyssa had helped her pick out, along with all the other gorgeous, talented contestants? They had planned to flip the traditional "beauty pageant" format — evening gowns first, then swimsuits — and exchange the talent section with an actual swimming demonstration in a swim tank on stage. Elyssa had had trouble getting past security even with all of her company passes, so she was later than she'd meant to be. Were the gowns she'd glimpsed on the contestants or the charismatic emcees? What part of the program had she arrived during?

In between curtains, silhouetted by the blinding hot lights, two males blocked her view.

Or, she should say, they filled her view. In jeans and black trench coats, they were tall, broad, and built. And tattooed, too. Were they rock stars? A pageant like this was certain to be attended by celebrities.

One was beefy like a pro wrestler.

The other was thinner and definitely had the lead singer vibe. His muscles stood out in sharp relief. A young quarterback who drew everyone's eye, or a star soccer player focusing on the winning kick.

Was he looking at her?

Crew members walked between them. She stepped out from behind the clothing racks. The beefy one spoke with a production assistant and moved onto the stage, disappearing behind the curtain.

The lead singer remained. He was definitely looking at her.

She stopped.

He turned and strode toward her.

Jeans hung low on his hips and his black trench coat flared, exposing a hard expanse of mouth-watering muscle. He was bare-chested. Silver tattoos slashed his torso in an intricate lightning-strike design.

He was intense. David Beckham-focusing-on-a-soccer ball intense. He must be a model. A movie star. Charisma oozed from his pores.

He was coming right at her.

Oh! She was in his way. Duh.

She stepped aside and stumbled into a young, clean-cut producer.

The producer's coffee sloshed on his black turtleneck. "Hey!"

"Oh my god, I'm so sorry!" She backed away, hands up.

"Watch it." The producer squinted at Elyssa. A back-stage staff pass hung from the producer's neck, but not from hers. "What are you doing back here?"

Crud. Elyssa didn't think about the pass. She backed over a thick cord. "Nothing. I'm just—"

Her sandals slipped.

She stumbled and fought for balance. Cord, cord, another cord, ah! She landed on bare wood and caught her balance. Whew.

The producer was still looking at her suspiciously. An assistant ran up and provided a distraction.

Thank god. Elyssa straightened her loose peasant blouse and lifted her purse higher on her shoulder.

The lead singer was still bearing down on her.

Huh? She'd gotten out of his way. Oh, maybe he needed to tell her something. She turned to face him.

Her sandal string snapped.

Her foot lifted but her sandal caught on another cord. Aaah! She fell forward, hands out to brace—

— into his arms.

His strong forearm crossed her midsection. His bicep bulged into her ribs. Pure waves of masculinity flowed over her.

Her heart slammed into her chest. She gasped and tried to push free. Her hands slipped and she stumbled harder against him. "I'm so sor—"

"Wait."

She obeyed.

He held her still and steady.

"I'm really very—"

"Calm."

His deep voice rumbled with command. Here was a

male who rippled with confidence. What was so she worried about? Panic faded. *Breathe in, breathe out, breathe in.* Her heart calmed.

The shaking started.

Still, he held her.

His scent was smoky like expensive leather and cognac, and also soothing, like vanilla candles, long baths, and sensuous massages. A sliver of awareness curled in her center. Was he wearing Axe? A movie star brand not available to the public?

And Elyssa was just hanging out in his arms.

Calmer now, she gently extricated herself and looked up into the face of the man she had fallen on top of.

His profile was cut with high cheekbones and a noble chin. His eyes were dark but flecked with the same silver as his tattoos. Unusual and compelling.

His intense focus on her never wavered. He was waiting for something.

Oh! He had caught her. Of course he was waiting to be thanked.

"Thank you." She sucked in a deep breath. "Like I was saying, I am so—"

"Come with me."

If voices were like food, his would be seductive as dark chocolate and rich as cream. She could just eat that up and lick her fingers afterward.

Wait. What?

She reacted about two seconds late. "I'm sorry?"

"Now." He took her hand and pulled her toward the stage.

She resisted. "I'm sorry. I know I'm not supposed to be back here, but I'm waiting for—"

Her broken sandal folded. She tripped and grabbed onto his arm. He stopped.

His bicep was so hard. She couldn't help squeezing it. He must bench press city busses.

He tipped his head to the side to stare down at her. "Are you unable to walk?"

"No, I can. Sorry." She straightened and unfastened the chunky white ankle strap. The toe part was broken. She really should have worn tennis shoes. "My strap broke."

"Ah." He turned and bent until his shoulder was level to her middle.

Oh. Had she dropped something?

His forearm snaked around the back of her knees. She crumpled against him. He tilted and lifted. Her butt flew up in the air and she hung off him on both sides like a limp piece of laundry.

"Hey! Wait!" She struggled. Her purse slid down her arm. She fumbled for it. "Just hold on. Whew."

He strode through the curtains onto the center of the stage. The dazzling, bikini-clad bride contestants stared up at her in shock. The TV crews, all pointed at a big water-filled swimming tank, swung to follow her.

Lights blinded her about the same time the truth did.

He was the merman king. And she was causing a human-merman incident.

Right now.

King Kadir bumped down the stage steps, through the surprised audience, and up the aisle into a private boxed wing.

Three powerful mermen rose to greet him.

"We are leaving now," he said.

Oh god. He was so offended by her touch he was leaving the pageant. The contract was off, humans and mer would never live in harmony, and all of Aya's hard work was in vain. Elyssa struggled.

"Yes, my king. Soren is in the tank."

She dropped her purse and sandals. Blood rushed to her head. Her legs were squeezed immobile by his impossible strength. "Wait. Please. Wait."

"You carry this woman. What is the problem?"

"She broke her footwear."

"Ah."

Another spoke. "My king, I believe she wants down."

"Yes!" Elyssa gasped. "Thank you. Please put me down."

He set her down and released her.

Okay. Whew. Her heart was still racing. She was all sweaty and out of breath. She was off-balance with one sandal and one bare foot on the cool tile.

Four hard-bodied, dangerously tattooed, dominant warriors stared down at her.

"Um..." She unpeeled her thin, sweat-stuck paisley blouse from her belly and flapped it. Her hair was probably a complete mess. "I'm very sorry for grabbing onto you. Twice. Please don't leave."

The warriors looked at King Kadir.

He jutted his chin. "My warriors need me in Atlantis."

"Yes, but the pageant is all for you. There's only a little left. We worked so hard on it. Please?"

He focused on her. It felt like he saw through her body to her very soul. "You worked hard?"

"Aya did. Please." She patted the plush gold cushion. Maybe this could be salvaged! "Sit for Aya?"

He looked at his warriors, then at the stage. "To you, Aya is...?"

"Like a sister to me. She's been working so hard. It would mean so much to us. Please?"

His mouth twisted to a corner. He nodded to his warriors and folded his large body into the auditorium seating with easy command. His shoulders strained the trench coat, and his leg muscles defined the jeans. His warriors sat in the row behind him.

Oh. Thank god.

"Well." She slid her bare foot behind her sandaled foot and eased backward. "I'd better let you get back to—"

He caught her wrist and pulled. "You sit here."

She thumped into the seat next to him. "Sorry. Okay. Thank you, King Kadir."

The reality TV cameras rolled from discreet angles. Production crew spoke into headsets. The other guests — celebrities and dignitaries — craned their necks to see into the private box.

Her in the hot seat was better than the mermen leaving empty seats. But it was still nerve-wracking.

Don't cause any more incidents. Rest your hands in your lap. Don't accidentally touch him.

Hey. Was that a piece of Captain Crunch cereal stuck to her capris? She picked at the bit. Yes, it was cereal. Weird. She hadn't dumped her breakfast on herself *this* morning. How long had it been...

According to her dad, she wasn't clumsy, exactly. Her head was just always in the clouds. The rest of her body self-piloted and she ended up in places she was never meant to be.

In comparison, Aya was perfect. Regal. Composed. Where Elyssa was a court jester, Aya was definitely the queen.

Now, she was down on the stage, in her sharp red bikini in the giant tank, swimming with the beefy merman.

The pageant was continuing despite Elyssa's interruption. Other contestants modeled swimwear while the loudspeakers described each woman's pre-written statement for why they wanted to become the mermaid queen. The statements were all noble, like how many lives could be saved with Sea Opals and how they would personally connect the races in peace.

The swimming demonstration was partly a test of swimming ability and partly to show that the contestants were not afraid.

Afraid, a person might ask? Why would anyone be afraid?

These were not your mama's mermen.

First, the mermen had two powerful kicking legs, just like humans. Second, they were all built like power lifters. Third, they were gorgeous, tattooed, and usually swam around naked. And fourth, there was this whole kidnapping-women-to-make-babies rumor in the ancient past. They were the original creatures from the black lagoon, only gorgeous instead of "finny."

Unnamed sources claimed the kidnappings still happened today.

The beefy merman in the glass tank kept his jeans on, which was pretty rare. Lucy had reported that the mermen of Torun's city swam buck naked. No bubbles emerged from where he floated near the bottom of the tank. His feet stretched so they were unnaturally long, curved, and graceful. From this distance, it looked as if he was wearing a pair of extra large, black-swirled scuba fins.

Aya dove below the surface and kicked smoothly, keeping her arms close to her body. The beefy merman tilted his head to look up at her. She held his gaze underwater, fearless.

Mermen swam like streamlined scuba divers, so Aya had practiced her form when Lucy and Torun visited a week ago. She was totally focused in the water. That was why she hadn't noticed Elyssa's entrance. Tall, toned, and graceful, Aya was never flustered or out of breath.

She just had to win the pageant. Only Aya could bring the races together and establish long-lasting peace. Elyssa would make sure King Kadir saw it.

King Kadir put his forearm on the armrest and leaned against Elyssa's shoulder.

Was it okay for him to touch her so much? Maybe, since she had already forced him to catch her backstage, he forgave the offense and relaxed the taboo.

His scent wafted over her again. She closed her eyes. Could she get it bottled? It would be called *hard, steamy fantasies* and she'd rub it all over—

"You are?"

Her eyes snapped open. He was holding out his wide, silver-tattooed hand.

Oops. She was being rude. She shook his hand. "Elyssa Van Cartier."

Her hand disappeared in his firm grip. His skin was dry and warm. Calluses roughened his palms. He felt human. Hard and bony and male.

"Elyssa of Van Cartier," he repeated. Slow and formal.

"You can just call me Elyssa. Your majesty. Sir. King Kadir."

"And you will call me only Kadir."

He seemed in no hurry to release her hand. His was just a powerhouse of strength. Her heart went *thump thump thump.*

Imagine those wide palms sliding across her body, squeezing her swelling breasts while he unveiled his hard cock. Desire curled in her belly and throbbed lower. She squeezed her thighs together.

He leaned closer.

Could Kadir sense her completely inappropriate desires? She pulled her hand away and quickly turned to his warriors. They were thickly bodied, like professional wrestlers or Maori warriors, while Kadir alone had an eye-captivating, lanky strength.

And they were all staring at her.

Again? Still? Uh, no matter. *Don't be rude!* She stuck her hand out. "Elyssa."

The closest one responded instantly with a handshake. He was older with clear, thoughtful eyes and lighter, timberwolf gray tattoos. "Lotar."

In the middle, Iyen was her age or younger. Deep maroon tattoos covered part of his well-muscled torso. His sharp gaze held hers for the moment he shook her hand, and then he returned to scanning the auditorium. He was like a secret agent, ever watchful, ready for danger.

The third merman, Ciran, had sandy brown hair and two-tone tattoos in coffee brown and leaf green. He straightened, jutted his hand precisely, and shook twice. And, he added, with a carefully clipped tone like a professor, "Pleased to make your acquaintance."

Aw. How sweet. "Pleased to meet you, too."

Actually, she really was pleased. She was sitting with four mermen! All of her fantasies came true in an explosion of rainbow confetti. She beamed.

The mermen blinked rapidly as though she was shining a flashlight in their eyes.

Kadir captured her hands. "Elyssa. You are my contestant choice."

Contestant choice? For what? She quickly corrected him. "Oh, I'm not a contestant."

He tilted his head.

She gestured at the stage with her elbow since her hands were secured in his grip. "Those are the contestants. They're all NASA scientists and Mt. Everest climbers. I've never done anything important."

And — reality check! — one of them would become his queen and rule Atlantis. Hopefully. Unless she screwed it up.

Don't think about his warm palm caressing hers, and how very much she'd love it to keep stroking her higher up her arm and then curve around her back and press her to him.

Focus.

"You are not a contestant?" he repeated.

"Yes. Nope. Sorry." She tried to tug her hands free. "The best contestant, in my opinion, is Aya."

"She is bright." Kadir started to release her. Then, just when she thought she was free, his fingers slid between hers, locking her into a deeper, more sensuous connection that made her heart throb. "But she is not the best."

Uh oh.

"Yes. Yes, she is! Aya's a born ruler. You can't go wrong with her."

He slid his wide thumb over the back of her hand in sensuous circles.

New delicious feelings curled in her belly. She babbled. "You can't tell from a distance. Maybe I should go get her. One conversation and her great qualities will shine through."

He paused and looked back at his warriors as though she had said something significant. "Humans cannot see great qualities from a distance?"

"Well, some great qualities are obvious. But, uh, some aren't. That's why you should get to know her in the normal way. Not in this distant, hard-to-get-to-know-you pageant."

Ciran shifted forward. "This pageant is not normal? You do not always initiate relationships by standing a hundred women in a line, changing dresses, and standing them in another line to select your mate?"

"Not usually. I mean, you could, but it's not the normal way at all."

Ciran and Kadir exchanged looks.

"What is the normal way?" Ciran asked.

"A date. Or, if you're meeting each other for the first time, a blind date."

Kadir took over, recapturing her gaze. "What is a blind date?"

"You meet up for something casual. Coffee or a movie. If you hit it off, you meet up again. And so on."

"Hit it off? What do you hit off?"

"Your feelings. If you get a special feeling in your heart." She tugged her hand free to place it on her chest. "You're meant to be together. It's fate."

In Kadir's case, her special feeling was also several inches lower, making her panties damp.

He had that deliciously unreachable rock star vibe. The hot, smart, talented athlete who breezed through the halls, making her wish that she were smarter and hotter and more talented so someday he would glance in her direction.

Now that he was actually glancing — more than that, he was holding one of her hands! — she wanted this moment to go on forever. The one moment she did something useful.

Entertained a gorgeous monarch, educated him about human dating, and helped him to find the one perfect woman who would make love grow in his heart.

"So you do sense the resonance," Kadir confirmed.

By "resonance," did he mean an inner glow? Torun had told her that mermen could see actual lights glowing in people's chests.

"We don't see it the same way you do, but I do think we can sense *something* when we hit it off. Love at first sight, or second sight, or tenth sight, or whatever."

He recaptured her free hand. "My warriors wish to blind date."

The mermen nodded.

"I'm sure you will." She smiled at him. At all of them. "You definitely all will."

They stared at her.

And although they were all mesmerizingly good looking, Kadir's gaze gripped her with such power she was unable to fully look away. She wanted to crawl into his lap and lick that silver lightning bolt across his broad chest. His intense concentration on her increased. He seemed to see straight into her soul.

But he was not for her. Maybe she could hit it off with a hot lieutenant. Or something. Did the mermen have low-paid jobs? In merman HR?

"The best way to meet women is to choose Aya for your bride," Elyssa said.

"You fiercely champion your cousin. That loyalty is admirable. But I will not choose Aya for my bride."

"But—"

"Because, Elyssa of Van Cartier." He arrested her with his dark gaze. "I choose you."

CHAPTER TWO

The luscious, enticing, brilliant woman sitting beside Kadir listened to his command for the second time with complete shock.

Had he used incorrect words? His English had atrophied in the jail, locked away from all interaction in solitary isolation, and he had labored to catch up with his studies on the journey to the shore.

If she did not understand his words, it was time to take more decisive action.

He shifted forward to claim her lips with his kiss.

Her lashes fluttered wide. She held up their joined hands to stop him. "Me?"

"You." He pressed kisses to her slender fingers. The chunky jewels that adorned them. "Are mine."

She took a deep breath. Her chest swelled beneath the thin shirt. Her soul light shone in her chest brighter than a volcano, brighter than a sun. Brighter than any other female in the pageant. Brighter, even, than the female known as Aya.

A distant chime, like the holy music of the Life Tree, tinkled across his consciousness.

Elyssa was *his queen*. The queen Atlantis needed. Destined to unite his warriors, crush the city's enemies, and lead their race to peace.

Then, her soul light fell dark. Shocking, like snuffing out all hope. "You don't mean me."

Hmm. How could he select a woman whose soul light fell so dark? But he had. And if his survival up to now had taught him anything, it was to trust his gut and act without hesitation.

"I do."

"But I'm not even a contestant."

"That is not my concern. You will join with me and carry my young fry."

"That's just not possible."

Behind him, the other warriors shifted in shock. They had also expected him to select Aya.

Kadir had spent the past several hours at this pageant debating women with his fellow warriors. Who best embodied the traits of their long-lost queens? It was a mystery.

A thousand years ago, a great catastrophe destroyed mer-human relations and drove mermen deep into the oceans. Mermaid queens, who were once as plentiful in cities as mer warriors, died out. Now, only sons were born.

The thousand-year-old covenant with the sacred islands saved his race from extinction. The islanders promised not to hunt the mermen or speak of their existence. They sent one bride every year to join with a worthy warrior in exchange for a mating jewel, which modern humans called Sea Opals.

When the sacred islands had been numerous across the

oceans, many young fry sons had been born every year in each city, and the mer had maintained their populations. They had not prospered, but they had survived. But now, many sacred islands were empty. Some cities received only one bride a year. Some had received no brides for a decade.

Hiding in the ocean and clinging to the old covenant was killing them. They had to seek modern women for brides. Now.

His treasonous vision had incited riots in the cities and landed him in the prison of the great, ruling All-Council. But it had also convinced a warlord to break his city's covenant and marry a modern woman. After the existence of mermen was revealed to all, a small army of warriors rebelled from their home cities and freed Kadir.

Kadir's Life Tree seed was planted in the shadow of the wrecked mer-human city of ancient times, Atlantis. His seed grew into a sapling, founding their new city and crowning him king.

Someday, they would raise the ancient city again. Mer and humans would mingle freely at the surface. Queens would once more flourish beneath the waves, and their race would thrive.

Starting today. His final vision was about to come true.

Their arrival at the crowded South Miami beach according to the instructions of the underwater broadcast had been nothing short of world shattering. Because fewer than one sacred island bride arrived in most of their cities every year, neither Kadir nor his warriors realized so many women *existed*. And a hundred were gathered in one auditorium to compete to become his queen? It was difficult to grasp.

The pageant's selection process was also difficult. In the past, the sacred islands provided one bride and the merman city elders pre-selected the worthiest warrior to receive her. It was all decided long before the participants ever met.

Here, Kadir was supposed to meet everyone and choose by himself. On their arrival at the auditorium, the organizer of the pageant, bright bride Aya, had explained.

"Written statements of the hundred contestants' skills and qualifications will be read while they model evening gowns. You will select the top twenty-five to change into swimsuits for a second round, and then narrow it to nine who will perform a swimming demonstration. From that, you select a final three and then choose your bride. Does this sound acceptable?"

"No," he said.

She blinked in shock. "No?"

"Show me all your brides now. I will select the one who is most resonant."

Her shapely brows had drawn into a frown. "Without knowing anything about their qualifications? Or goals? Or—"

"Only resonance is necessary."

So, with a nervous glance at the television cameras recording their conversation, she had led him down to the stage. He had met all the brides. Despite the unfathomable abundance of females, not one had filled him with certainty that she was most resonant. In the end, he had acquiesced to bride Aya's original plan and forced his warriors to select the brightest twenty-five, then the brightest nine.

Perhaps the problem was his health. He was still in a poor shape to take a bride. The humans must have noticed his thin arms, atrophied legs, and sunken chest. Were they counting the rib marks from his near starvation, or noting the scars of the beatings marring his tattoos? Nevertheless, they offered themselves to him as if they didn't see his weakness. It was very strange.

Many of these hundred contestants would make fine queens, but which was best for *his* queen? His queen must be confident. Radiant. She must shine her inner light and uplift all who looked upon her.

The instant he saw this Elyssa cowering behind the purple curtain, he knew. Finally. *She was the one.*

If Soren hadn't been swimming in the tank, Kadir could have simply carried Elyssa out of the pageant to the waiting vehicles. She would have understood her situation on her way back to Atlantis.

She was *his*.

But he had to acknowledge his physical state. She might question his ability to care for her. "Is my choice unwelcome?"

"No!" She laughed and shook her head. "No, but I mean, I'm no one. They're amazing." She pointed at the stage. "They're all...uh...they're...."

"Not you."

"No." She bit her lip, teasing him with the desire to bite it also. "I didn't prepare for this. I didn't even attend Lucy's mermaid bride training."

"I, too, did not attend a training." He squeezed her small hand. "We will learn together."

Her smile crept back onto her face. She shook her head as though to chase it away. "Me? As a mermaid queen?" Her light began to shine once more. "Really?"

Now she believed.

He pressed forward to seal their agreement with a kiss.

The lights rose abruptly in their section.

"Excuse me." The leader of Van Cartier Cosmetics, Chastity Angel, strode up the center aisle. She dressed all in cream, and her hair was white. Her face was bloodless like the dead. "Elyssa? Get over here. Right now."

Elyssa stuttered. "Auntie. Uh, I was just, uh...."

Chastity Angel's brow rose.

"Um." Elyssa pulled free and stood. Her soft eyes apologized to Kadir. "I'll be right back." She limped unevenly after Chastity Angel.

They were gone for too long.

Kadir rose.

His warriors rose also.

He followed.

Chastity Angel had corned Elyssa on the other side of their privacy wall. She was speaking in short, hard sentences. "... And on top of all that, you're also interrupting the pageant."

Elyssa hugged her elbows. "I just told you. It was an accident."

"Your 'accidents' have a way of turning into crises."

"Aya—"

"You've done enough to ruin Aya's life today."

Elyssa's light dimmed.

Kadir stepped forward. "Stop."

Elyssa startled.

Chastity Angel jerked up. Her narrow jaw clenched. "King Kadir. Elyssa apologizes for any offense she may have caused. She's leaving now."

The mer were leaving as well. "Good."

Elyssa's cheeks reddened. Her eyes filled with tears.

Did she still wish to watch her cousin? They had stayed as long as possible at her request.

"Return us to the seashore. We leave for Atlantis now."

"Now wait." Chastity Angel's steely eyes took in the

assembled warriors. "King Kadir. I won't allow my step-niece to ruin a mutually beneficial contract."

"She has ruined nothing." He focused on Elyssa. "She will become my queen."

Chastity Angel's eyes flew wide. "That's...well. What I meant to say was, I'm so glad my step-niece could entertain you. But you can't honestly intend to crown a woman who trips over her own feet."

Elyssa flinched.

He growled low in his throat.

"Excuse me." Chastity Angel touched the Sea Opal at her throat. What male had given her this mating jewel? Kadir had heard humans wore them for jewelry rather than utilizing their healing qualities, but the pearly iridescence looked out of place on the dark-souled woman. "Elyssa is a fine person within her abilities. We all know ruling a kingdom is outside them."

Elyssa stared at the floor.

She acted as timid as a young warrior in the old cities. Crushed down by a leader who cursed her. Forced to obey or face deadly consequences.

In Atlantis, Kadir abolished the old ways. Warriors were free to choose their own fates. Who to follow and who to lead. Soon, who to claim and who wished to be claimed.

Behind them, Soren strode up the aisle. Aya was only a few steps behind him.

Aya shone a clean, bright light from her narrow chest. She glowed with determination, and would certainly make a powerful queen. More powerful, perhaps, than Elyssa. Aya was the correct choice based only on the brightness of her soul star.

But Elyssa had a gentle, golden warmth hiding inside her.

Her soft skin had caressed his harder palms, and he wanted to draw her body into his arms and seal their promise with a kiss. Suck her lush, pink lips into his mouth and tease her with little bites, nibbling at her jaw and down her neck to the collar. Palm her small globes while his hard cock found her damp cleft and he surged into her, sharing the physical connection he craved until her soul shone brilliantly once more.

His warriors assembled. They were ready to leave.

"Accept my claim," he ordered Elyssa. If she had been beaten down, like some of his ragged-but-hopeful warriors, then he would teach her freedom once she joined with him in Atlantis. "You are mine."

Elyssa's light flared. She looked up. She would say yes.

Then, she saw Aya.

Aya's determined gaze focused on Elyssa. They seemed to be silently communicating.

Elyssa jerked her gaze away and bit her lip. Her soul dimmed. "Thank you for this opportunity, Kadir. I wanted to meet you more than anything. I'm sorry we got carried away."

Carried away? He should have carried her straight out to the sea without stopping.

Chastity Angel tapped her heel. "The rules of our agreement are simple. One shipment of Sea Opals for the provision and support of one 'bride' from among our contestants. Choose again."

"I will not."

He *felt* Elyssa's desire. If she were unwilling, he would conference with his warriors.

The king always took the first bride. But Kadir's vision *must* come true. They could not leave Miami without a bride. If his rejected him, another warrior must select the first bride. No matter how his warriors protested, this would be another tradition Kadir destroyed if he had to.

Perhaps Elyssa rejected him because he was not fully recovered. The long imprisonment had taken too much of his strength. She did not trust his capabilities.

His jaw clenched.

Whatever the reason, they had wasted too much time. Atlantis was not well defended. Every hour he prolonged the selection process was another hour that his sapling might be attacked or his rebel warriors might be kidnapped and forcefully returned to their home cities. Or, since their own traditions were not well-established, his warriors might fight amongst themselves and tear down the very city they were supposed to build.

He moved to the auditorium doors. "If Elyssa does not join with me as my bride, I return to Atlantis alone."

CHAPTER THREE

H e was leaving? Because he couldn't have her?
Elyssa's mouth fell open in shock.

"Let's not be too hasty." Chastity Angel was
cool and unruffled as Kadir began to storm out the doors.
"You need a bride to populate your city. We've brought
together the most accomplished, talented, and beautiful
contestants for your selection."

Accomplished. Talented. Beautiful.

Each word slammed into Elyssa. Shame made a squishy
lump out of her spine.

Chastity Angel's first words returned to scold her a
second time. *Did you come to this pageant, after I restricted
you, for the sole purpose of ruining Aya's chances?*

No, that was the one thing Elyssa had not come to do.
And yet, she *had* ruined Aya's chances. Messed them up to
the point that if Kadir didn't get Elyssa he was choosing
no one.

Now she could feel the heat of Aya's determined gaze.
She must want to shake Elyssa for turning Kadir down. But
didn't Elyssa have to? He was only "claiming" her because

she'd broken the taboo and fallen on him backstage. Aya was supposed to be his bride. Elyssa should never have gotten this far.

How could she look Aya in the eye? She couldn't.

The beefy one named Soren caught Kadir at the door and spoke near Kadir's ear. "She is not the brightest bride. Others are brighter."

See? Elyssa hugged herself tighter. A stranger could tell just by looking at her that she'd make a dumb ruler. Why couldn't he?

Kadir's eyes narrowed on her. "That is not what I see."

"It is obvious to anyone with eyes."

"Then since you see what is obvious, you claim the first bride."

Soren's mouth dropped. He blinked. An instant later, he snarled. "You are *king*."

"The old ways are dead in Atlantis, Soren. Claim your bride and we will leave."

"Never!"

"Or any of you." Kadir challenged his other warriors. "Choose now and determine our destiny."

They shuffled back, uncomfortable with his challenge.

"Please, noble warriors." Chastity Angel's smile curved. "There are plenty of women. Let's discuss this calmly."

But Kadir wasn't the kind of person to be talked into something. When Soren also lowered his head and growled his refusal, Kadir assumed control once more. "We leave now."

His gaze stabbed Elyssa. Molten hot. She couldn't catch her breath. *Choose.* She couldn't speak.

With a snarl, he turned and shoved the auditorium doors wide. His warriors exited behind him to the lobby.

Chastity Angel's eyes narrowed.

They were leaving. They were really leaving.

Elyssa's heart beat faster and faster. She clenched her hands to her chest. This was for the best. She could never be a queen. She could barely keep up with her filing. It was all for the best.

Aya made a panicked noise, grabbed Elyssa's wrist, and dragged her forward. "What are you doing? You have to say yes. Hurry."

Elyssa stumbled on her single sandal. "But—"

"Mermen are your obsession! Now's your chance."

"Don't bother." Chastity Angel's lips flattened. "He'll be back."

"Or he'll disappear to the bottom of the sea and another company will scoop up those Sea Opals."

"Dispassionate negotiation wins. Watch and learn." Chastity Angel scoffed at them. Her sharp stems clicked on the tile as she followed the mermen into the lobby.

"*You* watch *us* succeed," Aya muttered, near-silent under her breath. "Come on, Elyssa."

"It's fine!" Elyssa dragged her heels. "You catch him. He'll stop for you."

Aya frowned, brought up short by Elyssa's answer, and refocused on her. "I'm sorry this is so sudden. It isn't what I planned, and I was going to talk to you about — well, never mind that. You're not holding back because of me, are you? Are you really not interested in King Kadir?"

"I'm not a contestant."

"Forget about the pageant. Look me in the eye."

She could *not* look her cousin in the eye. "I told him to choose you."

"Don't think about me. Don't think about anyone. Take a deep breath. Think about *you*." Aya's hard, icy demeanor softened. Only in front of Elyssa did she ever crack her tough shell and show her true self. "Please."

Elyssa took a deep breath and held it.

"I'm sorry I wasn't here earlier," Aya said softly, still gripping Elyssa's wrist. Gentle, anxious, serious. "I'm sorry my mom got you all alone."

Elyssa exploded. "No, I'm the sorry one! You were on stage and I—"

"No, no. Focus. I'm sorry I didn't explain why I needed you to come today. *Please* tell me you're not turning this down because of me."

Well, that was one of the reasons. Not the only reason, of course.

Aya pushed on, accepting Elyssa's silence as tacit agreement and fighting it. "Forget me. You're the only one who can do this. He chose you."

"I can't boss anybody."

"King Kadir thinks you're fully capable of becoming his queen. I do also. He'll take you with him if you agree."

But Elyssa didn't agree. She remained silent.

Aya frowned hard. "Do you honestly not want to become a mermaid queen?"

Honestly?

"Oh, no. I'd love to. It's just that I..."

I don't need it. You want to. You're going to do great things. I'll never do anything important. The words died on her lips.

She didn't need to join Kadir as his mermaid queen? She didn't *need* it?

No. Elyssa did need it. She needed it so badly her chest ached. Her whole body did. She'd wanted to be a mermaid since she'd moved to Florida in sixth grade and her new step-cousin Aya invited her to join the Unicorn Mermaid

Girls Club. Her desire had only intensified after discovering mer people existed and she could actually become one. Denying she wanted to join the undersea kingdom would be like denying she needed oxygen.

But no way could she rule over anyone. She couldn't even match her socks.

Face reality. Accept your limitations.

Like Chastity Angel once said, Elyssa would not be doing important things anytime soon.

"I want it," she said firmly. "But I think—"

"You'll do great. Come on!" Aya dragged her into the lobby. "King Kadir, please wait. I have a proposal."

He ignored her.

Event staff, visitors, and cameras crowded around their rock star cool forms. Visible through the glass facade, black SUVs pulled up to the curb. Kadir pushed open the doors to the outside. Moist Florida heat barreled into the lobby.

"Excuse me!" Aya raised her voice. "King Kadir? If you could give us a moment of your time."

He didn't respond.

But that wasn't fair. Aya was trying so hard! How could he ignore her so coldly?

"Hey!" Elyssa called out. "Kadir, wait!"

He stopped and turned. The warriors moved aside, creating a protective aisle for Kadir to face them.

The intensity of his gaze once more stole her breath. In the full light of day, he was all hard muscle and broad height, dangerous power and inflexible steel.

Elyssa's legs went rubbery.

Why did he want her? Aya was better by every possible measure. Her icy blonde hair was slicked back in a wet, but perfect, bun. Her lips were still coated with a perfect layer of waterproof Van Cartier hot red *Checkmate*. She was dripping everywhere but she had a great body to show off in the bikini, and she'd taken the time to fix her matching heels. She was organized, put together, and imperious, and the fact Kadir didn't notice was baffling and unfair.

But Kadir's dark eyes fixed on Elyssa like an arrow pinning her to a target.

"Yes?" he said, putting more into a single syllable than she could put into a hundred sentences.

Behind them, Chastity Angel's disapproval crackled like a storm cloud gathering wrath.

The reality TV crew recorded every word.

Seriously. What was she thinking?

Aya pushed Elyssa forward, brave for the both of them. "Elyssa will sign the paperwork. Then, she'll become a contestant, and you can choose her."

"I do not care about your paperwork."

"You care about your honor. We're not abandoning her to you. The contract places her under our protection, too."

Kadir's eyes narrowed. He turned to Elyssa and set his feet. "Come, Elyssa."

Excitement pulsed through her. Longing entwined with fiery wishes.

This determined the next hours - no, days, no, years - of her life. Did she want it? Did she need it?

Elyssa walked forward.

Kadir's nostrils flared. He captured her hands in his. "Rule Atlantis as my queen."

Her doubts swirled. *I don't know how. I haven't had Lucy's mermaid bride training.* Then, there was his answer. *We will learn together.*

Elyssa squeezed his hands. "I'll try."

"You are mine." He tugged her into his arms and sealed her lips with his.

A thousand pounds of masculine strength embraced her, rock hard and implacable. His firm lips commanded her to lose herself in his embrace.

She gripped his bulging biceps. Her thighs pressed against his rock-hard jeans. Pulsing need pounded into her feminine center.

There was his scent again. Movie star delicious. Hickory and vanilla? His smoky flavor made her crave a deeper taste.

His wide hands cupped her cheeks. His teeth nibbled at her lips. Rivulets of need tingled to her hot center. She opened her lips. He dove into her mouth and branded her with his tongue.

Her body heated.

This was possession. All-consuming possession.

She wanted to climb onto Kadir. Wrap her legs around his taut waist. Lose herself as he plunged into her and rocked her to sweet release.

Their kiss changed everything. Her world shattered. All that was left was Kadir.

He freed her lips, kept his eyes closed, and sucked in a long breath.

She stroked the fierce planes of his rugged, silver-tattooed face. He swayed slightly and gripped onto her as though he were unsteady. As though their kiss had knocked him sideways just as hard as it had knocked her.

But he recovered quickly. His eyes opened. He glared at her with magnificent challenge. "My bride."

CHAPTER FOUR

My bride.

Elyssa's throat went dry. Never had she been so powerfully desired by a dominant male. She simply nodded.

Kadir straightened. "To the docks."

He moved her in a post-kiss dreamy haze toward the SUV.

"Hold it!" Aya grabbed Elyssa's other hand to stop her. "You still need to sign the paperwork. And before you disappear into the ocean, don't you want to tell your parents?"

Of course! Oh, god. Elyssa shook herself. "Yes. Sorry. I have to do that."

"We'll meet you at the dock tomorrow." Aya tugged Elyssa free from the mer king. "In the morning. After Elyssa and I have had a long discussion about her new role. See you then."

Kadir's jaw clenched and released. He conferenced with his warriors and finally, angrily, spoke to Elyssa. "Come at the dawn."

His taste remained on her wet lips. She nodded again.

He accepted her promise, gathered his warriors into the company SUVs, and was driven away.

Elyssa rocked back on her heels. Excitement bubbled in her chest. This was crazy. So crazy.

Aya stared after them. A shadow crossed her face.

Behind Aya, Chastity Angel glared with anger. She turned on her heel and tapped away.

Elyssa tempered her excitement. "Paperwork?"

Aya cleared her throat. "Yes. It's this way." She looked down at her tight, red bathing suit and grimaced. "Let me change."

In a private backstage room, Elyssa was interviewed by the reality TV crew about what had happened. Hopefully, her dreams and hopes would make a good sound byte and encourage more women to join the next pageant. The crew would follow her to the dock tomorrow and get their final footage for next week's exciting worldwide broadcast.

Then, she joined Aya and read through stacks of contracts.

Due to the secrecy of trying to prevent rivals from stealing away the mermen, only the highest levels of HR directors and lawyers had attended the bride contract meetings. Even so, Elyssa had managed to weasel out the main details from Aya. It was strange to read them in black and white.

She was to donate her share of Sea Opals to Van Cartier Cosmetics, where they would be used to develop life-saving medicines and health products. She'd receive a percentage of any profits after they passed clinical trials. In the event their scientists figured out how to synthesize the healing properties right away, the gemstones made amazing jewelry, and she'd get a percentage of those sales.

Kadir guaranteed Elyssa's safety in Atlantis. She would meet with Aya on a surface platform nearby — in the middle of the Atlantic — once a month to make sure she was still alive. That support ceased after two years unless Kadir provided a second shipment of Sea Opals.

So, Elyssa's new job was to make sure Kadir wanted a queen for longer than two years. This was only the starter package.

His kiss tasted like a thigh-squeezing promise of forever.

Elyssa lounged on the hard wooden floor behind Aya's privacy screen and filled out the forms. At the dressing table on the other side, Aya mixed an industrial cocktail to scrub off the waterproof makeup. The quiet was companionable, like back in school, when they worked on group projects.

Chastity Angel entered the room.

An icy chill of air conditioning wafted in with her. She faced off against Aya silently for several moments. They were like two cats hissing with hackles raised.

Elyssa peeked out from behind the screen. Did Chastity Angel know she was here? It didn't matter. She was coming to discipline her only daughter. Whether Aya was twelve or twenty-eight, this was always the same.

Chastity Angel picked up Aya's lipstick tube. "*Checkmate.* Do you know who designed this color? I did. And I designed it to hold up under pressure." She set it down with a click. "At least some of the things I've produced don't disappoint me."

Aya flinched. "The king was leaving. He meant it."

"And what if he did? A president can't so easily yield control. "

"I still have full control of—"

"No, you handed the entire project to a woman whose greatest honor was winning a T-shirt competition!"

Chastity Angel's rising voice echoed in the silent room. Elyssa hugged her elbows. A clock ticked loudly.

"The fate of your great-grandmother's company will now be decided by a woman who cannot follow my simple instructions to stay home, stay out of sight, and avoid causing an incident."

Aya's voice also rose. "That was—"

"He was right in front of you. You let him get away. You pushed that mediocre, useless—"

"He chose her! Out of a hundred of your 'highly quali-fied' contestants, King Kadir chose Elyssa. That is no coinci-dence. Her instincts with mermen are exceptional. She funded Lucy's expedition and was present for the final events. She should have been involved with this pageant from the start."

Elyssa's chest glowed. Aya always defended her.

"The male chose her because you let him. You are not a natural beauty, Aya, but today, your ugliness embarrassed me."

The clock ticked loudly again. Aya turned white.

It just wasn't fair.

Elyssa jumped to her feet and stomped out from behind the screen. "She wasn't ugly. She was beautiful. And it's not her fault Kadir chose me. It's mine."

Chastity Angel's fury froze Elyssa. "It *is* your fault. All you've ever done is ruin Aya's—"

"Stop it!" Aya flew from her seat. "Just stop. Mother. I promise you that whatever happens, I will take full respon-sibility."

Her eyes narrowed. "Losing our competitive advantage with the Sea Opals will destroy us."

Aya's lips tightened.

"Fail with this project, Aya, and you will no longer be my daughter."

Chastity Angel left.

Aya took a huge breath and let it out. Her shoulders slumped. She sat and rested her head in her hands.

Elyssa ached to go to her and enfold her in a comforting hug. But in this one way, Aya was truly the daughter of Chastity Angel. She would stiffen and try to pretend the argument hadn't bothered her at all.

Elyssa returned behind the screen to give Aya a few moments to get a hold of herself. Anyway, she knew better than to speak up. Chastity Angel only turned more vicious. It was usually better to take the abuse, remain silent, and weather out the storm.

Not much had changed over all these years. Elyssa wasn't any good, and Aya always had to try harder.

In junior high, Aya and Elyssa worked on a Sea Opal observation project for their private school science fair. Van Cartier Cosmetics scientists showed them the rare, valuable gems with unusual medicinal properties. They were supposed to write down the size, shape, and other observations for their simple report, but Elyssa noticed the gems seemed to brighten when held by certain people. Herself and Aya were two of the "brighter" ones.

She told Aya, and Aya told the scientists. It became a huge deal, not only within the company and the school, but internationally. Certain people "resonated" more with the Sea Opals. They also experienced the most healing effects.

Aya's mother kept saying that Aya had made the discovery alone. Aya doggedly insisted that she and Elyssa made the discovery together. Then, one day, Aya's mother visited Elyssa's parents.

"It would be better for all involved if you would tell Aya

you don't care about the credit," CEO Chastity Angel Van Cartier told thirteen-year-old Elyssa, in front of her parents. "Aya needs this for her future. She's going to be president. We all know you will never do anything important."

Her parents dismissed Elyssa to have a private adult talk. At the end of their talk, Elyssa's step mom received a promotion, her dad received a new golf membership, and Elyssa received a pony.

Yep. Her family had been bought.

Aya stopped correcting reporters about the resonance discovery. Elyssa's name dropped from articles, and journalists stopped trying to interview her. At school, Aya entered advanced classes. Their secret club, the Unicorn Mermaid Girls, disbanded. They saw each other less and less.

What if Elyssa's parents had held firm and insisted their girls share the credit?

Maybe they could have had the advanced classes together. Maybe Elyssa could have gone to Harvard and Yale too. Maybe the Unicorn Mermaid Girls could have stayed together, instead of one launching so far and the other watching in awe at the star trails she left behind.

Or, so Aya had confessed to Elyssa a few months ago when they banded together at the end of Lucy's expedition to take down the rogue company agent threatening her and the other mermen.

"We'll start a new division of the company," Aya told Elyssa in the helicopter. "It will be Sea Opal Acquisitions. I'll be president and you can do merman recruitment."

Elyssa had laughed. Spending time recruiting the sexy, beautifully tattooed mermen? Sign her up. "Do you think they have merman college job fairs?"

"If not, you'll have to start one."

But that had not happened. Aya didn't control the

company. Her mother and the board of directors did. Aya couldn't invent a division just because the two of them made starry-eyed plans over the pristine Gulf of Mexico. She couldn't even get Elyssa an official invitation to the pageant. The best she could do was sneak Elyssa in.

This time, rather than letting their parents divide them, they had to succeed together and prove Chastity Angel wrong.

Elyssa carried out her contracts. "I won't let you down"

Aya dropped her hands and forced a tired smiled. "Of course you won't. Don't ever think that. All signed?"

Elyssa set the thick packet on the clean dresser.

Aya stared at the first page for an unnaturally long time.

This had to be so hard. Aya's contract was probably already signed in triplicate. Now she was forced to read over another woman's, even though that other woman happened to be Elyssa.

"Aya?" Elyssa touched Aya's arm. It was cold. "I'm sorry we couldn't both be chosen."

She straightened, flustered. "What? No, I was thinking. Excuse me." She put on her reading glasses and lifted the papers.

Elyssa wanted to reach out again, but she curled her fingers to give Aya the space she needed. "You worked so hard on this pageant. You deserved to win."

Aya let out an exhale. She removed her reading glasses and rubbed the bridge of her nose. "Just because you work hard doesn't mean you'll succeed. You also have to have the right skill set. Kadir almost left today without selecting a bride. That's why I asked you to come."

What? So Aya knew he would choose Elyssa? "You planned this?"

"Not *this*. But you're good with people. Much better than I am."

Again, Elyssa wanted to pull her into a hug. She rubbed Aya's arm. "You're good with people."

Aya looked away. "You're the only one who would say that."

Elyssa rubbed warmth into her cousin's smooth skin. Aya had been the founder of the Unicorn Mermaid Girls. She surely wanted to be chosen today too. Who wouldn't? It was bad luck that Elyssa had stumbled in at exactly the moment Kadir was also backstage. Yeah. It was a coincidence that she had stumbled, and then Kadir had been forced to catch her, and then he chose her because they had touched.

"You're great with people," Elyssa said because it was true. Aya was a leader. She organized the pageant and managed the whole company as vice president. "That can't be why you asked me to come today."

"If Kadir tried to leave without a bride, I wanted you in the wings. I was going to throw you at him like a big ball of rubber bands and glue. You would keep him immobilized while I executed my contingency plans. By the end of the pageant, at least, I expected to know his type."

A big ball of rubber bands and glue. Heh. "Sounds messy."

"It sounds harmless and endearing, which is what you are. And I mean that in the best way. You did once stuff fifteen marshmallows in your cheeks and sing 'Baby Beluga' so we could win unicorn T-shirts in the lunch relay."

Elementary school memories. They had painted on mermaids riding the unicorns. Elyssa had run across the old T-shirt in her scrapbook only yesterday.

Aya thumped the contract packet. "But I didn't mean for *this* to happen."

Oh. Despite how she'd defended Elyssa to Chastity Angel, Aya also thought Elyssa wasn't capable.

She swallowed back her disappointment. "I'll try my best."

"I know you will," Aya said patiently. "If anyone's going to make this work, it's going to be you. No, the problem is, we don't know what's really down there." She tapped her reading glasses against the dresser. "Atlantis is a rebel city. It has unique problems, and apparently, it's considered anathema by the 'All-Council' ruling body. I can't even predict what might go wrong."

The thought Elyssa couldn't be queen had never crossed Aya's mind. Elyssa's heart swelled. She straightened her shoulders. "I think it will be okay."

"Name me one real life first-contact story that ends well."

"Sacajawea married a real, live English guy."

"She died of smallpox in England." Aya's eyes widened with sudden realization. "Do they have underwater diseases? You're not resistant. How will we handle medical evacuations?" She held her head and stared into space.

Another *it's-midnight-and-our-project-isn't-perfect-yet* freak out. How nostalgic. "You already thought of all this, right? At least twenty times?"

"But I thought of it was when it was other people. People I didn't know. Not *you*."

"Hey. I'll be alright." Elyssa grabbed Aya's shoulders. Aya flinched but endured the contact. "It's like you said. This is our chance! As soon as they accept me, I'll demand that they invite you. We'll be mermaid queens together. Just like we always dreamed."

Of course, that dream was from before mermen were real, and before Aya became vice president.

But her dreamy, hopeful cousin was still inside. The sharp, cold business executive who accomplished great things hadn't killed her dead. Yet.

Aya nodded slowly.

"Okay." Elyssa squeezed Aya in a soft hug. She couldn't help herself. "Enough doubts. This is going to be great. In one month, I'm going to be the most amazing queen."

Aya's shoulders remained stiff, as Elyssa had predicted. She couldn't accept comfort. She was always the strong one. "Please be careful."

"Of course. I've got people skills."

Aya snorted and Elyssa released her. Her eyes were red but she gripped the packet with new determination. "I've got no choice but to believe you."

"That's right." Elyssa grinned.

Her cousin started reading the packet with a small smile on her face. Good. Aya felt better. Mission accomplished.

Now, Elyssa just had to talk herself into believing everything she said was true.

CHAPTER FIVE

K adir waited on the dock for his bride. Early morning sunlight touched the bay. A sensation like electric eels pooled in his belly.

"Will she really come?" Soren demanded beside him.

They stood on the wooden dock. The tide was high, and waves splashed against the slats. On both sides, his warriors bobbed in the ocean. Although it was very unlikely any other city's warriors would come this close to the human-filled shoreline and engage an attack, his warriors were ready for danger from any direction.

Kadir rested his palms on his wet jeans. "She will come."

What Soren and the other warriors didn't know was that Kadir almost didn't want her to.

From a very early age, he had known the old traditions were wrong. Bringing his race into a new era was his destiny. He embraced and fought for it. Founding a new city was the first step. His actions now ensured his city's — and his race's — survival.

Yesterday, he'd glimpsed the end of the old ways. A

modern woman who possessed a cell phone and a television would transform by her own choice and stay on as a queen, dawning a new era of revitalization. His gut told him that human was Elyssa. All claims began with the kiss. So, yesterday in the auditorium lobby, when Elyssa vowed to rule Atlantis as his queen, Kadir had pulled her forward to claim her lips.

Now he couldn't get the memory out of his mind.

It consumed his thoughts. Distracted him from the plans he should have been making with his warriors for their return journey to Atlantis. Enslaved his soul.

As he waited for her arrival on the dock, the memory surged once more to the forefront. Unbidden and uncontrollable. The kiss had foretold danger, and he kept reliving it to fully identify exactly what was dangerous.

She'd stumbled. For a human who'd spent her whole life walking, she was oddly unprepared for it. He'd stepped forward to catch her.

She'd braced her hands against his biceps. Her small body fit into his arms as though she were designed to rest there. She let out a quick, surprised breath and looked up at him in apology.

Her expression froze as he lowered his head to claim what was his.

Their lips touched.

She melted against him.

Her softness felt like nothing he had ever prepared for. What he had intended as an imperial stamp of possession, perfunctory to complete the contract, intrigued him to linger.

He cupped her cheeks, holding her where he wanted her. Her lips trembled. What was her flavor? He had to know. He teased her lips. Sweet murmurs of hunger encouraged him to do it again. He nibbled at her gently with his teeth.

Her lips parted.

He surged into the opening, connecting with her deeply. She moaned, yielding completely to his possession. Feminine and gentle, with hints of sweetness and spice. For some reason, he couldn't get enough. She tentatively returned his thrusts with her own curious exploration. He took what she offered, claiming her wet interior, inside and outside, for him alone.

In her chest, her light flared to blinding. Something shifted deep within his soul.

What was that? He'd jerked back. Struggling to catch his inner balance, he'd rocked, even though he was standing flat-footed on the even tile floor of the auditorium lobby.

That was the moment his memories kept circling. What had shifted? This small thing, whatever it was, could change everything. He knew it. But how? All he was left with was the unsettled feeling of risk.

Risk to his city. Risk to his warriors.

Risk to his soul.

Yesterday, when he'd been reeling from the unidentified sensation, Elyssa had stroked his cheek gently. That small comfort was enough to give him back his center of gravity. He'd shrugged off the unsettling feeling and focused on what next needed to be done.

But when she had pulled away to complete the human's paperwork, he had spent a long night with his warriors mulling the situation over.

Twin feelings warred within him. One was hope and the other fear. One obsession and the other panic. One craving, and the other the need to crush that craving under iron control.

Both feelings were equally powerful.

Only one feeling could win.

A different bride would make his duty easier. One of the other pageant females would perform as queen admirably, require little attention, and Kadir could ignore her to focus on his city.

Kadir could never ignore Elyssa.

Her soul light fluctuated unpredictably. She had denied his claim and then changed her mind. Their kiss had unsettled him. His ongoing, obsessive reaction to her was frightening.

The life he thought he had been training for was gone. A glimpse of a stronger, more vibrant life beckoned — if only he had the strength to swim out and spear it.

And her craveable flavor once more teased his tongue. Her soft sweetness hooked under his skin. Would her second kiss feel as unsettling? Or would it show him a more direct path to his accomplish his vision?

Despite his concerns, he had to know the answer.

Vehicles drove to the isolated parking lot. Aya arrived first. Dark hollows bruised her cheeks as though she hadn't slept. She directed employees onto the dock. Some carried masks, tanks, and air-breathing gear. Others filmed for their TV program.

Soren couldn't take his eyes off Aya. "You are making a mistake."

Maybe. Maybe not.

Kadir ignored his first lieutenant.

Elyssa's car rolled to a stop at the marina. He sensed her presence inside. She climbed out and walked beside two older humans. A cloth in pretty shades of kelp-forest green wrapped around her body.

Aya posed her for filming, gave her black devices to fix

on her earlobes, and then led her onto the dock. The two adults remained with her. Elyssa's cheeks burned bright red and she, like everyone, focused on Aya.

Not on him.

Kadir fought the urge to storm across the dock, grab her chin, and force her attention on him. *I am yours. You are mine.* That was the danger, the obsession, the need to possess surging in his mind. He would not have felt this uncontrollable emotion with another bride. And he could not stop the feelings now. No matter how intently he pushed the thoughts at her, she focused resolutely on Aya and on the filming cameras.

Soren made the *tsk* noise. Because he sensed Kadir's unrest or because he took Elyssa's focus on Aya for submission to a more dominant female? Either irritated the first lieutenant.

Aya, in contrast, strode fearlessly to Kadir.

"King Kadir." A bold red dress clothed Aya's body, dark sunglasses hid her eyes, and white heels tap-tapped on the wood. "We're ready to make the exchange."

Kadir knelt. Iyen lifted the tightly woven bag full of Sea Opals into his arms. Kadir hauled it onto the wood at his feet.

"We give the bride her Sea Opals." Kadir untied the knot.

Aya's lips parted.

Inside, the smooth, white resin spheres gleamed.

Aya counted quickly and silently.

The foundation of a city was its Life Tree. As it aged, "Sea Opal" resin dripped from its branches and formed mountains around the trunk. At the appointed time of year, the worthiest warrior rose from the depths and placed a single Sea Opal in the sacred island's church as his offering.

Shortly after, a bride descended to join with him. Despite the abundance of gems, the covenant decreed only one, and the sacred island brides had never asked for more.

Van Cartier Cosmetics asked for a hundred.

The Life Tree of Atlantis was merely a sapling. It dripped tiny pebbles. Out of all the times to demand bags of Sea Opals, the founding of a new city was the one time a merman could not provide them.

Most warriors who escaped to join Kadir had been unable to bring much with them. A few plants from their home castle gardens, a rusty trident no one would miss, a dagger strapped to a thigh. But, out of hope for wooing a modern bride, they had all brought one mating jewel.

This was what Kadir gave to Aya. Because these thirty were from different Life Trees, they had different hues. Some were pink, iridescent black, gold, or his own silver.

She removed her sunglasses and counted again. "This is only a third of what you promised. Where's the rest?"

"Coming."

She withdrew her hand and stood, looking down on him. The hot sun haloed her head. She was angry but controlled. "That wasn't the agreement."

Her anger barely touched him. His warriors sacrificed much to gather this amount. "It is what we have."

"When will you have the rest?"

"We will pay as we can."

"You will pay at the first support visit. In full."

Distant sea-birds screamed on the salty breeze.

"You will have all the Sea Opals in Atlantis," he promised.

Aya huffed, took the bag, and struggled with the weight. She gave it to two suited men, who strained to carry the dripping treasure back to their SUV.

Kadir stood. Behind and below him, his warriors watched their mating jewels disappear with stony resolve.

These were the jewels of their home cities. The jewels which they had carried to claim their *own* brides. Van Cartier Cosmetics demanded an unprecedented ransom for a single bride, and after much debate, they had agreed to spend all on their king.

If Atlantis was on friendly terms with any other city, then the other city could easily provide ten bags of gems. Or twenty bags. Or even a hundred bags, each bag the size of a boulder. And the older Life Tree would quickly generate even more.

But Atlantis stood alone. Anathema. Constantly at risk of destruction. They would have no more Sea Opals until they received recognition as an official city from the All-Council and made effective alliances with their nearest neighbors.

Or until they excavated the treasury from the sunken wreckage of their ancient namesake.

That was what Kadir and the other warriors focused on. Giving away their precious gems now would lead to the successful debut of a mermaid queen. More warriors would escape to Atlantis, swelling their ranks to the necessary size. Their city would become recognized. Sea Opals would flow.

Enough to tempt a thousand brides. Enough to join with each and every one of his warriors.

"In exchange, my bride," he ordered.

Elyssa jumped. The older adults rubbed her shoulders.

Aya turned serious. "King Kadir. Please accept my cousin, Elyssa Van Cartier, as the first ambassador to Atlantis. I hope you will always respect her, be patient with her as she learns your ways, and treat her as precious to you..." Aya's voice cut out. A strange moisture filled her red-rimmed eyes. She cleared her throat and stiffened. "As a precious, and irreplaceable *treasure* as she is to me."

Elyssa's chest glowed with her cousin's words. Not a bold glow like Aya. A warm, gentle glow that sparkled.

"I will protect her with my life," Kadir swore.

Aya frowned hard.

He knelt again and reached over the side of the dock. Iyen ushered the precious, tiny white blossom he had guarded into Kadir's cupped hand.

He stood. "This nectar will permanently transform a human into a mer."

Aya blocked his path as though she had suddenly changed her mind.

Too bad. The time for changing minds was yesterday, and the only minds that mattered were his own and Elyssa's. Kadir strode past Aya as though she did not exist and presented his Life Tree's flower to his bride. "Elyssa."

Her soft lips parted. She sucked in a breath and finally, finally met his eyes. Tentative, fearful, determined. "Yes?"

"Drink."

"Now? Oh. Um..." She reached for the flower and then stopped. "Sorry. Do you mind?"

His guts twinged. So close. "Mind?"

"Before I transform, I wanted to introduce you to my parents. This is my dad, Baron, and my stepmom, Suzanna."

Her parents craned their necks to look up at him.

Baron brushed his thick, brown hair out of his eyes. "Hello, sir."

"Hi there," Suzanna said, her cheeks red.

"If anything goes wrong, send her right back." Baron

squeezed Elyssa's shoulder. "I mean if it doesn't work out. The whole 'water-breathing and ruling Atlantis' thing."

"Dad," she said softly. Her light proved she did not object to her father's kindness. She only felt love for him and her step mom.

"It's going to work out," Suzanna said with a short laugh.

Their anxious gazes pleaded with him to take good care of their daughter. Kadir had known Elyssa for less than a day, and yet, he was about to take her far out of their reach.

"I will protect her," he repeated softly. "She will return to you many times. Together, we will rebuild Atlantis. You will meet her often. And, soon, our son."

"Right." Her dad released Elyssa and held his wife for strength. "I'm too young to be a grandfather."

"Hush, Baron." Suzanna raised her chin. "We'll hold you to that promise, King."

The other warriors shifted. Even in the thin air, they must sense Suzanna's hope and longing, her anxiety and pride. This deep familial connection was what he hoped to secure for his young fry. To know the love and protection of *both* parents. Not only the father.

Now, thanks to Elyssa's insistence to introduce her parents, the warriors who returned empty-handed to Atlantis could hear the hopeful message for themselves. The future they clung to was also a future held tightly by humans.

Aya cleared her throat.

Elyssa's cheeks reddened like her step mom's. "I guess I've held the schedule back long enough. Um, how, exactly, do I drink this?"

"Cup the flower in your hand. Drink the liquid pooled in the blossom."

"Like this?" She pinched and lifted the flower.

Its thin walls collapsed inward. Precious nectar dripped out and stained the dock.

His heart pounded. He cupped the flower again. "Do not lift it from the water."

"Oh." Her light dimmed. "Sorry. I'll, uh, be more careful."

They maneuvered awkwardly. She finally rested her chin against his hand and tried to suck the blossom closer. He tipped his hand. The last drop of nectar poured into her mouth—along with the cupped seawater.

She choked.

Seawater streamed out of her mouth and dampened the front of her green dress. She coughed and hacked. Her step mom clapped her on the back. Her dad rubbed her elbow.

His warriors stared, stunned.

Soren lifted a brow. His authority-challenging lips curled into a sneer. Kadir could imagine his question. *Are you sure you chose the best bride?*

Elyssa hacked. She rested her hand on Kadir's forearm. "Is... it... always like that? When people change?"

He did not know. "The sacred island brides transformed before coming to us."

His warriors calmed. Yes, perhaps her reaction *was* natural.

But worry sliced into his confidence.

Had Elyssa received any nectar? At all?

She cleared her throat and met his eyes. Hers were red and full of tears from coughing. "Okay. I'm ready to try again. Let's drink."

"That was all the nectar."

"Oh." She sucked in a shaky breath and squared her shoulders. "Then, this is it."

She removed the kelp dress to expose a white bikini dotted with pink flowers. She hugged her stepmom, kissed her dad's cheek, and waved brightly at Aya. Aya waved back, worry tightening her body. Elyssa turned, marched past Kadir, and jumped off the dock, into the ocean.

Where she abruptly proceeded to drown.

CHAPTER SIX

The ocean was bouncy and salty. Southern Florida was as warm as a heated swimming pool this time of year, and the sandy beach below Elyssa stretched for miles.

Was it always so bright and clear? Could she always see schools of fish far away, suspended like flocks of birds against an endless blue sky? It had been a long time since she'd been brave enough to open her eyes underwater. So, maybe.

The transmitter earrings Aya gave her so they could track her location made an annoying, high-pitched humming in her ears.

She tried to take a breath.

Hot seawater slammed into the back of her throat. Her nose clogged. She gagged.

Elyssa thrashed for the surface.

The maroon-tattooed warrior known as Iyen hauled her out of the water and into Kadir's strong arms. Her throat burned hotter than when she choked on the nectar. Was there an instruction manual?

Kadir rubbed her back. "Breathe."

Everyone was watching. Aya. Her parents. The documentary crew and all the employees. Elyssa would transform. She would.

"Try again." Kadir shucked his jeans and trench coat and slid into the water. He helped her in and effortlessly treaded water. His gaze was so intense. Like he *needed* her to do this right. "Transform your body first."

They ducked under the surface.

He bent one leg at his knee to show her his foot. In the water, his toes flattened and elongated, and the thickly folded skin between them stretched tight. Webbing flared between fingers. Silver tattoos scrolled across the thin, delicate skin. His tattoos turned iridescent as a fish.

Her feet didn't flatten or turn into scuba fins. Her fingers did not grow webbing.

While the hours ticked past, Elyssa failed to accomplish anything more than holding her breath for a long time. And that was only when she forgot to think about it.

Even the mermen grew concerned.

Soren swam above her while she doggedly floated, holding her breath and focusing on her not-webbed hands. "Kadir, she is not trying."

She wanted to cry. If she tried any harder, she was going to burst a blood vessel.

"Give her time," Kadir rumbled beneath her, in a voice that both soothed and tingled, like a fingertip drizzling massage oil down her spine.

She had been so excited to do this, and so fearful of messing up in front of Kadir. And now, Kadir was her rock. Focused, calm, undefeatable. His faith never wavered. She *would* transform. If it were just the two of them, she almost thought maybe it would be possible.

He hung upside down. With his mouth closed in an encouraging smile, he somehow spoke to her. His voice vibrated inside her chest. "Now release the air trapped in your mouth and try to speak."

She opened her mouth. "I...agh...tr...agh." Air bubbles gurgled out and seawater choked the back of her throat. She gagged and bolted for the surface.

Soren's voice chased her. "She spilled all the nectar. You should have selected a brighter bride."

She broke free of the water and grabbed onto the dock. Gagging disguised her free flowing tears.

Her parents sat on shaded benches at the private company marina. Employees sprawled nearby. The scuba diver film crew had already used up their tanks of air and left.

Only Aya remained on the dock. Her face was red with heat, and her nose and ears were pink with sunburn, but she wasn't going home until Elyssa was.

"Hang in there." Aya patted Elyssa's hot, wet back twice. She was seriously worried. "Lucy said the first trans-formation is the hardest."

"Not this hard." Elyssa sniffed the salty wetness.

Kadir should have chosen Aya. She wouldn't have gotten distracted by introducing her parents. Aya would have drunk the nectar and been half way to Atlantis by now.

"I'll try Lucy again." Aya dialed her cell phone.

Elyssa thought she had pumped Lucy and Torun for everything they knew during the yacht ride from the Gulf of Mexico back to Florida, but obviously, she had missed a few steps. If she had been a bride pageant contestant, she would have attended their special training a week ago. Instead, Elyssa took them out for dinner afterward and chatted about silly, pointless things.

Kadir's head popped above the water. He addressed Aya. "Elyssa has failed to transform. I must return to Atlantis."

Elyssa cringed. He had to go back to Atlantis alone. The entire project failed. All because of her.

Aya stopped the call and scrambled to her feet. "No. You signed an agreement. You can't go back alone."

"I do not take orders from you."

"Take them from yourself! You signed—"

"It's my fault." Elyssa stopped the argument over the lump in her throat. "I can't transform."

Aya tore her gaze to Elyssa with effort. Her determination shone. "Yes, you can."

"We have wasted too much time on this." Kadir spoke the heaviness in Elyssa's own heart. "I will return to Atlantis and cultivate a second flower."

Elyssa hated this. But it was the only thing they could do. "Ok—"

"No!" Aya shook her head violently. She took it personally as if Kadir were insulting Elyssa. "Something's already changed. Elyssa, you've been underwater for more than nine-minute stretches."

"I've always been good at holding my breath."

"Not that good. The world breath-holding championship for women — without oxygen — is *eight*."

That couldn't be right.

Kadir frowned. "You believe there has been a change?"

"Yes. You are this close." Aya held her fingers together so they were almost touching. "And if you don't try a little bit harder, I'll be disappointed in the both of you."

Elyssa scrubbed her face.

She could go under again. She'd swallow a hundred gallons of seawater if it actually made a difference.

But Aya was fooling herself. In trying to encourage Elyssa, she was just making things worse. Elyssa was going to disappoint everyone. Kadir, the warriors, her parents, Aya ... and herself.

He spoke gently. "Elyssa. Your light is dimming."

And now, on top of everything, her light was dimming. "I'm sorry. I really am trying. It feels like I'm drowning. My throat hurts."

"Don't give up," Aya insisted.

His brows drew together. "Perhaps we may increase the nectar's power by increasing your resonance."

"Yes!" Aya latched onto the solution. "Increase resonance. What increases resonance?"

He thought hard.

Elyssa's chest rose. Maybe she was giving up too soon. Maybe there was still hope.

"It is something you are born with. I will conference with my warriors." He slipped beneath the waves.

Her hope crashed. The resonance studies also showed that resonance was something people had or they didn't. Those who had greater resonance responded to the medicinal effects of the Sea Opals. People who didn't, didn't.

She rested her forehead on the wet dock. The waves pushed her toward the shore. See? Even the tide rejected her. She pinched the planks. "Kadir's bride should have been you."

Aya was silent for a long moment.

Then, her voice was distant. "I'm sorry, Elyssa. But it couldn't have been me."

"Hmm?"

"For awhile, I thought maybe I could do it. But, no. In all honesty, I could never be a merman's queen."

She lifted her head. "What do you mean?"

Aya fixed on her. Trouble crossed her face. "There's something about this contract that you still don't seem to have realized."

What did that mean? "I read the whole thing."

Although there were an awful lot of pages, and she had been skimming while fantasizing about leaping like Flipper through the waves.

Aya grimaced and opened her mouth to speak.

Kadir burst through the surface beside Elyssa. The raw, fluid power of him in his element stole her breath and made her chest ache. She wanted to move powerfully like a mermaid. She wanted to do so with him.

She wanted it.

He coughed and wiped his face, sluicing the water away. His fine, silver-flecked eyes sought hers with an almost magnetic power. He had new answers. He focused intently on sharing them with her.

"My warriors reminded me that although we are all born with a set level of resonance, some actions can activate our deepest strengths." He held up his hand to enumerate them. As the water dripped off, the subtle webbing between his fingers melted back from his knuckles until they were completely separate, the same as any human's. "Vows of honor. Protecting the innocent. Joining with a bride. Pledging to defend the Life Tree."

Vows. Honor. Protection.

Joining.

She shivered. It was like reading a list of his best qualities. What could she do on that list? Vow something? She'd already promised to become his queen.

Maybe she just had to mean it.

She wanted to do this. She wanted to be with him. She wanted to be a queen.

He focused on her with brilliant intensity. "Continue."

"Connections," Aya mused aloud. "That's what all these have in common. Each act forges or strengthens the connections between people and strengthens the bonds of community."

Connections. Elyssa needed to strengthen her bond to Kadir by forging more connections.

Wait. She had a brilliant idea.

Elyssa turned to him. "Go on a date with me."

CHAPTER SEVEN

"**A** date?" Kadir repeated. Had he understood correctly?

"We can get coffee down at the promenade." Elyssa reached up a hand to Aya, who hauled her out of the water, relief obvious on both their faces. "Wasn't there ice cream? Maybe a movie."

"No movie." Aya studied her phone. "We missed the matinee."

The females retreated into their own world as they walked down the dock. If anything, they resonated with each other the strongest. Elyssa toweled off and tugged her sea kelp dress on over her bikini. She sucked in great gulps of air as though she could not get enough.

He rose from the water and dressed more slowly, fastening the button on his jeans as his warriors bobbed to the surface.

"My king?" Lotar's quiet question asked why they had left the water when every muscle screamed at them to finish this and return to Atlantis.

"We are going on a date," he replied.

Iyen and Ciran struggled to mask their concern. Lotar's expression was unreadable.

Soren's was not. "Better return to Atlantis now, grow another blossom, and claim a more resonant bride."

Kadir cut short his snap. Returning to Atlantis immediately was the responsible choice. But if he could increase Elyssa's resonance and force the transformation now, he had to try.

"Soren." Ciran cleared his throat pedantically. "We do not know if it is possible to grow a second blossom. Most Life Trees cannot grow a first blossom until they are in the presence of a bride."

And there was also that.

Everyone had been shocked when Kadir's little sapling put forth a blossom. It resolved the logistical problem of how to transport a bride across the ocean without a convenient sacred church or ancient pool of Sea Opal-infused elixir. Somehow sensing their predicament, his Life Tree had responded to the call of his heart.

Expecting a second miracle seemed more than presumptuous. It was disrespectful.

"I know that," Soren snarled. "But if raiders do not destroy the city, our own hard-headed warriors may tear it apart. Spending more hours here, with females who cannot transform, wastes our time."

Aya returned. "Excuse me. King Kadir." Her soul light was still bright, but her tone turned cold and imperious. "Elyssa is ready for your date. She will contact me when you two are ready to return. Your warriors will remain here."

Soren surged out of the water. Standing naked before Aya, he growled. "We guard Kadir."

She stared up at his face coldly. "If you all go, then it's not a date."

He towered over her. "We go."

Unimpressed, her hard eyes flicked down his bulky, seething, black-tattooed body and up again. "I don't think your presence will increase their resonance. In fact, it might cause us to waste even more of 'the mermen's valuable time.'"

Soren gritted his teeth. Surprise? Soren was not frequently taken aback.

Aya turned on her heel.

"Wait." Kadir shoved his feet into the flip-flops their company had provided. "I will go."

Soren stiffened. "Kadir—"

"How long will this 'date' take?"

Aya froze and narrowed her gaze on Kadir. "That all depends on you. Don't you think?"

He did not take her meaning. So, he skipped to the point. "We have a long journey ahead. If my warriors are stuck here waiting, they cannot hunt."

"Of course. You are still our honored guests." Her words were clipped. "Food will be provided."

She stalked off the dock. Every ounce of former friendliness was stripped from her stiff spine. She reached the car where Elyssa was already waiting, climbed in, and slammed the door.

Soren stared after her.

The others bobbed in the waves. Uncertainty filled all of their faces. It was clear that Soren had made a new enemy, and her fury rivaled even his. Perhaps now they were grateful Kadir had chosen a gentler bride.

"Eat well," Kadir told his warriors. "Rest. I will not be gone long."

"What should we do if we meet brides in your absence?" Iyen asked.

He was requesting guidance on a question they had wondered on and off through the entire journey. Although there was no more nectar, they could meet a bride and make an arrangement to return for her. If Elyssa did not transform now and they had to return to collect her, perhaps they could also collect two brides — or more— on their next journey. Iyen asked whether Kadir wanted him to make this his mission in Kadir's absence.

Soren snapped. "End your dream. They would not become ours. All the mating jewels are gone and we have nothing to offer them."

Iyen tightened.

He was from Rusalka originally; a strict city with a clear hierarchy. He did not like Soren answering for Kadir. He didn't realize it was evidence of a deep wound in Soren's soul.

Soren used to respect rank more strictly than any other warrior. While Kadir had been imprisoned, something terrible had happened — something which even now, Soren refused to tell him — and which had shattered his honor, destroyed his loyalty to Dragao Azul, and led him to challenge the All-Council itself. He stayed with Kadir now because they were old friends and because Kadir begged him.

"Atlantis needs a great warrior," Kadir had urged Soren shortly after their prison break. "If denying your honor is so important, remember that Atlantis is anathema and I am a ruler in exile. My first lieutenant will surely be regarded as a disgrace."

Only when Kadir promised not call him by his title of

first lieutenant would Soren agree to remain. Uncontrollable flares of temper was a small price to pay for his loyalty.

The other warriors in Atlantis had equally unusual backgrounds, and uniting to make a new city did not come easy. Soren had selected Ciran, originally from the proper city of Undine, and Lotar, originally from the independent city of Syrenka, to join Iyen as guards for this journey because they were least likely to harbor resentment for the small offenses that were inevitable while working together.

Now, after the long morning of carefully not snapping at each other, Iyen's idealism was inspired. Kadir delivered his ruling. "If any of you meet a potential bride, talk with civility. You could use the practice."

Iyen looked up to check whether he was serious. Ciran retreated into deep thoughts, as though he were reviewing his entire catalog of memorized civil phrases. A small smile curved Lotar's lips.

Soren shook his head.

Kadir tugged on the white T-shirt and crossed the shoreline to join the women.

The car ride was short and quiet. Elyssa navigated and Aya drove. They stopped in front of a dark store with a green female on the sign. Aya's parting comment to Elyssa was quiet and not meant for Kadir's ears.

"I'll call as soon as I hear from Lucy. Have fun."

"I'll try." Elyssa pressed her phone to her chest. "I really am trying. I promise. I'm trying so hard."

"Of course *you* are. It takes two people to forge a connection." Aya's gaze lifted over Elyssa's shoulder and settled hard on Kadir. "Remember, even a Sea Opal can't resonate in an empty room."

Kadir returned her gaze evenly.

She hardened and drove off.

"Have fun, she says," Elyssa muttered. She took a deep breath, let it out, and turned to him. "So, have you ever had a coffee?"

Brilliance glowed in her chest like the sun.

It speared him like a blade.

How dare she resonate now? Here? So far from the ocean, when it was least important to do so?

He barely heard his answer. She led him inside the building, pointed out artwork and tables and chairs, and took him to a counter. Some noises—music? —played.

"Here." Elyssa handed him a frothy brown drink with clinking ice. "This is an iced white mocha. I hope you like it."

He gripped the cool plastic. She turned back to the counter.

Anger sliced him again. How dare she glow so brilliantly inside a building? Kadir's gut instinct had been wrong. He should have followed his head over his...what was it? What had assaulted his senses so thoroughly at the auditorium?

An impulse? Lust?

Elyssa had *not* drunk the nectar. She could not transform into a mermaid. He had traded all his city's Sea Opals for a female who could not transform.

And now they were standing in a building drinking coffee.

He drank the cool liquid in one gulp.

Elyssa turned from the counter with a tray of cookies. She blinked at his empty cup. "Oh! You're supposed to drink it slowly."

He nearly crushed the cup. "How slowly?"

"As slow as you can." She grinned. Her light flared

again. Pretty, golden, intoxicating and *useless*. "It's so you have an excuse to hang out."

He swallowed his impatience. Barely.

"Find a seat. I'll get you another one." She gave him the tray. "This is something I can handle."

He forced himself into a seat at a small corner table and sprawled his human legs. After the first curious glances, the humans did not seem to notice him. A tall male in jeans and flip flops, with silver tattoos poking out beneath a tight, white T-shirt, did not rate much attention.

Elyssa took a prim seat across from him and handed him a second drink.

He held it without drinking. She chatted about meaningless things. He counted every second.

His warriors would at least be fed. They'd take the fastest current back to Atlantis. Without sleeping, it was possible to traverse the distance in less than two weeks, and—

"Do you think the logo makers knew the truth about mermaids?" Elyssa asked.

Her question jolted him from his calculations. He focused on the green logo. A smiling female with two scaly legs.

"It's funny." She sighed. "To think of all the hours I wasted practicing to be a mermaid with a monofin swim tail when I should have been practicing with scuba fins all along."

Through his anger, he found himself curious about her answer. "You practiced being a mermaid?"

"Aya and I both." She sipped her drink. The ice jingled. "When we were kids, it was this dream. Then, to think it was real...Well." She set the drink down and stabbed the ice with her straw. "Real for some people, I guess."

She had practiced swimming as a mermaid just as the mer secretly practiced walking on land. "How else did you prepare?"

"Prepare to be a mermaid? Well, last night I wrote out my last will and testament."

He did not know those things. "What is it?"

She straightened nobly. "If anything happens to me, I will all of my savings and everything I own to Lucy's Mer-Human Alliance for constructing a merman dating website." Her shoulders rounded. "I stayed up way too late. This coffee is exactly what I needed."

It was a planned gift. That was the last will and testament. "If anything happens to you?"

"When I'm underwater, in case I meet an untimely end. It's probably why my family freaked out and had to see me off today."

He didn't understand.

"You still look confused," she said.

He nodded.

"If I die," she said. "I want my parents to sell my stuff and give away the money."

Die? If she should die underwater with him?

He felt...he felt...

He didn't know how to feel. Shocked. Hardened. Jumpy inside, like his bones wanted out of his skin. Like the water he swam in was so cold he could barely think.

She sipped her drink.

"I swore a vow," he finally said. "To protect you."

Her brows lifted. "Oh. I know. But Atlantis is a rebel city and I'm 'anathema' to your All-Council."

A streak of fire blazed across his chest. The entire building heated under the focused rays of the sun. "No mer would *dare* attack a *bride*."

"Maybe not a bride, no." She was strangely upbeat. Despite insulting his honor, his loyalty, his city, his ability to protect her, and forecasting her own death, her smile was gentle and warm. "But I'm supposed to be your queen. Right? So the old rules might not apply."

For a moment, the world stopped turning.

Could that possibly be true? Was she right? Kadir had ended many traditions already and planned to end many more. Could the rule about not harming brides ever be broken?

No.

Even in the heat of battle or the jaws of a megalodon, a warrior would give his life to save a female. She might carry a young fry. And a young fry could grow up to become a warrior of any city, not only the city under siege.

But Elyssa didn't know that.

A new shock slashed through him. She had stayed up all night worrying she might be going to her death. No wonder her father had asked for Kadir's vow. No wonder her stepmother weighed all his answers. No wonder Elyssa fumbled the nectar and could not transform.

She feared deeply for her life and chose to come with him anyway.

Few warriors were so brave. Her determination stunned him. How petty his own doubts and fears looked in the face of this small human's dedication.

"They are not different," he said firmly. "Any warrior would give his life to protect yours. Even my worst enemy would ensure you remained well."

"Well, that's a relief." She smiled cheerfully. "Try the cookie. It's my favorite."

He bit the soft, chocolate-filled dough. Sweet, like her. She watched carefully for his reaction. "Do you like it?"

He liked sitting here with her. "I do."

Her soul glowed like a nova. "I'm so glad we got to do this."

"A date?"

"Yes. And." She jerked her chin at his crumbs. "I understand that this is my one chance to share my favorite food with you. Underwater, I'll be fully reliant on everyone else."

His stomach lurched again. "You will never go hungry."

"Ha! I could stand to go a little hungry. But that's not what I meant."

"I will provide for your every need."

"No, no. I know. That's—"

"If you fear I will fail you, my warriors will—"

"Kadir!" She reached across the table and grabbed his hands in both of hers. "I trust you will take care of me. Completely. *That's* why I'm glad right now I can do this little thing to take care of you."

It was such a strange way of thinking. Mermen always took care of their brides. Brides were helpless beneath the water. To believe differently was to dishonor the warrior. "It is different from the air world."

"Sure. Although I'm not fully independent in the air world. I'm still living with my dad and stepmom. I just meant it's nice to do something for you."

Hmm. It was the deepest fulfillment of a male to solely provide for his bride. Was that a problem? By taking over everything, were mermen preventing their brides from the same satisfaction?

He would have to think upon it more.

Elyssa studied him carefully. Her brows, wrinkled from worrying, smoothed. She squeezed his hands and let go. "Sorry. We're supposed to be increasing our resonance but I feel like I'm just putting my foot in my mouth. I hope it's not stressing you."

Her light dipped. She picked up her half-empty mocha and sipped.

If he were honest with himself, her light hadn't increased because they were inside a building or on solid land. It increased because Elyssa focused on him. She focused on his words, his actions, his thoughts.

Resonance cannot increase in an empty room.

Finally, he began to see what that truly meant. Now, when it might already be too late.

CHAPTER EIGHT

Kadir tried bridging the distance using a topic he knew she cared about. "Your parents are close to you."

It worked.

Elyssa brightened immediately. "We're all close. I'm so lucky. How about you?"

"No."

Her brows lowered. She looked down at her drink. "Oh. Sorry."

Her light dipped.

Sorry. That was a word he must strike from her statements.

But more importantly, she reacted to his feeling. Pain and anger. He forced past the pain of his situation to give her an important truth. "My mother died. Since then, my father has been castle-bound with illness in my old city, Dragao Azul. I have not seen him since my exile."

Her light flared. "Oh, I'm so sorry." She started to reach out, then hesitated.

He opened his palms.

She took them. Her light flared even brighter. Her dark eyes studied his intently. "You're all alone."

"I have my warriors. Soren." He slid his thumb over her delicate cream fingernails. "Like you, I was lucky. According to the old covenant, brides must return to the surface as soon as their young fry is born, but my mother made a secret request. Once a year, my father took me to the surface. There, she would be waiting on the shore."

She would always be sitting on a folding white lounge chair, in a full dress, with a book and a beach blanket. Her hair was black like Kadir's, and she kept it in one braid down her back.

"You met her?" Elyssa asked, eyes glowing.

"No." He focused on the lighter crescents of her nails. "We watched."

Contact was restricted by the covenant. This annual trip had to remain secret, and bobbing in the distant waves was as much as he dared. Hour after hour on those long days, Kadir and his father watched her turn pages, eat her lunch, hike up her skirt, and carefully wade.

The year Kadir determined to end the old covenant and forge a new one with modern brides, his father was struck by the mysterious illness. At that time, Kadir didn't realize what it meant. He was only grateful to have solitude as he swam to the surface and planned how to reveal himself to his mother. But his planned rebellion never occurred. His mother wasn't there. A small group of aunts and uncles and cousins circled her empty lounge chair and tossed white flowers onto the waves.

Elyssa sighed. "That's so sad. Too bad it wasn't a little later."

He fixed on her. What did that mean?

"Because now you're revealed," Elyssa said. "Everyone

knows there are mermen. Oh! If you wanted to visit her last resting place and say goodbye, I could look that up for you."

He shook his head immediately.

"Sure?"

It no longer mattered, and after all the years, crossing the final distance felt like it dishonored his father's commitment. "It is too late. I should have crossed to the shore much earlier."

Or not at all.

She softened and stroked his cheek. Pure kindness radiated from her. "She must have loved you very much to make your father break the rules like that."

His chest throbbed.

How strange. He had often thought that his life was harder because his mother and father had broken the rules. Better not to know her at all than to be forced to watch her and long for something he could never have.

"I could never leave my children," she said. "She's amazing. Truly."

His chest throbbed again. "It is different in each situation."

"Yeah, but no." Elyssa dropped her hand and straightened. "You see, I've had a lot of opportunities to think about it. I only see my mother once a year too."

He focused on her completely. She had the love and devotion of her father and stepmother. Two parents. He had assumed the mother died. Did Elyssa mean to say she had a third in her biological mother too?

"She's this complete free spirit," Elyssa explained. "My dad thought my birth would tie her down, but that never happened. He's way better off with my step mom. And Julianne—my biological mom—is always on the move. She's super fun when she's around, but at the same time, it's kind of exhausting. I'll never do that to my kids. When I settle down, I am settling *down*."

She spoke firmly, with a golden fire glowing in her chest and lighting her eyes with sparkles.

A tug of rightness gripped him.

Elyssa was, truly, everything he wanted in a bride. And she spoke so calmly and competently about critical things. She would be an excellent mother.

His cock twitched.

Now. He wanted her in his arms pledging herself to carry *his* young fry. As his bride.

"You have two mothers and one father," he repeated, trying on the family for size. "That is an amazing ratio."

She bit her lip. "Well, actually, the ratio goes the other way. My mother collected husbands like animal sanctuaries collect strays."

He frowned.

"Don't get mad," she instructed. "Our culture has divorce. And it's totally normal. There's no, 'your original husband is justified in murdering any guy who touches you' thing that mermen have."

He accepted her words while refusing the concept. It was slowly becoming less shocking that the female cashier touched everyone to give money and coffee, and no humans reacted. But surely it would be different to be intimate. Yes, in merman culture, a male could be punished for touching another warrior's bride — even to save her life, the husband was justified in calling for her savior's dismemberment. But if any male attempted to claim Elyssa now in front of Kadir, that male would be asking for death.

"All this is to say that my dads kept me in the divorce. I live with my biological dad and my stepmom — they're the most stable — and it's all complicated, but suffice it to say I have three moms and five dads."

Three mothers and *five* fathers? Eight parents? For one daughter?

"And that's how I know I don't want that. I love all my parents, but I don't want to make my kids divide their holidays up. My sweet sixteen was held at a community center just so it could accommodate all of my grandparents! I want one husband, two to five children, and a couple of big dogs."

She said it decisively, giving the truth to how deeply she'd thought of it, and finished her mocha.

Once more, he felt like the conversation had tipped in a direction he hadn't even fathomed was possible.

"Five children," he repeated.

She hunched her shoulders. "Is that a problem? I was going to say two or three, but I'm okay with big families, and you have a shortage."

Five.

Humans had multiple children. But mermen had one.

Because of the old ways. The covenant. That was why the cities atrophied. Why the young mer rebelled and joined him in Atlantis.

He could have more young fry. He could have five.

So could Soren.

Lotar. Ciran. Iyen.

His city could grow and thrive. The mer race could expand to its greatest height. Fill all the empty castles with warmth and all the cities with community. The vision Elyssa unveiled stunned him. Never in his wildest dreams had he thought it possible.

"Are you still hungry? Did you want to go get ice cream?" She reacted to his silence by retreating into her nerves and smoothing her kelp green dress. "Don't you like the mocha?"

He looked down at his untouched second coffee. "I am drinking it slowly."

Her smile radiated like the sun. "Oh."

His distraction from before, when she was revealing her light to him so generously, shamed him. The one who was wasting time was not her. It was him.

He must convince her now to increase her radiance. That responsibility was his. She was his bride. *He was her husband.*

He picked the coffee up and drained it in one gulp.

She laughed. "You did it again! So, how did you find the coffee?"

"Cold." He stood. "We must return to the dock."

Her smile faded. She rubbed her chest. "Already?"

Ah. Did she not feel the resonance? Then he would not force her. Not until she felt what he knew.

"No. I am still hungry."

She stood also. "Sorry! What can I get you?"

"A favorite food that only you will provide."

She sucked in a breath. Yes, he had listened carefully. She wished to care for him. For a short time in the air, he would make it so.

Elyssa rewarded him by slipping her arm through the crook of his elbow and tugging him to the exit. "I know just the place."

The strolled along the promenade, arm in arm, and he strove to increase her resonance as she asked about Atlantis. Did they have coffee shops? Did they have shopping malls? Did they have movie theaters? Did they have ice cream?

No. To all of the questions. He was beginning to worry

that the difference in their ways of life might be a larger problem than he originally thought.

She stopped at a stand and purchased him a cone stacked two high.

He consumed the cold, dark chocolate scoops with his usual single-minded approach.

She put a hand on his elbow. "Slow down. Don't you want a bite of mine? I bet you've never had Monkey Chunk before."

He did not trust a food made out of pulverized jungle creature. "I would not steal the food out of your mouth."

She laughed again. "When you put it like that, I almost wish you would."

He stopped.

Her laughter faded. Her lips parted. Her chest burned bright.

A cool drip of melting cream landed on his wrist and traveled.

"You have a drip." Holding his gaze, she touched his forearm. Her tongue caught the cream and traced a hot, wet trail up the back of his hand to his knuckle. She swallowed and smiled. "Delicious."

His cock, already alert by their thighs brushing and her enticing nearness, hardened to granite.

"You also have a drip." He lifted her wrist and nipped the bare skin.

She caught her breath with a little gasp. "I do not."

"No?" He sucked the fast blood-beat underneath her skin. "I am certain."

Her soul light flared.

His cock pulsed hot. How was it possible to crave her even more than when his soul claimed her in the auditorium yesterday? But now, after this day, brushing against her sweet, succulent thighs and falling under the spell of her playful, sparkling smiles, he needed her.

He pressed forward.

She smiled, playful, and backed away. "Where are we going?"

He didn't care. Down the side of the ice cream stand and around the back corner, into a shadowed alley. Her back hit the dead end with a thump. He pressed her against the shop wall.

Her light flared and her gorgeous, clear eyes fixed on him. "Kadir?"

"Elyssa." He rested his forearms on the wall on either side of her head. "You are mine. I must join with you."

Her lashes fluttered. Her light flickered radically. "I want that..."

Yes. She wanted that.

He swooped to claim her mouth.

Her eyes widened. She moved, and his lips met her chin. "But are you sure it's a good idea?"

He kissed her chin.

She giggled and wiggled, resisting with a laugh.

He pressed her harder into the building and tasted her jaw. Salty and sweet, coffee and cream. He followed the bone to the delicate ear and tugged the hot flesh.

She gasped. Her light glowed.

His cock pulsed. *He made her glow.* He moved her silken hair away from her neck.

She caught his hand. A question remained in her worried eyes.

He would hold her like an anchor and drown her with passion until all her fears were gone. He cupped her jaw and rubbed his wide thumb across her lips. She parted for him.

He bowed his head. This time, she would not turn away. "It is a very good idea."

"Um, but, what if I can't transform?"

He was not leaving this shore without her. Between nips, he ordered. "Feel our resonance."

"Well, but..." She glanced at the half-melted ice cream in her hand, nearly forgotten against the building.

He plucked the ice cream from her hand and crunched it in three bites. The yellow cream was thick and sweet.

She licked her lips. "If I can't, you'll have to give the new blossom to a woman who can. A woman who's better suited to ruling with you."

"There will be no more blossoms. The Life Tree needs you, Elyssa."

"It does?"

"Atlantis needs you."

She resisted. "Atlantis needs a strong queen."

"You will become a strong queen."

"No."

"Yes. You are what I need."

His words melted her resistance. Brilliance overflowed her chest, wrapping them in a private blanket of pure hunger. Her lashes fluttered closed and she tilted her lips up.

He took her mouth. The cold cream mixed with her natural sweet flavor. He captured her mouth and plunged in, sealing their bond. She clung to his forearm. He squeezed her curves. The soft breast ripe for palming. The wide hip perfect for gripping. The feminine curve of her thigh.

She sank into his caress.

He gripped her thigh, hiked it higher, and pressed his hard cock against her soft cleft.

She shuddered.

He released her mouth to taste the pulse-beat at her throat. Tease it with his teeth. Mark her as his. He shoved aside the green cloth and bared her skin. She gasped. The intensity of her light increased.

Her small, beautiful breast mound was perfectly shaped, like a scoop of iced cream with a dusky cherry. What was this flavor? He swiped his tongue over the pink peak.

Her fingers stroked his hair. Soft, gentle. Tentative.

He needed her brighter. Much brighter. And harder. Writhing against him.

Kadir lifted his head. She looked at him with soft, parted lips and unfocused, passionate eyes. A powerful wave of domination clenched him. She would not escape.

He ripped the green fabric out of his way and kissed the soft rise of her belly. She trembled.

Somehow, although she was right here, it felt like she was also far away. He hesitated. One hand gripped his forearm. The fingers stroking his head dropped away.

He surged up her body, slamming his forearm into the wall beside her head, making her jump. She was surprised but focused on him.

She focused on *him*.

And then she didn't. Her chest rose and fell. She licked her lips and started to straighten her torn dress.

He gripped her hands. "You are mine."

She did not protest. She also did not draw him closer. She waited.

His chest agitated. She was slipping away again! In desperation, he dropped his palm to her hot cleft. She gasped. There, the thin strip of polka dotted fabric. He moved it aside and cupped her feminine heat. "You are mine."

She moaned and thrust against his hand. Her light almost blinded him. "Yes."

"My bride."

"Oh, yes."

"My queen."

Her light dipped.

He released her as though she had burned him.

That was the problem. That was how she escaped him. He demanded she be his queen and her soul light went out cold.

CHAPTER NINE

E lyssa's thundering heart skipped and crashed into her chest.

My queen.

Kadir sensed her doubt and stopped his passion, stilled as though she had cried out. With his deep awareness, he always seemed to know exactly what she was thinking.

Now, of all times, she wanted to be his. She wanted to make him happy. She wanted to experience again his incredible passion, which flowed over her like a typhoon so hot and furious all she could do was hold on. He'd ripped her dress nearly in half without even thinking about it. All that hard, hot, masculine power focused on pleasuring her made her swoon. She wanted *You are my queen* to be true.

But then it struck her that everything depended on her. Everything. She wasn't Lucy. She wasn't Aya. How could the entire future of merman-human relations rest on her thin shoulders?

"Elyssa." The fierce warrior frowned and stroked her cheek. "You vowed."

Fear stopped her from transforming. It hurt Kadir. It hurt her.

But she couldn't just *think* her way to success, or she'd already have displaced Chastity Angel as CEO and promoted Aya. She'd already have transformed. And she'd already be a great ruler in every way.

"Very well." Hard darkness set his jaw. "I will talk no more about you becoming my queen."

"No, you have to!" Him giving up on her would be the ultimate failure. Elyssa squeezed her eyes shut so she didn't have to see Kadir's disappointed face. "I'm sorry. I just, um—"

He growled. "You are restricted from saying that word."

"Um?" Of course Kadir was right. A queen should speak confidently, not stutter. "Sorry."

"That word."

"Sorry?"

"Stop." He stroked her cheek, forcing her eyes on his. "It is one of the words that dims your light."

Oh.

When he studied her with such intensity, she melted a little. "Sorry."

His intensity increased, and so did the pressure on her cheeks. "Elyssa."

"What?"

"You said the word again."

"I know! Sorry. I can't help myself. I just—sorry."

He rested his forehead against hers. "You are the most confusing, intriguing, enticing bride who ever joined with a merman."

That...didn't sound like a compliment.

"I expected to begin the journey to Atlantis. But instead, I have spent today sitting with my bride. Talking.

Connecting. You have shown me a world I did not understand."

It sounded worse and worse! "I'm so sorry."

He eyed her intensely. "Use that word again and I will take it from your mouth with my tongue."

A shocking pulse of heat rolled through her.

He continued speaking. "I have always wanted one young fry. Now, you have taught me to want five. I have always wanted a queen. Now, I want only you."

Wait. That was the world he didn't understand? Multiple kids and her as his wife?

She knew she'd been losing him back at the coffee shop. The harder she tried to prove her worth as queen, talking about her qualifications for ruling and that one political science class she almost flunked in high school, the less impressed he'd seemed. Finally, she'd realized it was all over. She had nothing left to lose. And so, she started talking about pointless things. The logo on the coffee cup. Her hopes and dreams.

Now he wanted only her.

Tingles of destiny warred with disbelief.

That was what had touched him? Turned his monotone grunts into full conversations? Lit a fire in his silver-flecked eyes so hot it made him back her down an alley and crash over her in a tsunami of passion?

"Don't forget the two dogs," she said faintly, her mouth talking while her brain struggled to catch up. "Oh, I guess you call them 'house guardians.'"

"Elyssa." He pulled her lax hand from his hard bicep and kissed the center of her palm. A naughty edge of teeth made her shiver. "I vow to honor you. Protect our innocents. Join with you. Defend *our* Life Tree."

His words stole her voice. She whispered. "Even if I can't transform?"

"You must."

"But—"

"You will return to Atlantis with me. Now, or when I have returned with another blossom."

Her chest warmed like the full sun shone down on her. He'd return even though she'd messed up today. He wanted *her*. She sucked in a deep breath and threw her arms around Kadir. He caught her and crushed her to his hard pectorals.

With his steady faith, she could overcome anything.

He drew back. His lips nuzzled her, changing the glow into a steady, hot pulse-beat. She melted into the promise of his kiss.

Her phone jangled and vibrated in her torn dress pocket.

Kadir tensed.

She straightened and dug out the phone reluctantly. They were almost connected. She could feel it, finally. A new, powerful strength beat in her heart. With just a little more focus, she could certainly get over her doubts and transform. "It's Aya."

He stepped back.

She answered. "Just give us a little—"

"Come back right away! Lucy says you're already a mermaid. She'll prove it."

She couldn't stop her shocked, "What?" but Aya just tossed meeting instructions at her and hung up.

Could she become a mermaid queen in spite of her doubts? Really? Then everything was on hold. She raced to follow Aya's directions, tugging Kadir with her.

A driver picked them up and drove them back to the

private dock. Butterflies fluttered in Elyssa's stomach. What would Lucy have to tell her?

At the private marina again, Kadir's long strides closed on the dock. She hurried to keep up. Everyone was gone now — her parents, the filmmakers, everyone. They reached the wooden slats and Aya met them.

Aya shoved her phone at Elyssa, bright with excitement. "Talk to Lucy."

Elyssa held it in both hands. This was it. She took a deep breath and answered.

"You're a mermaid too! I'm so excited." Lucy was older than Elyssa. She was also much more accomplished, a boat captain and expedition leader who dove for treasure before becoming a mermaid. But on Aya's phone, the difference between them melted away. She giggled like a teenager. "You're going to have a blast. And you're going to a mer city where they want you! We got run out of Sireno. We're coming to visit."

"Ha ha. We'll see if the city actually wants me." Elyssa twisted away from Aya's frown and Kadir's matching expression. "I, um, still have to get there."

"Transforming is hard. The first time is the worst. What's going on?"

Elyssa told her the details, strolling down to the end of the dock for privacy. Lucy uh-huhed and hmm'd through the whole trauma. Just speaking all her doubts and fears aloud was deeply cathartic.

"And I keep feeling like I'm drowning," Elyssa finished.

"That's natural," Lucy said immediately. "But listen, you understood them speaking underwater. That's impossible for a human. We only hear a weird humming. You're already transformed."

"I half-transformed."

"There is no half-transforming."

"Are you sure?"

"Positive."

"They think I didn't drink any nectar and they're pretty sure I'm not smart enough to be queen."

Kadir made a noise.

Oops. Had he heard? She thought she was far enough away. She quickly turned and headed down the dock to the abrupt end. When she was whining like this to Lucy, she couldn't hold his strong gaze.

"Well, that's rude of them, and it's also completely wrong," Lucy said though Aya's cell phone. "Your fins and webbing are already there, waiting for you to make them come out. It might take months to train them to emerge on command. Speaking and breathing are easier because it just happens. And didn't you see more than usual? Or hear the plants and animals making music, maybe?"

She *had* seen awful far. "But the drowning—"

"Will never go away. Have Kadir distract you. The next thing you know, you're six feet under. I like to lose myself in Torun's kiss."

Her chest heated. "Kiss?"

"Make out like there's no tomorrow. If your king is half as hot as Torun, it shouldn't be a problem."

Her desire twisted. She'd been reliving his kisses every time her mind wandered. "Oh, it's no problem."

"Good. Have fun. I'm so excited for you! You deserve it."

You deserve it.

It was nice to hear those words from Lucy, who only knew her from the short time they spent together on the Sea Opal expedition. It meant more than any encouragement from her family, who often seemed to tinge theirs with sympathy for whatever mistake she'd just made.

Maybe she would handle the ruling thing after all. First, she had to get to the city.

"Oh yeah," Lucy added, just before hanging up, "and get naked."

"Naked?" Elyssa squeaked.

"It helps. Especially the first time."

They finished their goodbyes. Elyssa handed the phone back to Aya.

"Apparently I've been a mermaid this whole time," Elyssa said. Awkward! "Um, thanks for going out on a date anyway."

"Elyssa." Kadir's eyes glimmered with strong emotion. But which one? "Soren's words dimmed your light."

So he had heard her. "Soren spoke the truth."

Kadir's mouth flattened to an inflexible line. "From this hour forward, only honorable words will be spoken in your presence."

"Hopefully I can keep from screwing up so you don't have to worry."

He focused on her again. Clearly, he intended to protest.

But she had already wasted enough of everyone's time.

She took a deep breath. "I'm, um, supposed to get naked and then make out with you. Will you help me?"

His protest died. He tipped her over the side of the dock. Together, they plunged deep into the startling blue depths.

Sunlight from the waves overhead dappled them. Kadir's body shimmered, slippery as a fish. He shucked his shirt and kicked free of his jeans. Silver iridescence scrolled all over his lithe body, even down the length of his... Elyssa stared. She'd been so distracted before by trying to transform that she didn't notice his total nakedness or his long, thick cock. It was, like the rest of him, proud and commanding.

He focused on her with hard intensity. "Off."

She removed her dress and it floated away like his clothes. She struggled free of the bikini. Warm ocean flooded her secret nooks and crannies. It felt illicit and naughty. She was skinny-dipping in public with a hunky merman.

Far below her toes, the sand glowed brightly. It really did spread forever in every direction. If she squinted, she could probably see the Keys. The Caribbean. Texas. And, diving through the ocean like swallows and ravens, every single fish in between.

She'd been a mermaid from the very first plunge off the dock. She'd just failed to believe it.

Elyssa floated in perfect equilibrium. Currents tugged her to and fro like strong breezes. Unlike breezes, however, she could see their movements. They swirled with tiny, sparkling plankton.

She *was* a mermaid. A very human-shaped mermaid.

Kadir tugged her deeper. For once, her single-minded warrior seemed to relax. He stroked her cheek. His touch was feather-light and deeply moving. Tenderness she had never seen calmed his hard, silver-streaked brow. It whispered secret promises into her soul.

He twined her in his arms. "Kiss me."

His voice thrummed from his chest directly into hers. Lucy had told her about this. Elyssa needed to speak without speaking. Think her words, and push them across to Kadir in the same cavity where she heard them.

"You...were eavesdropping," she said cautiously.

It worked.

He drew her closer. His lids lowered and he kissed her fingertips. "I will always listen to you, Elyssa."

Her chest squeezed.

Could she really give herself completely to Kadir like this? The rock star fantasy had peeled back to reveal a complex, thoughtful, commanding mer king. Could she really stand beside him and rule over his kingdom?

Again, in the way that he seemed to read her thoughts, a shadow passed his face. "Do not think about becoming a queen. When that time arrives, you will be ready. From now until that time, I will not speak of it in your presence."

He did that for her. Even though it pained him.

She entwined with him. Command stamped itself on his chiseled cheeks, his strong jaw, and his broad shoulders. He would keep his word, sheltering her from her fears, for all eternity.

He nuzzled her gently. His lips teased her to open. To let him in.

She sank into his kiss.

His tongue stroked her hidden crevices, just like the water. He tasted salty as the ocean and also richly smoky. His flavor coated her lips in liquid sugar. His hard cock pressed against her soft belly with delicious demands.

This was what mattered. Not the future. Not the past. Nothing but Kadir. Her merman.

Her king.

They sank into the depths together, twirling slowly.

"Breathe out," he ordered without lifting his lips. The words vibrated in her chest.

She trusted him.

Bubbles erupted from her mouth. Ocean poured down her throat.

Her chest convulsed.

She jerked, coughing out bubbles and sucking in thick water.

His arms tightened. "Stay with me, Elyssa. Listen to the song."

She thrashed. Listen to the song? What... oh.

Symphony music swelled like a radio turning up the volume dial.

The mosquito hum of the earring transmitters still buzzed in her ears. But beneath it, a hum-hum-hum of silver fish flew in a school, a boom-boom of crabs scuttled along the sand, and a chuga-chug of sand dollars dug beneath the sand.

In fact, it felt like she could see *through* the sand somehow. Behind rocks, even though normally light didn't bend that way. Her senses were expanding. She was "seeing" things she couldn't possibly see. The animals glowed like Christmas lights, brightening the already brilliant ocean. A giant laser light show, from the tinkling patches of kelp beds that illuminated several miles off-shore to the surprised shouts of Kadir's fellow warriors, swimming toward them furiously, a few miles down the beach.

Slowly, by degrees, she let go of the panic.

The ocean caressed her body inside and out. And she was still alive. Everything was fine. She did not need air to breathe.

Her hands crept to her lower back. Hard ridges formed the vents for gills. At her touch, they closed up tight, sealing her body. This was how a mermaid held her breath.

The mer warriors swam around them. Unlike Kadir, who was unarmed, the rest of them carried long metal tridents; Lotar also carried twin daggers strapped to his biceps. They were otherwise naked, but it didn't seem weird or awkward. Of course, she couldn't help checking them out. Their cocks flew loose and free, as intricately tattooed as the rest of them, all different sizes and shapes. In contrast, she didn't feel like they were checking her out at all.

Soren noted her feet. "She has not transformed."

"Apparently the feet and hands are a later stage transformation." Kadir rested his forearm possessively around the curve of her buttocks. "She no longer requires air. Only that matters."

Soren grunted. "Carrying her will slow our return."

"We expected this possibility. Brides never fully transform."

"She is shining." Ciran studied her upper back. Although she glanced down at his coffee-and-green swirled cock, he seemed uninterested in her attributes. The vertebrae between her shoulder blades, which didn't seem any different to her, drew his eye. "This level of brightness suggests she is happy despite being under the water."

"You can ask her, Ciran. She could hear our words from the beginning."

They all fixed on her.

Oops, she was exposed. She clung to Kadir more tightly. "Hi."

Ciran licked his lips as though he didn't know how to repeat his question.

Iyen asked for him. Intent as a special ops soldier who needed to know whether or not he had completed his mission. "Are you happy?"

Well, a few minutes ago she'd thought she was a failure who'd wrecked the mer-human project and destroyed Aya's great grandmother's company. "I feel great right now."

They all seemed...peaceful? Like exhaling a huge sigh, only no one was breathing air.

It would be useful if she could see some sort of inner-chest-glow in them like they saw in her. Lucy had been unable to see the glow. Now Elyssa couldn't see it either. Maybe only mermen could see it.

Soren broke the peace with a flick of his fins. "We must go, my king." He shot through the water.

A splash broke the sea by the dock. Aya. She wore her red bathing suit and snorkel set, and she gestured to Elyssa urgently.

"Just a sec."

Elyssa let go of Kadir and swam to Aya. Her cousin didn't seem to see her until almost the last moment when Elyssa nearly grabbed her shoulders.

Aya pointed at her underwater camera. Scientific documentation, of course. It made the same mosquito whine as the transmitters. The red light blinked. It was recording.

And...she was naked.

Oh well!

"Cheese." Elyssa swam loop-de-loops. If this got broadcast with the rest of the reality TV documentary, they'd fog out her private bits.

Unless a cable channel bought the rights. Best not to think about it too hard.

They splashed around each other like the old days in the pool. Aya was still the stronger swimmer. Her red plastic fins easily out-paced Elyssa's barefoot butterfly kicks. But this time, Elyssa was the one underwater, with the whole undersea world opened up. She dove down, down, down. Aya had to turn first and go back up.

The mermen waited.

Right. Enough messing around.

Aya pointed to the surface. She wanted to tell Elyssa something.

"Say your farewells," Kadir called.

Soren's grumble carried. "You will see her in a month anyway."

Right. The first check in was in a month.

Aya got her breath at the surface, descended again to Elyssa's level, and pointed upward more insistently.

Elyssa did not want to go through the transformation again. What if she *couldn't*? Okay, that was a silly fear, but Lucy said all transitions were hard. The first was only the hardest.

Aya's insistent gesture slowed and stopped. She must realize Elyssa wasn't coming up. She made her hands into fists that seemed to mean, *Good luck.*

Elyssa gripped her fists and pulled her into a hug.

Aya stiffened, then her arms went around Elyssa's back. For the first time in their long friendship, she squeezed Elyssa.

A lump formed in Elyssa's throat.

Aya quickly released her, trying to pat her back awkwardly under the water. On the surface, she'd have been red as her signature clothes. Even underwater, behind a mask, holding her breath with a snorkel clamped in her teeth, she looked everywhere but directly at Elyssa.

"I'll find a way for you to become a mermaid queen too," Elyssa whispered. "I promise."

Aya couldn't understand her, but that was okay. She waved and kicked to the surface. Unlike Elyssa, she couldn't hold her breath forever.

The warriors were waiting.

She swam to Kadir. "I'm ready."

He drew her to his broad chest. "Hold on."

She slipped her arms around his neck and fit to the hollows of his body, squeezing and squishing like two puzzle pieces snapping into place. His erection, which had gone down after she left his arms, hardened again with her nearness.

He made her feel beautiful and desired. He didn't just say he wanted her. His body meant it.

She snuggled against him.

He kicked. They flew through the water like a plane accelerating for take off. The seafloor rushed past and the dock, with lonely Aya kicking at the surface, shrank tiny. They crossed miles in minutes and entered the greater echo chamber of the ocean. The coastline disappeared.

She was on her own.

CHAPTER TEN

K adir carried his bride into deep water.

The surface trials were over. Elyssa held onto Kadir's body trustingly. A powerful, protective urge pulsed through his muscles. His fins pumped across the treacherous shore-hugging current.

He had wanted her to transform completely right away. Brides never did this. Some could not make their fins even at the end of their stay. If Elyssa had, it would have encouraged them that Kadir's vision was right. She was destined to be more than a bride who returned to the surface. She was destined to remain forever as his queen.

But his focus on her fins had blinded him to the parts of the transformation that had already taken place.

Her doubts — and his — slowed them.

Aya had given Kadir a meaningful gaze on the dock while Elyssa had learned the truth of her powers over the cell phone. Her hard gaze blamed him for the delay. She was not wrong. They could have been on their way to Atlantis more than half a day earlier if he had held tighter to his faith.

Faith in the Life Tree nectar. Faith Elyssa's transformation happened at its own pace. Faith in himself.

Now Elyssa stared in wonder at the passing ocean. She breathed, she saw, she heard, she spoke. Someday, the rest would come. Rightness gave him a burst of speed. He would not forget this lesson soon.

"Will it take long to get to Atlantis?" she asked.

"Yes." In surface time, their arrival took over two weeks. "Shorter because we will not sleep."

"Sounds like a long night."

"Many long nights."

She caressed his neck and shoulder blades with soft, insistent strokes. "You're holding me tight. Is there something I can do?"

He found the most aerodynamic shape to press her abdomen to his and let her human feet dangle between his long fins. "Rest your head against my shoulder."

"Like this?" She touched her forehead to his collar.

He pushed her head closer to seal the gaps. She shifted with his pressure and suddenly they smoothed into a shape coiled with power. He shot through the water twice as far using only half of the kicks. His warriors noticed and perked up. They had been holding back because of him; now, they kicked hard.

"Is this really helping?" she asked. "I feel like all I'm doing is weighing you down."

Ciran fell behind. Soren looked as though he were struggling.

"It is the best we can do. Do not move." He summoned Ciran. "Why were you not fed and rested?"

"We were."

"Then why do you struggle to match my pace?"

Ciran looked ahead at Lotar and across at Iyen. All

showed signs of exerting their maximum effort. "My king, you are swimming excessively fast."

That made no sense. On the journey out, Kadir had struggled to keep up with the slowest pace. The warriors had held themselves back. They had all experienced the same rest, and now Kadir was burdened with a second weight and mass. How could he possibly be going faster?

Soren finally motioned for Ciran to return to his position, and he swam beside Kadir to gruffly admit the truth. "We did not rest as long as you ordered."

"Were you not treated well in my absence?"

"Aya treated us fine!" The slash he made in the empty water with his trident was suspiciously defensive.

"But?"

"There was a disagreement."

"With Aya?" Elyssa lifted her head.

Their aerodynamic shape collapsed. Current slammed into them. The other warriors soared past.

Soren fell back. Concern struck his face. "My king?"

"I am fine." Weakness was to be expected. "Continue your explanation."

"Aya took us to a 'fifties diner'. We consumed grilled, macerated cow 'burgers' and salted potato wedges. Also, a glass of a cold substance sucked through a straw. Chocolate something."

"Chocolate ice cream? Yes, I also enjoyed this food."

Soren grunted.

Elyssa dropped her head to Kadir's chest again. Their aerodynamic shape improved. "Did you have a good time?"

"No."

"No?"

"She is infuriating."

"Infuriating? Aya is? You were offended by Aya?"

"Stop saying that name!"

She started.

Kadir growled deep in his chest.

Soren fell back, chagrined, and kicked hard to catch up. "You are swimming fast again, my king."

He was? Kadir lengthened his strokes. He did not feel any stronger in his back or his legs. "I have found a faster micro-current."

Elyssa nestled against Kadir. "I just can't believe A—my cousin, uh, made you angry. She's a master of diplomacy and she's never ruled by her emotions."

Soren huffed. "She insisted... She insulted our ability to protect a bride."

Kadir grunted. On the sacred islands, brides were raised never to question the covenant. "She is a modern female."

"Even so." He seethed. "We left and secured the swimming areas while we awaited your return. Do you know humans pay no attention to predatory signs? They dangle young fry in the same currents as bull sharks! Madness."

"Sharks!" Elyssa reared back. They flew hard off-kilter, throwing the other warriors off. Her white face darted in all directions, high alert, seeking an enemy. "I was so excited about becoming a mermaid that I forgot. The ocean is teeming with *Jaws*."

"Jaws are easily avoided." Soren frowned at Kadir's abrupt struggle. "Most sharks live at the top of the water column. Those are easy to outrun."

"Oh. Good." She partially relaxed. "We can outrun them."

"Not you."

She jolted.

Conscious of his vow not to allow dishonorable words in her presence, Kadir amended Soren's statement. "Not anyone with human feet. The mer can easily outrun sharks. You will also when you can make fins."

She tightened on Kadir. Her earlier relief was gone; she remained stiff. The current turned rough against him.

"I will protect you. Believe."

"I do."

"Do not let human fears poison your new life."

"I'm not. Totally not."

But her body remained stiff and her light remained dim, giving up the truth of her lie. With Lotar in the front, Soren and Iyen parallel, and Ciran behind, they made the safest possible formation through the rough, wild seas. She could not trust in that.

She could not trust in him.

Soren finally realized his role in alarming her and kicked. "You will see the truth. Lotar will find sharks for you."

"Oh, uh, you totally don't have to. Don't go out of your way on my account."

"It is not out of our way. We are crossing shark fields now."

"Shark *fields*. Oh god. Tell me you're kidding."

"No." Soren swam ahead to Lotar easily.

Kadir labored. The water pressed in, heavy and not. Her fear was like a weight dragging him down. "Rest your head on my shoulder again."

She obeyed reluctantly. The currents eased, but her stiffness remained.

"Release your fears," he ordered. "We do not fear sharks at the surface."

"It's not only that. I just can't believe it." Elyssa traced the silver tattoos to the jagged scars interrupting them.

"Aya's so careful. If even *she* made you guys angry, what hope do I have?"

"You are not Aya."

She snorted. "That's what I'm saying!"

He tried to formulate his true thoughts. That he had chosen her because she was not Aya. Her strengths were different.

Her tone dropped. "There's just no way I can be a queen."

His heart thudded heavily. Even though she was in his arms, speeding toward Atlantis, her wishes placed her miles away. The surface. A sandy shore, and a white lounge chair, and a distance he could never cross.

"You do not have to assume that role," he said, even though the words cut his throat like little shards of broken shells. "In Atlantis, you will be accepted the same as any warrior until you are ready for more."

He deliberately said "warrior." Although she would automatically be accepted as a bride, he wanted her to fly freely through the city, confident of her place. Queens belonged. Warriors belonged.

Finally, he broke through her resistance. She eased against him with trust. The water didn't feel quite so thick. He propelled them onward.

"I do want to try to be a queen," she insisted, even though every fiber of her being — and her soul light — declared that she did *not* want to try, and in fact, accepted Kadir's offer with her whole heart. "I'm just terrified that I'll get off on the wrong foot. Or wrong feet."

"Your feet are not wrong. Some brides never make their fins for their whole stay."

"Which is two years? I read the contract."

"Yes." That was roughly the same time as the old covenant. "But it does not have to be."

"It doesn't have to be two years?"

"Correct." He hoped it would be the rest of both their lives.

"So it could be a lot shorter?"

Unease slid into his spine. Why was she asking this? "Yes."

"What would, uh, cause that?"

The bride's wishes. The dissolution of Atlantis. Kadir's death.

He enumerated the reasons under the old covenant. "If the bride cannot adjust. If the pairing is unsuccessful. If her warrior is gravely dishonored."

She dropped silent. Thinking hard about her wish to be only a bride? She clearly held that preference. But he did not wish to return her to the surface. Not now, not in a month, and not in two years. They had barely begun this journey and already he felt like she was slipping away from him. Even within his own arms.

"I will instruct the others to treat you as a warrior if that will ease your discomfort."

"Oh." She was distracted. "Thank you."

"A great feast awaits your arrival. You will make the welcome speech of a warrior and receive all the appropriate honors."

Her tone flattened. "Speech?"

The water grew rough again. Kadir focused on maintaining his speed.

Soren dropped back to their position. "Lotar senses a migration of hammerheads." He pointed off the current. "It is a short distance."

Elyssa's light flickered. The water dragged. Neither his

body nor his soul could compensate for the heavy doubts of his bride.

Lotar looked back.

Kadir signaled. "We will detour."

She relaxed. "Thank you. I'll see them later. Thanks."

"He meant detour closer," Soren said.

She stiffened.

"Relax," Soren snapped. "Why do you insult us? We have already told you sharks are not to be feared. And even if they were, you further insult our ability to protect you."

She wriggled away from Soren. "I'm sorry! I watched too much Shark Week, okay?"

"No, it is not okay. Every vigorous movement like you are making injures Kadir."

She stopped. Her soul light dipped. "What?"

Kadir growled. "Speak honorably in front of my bride."

"It is truth." Soren's dark eyes snapped to Kadir. "Lotar sensed she is the reason for your uneven swimming. When she moves wildly, it increases your weakness."

Her light dimmed. She sank heavy in his arms. This was the cost of Soren's dishonorable words. Even if they were truth.

No male would injure his bride.

His anger grew. "I warn you."

"You drag your bride through the water like pushing the flat side of a wall."

Kadir snarled, dropped Elyssa to one arm, and surged forward. She gave a surprised shriek.

Soren jerked away, his trident rising instinctively to protect his face. Kadir grabbed Soren's throat and dragged him close to his enraged face. The powerful warrior twisted his trident at the last moment to thump Kadir's forearm with the flat side of his blade.

In any true battle, Soren was the superior warrior. They had been friends since they were youths. Soren was the one who had planted Kadir's Life Tree seed and led the band of rebels who rescued him from prison. But Kadir had the superior rage.

"Do not speak dishonorable words to your future queen. You will honor her!"

Soren's deadly black-tattooed face clenched. "She refuses those honors. Everyone has seen her soul light darken. She does not love Atlantis."

"She will love it in her speech."

"Words mean nothing! Only action matters. She is no queen of mine!"

White hot anger burst in Kadir's chest. He bared his teeth to make Soren submit or die trying.

"Stop!" Elyssa wrapped her arms around Kadir's chest. Her legs secured his waist and she hugged him from behind. "You have to stop. I'm so sorry. I'll try harder. Please don't fight."

Soren snarled as if he didn't hear her.

Her desperate heart raced in her chest, sounding an alarm call in his head that could not be ignored.

Kadir released Soren abruptly.

The other warriors hovered around them. Frightened and unsure.

This was a mistake.

He sucked in cool liquid and tried to get his calm back. Defending Elyssa hurt his warriors. Injured his friendship with Soren. Ripped their fragile alliance apart and threatened the integrity of Atlantis.

She crawled around to his front and cupped his cheeks. "I'll make the speech. I'll look at the sharks. I can adapt to the ocean. I'm not afraid anymore. I promise."

His stomach turned.

He should have listened to his warriors. He should have selected another bride. Choosing Elyssa and forcing her to come had driven her to this. Pain. Sadness. Desperation.

"I'm not afraid." She stroked his cheek. "Let's go. Let's go right now."

Lies.

Sweet, honest, heartfelt lies.

And despite all that, he received comfort from them. Tension deep in his soul eased. She saw him. She cared for him. She felt concern because of his actions and her worry made him feel good.

He disgusted himself.

Kadir peeled her hand from his cheek and ignored the stab of sadness. He did not deserve to feel happy. "Lotar. Resume our course. Forget the detour."

They turned to make the formation. Soren kicked back to his position. His rage silently seethed. Kadir had never treated him so roughly. It was too late to undo his actions. They were done.

Kadir kicked. His chest felt dull. His body ached. "Rest your head on my shoulder."

"But wait." Elyssa placed her hands where Kadir put them but she would not mold to him. She kicked, as though her human feet would help him, and sought his gaze. "I told you I want to see the sharks."

"You have seen enough for one day."

"I mean it."

"You are frightened. There is no need."

"Please!" She grabbed his cheeks and forced him to look her right in the eye. Hers were not white with fear. Her expression was fiery with determination. "Please take me to the sharks. Now."

CHAPTER ELEVEN

E lyssa had done everything wrong.

She had promised to be a queen, and her fears had caused a fight with Soren. She had promised to try to help Kadir, and she slowed him down like pushing a wall through the water. She had promised to try her hardest to fit in, and the moment they offered to show her their world, she closed herself off in fear.

Right now was the moment. She gripped Kadir's silver-streaked cheeks and held his matching silver-flecked eyes. There would not be a second chance. She had to prove her dedication to him and to herself.

"Take me to the sharks," she repeated. The tremble in her tone was just the unfamiliar feeling of her chest vibrating. "Please."

He studied her for a long, hard moment.

If he said no, then she would know it was already too late. She had failed to reach him. He would take her to the surface as soon as her presence caused the Life Tree to grow a new blossom.

She tightened. He had to give her this chance. She

would make it matter. *Please. I believe you. Please.*

He nodded slowly and gestured to Lotar. "Go."

Lotar cut sharply to their left.

Kadir followed. The others moved also.

Relief made her tremble. She had another chance. It wasn't all over.

He pressed her head to his shoulder. "Increase your glow."

She collapsed onto his hard, solid strength. He pushed her head deeper into the comfortable hollow by his neck and shifted her thighs so they straddled one leg. It was too intimate. Nerves fluttered and warmth glowed in the places he touched. His heartbeat seemed to sync with her chest. She was warm and safe, embraced and loved. The promises this intimacy whispered to her were dangerously appealing. She could love him. Trust him. Give him everything.

That was why she kept stiffening and reacting. It was all in her head. The promises were poisonous but seductive. Resisting them was like trying to resist sleep. They were so deliciously hypnotic.

Worse, when she gave in, Kadir seemed to move more easily. So she had no choice. She tried to force the tenseness to leave while still resisting the overwhelming desire to give in.

Kadir's voice rumbled in his wide chest. "Relax."

She tried. While still resisting. "I'm sorry."

"That word."

"Hm?"

He was silent for a moment. It felt as though he changed his mind about what he was going to say. "On the surface, you fear sharks because they are hidden beneath layers of water. But now, you can penetrate what was hidden. Look and listen."

She opened her eyes. The sea stretched like a limitless sky and they flew across it, free and uninhibited. Fish sang all around them. In the distance, the mass of sharks formed a gray river. Their song was unique yet strangely familiar.

"It sounds like a fire truck," she said, finally. "The second half of the siren. It goes down in pitch."

"It is loud and easily avoided. Yes? If we persist, as now, the tone changes."

The hammerhead siren grew louder and the pitch began rising. Several sharks darted out of the stream, feinting at Lotar.

She tensed.

"They are establishing borders and warning off interlopers."

Lotar swam straight for them.

Elyssa's heart thudded. "We're not stopping?"

Kadir's jaw clenched in iron determination. "These sharks are shy. They will move away."

She was making it harder for him to swim. She knew that. But there were *sharks*, hundreds and hundreds of sharks, and Lotar was swimming *right for them*. "There's so many!"

"Trust, Elyssa."

She bit the inside of her lips. It was possible to trust and still be scared spitless, something none of these arrogant, overly-muscled males appeared to take any notice of.

Kadir gestured.

Even though Lotar faced away, he somehow sensed Kadir's order. He canted up, swimming toward the glistening surface. Kadir and the other warriors followed. Beneath them, the hammerheads dove deeper, avoiding the mer.

And he was right. The sharks did not attack.

Their flat heads and long bodies undulated beneath her. They were migrating, traveling just like her, from an old home to a new one. Their gray fins fluttered and they were suddenly, strangely beautiful.

The two groups passed by each other cross-ways, the mer headed deeper into the Atlantic. The sharks journeyed north in search of cool.

She melted against Kadir once more. "They did move away."

He seemed lighter and stroked her back gently. "Yes."

"Are all sharks like that? Or all undersea creatures? Am I like a master of the sea?"

"No." His chest moved. He was laughing at her. "We travel in groups this size because it discourages most predators."

She let out...well, not a sigh because her lungs were full of water. A watery sigh. "I want to see more."

"Predators?"

"Everything. I mean, if it's safe, like the hammerheads."

His hand paused. "You trust us?"

"I always did."

Lotar looked back at them. Was she tensing again and slowing Kadir down? She tried to relax more. But it was hard like this, having an argument.

"You did not trust us," Kadir said.

"I so did."

His low rumble disagreed.

Maybe her problem wasn't that she made mistakes.

"Fear and trust aren't opposites," she said. "If you pick up a hot coal, you're going to get burned. There isn't a way to talk yourself out of it. You told me to pick up the hot coal anyway. I trusted you."

He grunted. "A shark is not a hot coal."

"Sorry, I'm not explaining myself clearly."

"That word is forbidden."

Huh? Oh. Right.

"Sorry."

"Elyssa."

She tightened her diaphragm. "The point is, I'm scared of a lot of stuff. Like the speech. I'd never want my first meeting with someone to be a speech, and I'm terrified I'll say something wrong and offend everyone. But I'm still going to try. Actions are more important than words, right? I'll try not to complain."

He was silent for a long time.

"How do you normally meet someone for the first time?" Kadir asked finally.

"A personal introduction. Like, you know. 'Hello, my name is Elyssa, nice to meet you.' One by one. That kind of thing."

"For us, it is traditional to give a speech." He ground his teeth. But he was thinking about her, which touched her. "It is normal to explain why we have been exiled and demonstrate what strengths we pledge."

"Exiled?"

"No warrior willingly leaves his Life Tree." His lips pulled back in what was almost a smile but didn't quite reach beyond a grimace. "Except to come to Atlantis."

If it was tradition, it was tradition. Heads of state always made speeches. "I'll make the speech."

"It causes you great fear."

"Yeah." Because, as Aya would say, it wasn't in her skill set. "But if your warriors won't toss me out when I put my foot in my mouth, I'll do my best."

Even if it killed her.

CHAPTER TWELVE

W hile the endless ocean passed, Elyssa fell into and out of sleep.

Normally, she didn't go longer than a few hours without snacking, and she kept waking up hungry and apologetic. Kadir didn't eat — or sleep, or stop — so she wouldn't complain The hunger floated away when she told it to go. Although, it left reluctantly, and at some point soon, she could tell that she wouldn't be able to push it off much longer.

Exactly how long was the journey?

She could see forever in every direction, bright as a summer afternoon. Animals and plants and rocks and currents all glowed with extra sparkles. The day never changed into night. Her only marker of time was her catnaps.

So, she used the time productively.

Whenever she was awake, she traced the same letters over and over on Kadir's silver-inked chest.

Fall in love with me, Kadir. So deep, you can't ever let me go.

Because she was going to screw up. She could sense the screw-up coming like a hammerhead shark siren. She was going to offend Soren. She was probably going to offend Kadir. And when she did, if she wasn't already embedded like the silver under his skin, he would use that under-two-years escape clause. This was going to be a very short trip.

Especially if it depended on her welcome speech.

The first day of her new elementary school in Florida had coincided with Parents Day, so her accidentally vague welcome speech — "I have three moms and three dads" — branded her a hippie weirdo until well after high school. And that was before her mom brought home a few more soon-to-be-ex dads to join their extended family.

Her step mom Suzanna said Elyssa's biological parents were weird. "If your father divorced me, I would throw his golf clubs into the Everglades and park his cart under a nest of hornets. We would *not* remain friends."

She barely understood why Suzanna was so emphatic. Elyssa had inherited the easy-going gene. She was friends with all her exes. Sometimes, hanging out after a breakup felt the same as hanging out when she was dating.

But now, finally, she glimpsed what her stepmom had meant. She couldn't imagine remaining friends with Kadir. Two days together felt hotter and intenser than two years of past relationships. It was impossible to imagine what "after" would be like with him.

That meant she had to wow him during the speech.

"Observe the mermen closely," Aya had told her on the last night. She'd followed Elyssa home after signing the contract and stayed late to drill her in every important underwater scenario—except how to face down sharks—while Elyssa had drafted her will. "Small clues can tell you their values. You don't want to insult something of great importance."

Good advice. Too bad she'd already missed several clues. Elyssa doubled her efforts now and studied.

Ciran spoke precisely and didn't smile often. He had the manners of a young Mr. Spock as played by Zachary Quinto. Iyen zoomed toward danger with a serious look on his face like Jason Bourne. Soren was The Rock set to furious mode; he spent his time growling or throwing orders. He also looked like he could snap a whale in half, so even though he glared at her for slowing down Kadir, she still felt safer having him around. Lotar was a bit of a mystery. He swam at the outer edges, always roaming furthest. A lone wolf.

As she studied, they zoomed to the ocean bottom. The whine of the Van Cartier Cosmetics transmitter earrings went silent. Was that bad?

Normally the pressure on the bottom of the ocean could crush a zeppelin down to the size of a thimble. But it didn't crush her at all. No ears popping or painful compression. The pressure was like...colors, maybe? If colors had a weight. Heavy blue to tangerine orange to sunshine yellow.

Another thing that didn't bother her was temperature. The Florida coast was swimming pool warm. Wasn't the floor of the Atlantic only a couple degrees above freezing? Instead of cold, the water felt thick, like swimming through wool blankets.

She saw uncountable fish and so many other amazing things — shipwrecks, mysterious spheres, volcanoes, crevasses, indescribable creatures — that they blurred together into one solid sense of awe. How could she report back to Aya and the rest of humanity what was really beneath the sea? Every time she tried to catalog it all in her head, she fell asleep and woke up knowing she'd already forgotten several unforgettable sights.

Finally, after one of her longer catnaps and when her hunger was really starting to pinch, they rose into thinner, warmer water and left the fast current. Kadir kicked warily. His mer guard tightened close, tridents out.

"Is everything okay?" she asked.

"Yes." But his intense frown deepened. They passed over a field of giant tube worms flicking hungry, barnacle-like tongues into the current. "We are approaching the city."

Thank goodness. Finally. It felt like two weeks had passed. She was hungry enough to eat a tube worm.

Oh, wait. She'd been trying to catalog her surroundings so long she'd forgotten it was speech time. "Already?"

"What is wrong?"

"Nothing."

His eyes flashed. Real anger, and something else. "Elyssa—"

"Kadir," Soren growled low. "Someone has hunted in that field."

He tensed. "Our warriors?"

"No." Soren slashed the water. "These hunters gathered paralyzing poison surrounding the worms' tubes. See the scrape markings near the mouths. It is another raiding party. Eyes out!"

The others closed in, forming an impenetrable guard.

Butterflies fluttered in her stomach.

"You are protected," Kadir pushed. "Relax."

She wasn't nervous about the raiding party, whatever that was. "I'm trying."

"Trust in us. Think of your speech."

Gah. Her butterflies poured mimosas and started a dance party.

Wait, that wasn't dance music, and it wasn't in her belly, either. "I hear a shark."

"To your left."

From across fifty football fields, a startling goblin shark veered toward them. Even though it was forever far away, its hollow, eerie air raid siren was as surreal as its appearance, like something out of the *Aliens* movies. She had seen them before on Shark Week. They were like big, ugly eels with pale, sightless eyes and a gaping fake mouth rimmed by false teeth. Just when they'd suckered their prey into thinking the fake mouth had missed, their real mouth flew out and crunched the unsuspecting prey. Freaky! But they were not dangerous to people because they were pretty small.

The animal slithered through the water toward them. It grew bigger and bigger.

Her nerves twinged. "I thought you said sharks aren't dangerous."

"It has been driven to this location," Kadir said grimly. "The raiders drive these types of sharks into a frenzy within our borders to tire and harass us."

Wait. "So that means it *is* dangerous?"

"Elyssa." He sounded strained. "Trust."

It was coming straight at them.

Lotar dropped from the group and darted beneath the shark.

Its mouth loomed. Teeth. Endless teeth. It was coming! Kadir barked. "Elyssa. Trust—"

She strangled Kadir and closed her eyes. It wasn't real. This was a scary movie.

Something rough scraped her shoulder.

She was going to die.

Kadir shouted. "Soren!"

Soren snarled. Her eyes snapped open. Iyen rammed into her and Kadir, shoving them sideways. Soren and Ciran turned. The goblin shark cut between their two groups. It was the size of a city bus.

It wheeled.

"Fly!" Soren shouted. He stabbed the goblin shark and aimed for its nose.

The goblin shark's fake mouth opened wide. He missed. The inner mouth closed on his trident. He tugged. With his trident immobilized, the inner mouth pushed him back, hard. Real teeth snapped at his shin.

Soren's legs swung back, to safety.

The goblin released his trident and lunged for his head. Teeth grazed his forehead. Soren screamed in rage. The water streaked with his blood.

Kadir slowed.

Lotar zoomed up and slammed the base of his trident into the belly of the goblin shark. The shark forgot Soren and pivoted.

Kadir kicked to speed. "Iyen! Guard."

"My king." Iyen lowered his trident and faced the attack, watching Lotar and Soren with the goblin shark.

"Ciran. Report."

"I see no enemies."

"Take point."

Ciran flew ahead.

"Soren! You are injured."

Soren kicked, leaving Lotar behind. "A scratch." His forehead trailed blood.

As a unit, they moved in battle-ready formation.

"What about Lotar?" Elyssa asked. Over Kadir's shoulder, he alone remained with the shark.

"Lotar ensures our escape."

The lone warrior faced off against the goblin shark. The shark roared. Underwater, it sounded like a lion crossed with a grizzly bear. The goblin wheeled to attack Lotar.

He dove and popped the base of his trident to punch the shark's nose.

The shark's bugle cut off. It turned aside and thrashed.

Lotar wheeled and waited.

The shark shook its injury off and moved in for a second attack.

She and Kadir accelerated away from the fight.

"Is he going to be okay?" she asked.

"Trust Lotar."

"But the shark bit Soren."

Soren bared his teeth. "Because you lacked faith!"

What?

Kadir snarled.

Soren growled and flicked away.

"What did he mean, I lacked faith?" As the adrenaline drained out, leaving her cold and shaky, she was actually pretty pleased that she hadn't freaked out and tried to claw her way free. "I held on."

Kadir did not answer.

Ciran cleared his throat. "You moved."

"Huh?"

"We counted on Kadir's ability to maintain the faster speed. You changed your shape, increasing the water's drag—"

"Ciran." Kadir snapped.

The warrior dropped silent.

But he was too late. She got it. A horrible shaking hollow emerged beneath her and everything tipped in.

She had pushed through her fears. She had trusted in Kadir. She had done her best and it *still* wasn't enough. Soren got injured. They nearly all got killed.

She had done her best.

This was never going to work.

"Rest against me," Kadir ordered shortly.

He sounded exhausted. The bone underneath his pectorals was too near the surface. While she'd been sleeping and daydreaming, he'd been carrying her for hours. Hours that felt like weeks.

"Now."

She collapsed. Reducing his drag was the least she could do.

Lotar caught up to them as they flew over a rise.

Off to their left, strange architectural shapes, like towers and domes, walls and windows, formed a geometric pattern in the rocky seafloor.

"This is what remains of the ancient city," Kadir told her. He did not sound angry. Maybe he forgave her. "Someday we will raise it to the surface once more."

A terrible grinding noise emanated from the wreckage, like a garbage truck backing over an accordion. "What's that?"

"A cave guardian."

Oh. Lucy told her about those and she'd seen grainy footage on a Facebook live broadcast. Cave guardians were mammoth octopuses. In comparison to the harmonious fish, bass-heavy crustaceans, and pleasant cymbal-like jellyfish, octopi stood out as the tone-deaf, flatulent members of the undersea choir.

Kadir's tired tone lightened. "Now we enter our territory."

On cue, the ocean floor beneath them changed from monotone gray rock to gorgeous, colorful corals and vibrant grasses. The undersea song changed to a deep, beautiful aria. The mermen soared overhead like eagles soaring over their forest. Rainbows of singing fish wove through the kelp below. Tiny silver fish flew up and swirled around her and Kadir like twittering butterflies before descending back into the concealing forest.

In the distance, anchored to the ground but floating high above the forest, a single orb glowed. Radiant as a silver sun, it soothed the ocean with healing silence. Her chest lifted like she was stepping onto holy ground. Her heart swelled with awe.

Wait Was that it?

Elyssa was expecting a Life Tree like Lucy had described in Sireno — an actual white tree with bare branches, like a ginormous albino bonsai on a dais, floating in the middle of the city. Around it was supposed to grow fifty or a hundred giant, floating, bubble-shaped castles arranged in concentric circles. The king and important elders lived in the inner ring. The outer castles were ruled by warlords and had their "flavor." Lucy could sense which was Torun's by its gold, cinnamon-chocolate aura before he took her inside the first time.

In fact, a Life Tree was the stamen of its city, and the bulbs were its leaves. If anything happened to a Life Tree, the whole city would blacken and wither. So would the mermen who lived there and formed a symbiotic relationship with it, unless they quickly scrambled to get accepted at a new Life Tree.

But this small, glowing, silver bulb was no actual tree. It

was like...a closed tulip? Like the Life Tree was hiding inside, and petals were still closed over it, keeping it safe.

Also, only one castle floated behind it. The castle was like a giant green planet caught in the Life Tree's orbit. Its anchor also stretched straight down and disappeared into the forest below.

That was Kadir's city. Atlantis was two floating orbs. One radiant silver, one larger green. One hidden Life Tree and one castle.

And that was it.

Kadir swam toward the glowing Life Tree orb.

Yay. They made it.

Oh god. They made it.

"Do not fear," he murmured. "You are safe here."

It wasn't her safety she was worried about.

Warriors erupted from the distant green castle, zoomed across the vast, open distance, and swarmed their party. The ocean filled with light, sound, and gladness. The warriors of Atlantis darted and swooped, whooping. Her patrol broke formation to greet their comrades.

Kadir swam determinedly on. A smile curved his lips. The white light of the orb reflected in his silver-flecked eyes.

As they neared the orb, it grew to the size of a huge cathedral. Kadir swam past the curved outer walls. She could reach out and touch them. They looked smooth as marble.

Maybe it was just the last peace before the storm, but she almost felt like everything would be okay. Kadir had chosen her. Despite his doubts and her fears, she had arrived. *She was chosen.* She belonged.

They left the Life Tree and crossed to the castle.

Now, in perspective, the Life Tree was like a cathedral and the castle was like the Death Star. It was just huge. It was also no longer solid, flavorless green. A gentle, silvery-green light radiated hints of vanilla and hickory. Yum. This was Kadir's castle.

Kadir swam to the entrance. A tiny dot in the center of the bulb was actually a grand hallway tall and wide enough for two cars to drive through.

They entered and flew down the long hall. It opened into a large inner courtyard.

But it wasn't actually as vast as she expected. It wasn't like a football field or even a soccer pitch. It was more like a baseball diamond. The inner diamond, not the outfield.

That meant the walls were thick enough to hold conference rooms. Doors and windows grew organically from the inner walls, but she couldn't see very far inside, as if they hadn't been fully carved out. Some hinted at mysterious corridors inside. One would lead to the castle's "heart chamber," the most protected room deep within, where Kadir would take her to consummate their marriage. It made her squeaky with anticipation.

Kadir swam down. The floor of the courtyard was blanketed in a leafy garden. Rows of plants radiated from a central dinner plate-sized pedestal.

"The Life Tree will soon grow its first seed," Kadir told her. "It is a symbol of citizenship and great honor. As a castle makes a warrior into a warlord, his seed is the heart of his castle. All the warriors you see today will be warlords of Atlantis who possess queens and seeds." He stopped before the pedestal. "Our seed will rest on this pedestal. Practice honoring it."

He released her, bowed his head, and hovered his hand over the empty pedestal. "I vow to defend this seed as I defend my home." He kicked back. "Now, you."

She paddled to the pedestal, her feet brushing the

garden leaves, and held her hand out, palm down. Deep breath — well, not literally. Hah.

Around them, mer warriors flew into the courtyard and suspended in front of her and Kadir, just above the garden. They formed an iridescent, well-muscled, impressively endowed ring around her. They eyed her curiously, edging each other out for the best view. Elyssa was on display and she hadn't even met any of them yet.

Oops. In her distraction, currents buffeted her away. She paddled back. Currents pushed her into the pedestal. It rocked and started to fall. Aah!

Kadir righted it.

She spoke quickly. "I also vow to defend this seed as I defend my home."

The mer fell silent.

Uh oh. Had she done it wrong?

Kadir broke the silence. "Welcome my bride. Elyssa of Van Cartier."

Her heart sped. Her mouth went dry. Her tongue went numb.

"Now, the speech."

Someone in the back protested. "Speeches are for warriors. Brides do not give speeches."

Kadir hardened. "They do now."

The warriors quieted.

Kadir looked at her. Not angry. Maybe tired. Definitely expectant.

She was supposed to be his queen. She was supposed to represent humanity, Van Cartier Cosmetics, and Aya. She had to make the best impression now or ruin her image forever.

And that old trick of imagining her audience naked? Well, they *were* all naked — displaying large, at-ease, tattoo-swirled cocks as far as the eye could see — but it didn't help at all.

Her palms couldn't sweat underwater, but her belly crunched like her insides were made of aluminum foil.

"Hi. I'm Elyssa. Uh...I'm very pleased to be here. I've wanted to be a mermaid since I was a little girl, and so this is like a dream come true. But I have a lot to learn, and I still can't make my feet transform. It's hard!" She laughed.

No one cracked a smile.

Oh, god.

She scrambled for a serious tone. "Um...I'm sure you'll all find brides of your own very soon, and we'll rebuild Atlantis into a great city with Kadir. Thank you."

They continued to stare. Not aggressive. Just waiting.

She edged to Kadir and whispered, "I'm done."

He rubbed her back. He seemed...satisfied? Not unhappy, at least. And his casual touch and easy acceptance gave her so much comfort. "Now, form lines and perform the personal introductions common among humans."

A burly, gray-haired warrior swam forward with a critical eye. "Why personal introductions?"

"Because Elyssa greeted us as is custom for our people. We will now greet Elyssa as is custom for her people."

"This is highly unusual."

"You do not have to make my queen feel welcome, Adviser Creo. The All-Council must do what it considers best." Kadir's steely gaze settled his warriors, silencing any protests. "*We* will welcome her to *our* city."

Awkward.

The adviser huffed. The extra skin at his throat looked like a turkey's wattle. Although he was a large, muscular, nude male just like the other warriors, he seemed better fed and more opinionated. Kadir's pointed remarks ruffled his feathers. "A bride must always feel treasured. What is this human greeting?"

"Stand as you are. Elyssa will lead you in the proper action. This is Adviser Creo of the All-Council," Kadir said to Elyssa. "He is a neutral observer who guides us so we may be recognized as an official city."

Right. A VIP. She stuck out her hand. "Pleased to meet you."

Adviser Creo jerked back and frowned at her hand. "You wish to caress me?"

Oh, no. Mermen didn't touch. She knew better than to do that!

Elyssa's heart slammed into her rib cage. She pulled back and curled her hand into a fist. "Sorry. My bad. I just wanted to say hi." She pressed her fist against her chest.

The burly, gray-haired turkey floated back, staring her up and down, confusion building upon confusion. "What is this? Now she is gesturing at me. Rudely."

Great. The last person she wanted to piss off was the very first person she met.

Kadir uncurled her fist and smoothed her palm in his larger ones. "Modern brides shake hands, Adviser Creo."

"Lies."

Kadir growled. He was, Elyssa was starting to under-stand, a young king with no experience—and, if Atlantis wasn't a recognized city yet, maybe even no legitimacy—but it still seemed brave of Adviser Creo to dismiss him outright.

He turned to his warriors. "Ciran?"

Ciran straightened and swam forward. "It is true. All humans shake hands. Brides included."

"Not mated females."

"Yes, even those already joined to other males. It is a

simple greeting. We observed it many times and partook it ourselves." He puffed out his scholarly chest. "I, as well as Lotar and Iyen, have already shaken bride Elyssa's hand."

The adviser narrowed his eyes.

Kadir lifted his chin, having proved his point. "Surely, as the representative of the All-Council, you knew this?"

"Well. Of course." Adviser Creo harrumphed. "But it is not done under the water. She is too forward."

"Shaking hands is allowed in Atlantis. Its meaning is the same as on the land." Kadir's powerful resolution echoed across the full courtyard. "Whether above the surface or below, my bride resonates for me alone."

All eyes returned to her.

Great. Now she'd forced Kadir to rewrite merman law over the first split-second of a handshake. What else would she do wrong?

Kadir gestured for the next male to swim forward. "Faier."

Faier was older than Kadir but not as old as the adviser, and he kicked using only his left leg. His right dragged in the water. Scars raked his torso and obscured his mauve tattoos. He had a cautious, friendly face, as though he had once been outgoing, but had been beaten down too many times to trust openly.

He stopped in front of her and hesitated.

Okay. She was going to do this one right.

"You don't have to shake my hand," she said. "I didn't mean to be weird. How is the official warrior greeting supposed to go?"

Faier blinked at her. "We do not do this greeting."

Oh. Right. Jeez. "Sorry."

Kadir answered. "Do not apologize."

"No. I mean, I won't." That was not very queenly. She shook her head. "Of course. Sorry."

Kadir rotated to her fully. "You apologized again."

"Right. Sorry."

"Elyssa."

Ah! She couldn't help herself. She was all messed up and everyone was staring. "I'm sorry! That's the last time I'm apologizing." She flapped her hands in distress. "Sorry."

Kadir captured her hands and tugged her into his kiss.

He was calm. He was centering. He was everything she needed, her one anchor in the swirling chaos.

She rested her hands on his broad shoulders. It felt natural fitting herself into the position she had assumed for so long when he carried her safely to the city. His arms slid around her back and tightened. Her thighs wedged against his.

Her gratitude — he wasn't angry, he was totally support-ive, he was safe — swirled into a ball of fire that ignited in her core. Her need of the kiss changed. She pressed against him, squeezing him with her thigh.

He tightened.

The sweet, hot pressure of his lips slid into her like a shot of liquor hitting her vein. Sizzling heat flowed into her center. A tinkling cry, like a distant wind chime, sounded throughout the ocean.

Throbbing need twisted into an ache. She was suddenly all too aware of his nakedness. And hers—

He released her.

She floated back, torn free when she least expected it. Conflict chased across his hard face, and his gaze flicked over her shoulder.

Oh. Right. They were kind of in the middle of some-thing. She rubbed her head. He wasn't the only tired one.

She turned back to face the warriors.

Everyone was frozen.

Oh, god. What had she done now? She had stunned them all.

Faier, who she was supposed to be greeting, shifted uncomfortably.

"Continue with the greetings," Kadir ordered gruffly. His erection was hard and obvious, probably like her throbbing flush.

But the other warriors weren't too bothered. Even though everyone was naked, the arousal connecting her and Kadir was somehow contained. Their faces relaxed. Oh, maybe they weren't stunned. Maybe they were just waiting.

"Hello, Faier." She grabbed the mauve warrior's large hand. His eyes widened. She pumped it once. "This is a human handshake. What do I say?"

The warrior looked helplessly at Kadir.

"Use your usual greetings." Kadir brushed her shoulder. "Your name and where you are from."

Okay. Yes. She could do this.

"I'm Elyssa. From, uh, America. I used to work in HR, but...you know, never mind what I used to do. Nice to meet you."

His mouth dropped open. His voice was pleasant and commanding. "I am Faier. I am from..." He frowned and looked at Kadir as though uncertain of what to call this place.

"You're from Atlantis," she said.

"I do not have a Life Tree seed."

"Nobody does. Right? You can still be from here."

He blinked and straightened. His shoulders went back and his chest puffed out. "Then, I am from Atlantis."

Kadir nodded his acknowledgment. The warrior Faier

swam away proudly on his left leg, and the next warrior moved forward.

Her head swirled with the names, but everyone else went smoothly. Shy smiles were kind of endearing on the massive tattooed faces of the powerful warriors. Maybe, just maybe, she could get through this after all.

But she had a guess that she'd still be stuffing feet — many, many feet — into her mouth with dinner.

CHAPTER THIRTEEN

"That was skillfully done," Kadir told Soren. They floated outside the ring of feasting warriors to discuss the security of the city; Balim silently healed Soren's shark injury while they talked. "She has performed the welcome as well as any warrior."

Soren growled. "You prepared her for the first test."

"I did nothing, Soren."

He eyed Kadir skeptically. "She resonated with your kiss."

Yes. The warm memory of it lightened Kadir's chest.

The warriors who had accompanied them to Florida met many humans before greeting Elyssa in the auditorium. They reacted appropriately to her casual handshake that day. Kadir had not realized she would carry the tradition here.

Adviser Creo's shock and horror were echoed by others in this castle. If a warrior touched another's bride to save her life, her husband was justified to take revenge. Cutting off the offender's parts and banishing him to exile were common punishments.

In the face of that surprise, Elyssa had struggled with her fears. Like when they were attacked by the goblin shark outside the city, her effort to combat her fear was not sufficient. Her anxiety leached into the water, affecting all the other warriors with dangerous levels. They fidgeted and twitched, agitated. Kadir sought only to calm and refocus her with the one action that always worked.

But their kiss changed into something more. A reaffirmation of why she had come. A promise to the warriors of what could be theirs.

And she had emerged from it stronger, calmer, and glowing with his resonance.

That was why he felt comfortable leaving Elyssa's side now. She smiled for the warriors but her eyes continually turned toward him and, when he met her seeking gaze, she lit up. All the warriors understood. A handshake meant nothing. It was not a punishable offense. Her passion was only for Kadir.

But he had not prepared her to demonstrate that. "Our connection is strong."

Soren frowned.

"Do not scowl," Balim ordered. "You still have embedded teeth."

"Finish quickly. I must interrogate the last patrols."

"You are lucky you have a thick skull." He removed another tooth fragment from Soren's forehead, reopening the wound and causing blood to flow. "And you are lucky to have only suffered one injury in the open ocean."

"I received it near our city. Which sea slugs need a lesson in border defenses?"

Balim's lips twisted to one side. He preferred to concentrate silently on his work, but he was also used to being questioned. His dark, heart-blood red tattoos tallied the lives he had saved through his work. "The last patrols were Nilun and Zoan."

Soren growled. "Untrained young rebels."

"They are young, but Nilun comes from Djullanar." Like Rusalka, Djullanar was a city known for strictness; even now the hot-headed young male Nilun sat with a stiff back and his head at a military angle of respect as he took precise portions of the feast. It contrasted especially with the cheery male sitting beside him, Zoan, digging into Nilun's stiff ribs with a teasing elbow. "And Zoan stormed the prison right behind you to free Kadir. While you were gone, they engaged the raiders and interrupted a kidnapping."

So, the raiders who drove the sharks across their borders had also attempted to kidnap Kadir's warriors. Then, he would know which city they were from. Not that it mattered. Any city that could muster a squad would come to Atlantis to demand its defectors back.

"Neither complained about the extra shifts required for patrol," Balim continued.

Soren grunted. "There were complaints?"

"None that I took seriously." Balim removed another tooth. "Especially considering their situation."

Truly, these warriors did Kadir proud. They put aside their differences and worked toward a common goal better than any army.

Soren's black gaze flicked back to Kadir. "You prompted your bride to tell the warriors to claim *this* city as their own."

"I did not." He would have done so if he had thought of it.

That action was perhaps more important than demonstrating their special resonance. She encouraged the warriors to claim Atlantis as though it was already a recognized city, and they were its warriors.

To take just one example, Faier had been born in Nerissa, a city suffocated and buried by toxic slides after the unexpected emergence of a nearby volcano. His refuge city, Rusalka, passed him over for a bride after he was wounded in honorable combat.

Elyssa told him that Atlantis claimed him as a citizen, that *here* was where he belonged. She did more to reverse Faier's discouragement and discrimination in a single sentence than Kadir would have thought to do in a hundred years.

The light of a mer warrior held steady. It was not so easily knocked dim like the humans'. But, it was still possible to change. When Elyssa recognized Faier for Atlantis, he brightened a full notch. The others did as well.

Now, Faier served Elyssa with his usual friendly calm, but he moved more fluidly, as though his injuries bothered him less, and he seemed more at peace.

"It was her idea," Kadir emphasized.

"It was a *lucky* idea," Soren grumbled.

The snarl formed in his throat. He was tired of fighting about whether he had selected the best bride. "Was it? Did luck speak what our hearts need?"

"Her friend joined with a Sireno warrior. He could have prepared her."

"Her friend is not here now." Kadir thrust his hand at Elyssa. "Look at my queen. She is your future."

Elyssa floated in a place of honor surrounded by mer warriors. She smiled, laughed, and talked as she sampled dish after dish of the feast.

Soren said nothing.

Balim sealed Soren's forehead wound with a strip of

healing paste and collected the goblin shark's teeth. He looked at Kadir's bride for one long, inscrutable moment. "I hope a queen is all you dream it to be."

Kadir straightened. Was that a challenge? But Balim simply nodded to him, "My king," and stowed his healing supplies to join the feast.

He suddenly felt far too tired. He had brought a bride to Atlantis. A modern bride, who chose this life on her own, and promised, despite her fears, to try to become a queen. It was more than any of them could have received in their home cities. And yet, the undercurrent of anxiety seemed to poison everything.

"Where is your faith?" Kadir asked softly.

Soren made a rude noise. "Our faith was traded to be fashioned into jewelry for dark-souled women."

He meant that the warriors had lost faith when they gave up their Sea Opals for Elyssa. The image of Chastity Angel wearing the mating jewel irritated Kadir too. But worse was Soren's dismissal.

"This is only a short limitation. The ancient city was full of treasures. We will excavate the ruin and discover enough Sea Opals for a hundred brides. For a thousand!"

"If you can hold your new city from deadly enemies circling just outside."

Kadir bit back his anger.

The adviser swam up to them. Disagreement pinched his face.

Yet another complaint.

Soren put himself in front of Kadir. "Adviser. Problem?"

"Yes. You are in my way."

Soren did not move. Adviser Creo growled. The two regarded each other with snarls.

Kadir spoke mildly to defuse tensions. "Does the All-Council have guidance, Adviser Creo?"

"It is your bride!" He glared up at Soren, still partially blocking his way. "You should not put her on display this way. It is tiring and dangerous. And you should not encourage her friendship or casual touch. There are countless tales of warriors driven mad by the unguarded presence of a female!"

Another slice of anger burned hot in his chest. He understood Adviser Creo's fear, but he could not allow the insult. "She is not unguarded. She is surrounded by thirty loyal warriors and *me*."

His words carried. Those nearest glanced behind them.

Let them know that Kadir, at least, had faith.

Adviser Creo lowered his tone. "Your bride's speech was also irresponsible. She toys with their hopes."

"No one complained," Soren snapped, forgetting his own criticisms from a moment before.

"Because they are blinded."

"Her speech was inspiring." Kadir controlled his own anger to balance Soren's dark rage. "They work hard to guard Atlantis and excavate the old city. Remembering the reason is what they need."

"They must wait years until your Life Tree matures enough to put forth suitable mating jewels."

Kadir's hand flexed to choke his fat throat.

"We will possess a hundred brides," Soren growled, changing his answer in the face of Adviser Creo's attack. "The 'old ways' can swim with stinging jellyfish."

The adviser harrumphed. "Your Life Tree is only a sapling. This bride is a mistake. Both are vulnerable. You will regret not listening to me." He swished away.

Soren glared after him.

"We will soon be recognized." Kadir placed a steady hand on Soren's taut forearm. "More warriors will come. Then we will have our own representative in the All-Council."

Soren slowly relaxed.

Adviser Creo's self-righteous attitude made Kadir want to turn him into chub, but even Soren recognized his importance. After the All-Council approved the city, Atlantis would receive additional protections. Treaties with the other cities would be honored. Raiders would be outlawed.

And his bride — Atlantis's future queen — would be safeguarded. Even more than she was now.

He studied her silently with Soren.

After the human introductions, the warriors produced the wedding feast. Normally a wedding feast was held with only the bride and her warrior present, but the expedition was starving and everyone was exhausted. It was cruel to force them out on a night meant for celebrating the arrival of their first queen, and Elyssa demonstrated great interest in getting to know the warriors better. So, he ordered each male to present foods they had replanted from their home cities.

The offerings continued even now.

"This one tastes like fava beans." Across the courtyard, she crunched a bulb kernel. "You grow these yourselves? All of them? Wow. And this plant ... this one tastes like ... rootbeer?"

"What about this one?" Ciran's close friend Gailen eagerly offered her a precious leaf.

She bit down. Shock filled her face. She clapped a hand over her mouth. Her eyes watered.

"Horseradish." She spat out the mouthful and gagged. The green chunks floated away and descended for the courtyard garden, where they would turn into mulch. "Way too much. Hand me the rest of those fava beans. Quick!"

The others hurried to help her. She desperately chewed the beans and swallowed. They watched her closely.

Gailen's shoulders drooped. "You do not like my food," he said dully.

She shook her head violently. "It's not food."

His eyes widened in shock.

Soren bared his teeth and began to move, crossing to her side to stop her from inflicting any more pain. Elyssa could not know that Gailen had stolen this special plant from his father's gardens, on pain of death, for the sole purpose of giving it to a bride. She could not know his father had disowned him for daring to cross his city's council. She could not know how he'd worried over the stolen plant here, tending it as his sole tie to the heritage he had been forced to leave behind and his hope for a brighter future.

Kadir stopped Soren. Elyssa's tone and posture were not cruel. Soren's interruption would destroy any chance at reconciliation. Kadir had faith.

"You can't eat it whole," she said, unaware of the reactions taking place across the courtyard from her. "Horse-radish goes *with* other food. It's a condiment."

"Condiment?" Gailen repeated.

"Only eat a small amount. It brings out the flavor."

"Of what?"

"Prime rib, for one. Most beef is good. Um..."

"What is 'prime rib'?"

"The most expensive meat. It's so delicious. Pretty rare."

"Rare and expensive meat?" Gailen slowly straightened. "Like wedding meat?"

"They would serve prime rib at a wedding reception. Absolutely."

Gailen brightened.

Soren relaxed.

Elyssa pressed the other leaves into Gailen's hands. "Don't feed anyone a big leaf. Serve a tiny amount. Just a taste."

"For a wedding feast." He nodded and tossed an arrogant grin at Ciran. His enthusiasm was infectious, and the other warriors all smiled. "My offering is not ordinary. It is only for rare, expensive meat. A bride will like that."

"Anyway, don't worry so much about giving your bride an offering. Most important is your feeling here." She pressed her chest.

A hard punch of longing twisted Kadir's chest with bittersweet. They had been trained their whole lives that brides must have a mating jewel to consider a husband. No male was worthy without a jewel. To hear that a bride could love him without any offering at all was hard, frightening, and haunting. It was what they all longed to hear. She gave words to their deepest held dreams.

"Hmm." Her eyes were unfocused, her mind clearly elsewhere.

Gailen was listening to her so hard he nearly collapsed on his own elbows. "What are your thoughts?"

"Wasabi." She pursed her lips. "Real wasabi is so rare it's only served in fancy sushi restaurants. It goes for hundreds of dollars an ounce. This leaf could be worth as much as your Sea Opals." She ripped off a tiny piece of the leaf, pressed it to a chunk of freshly hunted albacore, and chewed thoughtfully. "When you raise Atlantis, you should open a restaurant. You'll serve the freshest sashimi ever."

She spoke so convincingly about things even Kadir

sometimes considered impossible. He focused on his vision because he could not face the daily discouragement of their present situation. Her casual acceptance of an inevitable future was both inspiring and terrifying.

Soren finally rocked back. He lowered his voice for only Kadir's ear. "She *should* be hidden from display."

Kadir's anger flared. "You doubt our warriors' honor to treat her well?"

"Not for her protection." He lifted his trident. The metal was heavy as his scarred brow. "For ours."

Because she raised the warriors' hopes. Because they believed every word. Because they would be crushed if she was wrong.

That stopped Kadir. A large, deadly warrior like Soren studied Elyssa like a new type of threat. One he'd never considered before. And he considered all threats. All of them.

Kadir growled. "Words mean nothing." He threw Soren's back at him. "Only action."

"Words can cause action." Soren regarded him from the side of his eyes. "We are all here because of yours. What will you do when she demands to return to the surface and refuses, for the final time, to become our queen?"

CHAPTER FOURTEEN

K adir was fighting with Soren.
Elyssa felt it, even though she couldn't hear the reason. They swam together into a hallway and disappeared.

Hopefully, it wasn't about her again. She rubbed her bare arms, striving for the calm that she felt when he had kissed her.

There was no reason for her to feel this nervous. The warriors were overwhelmingly kind. As soon as they started coming up to talk to her, the distance melted away. They were like any eager college grads wanting to learn all about adult life.

How silly that she had been so afraid of speaking to them. Some hung back shyly, but others were more overt with their offerings and their smiles.

The orange pepper-tattooed warrior named Gailen, who'd accidentally served her a giant mouthful of horse-radish, seemed close to college recruit age and was just as eager to understand everything. "Why do you describe these like foods you eat on the surface?"

"Well, this fruit really does taste like a cran-cherry. I'm trying to fix it in my brain so I can describe it to everyone."

They stared at her.

Had she said something wrong?

"Who is 'everyone'?" Gailen asked. He was enthusiastic and puppyish — and also a hard-bodied, ripped warrior. He reminded her of teen Chris O'Donnell, Elyssa's earliest crush. A gentleman, and trustworthy, like he would carry your book bag while making your heart pound.

"Aya. She's my cousin. And my parents, of course. They'll want to know."

Everyone's brows raised. She had said something truly shocking.

"And it'll have to go in my reports," she continued, babbling now. "There's so much interest."

"Your people are interested in us?" Faier asked, scratching at his deeply scarred left arm.

"Fascinated," she said. "Three months ago everything was normal. And then, boom, mermen have been living in the oceans for thousands of years and we never knew. When I was growing up, there were mermaid crazes, and we used to dress up in mermaid costumes, or me and my cousin Aya took mermaid swimming lessons, where we pretended we *were* mermaids and we wore swim tails. But it was all mythical make-believe. And now, when we find out it's all real..."

Food floated in the water before her, mermen warriors flexed their iridescent tattoos, and dinner was in the courtyard of a gigantic, living castle.

"It's a dream come true."

The mermen seemed to exhale, even though no one was actually breathing.

"Not everyone feels that way." The skeptical healer, Balim, lifted a superior chin. He was a bit like Benedict Cumberbatch showing off as Sherlock Holmes. "The water is different from the air. This dream of uniting them is rare."

"Maybe not everybody in the world wants to become a mermaid. But there was a whole pageant full of people." She pointed at timberwolf-grey Lotar, who was standing apart from the group. "You saw."

He said nothing, neither acknowledging or denying. Ever the lone wolf.

Ciran grimaced. "What Balim says is also true. Not every woman wished to be there."

Some people just had to be precise all the time, even when they missed the point.

"Okay, but there were tons who *did* wish to be at the pageant, like my cousin Aya, and there were tons more who weren't allowed to compete, like me."

"Compete?" Gailen turned to scholar Ciran. "What is this 'pageant'?"

"Women walk in a line across a large stage. They turn and smile. Then, they change clothes and walk in a new line."

"I want to see it."

"At first, it is interesting. Then, it is very boring."

"Ah!" Gailen's eyes widened with sudden realization. "Many were assembled for this pageant and were not chosen? That means brides are still awaiting us. Let us go *now* and claim them."

A fever of excitement swept through the feast. Warriors packed away their food and prepared to leave immediately.

Where was Kadir?

Ciran gripped Gailen's forearm to prevent the warrior

from swimming straight for the door. "You forget. We have no mating jewels for offering."

He considered the problem for a moment. "I will offer my horseradish."

"A bride will not accept your claim for horseradish."

"A modern bride will. Queen Elyssa has just said they do not need an offering if you can convince them with resonance." Gailen turned to Elyssa. "Right?"

Everyone stared at her.

Well...She didn't like how everyone was always talking about "purchasing" brides with offerings. Even though it was a bit ironic because Kadir had given Van Cartier Cosmetics a large bag of the precious gems. That wasn't *for* her, though. That was for the ocean platform and infrastructure to support her experience, like an astronaut that had to pay for their own rocket fuel to launch into space. She would have done it for free, and she wasn't the only one.

"For most people, the important thing is your feelings," she said. "But—"

"Then we will offer feelings." Gailen dropped his horseradish. "Come, Ciran. You never tried to claim a bride, did you?"

"For me to do so before the king is not tradition."

"Now the king has a bride, so you can."

"But, all at once like this, it is also not tradition."

"Atlantis has no traditions. It is a new city. We can make them ourselves now."

Swept up by Gailen and the rest of the warriors, Ciran was carried by the mass toward the door.

Uh oh.

"Wait," Elyssa said, paddling after them. "Let's, uh, talk about it some more."

"There are no rules," Gailen shouted. "Not in Atlantis."

The whole mass of warriors kicked toward the exit.

"There are rules. There are rules!" Adviser Creo kicked in front of their path, blocking the exit. He raised his arms and shouted. "Warriors! Wait. This is madness."

"It is not mad. We want brides," Gailen said simply. He was reasonable and heart-meltingly enthusiastic. "They want us."

"If you all leave, who will complete the duties to make this castle into an All-Council recognized city?"

"We can draw lots and claim our brides in turns."

"Then where will you store them? There is only one castle!"

"Bride Elyssa is here now. The Life Tree will grow more castles soon."

The warriors began negotiating who would go to claim their brides and how many would stay behind for the next turn.

Kadir's city was dissolving around him — all because of her! — and he wasn't even here to stop them. Oh, no, wait! Kadir flew from the hallway with Soren, cast a glance at her, and swam to the warriors massed and debating. He kicked forward to stand beside Adviser Creo.

Kadir held up his hands. "Before we claim these brides, we must uphold our agreement. The humans must know we act with honor. We will excavate the old city, uncover the Sea Opals, and then seek the next bride."

There were darker rumbles of disagreement. Someone muttered that they should never have agreed to the Van Cartier Cosmetics demands, and another muttered at how convenient it was that Kadir did not push for more brides now that he had his own.

Gailen stood indecisively.

Adviser Creo huffed and focused on him. "Take proper care of the bride you have before you go to solicit any more. Excavating the old city while bride Elyssa adjusts to our ways is the safest way to proceed."

Galen's jaw shifted in disagreement but he did not argue.

Someone hidden within the mass shouted, "Getting brides now will convince more warriors to join us and then excavating the old city will be easy!"

The hidden speaker exploded their anger. The warriors surged to the exit. Kadir and Adviser Creo braced. Two mermen could not stop the tide.

Soren's voice cracked. "Who damns their bride to death in the open ocean?"

The warriors slowed and turned.

Soren bellowed, alone, in the middle of the courtyard. "Who abandons this city on a selfish quest?"

Gailen twitched and faced Soren. "It is not selfish. Claiming a bride is why we—"

"You plan to carry brides across the open ocean. None will guard against predators which took all five of *us* to face." Soren's scarred visage was a testament to just how lucky they had been. "Even if your brides survive the crossing, you will return to what? A barren patch of seafloor littered with the wreck of this city and the skeletons of the warriors you left behind."

Gailen's jaw flexed.

"Wait until you can *protect* the bride you so desperately desire. Until that day comes, you are not worthy to offer yourself as a husband."

He flinched. The other warriors agitated with new anger at Soren's rough insults.

"Your passion is admirable." Kadir's rumble silenced the

warriors and soothed Gailen's frown. "You are all worthy of claiming brides. And now we know that it is possible to claim brides without Sea Opals. In future, we will find these brides. Now, we must prove Atlantis is a city founded upon honor."

They murmured in agreement.

Soren swam over them to the doorway. "Change patrols."

The rest of the warriors obeyed. Gailen, still flinching, chased after Soren. "Are we so unworthy? If you could have a bride, you would—"

"*I will never have a bride.*" Soren swam out. His voice echoed back. "Patrols, with me. Now!"

Three warriors separated from the crowd and swam after Soren. The others shifted somberly. No one was leaving to claim brides tonight.

Gailen glared at the absent mer. His shoulder slumped. He scratched his nose.

Ciran squeezed his shoulder. "Soren is a dedicated warrior."

"He is no warrior," Gailen grumbled. "He is a monster risen from the blacknight sea."

"Gailen." Iyen snapped. "Stow the food."

He obeyed without complaint, and many of the other warriors helped him, chatting in a lowered voice. Apparently going on patrol after having crossed the ocean without rest proved that Soren was a beast.

Was Kadir very angry? He spoke with Adviser Creo and looked tense and busy, as expected of a king.

Elyssa tried to help the cleanup effort. The warriors darted easily around her, plucking dishes just out of reach and collecting stray food before her fingers could close around it. She finally wrested a small serving dagger away from Faier, who let her have it with a friendly smile. Then, she had to be shown where to stow it — a pocket growing into the castle wall — and one of the more muscular warriors, Nilun, had to wedge it in.

"Is it okay? The cabinet seems kind of full already," she murmured.

"Cabinets deepen as the castle ages," Faier told her. "The castle is young and undeveloped."

Oh. A house that grew storage as it got older? "Magical."

He smiled.

A merman whose name she couldn't remember — Pelan? — made an exasperated noise as he shoved closed the last cabinet closed, cleaned his daggers, and affixed them to his bulging black-and-red-striped biceps and calves. "Another huddle on the seafloor trying not to become crab cake. You know what I miss most about Sireno? A good, long sleep."

"Sleeping in the open ocean is an adventure," another grinned. Zoan? Peach tattoos scrolled across his tanned chest. "Here, we are near a Life Tree. It is a luxury, believe me."

"And yet, every time I close my eyes, on the back of my neck I feel teeth."

"That is Nilun, giving you a goodnight kiss." Peachy-keen Zoan threw his arm around Pelan and pretended to gnaw on his neck.

Pelan shoved the teaser away and gripped his bristling daggers. "If that is what you think is a kiss, I hope you will receive a bride last."

"Straighten your lines," their hot-headed friend, Nilun, snapped. "Obey your orders with honor."

"You say that Nilun, but you huddle like a water bug." Zoan demonstrated, rolling into a ball.

Nilun reddened. "That is the strongest form for defense! You will value it if you are awakened by vent feeders."

Faier grimaced at Elyssa as though silently apologizing for the warriors' roughness. Obviously, they were the Three Amigos; a known trio of troublemakers. He kicked on his functioning left leg and shooed them. "We sleep in shifts. There is no biting. Go now."

They began to swim to the exit.

Why were they swimming out in the ocean when they had a whole castle? Elyssa paddled to Kadir.

He was ordering Lotar and Iyen. "Rest for two shifts. Forget the excavation for now. I need your strength for the coronation. A goblin shark attack is likely."

They nodded and kicked to the rest of the mermen filing to the exit.

Kadir turned to Elyssa.

She paddled — about ten more minutes it felt like — to reach his side. "Where is everyone going?"

"They are leaving the castle to our use."

"Why?"

His arms, which had been open to embrace her, moved closed. He held out his forearm for her to grab onto and steady herself. "It is custom."

"But isn't it dangerous out there?"

He hardened. "You will be protected in my city."

"For them," she clarified. "Didn't you just say there were goblin sharks and attackers?"

"We are warriors. We can endure any hardship."

Of course they could. "This is their city. We have a castle here. They should use it."

A muscle in his jaw tightened.

Don't tell her she was insulting his warriors' endurance. "I'm just asking if it isn't better for them to sleep inside the castle. How can anyone rest if they're afraid of vent feeders?"

One brow rose. "Vent feeders?"

"Or whatever. If I'm wrong, please tell me." She gripped his forearm.

His hand clenched tight into a fist.

She wanted to stroke him so that he released his fist, pulled her into his arms, and accepted her apology for nearly fomenting a rebellion and now turning his warriors out of their own home. "I just don't want my presence to cause any more disruption."

"Very well." His other palm rested on top of hers. The hardness eased. It was replaced by something she didn't expect. Sadness. And resignation. "I will call them back."

He turned to the exit, the long tunnel that led through the wall to the outside.

She tightened her grip.

He glanced back. His sadness eased. He captured her hand and flew with her to call the mermen back. Across the clear, bright seas, the marble cocooning the Life Tree glowed like a brilliant moon, bathing them all in effervescent moonlight and tinkling beauty. It eased her heart and cast a kinder glow on the surprised faces of the mermen recalled to the castle entrance.

"You will sleep inside the castle this night," Kadir informed them, his hand entwined with Elyssa's.

"And every night," Elyssa said. They all turned to her. She firmed her stance. "Until another castle is grown and it's safe."

The warriors looked at each other, then at Kadir again.

He was noble and implacable in the Life Tree's holy light. Truly a king.

Iyen frowned with hard concern and spoke to Elyssa. His expression said he was breaking self-imposed orders. "Do not worry about us."

"I do worry about you." All of them had been so kind. She looked from face to face. Their cuts and bruises were an obvious reminder of the dangers. "And I'm not going to rest easy if you're out there, risking your lives when you could be safe inside."

He turned his worry on Kadir.

Kadir motioned Iyen to pass into the castle. "Your queen has spoken."

Iyen lowered his head and led the warriors in. They made a silent, solemn procession of fin flicks and metal tridents. Were they insulted too? But better to be a little insulted than to be attacked and exhausted. Right?

At the back, Faier rested his old injuries beside Kadir. He looked away from Elyssa. Concern was palpable in his voice. "Where will you rest, my king?"

Huh? She made a noise.

They both looked at her.

"I thought..." Did she misunderstand? "Aren't we supposed to sleep in the, uh, the heart chamber?"

Kadir's eyes widened.

Faier blinked and then a deep flush crept up his cheeks. He ducked his head. "Ah. I see. Good rest." He kicked his left leg hard and disappeared inside with the others.

Kadir turned to her with the intensity of a predator focusing on prey. The Life Tree behind him loomed like a werewolf moon. "The heart chamber..."

She instinctively paddled back until she hit the firm inside wall. "Am I wrong?"

"...has yet to grow." He kept hold of their entwined hand. He rested his other arm on the wall above her head. "It is undeveloped."

Oh!

Ohhh. She *was* wrong. There was nowhere for them to sleep. No wonder the other warriors were so worried. No wonder Kadir had looked at her like she slapped him in the face.

His lean, hard thighs pressed against hers. "Do you know what we do in the heart chamber?"

Her heart thumped. "I...I think so."

His lips hovered over hers. His silver-flecked eyes snapped with intensity. "We join."

Anticipation tightened her thighs. Blossoming awareness swelled her breasts and tightened her nipples. He looked like liquid silver sex and yes, she wanted him.

His nostrils flared. Was he scenting her desire? Through the water, somehow?

She licked her lips.

His gaze dropped to that motion. "Do you understand what that means?"

She tried to nod.

"Do you intend to join with me?"

Her mistake had made him doubt whether she really wanted to be with him. Now she had to reassure him. She lifted her chin to protest. "Of c—"

He pressed her into the wall and cupped her cheeks with both hands to take his full-body kiss.

She clung to his wall of masculinity. His hard biceps caged her in. His powerful thigh lanced between hers, pressing demands to her throbbing, hot cleft. The powerful thrusts of his tongue controlled her, branded her, claimed her. The undeniable length of his cock hardened into an unstoppable promise.

She had made him this desperate. What was supposed to be their wedding night had turned into a big sleepover. She needed him to know that she *did* desire him. Not for his position or his power or what he could offer her. Not as a king or a mer or a warrior. As a man.

But she was only clinging to him. Holding on to his flexing biceps like before. To prove it, she needed to ease his fears with action.

She slid her hands up the mountains and valleys of muscle to his broad shoulders. Then, she splayed her hands over his massive pectorals. He felt like a work of art.

His kiss slowed and his lips formed a smile against hers. He enjoyed her touch.

So, she touched more. He felt amazing. With his slow, languorous kisses taking her mouth, he left her hands free to trace the breadth of his ribs, the iron muscles of his taut abdomen, and the flat plane below. There, thrusting proudly, nested the base of his prominent cock.

She wrapped her fingers around it and squeezed. He felt warm and thick. *Hers.*

A tingling sound, like cymbals building and dying away again, sounded in her ears.

Kadir pulled back abruptly and looked over his shoulder.

She collapsed against the wall. Her lips throbbed from his commanding possession. Her feminine center throbbed with need for it. She flexed her empty hand, remembering the long, hard feeling of his cock in her grip, and she struggled to balance upright. He was still looking out over the open city.

"What is it?"

He turned back. A possessive smile curved his lips. He smoothed her hair and tugged her off her feet to fly into the protected castle. "Nothing that cannot wait for tomorrow."

Their wedding.

Her coronation.

CHAPTER FIFTEEN

K adir led Elyssa down the long corridor into the castle. She was hot and her pulse beat fast, promising her readiness to join with him. How different from when they exited, and he believed she did not wish it.

How unfortunate that the heart chamber had not grown yet, and they could not join together until tomorrow.

"Too bad we can't sneak away or sleep with the Life Tree," she said, mirroring his thoughts.

"The sanctuary is holy ground. Access is limited."

Iyen met them at the inner entrance. "I heard a noise."

"Noise?" Elyssa tilted her head.

Kadir assured them both. "It was nothing."

Iyen allowed them to fly past. He stared out the entrance on full alert. His capable maroon-tattooed hands gripped his trident.

Tomorrow, joining would connect their souls. All doubts would fly away, and his warriors would treat her as their true queen.

Below, the warriors sprawled in hollows amid the rows

of cultivated plants and in the doorways to unfinished halls. Whispers ceased at their appearance and overly loud snores — chest vibrations — soon followed.

Kadir settled in the hallway that would lead to the heart chamber. They reached the dead end. A soft glow suggested maybe the rest of the route was growing even now. But until it completed, they would have no more passion. Only ordinary rest to prepare for the wedding ceremony.

"What noise was Iyen talking about?" Elyssa laid her head in the hollow of his shoulder, where she had kept it on their journey. "I thought I heard a crescendo."

"It is nothing to worry about."

Kadir had heard the crescendo too. The Life Tree had responded to their passion with a vibration like a strong breeze blowing through its limbs. He had not heard it before today. Was it common? Perhaps it explained why mermen always joined with their brides only inside a heavily shielded heart chamber.

"You know, I shouldn't be tired." Her fingers traced his chest tattoos. She wrote secret symbols with an unknown meaning. "I slept half the time you carried me."

"It is our resonance." He was tired now, so she also felt tired.

"Really? Good. Then, I hope I slept enough for the both of us." She relaxed and melted into sleep against him.

Slept enough for the both of them?

She meant that she was not only sensing his tiredness but that she had also given back to his strength. Was this possible? He thought back to those times. When she slept, she was easier to carry. Was that not because she released her stiffness and assumed the more aerodynamic shape? Had she truly given him energy?

Mermen did not travel with their brides.

He would have to test it.

But now, on what was supposed to be their wedding night and first joining, his bride snored softly on his shoulder and he easily collapsed into sleep.

They slept four days. His warriors woke him to notify him of dangers and signs found on patrols. Elyssa slept straight through.

When she finally awoke, she yawned and stretched. "Ahhh, I feel great. Like I slept for two solid weeks."

"It was not that long."

She blinked and grinned.

"Four of your days and nights. Only."

She laughed. "Oh, was that all?"

"That was all." He helped her to rise and swam through the gardens together, briefly showing her how to gather the fava beans and root beer bulbs she had eaten at the wedding feast. "Surface days can be measured by tracking the movements of fish who migrate according to a diurnal clock. But the mer usually anchor time to important events."

She stopped him. "Are you saying I actually went without eating for two weeks and didn't notice? And just now, I slept for four days?"

He nodded.

She took a huge bite of the giant root, chewing with her mouth full while her chest vibrated her words uninterrupted. "This is crazy. I don't feel *that* different." She suddenly stopped and put a hand over her chest as though it had just occurred to her, again, that she could speak without opening her mouth.

"You also 'see' in an enclosed castle at a depth where no surface light penetrates."

She chewed more slowly.

"Today is an important ceremony." He held out his hand. "It will be an anchor for our city for all time."

She finished eating quickly and took Kadir's hand. "Here goes nothing."

She had such a funny way of phrasing. "You are not nothing to me."

"Oh!" She blinked and laughed. "I'm nervous. That's not what I meant. I should say, 'here goes everything.' Or is that worse?"

She was babbling.

It was endearing.

He flew her to the castle entrance. His warriors formed an honor guard, lining a tunnel to the Life Tree by protecting above, both sides, and also below. Their faces were solemn and posture full of honor. Elyssa slipped her arms around Kadir's shoulders.

A distant siren caught his ear.

She looked over her shoulder. Her lips parted. "Aren't those sharks?"

"Tiger sharks." And because Kadir had pulled off all the patrols for this ceremony, they circled well within the city perimeter.

Adviser Creo saw them too. His lips thinned.

Curse these foreign raiders.

Kadir had to protect the city's boundaries. Failure to protect them meant Atlantis could not be recognized. If Atlantis failed to be recognized, they would remain anathema and the other cities would pressure the All-Council to destroy his Life Tree — and Kadir. His mer would be forced to return to their origin cities and face punishment for their rebellion.

Soren had stopped his warriors from abandoning the city the other night. Such enthusiasm to claim brides was admirable but dangerous when raiders pushed sharks into their boundaries and threatened patrols. Kadir's tightened his arms around Elyssa.

She looked up at him.

Atlantis was already an unprecedented experiment of mer from different cities uniting. It was unusual, dangerous, and prone to misunderstandings. Elyssa's arrival was supposed to strengthen their bonds. Instead, during her wedding feast, her revelations had almost torn them apart.

Now, she would be recognized as queen and join with him. Soren, Balim, and Adviser Creo would stop questioning her presence. Her doubts would be replaced by confidence, and his city would strengthen with her glow.

From here forward, everything would be different.

Kadir flew down the tunnel of warriors, carrying Elyssa to the Life Tree. It was so young and fragile that thick guard petals hard as granite still enclosed it, keeping it safe. He slipped into the narrow entrance between two petals and pulled her inside after him. They flew down a narrow corridor. Behind them, the rest of the warriors of the city entered also.

At the end of the corridor, the inner sanctuary opened on a small, white dais. In the middle glowed the pure Life Tree.

His sapling had one central trunk and three sturdy branches. The upper branch almost crested his forehead. Its arms were dotted with tiny pebbles of Sea Opals. Smaller pebbles dusted the dais around the trunk.

Every Life Tree began as a sprout. His Life Tree, grown from the Dragao Azul seed, was intricately tied to the blood flowing in his veins.

Kadir retracted his fins into human feet and bounced on the soft, white courtyard. The water was so still and clear in the sanctuary. Elyssa stood beside him and gazed at the thin tree in awe.

The rest of his warriors left their tridents just outside the sanctuary and formed a ring around the edge of the dais, leaning against the curved petal walls.

Elyssa's eyes glittered. Amazement and joy emanated from her and increased the white glow of the tree. They were finding each other and growing their resonance. Kadir's heart swelled painfully in his chest. This was why he had brought Elyssa here. So they could find each other and thrive.

"Now perform the vow. Watch me." He knelt and bowed his head to the thin, white trunk. "I, Kadir of Atlantis, present Elyssa as my chosen bride. Shower your blessing and healing on our union so she may give us a young fry."

He bent low, kissed the skinny trunk, and stood.

She glanced behind her at the other mermen. A small doubt crossed her face, swift as a shadow.

A shiver of unease tinkled in the branches.

He gripped her shoulder. Atlantis needed her to perform this. He would encourage her confidence — somehow — if he had to.

Elyssa smiled at him, squared her shoulders, and walked forward. Her feet bounced lightly on the thick dais pad. She knelt. "I, Elyssa of America, present Kadir as my chosen groom. Please shower your blessing and healing on our union, and give us a baby." She kissed the trunk.

The Life Tree made a loud *sching* sound, like two pieces of sharp metal rubbing together.

What was that?

Elyssa looked up at the tree, her eyes wide and worried. The mer shifted and glanced at each other.

Adviser Creo harrumphed. "Modern brides have a strange resonance."

Soren growled. "Respect."

The sound faded. An unsettled feeling remained.

Everyone quieted.

Elyssa stood and padded back to Kadir. Her smile was nervous. "Does it always make a noise like that?"

No. The Life Tree never made that noise. It sounded... what was it? If she were a warrior, it would have sounded war-like. As though the Life Tree were preparing for a great battle.

But she was not a warrior. She was his bride. And the battle for her status was nearly over.

He reached out to take her hand. "We will complete the ceremony and you will rule as my queen."

"Great. I'm absolutely ready." Her light dimmed with her lie.

The tree shivered. *Ching-ching-chang!* Harsh tinkles threatened to rip leaf buds off.

The mer shifted to fighting stances.

A piercing sensation, like a needlefish, lanced Kadir's chest. He put his hand over the center of the pain. What was this warning of his doom?

Elyssa jerked her head side to side as though searching for sharks. "This can't be nor—Kadir!" She stroked his cheeks. Her worried face seemed to ease the pain.

The shivering stopped. The Life Tree's tinkling echoed to silence.

He recovered and clasped her hand. Her worry only deepened. "It is fine. We will continue."

Adviser Creo darkened. "No Life Tree has ever made such a strange noise. Brides should be hidden and treasured, not displayed like warriors. Your actions are reckless and dangerous."

One of his warriors made a face.

Kadir focused on him. "You heard this noise in your old city, Warrior Pelan?"

"Yes. When Lucy came to Sireno, the Life Tree did make a strange sound."

Advisor Creo's mouth dropped in shock and horror. "Sireno's Life Tree was destroyed! Do not allow your bride so close, King Kadir. Her strange resonance is dangerous."

Kadir bared his teeth. He had felt the needlefish pain, but he would not allow the adviser to insult his queen. "Strike those words from your lying soul."

Adviser Creo drew himself upright. "I will not ignore the truth. Sireno's Life Tree *did* die. A bride, who was also a so-called 'queen', caused its death."

Gasps and mutters filled the sanctuary with discord.

"Do not listen!" Pelan's face reddened. He gripped his daggers. "Sireno's Life Tree gave a warrior's cry when Queen Lucy used its power. It was not this weak, little chime."

"The sound is the same. Modern brides must be protected the same as the sacred island brides were protected. Neither are allowed near the Life Tree. It is for everyone's protection."

"The sounds were not the same!"

The adviser ignored him. "It is the same."

Nilun growled in defense of his friend. "Pelan is a careful observer. I will fight any warrior who disagrees."

"Do not fight on holy ground, Nilun." Zoan grinned as he took his friend's other side. "Wait until you are out of the sanctuary. Then you can use weapons."

Adviser Creo snarled at Zoan. "Do not speak out

of turn."

The trio bowed their heads. Pelan and Nilun were furious but obedient; Zoan maintained the irrepressible gleam in his averted eyes. In the older cities such as Sireno and Djullanar, speaking up was harshly punished, even when it helped. And Zoan's home city had recently been taken over by another, Siyokoy. They also enforced the hierarchy harshly.

Soren eyed the adviser. He made a point of not enforcing such rules, but home city training was deeply ingrained.

Elyssa pressed her fist to her chest in the universal insult. "The problem is me again. Isn't it?"

Kadir uncurled her fist. "It is not you."

"Me. Because I still get nervous when I think about ruling as your queen."

Kadir considered his words. "No—"

"Yes!" Adviser Creo blazed with righteous indignation. "Why force your bride to shoulder such a burden? She trembles at *your* insistence and her soul darkens like a moonless night."

"No," Elyssa insisted. "It's not true. Kadir isn't forcing me. I want to."

The Life Tree began to tinkle again. Sharp, unsettling warnings that made her eyes widen and protests stop. The harsh chimes immediately proved her words for lies.

Adviser Creo lifted his chin. "Look at how her soul fades to darkness."

She gasped and covered her mouth, even though words vibrated in her chest underwater.

"Your king's orders make her suffer. I will not call her queen." Adviser Creo turned to the other warriors. "Am I the only one who cares for this gentle, fragile bride?"

CHAPTER SIXTEEN

Kadir's heart cracked in half.

Elyssa's brows folded into agony. She looked as frightened and sad as the brides of his memory. Frightened by the old covenant. Refusing their destiny. Crying.

This ceremony was supposed to fill Elyssa with power. It was supposed to strengthen their love and prove her rightness as ruler. She was supposed to shine so brightly that no warrior would doubt her need to remain as queen.

But that was not what had happened.

Adviser Creo was correct. Kadir had selfishly focused on acquiring a queen. Any queen. Elyssa told him over and over ruling wasn't her wish. He pushed her into the blade of a trident and then chided her for writhing and screaming.

That was his love for her. It was as sharp as a blade.

"Fine," she cried shakily. "Don't call me queen. I know what it looks like and I don't blame you."

Even now she was suffering. Redness and shinier moisture rimmed her eyes. Kadir started to try to calm her. Before he could, something strange happened.

Her chest glowed brighter.

She swam forward and stabbed her finger at Adviser Creo. "But don't try to pin my problems on Kadir. Or Lucy! Lucy is the smartest, nicest, most capable person you will ever find. And if Aya were here, we'd all be fine. My problems," she pressed her hand flat against her chest, "are *my* problems. So don't call me queen if you don't feel like it. But, honest to god, I'm one hundred percent trying."

Her fiery commitment, yelling at the shocked adviser and the rest of his stunned warriors, eased the sharpness in Kadir's soul. This golden light was what had intrigued him.

But Adviser Creo was still correct. She tried *because* Kadir forced his will upon her. In the beginning, he hadn't cared. He had caused her suffering because he had not cared beyond his own selfish vision.

"Elyssa's wishes will be obeyed," he ordered. "You will not call her queen."

"Unless you feel like it." She abruptly sat next to the slender trunk of the Life Tree.

The mer shifted uneasily. Gailen glared at his feet.

Kadir selected him from the crowd. "You protest my order."

Gailen's head snapped up. His enthusiasm burned hot as the bright orange tattoos scrolled across his broad chest. "Yes, I protest. Queen Elyssa is a queen. She is here, and she is here to stay."

The words, which Kadir wanted to be true, nailed into his selfish heart. He struggled to formulate his response.

Elyssa answered instead. "Yes, but, you don't have to call me queen until I've done something to deserve it."

"Deserving it is not the issue." Gailen glanced at Nilun, who stood out because he was the only warrior who'd remained in a military precision stance despite all of the wedding day's shocks. "Some warriors even address Soren as first lieutenant, even though he—"

"Enough!" Soren snarled.

Gailen stopped.

Kadir found his response. "Titles have never been compulsory in Atlantis. When you call me king, it means you acknowledge my right to rule. Every time you call me king, it holds this meaning. And the day you stop calling me king, that will also have a meaning."

He held their attention. They stilled, full of honor, chests risen.

"Elyssa comes before you not as a title. She comes before you as herself. She is *my* queen. When she has your honor, then you call her queen also."

Gailen lifted his chin. He and others, like strict Nilun, would call Elyssa a queen right away. Roles and honors must be clearly established.

Brides came and went. Queens stayed and ruled.

This solution seemed to please Elyssa. She stroked the Life Tree's trunk. Her chest glowed with firm resolution.

Only Adviser Creo worried. "You are making a mistake. Your bride is a treasure that must be protected. Do not force her into an unnatural role so roughly."

"It's not rough," Elyssa protested.

He stared at her pityingly. "He asks you to do hard things. You struggle."

"Well, I know I should do better."

"You should not have to try. The role he forces you into is unnatural."

"There were queens in ancient times," Kadir growled.

"Yes. *Ancient* times. Not modern." Adviser Creo softened as he regarded Elyssa. "That is why you suffer."

"Really? But...I am trying..." Elyssa rested her head on the trunk. Her soul light darkened.

It stabbed Kadir in the chest.

The adviser's words hurt her. Kadir jerked his chin at Soren to take control of the warriors. "Leave us."

Soren swam to the tunnel. "The first group, to patrols. Second group, assist. The third group, join me in the old city." The warriors swam out of the sanctuary, emptying it.

Adviser Creo lingered.

Kadir ignored him. He had no words for the All-Council representative. Especially because Kadir knew, deep down, he was right.

Soren swept the sanctuary. His eyes were sharp. "Adviser. Leave."

The adviser puffed up. "King Kadir must hear—"

"Now!"

Adviser Creo huffed.

Soren bared his teeth.

The adviser fled from the large, angry mer. Soren swam after him. They were alone. The sanctuary fell silent.

Elyssa's soft, brown hair floated into the Life Tree branches like a sea dragon curling among leaves. She stroked the tree, her light fluctuating unsteadily.

"Elyssa, your light is flickering," he said softly.

"I'm afraid."

Fear spiked in his heart. She had taken the vow. He had tried to calm her by not forcing the other mer to address her by her proper title. Now she feared their new life?

"What is your need?" Although he meant to be soft and entreating, his tone seemed harsh. A reflection of his disturbed heart.

"My attitude. It's always the same. 'I can't do this.' It's the problem."

His heart beat in his ears as loud as a predator attack. She couldn't be his bride? She couldn't be a mer? She couldn't give up the air world and join with him?

His chest panged.

This wasn't supposed to happen.

As soon as he brought a bride to the Life Tree and they performed the ceremony, she was supposed to reassure the warriors. She was supposed to join with him. She was supposed to carry his young fry son, win over the All-Council adviser, and establish Atlantis as the chosen city of a new era.

Instead, the ceremony went wrong, his warriors were confused and worried, Adviser Creo had stopped an outright rebellion during the wedding feast, and his bride was afraid.

He barely heard what he said next. "You cannot?"

"It's like how I messed you up during the goblin shark attack. I stiffened and almost got Soren killed. I keep *saying* I'm trying. But you can see this glowing light in my chest that shows how I really feel." She smoothed her hair and played with the branches. "I finally get it. Words aren't enough."

What was she saying?

"Words are vows," he growled.

"Vows only matter if they're backed up by action."

Was she saying her words were empty? They would have no action?

"I'm trying to be a mermaid, I'm trying to be a good bride, I'm trying to be an impressive queen. All my words are saying, 'I'm trying,' but all my actions are saying, 'Stop, quit, I'm leaving.' That's the problem. Don't you think?"

She wanted to stop. She wanted to quit. She wanted to leave.

Now.

Although he was standing upright on two human feet, the Life Tree dais seemed to tilt backward. He staggered.

"So obviously what I need to do now is stop talking," she rose and turned to him, nervous but determined, "and start acting."

Elyssa smoothed her hair and stroked her hands down her body, curving over the swell of her small breasts and dipping to her waist, flaring over her feminine hips and down her thighs.

She was so beautiful and all he could see was that she was going away from him.

It was like on the swim where he had determined to reveal himself to his mother and discovered he was already too late. Even though it was impossible, it felt like his intention had caused her death. On the long, solo swim back to Dragao Azul, every gasp of seawater had choked him.

It felt the same now.

He had no tools for this. No weapons to fight this shock. No plan to evade her pain.

Elyssa licked her index finger, teasing the digit between her teeth, and glanced over her shoulder, up at him coyly, from the corner of her eyes. What she saw in his face shocked her. Her half-lidded pose abruptly straightened and she bounced to his side. "Hey, are you okay? You're looking white."

He couldn't make words.

She took his hands. "You're trembling." Her frown cleared. She sought his gaze. "What's wrong? Are you going to be sick?"

He shook his head.

"Kadir?" She stroked his cheek. Only moments ago, those smooth fingers had been stroking the Life Tree. As if she carried healing balm in her fingers, each stroke calmed his thudding heart. "You're frightening me."

He gripped her wrist. Arresting her. "You wish to leave."

She tried to pull free. "No, I'm—"

"You cannot do this. You wish to quit. I frighten you."

"No!" Her eyes flashed. "Just a minute."

"You refuse to be my queen."

"You're not listening to—"

"But it is too late. For all those things, I want you." He forced her to his chest and captured her mouth with his kiss.

His.

She struggled.

He kissed her harder.

She put her palms on his chest. *Bang!* A force shoved him back. He stumbled and fell, landing flat on his back on the soft, white ground.

It felt like he'd been slammed with the flat base of two tridents. His lungs collapsed. His eyes burned with tears. He struggled to draw in water.

She had pushed him away. Used the force of the Life Tree to incapacitate him.

Elyssa rejected him completely.

"Stop! Will you listen?" Her face scrunched, and she balled her hands into fists. "I'm trying to say I want you too!"

No. He misunderstood. She wanted to flee to the surface, not sink down to the muck with him.

"I do so want the muck." Somehow, she knew his words, even though his chest was constricted from the force and he was unable to form sounds. She pounced on top of him. Her legs straddled his abdomen. His back pressed deeper into the soft, white loam of the Life Tree, flattening his gills and cutting off his non-existent breath. Her eyes shone brightly. "The muck has you."

No. She did not feel like he did.

"Don't tell me how I feel. It's hard enough when you consider how you're a literal king and I'm somewhat below ordinary."

She splayed her hands across his pectorals and dipped her mouth to one nipple. Her mouth was hot and her teeth hotter. His cock flooded with arousal.

"What...are you doing?" he managed, regaining control of his chest vibrations.

"I told you I'm done with words." She swirled the other nipple with her tongue and moved lower, leaving a heat trail. "I was trying to seduce you."

That was why she had stroked her body and looked at him coyly over her shoulder?

He slowly regained the use of his hands, although the grip that arrested her hands barely held her. "Stop, Elyssa. Not here."

She yanked her hands free and nearly growled. "Don't underestimate my determination."

Her gaze arrested him. The Life Tree chimed once, gently. Did she then truly want him? Yes. He released her.

She dropped her mouth to his flexing abdomen and licked. A warrior matching him for raw sexuality.

His cock pulsed with arousal.

Her soft breasts slid over his hot skin. She was so beautiful. Her tongue traced the silver lines down his legs, sliding over the prison injuries and scars. He had endured the beatings because of this day. Because he would not give up his vision. Today, his queen joined with him.

A powerful sense of rightness anchored his body.

She wrapped velvet hands around the thick mushroom head of his cock.

He surged into her hands. Ready.

She smiled at his eagerness — smiled, like sunshine — and lowered her mouth. He thought that she would kiss him and tensed in readiness. But instead, she swirled her tongue over his head and took him into her mouth.

He had never imagined such a thing.

Her tight, slick mouth heat encompassed him. Her tongue moved, slippery and curious. She tasted him, appreciated him, savored him.

His balls clenched.

He gripped her hair and dragged her face to his.

Her eyes were half-lidded and a smile curved her gorgeous lips. "Tastes—"

He stole her thoughts with his kiss.

Her willing mouth opened and her tongue joined his, tangling and wrestling, stroking. Delicious moans fed the arousal pulsing in his blood. He needed her now. Craved to join with her. He shoved his shoulder into hers to roll her over.

She resisted, clamping her thighs around his waist and forcing *his* shoulders to the ground.

He stared up at her.

There was no doubt that she wanted him.

With powerful knowledge of how she commanded his body, she twisted to capture his iron-hard cock in her small hand.

Her pink nipples floated tantalizingly close to his face.

He curled tight and caught one sweet nipple in his mouth.

She cried softly. Delicious arousal. Her fingers tangled in his hair, pulling him closer.

He cupped the other breast and pearled its nipple between his thumb and index finger.

She moaned and arched, opening herself to him completely. This was trust. This was love. This was his bride's true desire. He chased her pleasure, sensing it the way he sensed her rising heartbeat. His cock slipped closer to her channel. He needed her in every way. In his soul, in his body, in his heart.

But what about her? She closed her eyes.

"You want me," he declared.

She licked her lips and moaned.

He marked her with kisses. Her beautiful, soft belly and her gently mounded breasts and her pink nipples, her curved shoulders. Her long neck and her playful smile and the hunger in her pleasure-closed eyes.

She wrapped her legs around his thighs. Her slick cleft teased the head of his cock. Still with her eyes closed, she moved her hips, urging him to enter.

He arrested her. Forced her face to his. "Tell me."

She blinked and struggled to focus. "I need you."

He eased in the tip.

Her eyes rolled back in her head. Bliss illuminated her. She moaned and tilted to take him deeper.

He grabbed her waist, slowing her. She felt sweet, hot, and slick like her mouth, but deeper and more yielding and tightly feminine. His cock throbbed. She would not run away.

From this moment forward, everything was different. From this single life-giving union, their bodies and their souls became one.

Her sunlit smile wavered. Her lips trembled. "Kadir?"

He held her tight. This moment would never be

repeated. What came after? Did anything come after? No. Only Elyssa. In his arms. Forever.

Could he reach the shore?

"Please." She nipped his lips again, teasing him with her sweet entreaty. "Kadir. Please."

He released her waist.

She speared herself deep on his hard cock. Pleasure shuddered through both of them. It was done. They were connected now, fully and completely.

She slipped away from him. He surged to meet her. Rocking, like the eternal surface tides slapping the wet shore.

Their rhythms matched. His long male cock massaged her tight female channel in a dance as old as life. She writhed desperately. Her light pulsed brilliantly, bathing him in awareness of her uncontrollable pleasure.

A gathering sensation clenched in his spine.

She dug both hands into his hair and screamed.

He pounded into her, giving her what she begged for, what she needed.

She cried his name and threw back her head, bucking and grinding with abandon. White light flashed, intense and brilliant. She collapsed. Passion whipped through her, trembling her to completion.

His balls pulsed and the clench released. He poured his seed deep into her with one final long, hard thrust.

It was done. They were united.

She lay against him and rested her head on his shoulder. A satisfied smile curved her small lips. She kissed his jaw and twined their fingers.

The Life Tree branches glowed down on them as though questioning. What were they doing here, joining in this holy sanctuary? Yet another taboo he had broken.

With his still-hard cock embraced by his Elyssa, a deep sense of peace flooded his heavy limbs.

His warriors would overlook this. No, he would make a new tradition, one where the bridal night was always spent with the Life Tree.

The warriors would accept Elyssa as their queen. She would accept herself. Adviser Creo would approve their city.

Kadir willed it. He willed everything else to come true. He would make new traditions, and all would accept it as he had done so.

CHAPTER SEVENTEEN

Elyssa was well and thoroughly satisfied. For once, things had gone very, very right.

She stretched in Kadir's arms. Ahhh. Her muscles were sore in unusual places, but the sex was great. She had known it would be from the first moment he had commanded her with his imperial kiss.

And for their first time, she had been the one who initiated it. That never happened. She never initiated in the past because her past lovers were too quick to get their own pleasure. It was always casual. Never this soul-shatteringly intense.

Maybe she had never really loved any of her boyfriends at all.

Kadir stroked her curved waist and trailed his fingers down her thigh. His forehead wrinkled.

"What?" she asked.

"I will protect you. No one will take you from me."

"I wouldn't let them even if they tried."

His frown deepened. "Not your people. Not my people."

"Not nobody." She kissed his forehead wrinkles. He snorted in surprise. So serious, his silver-flecked eyes. Just like when he had told her that he would never let her go.

She never wanted to be let go. And that was the moment she realized that the only way she could truly prove her devotion to Kadir was to take action. Like when she had begged to see the hammerheads, she had reached a crossing point within herself. If she didn't take the next step, she never would.

She needed to be regal. She needed to be imperious. She needed to match Kadir's confidence with her own. She needed to not just agree with whatever anybody told her. She needed to go forth and grab what she wanted with both hands and not let go. The same as Kadir.

"So, I'm an official mermaid." She rose from their resting place, bounced up, and pointed her toes.

They remained human.

Aw.

Kadir rose up on an elbow. "What do you mean?"

Apparently, she meant nothing. "I thought after we joined I'd be able to make my fins." She flexed her feet, her toes, her ankles.

He pursed his lips. Was he also disappointed?

She hunched away and muttered. "I'll keep trying."

He rose. His toes effortlessly separated like spreading wings and silver swirled webbing transformed his human feet into fantastic fins.

It wasn't fair. He made it look so easy.

"Perhaps you will resolve it tonight in the heart chamber."

"The heart chamber?" She reached for his hand, missed, and spun in the still sanctuary water. "I thought it hadn't grown yet."

"It was growing." Kadir took her hand to steady her. "I expect it finished after we exchanged vows."

They should consummate their marriage in the heart chamber properly. "I feel like things are a little out of order."

"Things *are* out of order." He swam with her out of the inner sanctuary and down the corridor. "Normally a bride drinks a temporary elixir and transforms for her journey through the ocean. She arrives at her husband's castle and joins with him in the heart chamber. If all is well, the Life Tree reacts to her energy and grows a blossom full of nectar, which she then consumes to make the change permanent."

But Elyssa had skipped all the steps. "I drank the nectar first. Sort of."

"And we are the first to grow the heart chamber." They reached the exit. "It is shielded so no noises leak out."

Wait a minute.

"Noises?" she repeated.

The guard, Nilun, greeted them outside. His eyes averted. "King Kadir. Queen Elyssa."

Queen Elyssa. Wow. He accepted her already! Tingles ran down her back.

But his awkward refusal to meet her eyes was very suspicious after Kadir just mentioned noises.

Kadir kicked, leaving Nilun behind and easily flying them across the open water to the silver-green castle. She lowered her voice. "Are you telling me that other people heard us just now?"

"The Life Tree dais is built for amplification, not shielding. Although it is now enclosed, I think it simply amplified our passion louder."

What?

Her first act as queen was to have *amplified* public sex?

A heat wave rolled through her body. Her cheeks turned the approximate temperature of the surface of the sun.

She was going to die. She was going to die. She was going to die.

Kadir glanced over his shoulder. One brow cocked. Arrogant. Proud almost. "Problem?"

She was going to kill him. "You could have told me!"

"I tried. You were insistent."

Oh, god.

"Take me to the heart chamber." At least no one would hear her when she screamed. "Now."

"Yes." His lips curved as he twisted away. "My queen."

She was seriously going to kill him.

Well, she had been trying to prove that she wanted him and it was more than just pretty words. At least her unqueenly performance was confined to the guards outside the castle and the Life Tree. Oh, and the warriors inside the castle courtyard, apparently, because they also averted their eyes and turned nearly her shade of red. Everyone else was out on patrol or at the wreckage site.

Kadir flew across the courtyard into the narrow hallway. Last night — if it really was last night, now that she knew her sense of time was all screwed up — the hallway had terminated before he could take three kicks. It now wound through the inside of the castle like a labyrinth, and they flew around and around in spirals. There, at the deepest dead end, Kadir placed his and her linked hands on the wall. The living green wall glimmered silver, recognizing them, and parted inward.

Inside was a chamber barely big enough for the two of them.

Kadir's fins shifted to human feet and he stood intimately near. The water tasted smoky, like his flavors. Hickory mixed with vanilla.

Desire rose and twisted in her center.

She reached for his hand. He caught hers and gazed down at her with intensity, twining their fingers. Maybe they should christen the room they were supposed to use—

"King Kadir." A voice interrupted their silence.

Kadir swung her behind him, deeper inside the chamber. "Who dares approach?"

"I am under orders from Soren." Balim reached the chamber cautiously, his eyes averted, his cheeks also red. "How is your health?"

Kadir did not relax. "Why have you returned from the wrecked city?"

"We saw flashes of light. Soren asked me to check your condition."

"Flashes of light?" His shoulders slowly relaxed. "The Life Tree amplified our joining all the way to old Atlantis?"

Balim's chest was now so hot, his blood-red tattoos blended into the rest of his body. "You did not notice?"

"I was distracted."

And she was literally going to die. Of embarrassment. Forever.

Balim deliberately did not look at her. "May I inspect?"

"Soren worries too much." Kadir exited the chamber and stood patiently.

Balim examined his ribs, his arms, his spine and hmmed. He needed a clipboard and glasses to push up his nose and he would be any other physician.

"How do you feel?" he asked finally.

Kadir smiled with his teeth. "Energy flows in my veins."

Balim raised one brow skeptically and shook his head. "Sure it does. Rest now."

"Truly, Balim, I am ready to join the work site at the old city."

"Do not insult my assessment. The journey across the Atlantic set back your healing and now you have once again taxed yourself. Rest."

Great. They had loud, public, acrobatic sex at the Life Tree and it had set back Kadir's healing.

Healing?

Elyssa tilted forward and touched his forearm. "Another day can't hurt. Let's sleep in here."

His lips quirked and his gaze darkened. "I obey my queen."

Delicious tingling filled her veins.

"I said to *rest*," Balim said dryly.

"By the way, what are you healing from?"

Kadir looked down at her. Startled. "My imprisonment."

"Oh, I'm so sorry. I never realized." He was so powerful and intense, whether pressing her against a wall, pinning her with his imperial gaze, or swimming her across an entire ocean. It never occurred to her that he might not be feeling one hundred percent. He masked it so well. "Where are you hurt?"

"You cannot see?" He looked at Balim, whose eyes were equally wide. They were shocked. She clearly won the worst girlfriend-wife award for never noticing.

"I'm sorry." As she spoke, Kadir's brows darkened. Was it really obvious? "Um...is it your head?"

"My head?"

"Sometimes you look really angry like you might have a migraine."

He blinked.

Okay. Not his head. She held up her hands before she

stuck her completely-human-not-at-all-mermaid foot any further into her mouth. "You have to tell me. I'm going to get it wrong."

He pointed to his ribs.

Broken ribs were the worst! Or so she'd heard, from people who cracked them horseback riding or skiing. And she'd been holding onto him really tight, and gripping him with her thighs. How had he stopped himself from screaming?

She winced. "How many did you break?"

"No, they are not broken." He placed her hand flat against his rib cage and, when she still didn't get it immediately, he slid it to the side. "Do you now feel?"

Hmm. There were scars across his tattoos where the skin had been torn and healed. It must have been rough in prison. "Your scars healed pretty well already. I thought it was the pattern of your tattoos."

His eyes bugged.

She was still getting it wrong.

Balim cleared his throat. "Kadir was starved. His ribs protrude and he has not regained his muscle. Soren stormed the prison in his final moments. He nearly died."

Ohhhh. Then, his leanness wasn't his body type or his rock star personality. Maybe she could see it now. The cheeks that ought to be fuller. The eyes that were intense because they were slightly sunken into dark hollows.

And he had nearly died.

A lump formed in her throat. She struggled to swallow past it. His body was beneath her hand. His heartbeat on her palm proved he was still alive. But he nearly wasn't. They almost hadn't met.

She slid her arms the rest of the way around him and hugged him. His heart thub-thubbed steadily beneath her ear. She closed her eyes. He was hers. She would pay more attention, and help him, and treasure him.

His warm palm stroked her head. "You truly did not notice."

"I thought it was your body type. Besides." She disentangled herself to look at him. Really look at him. "It doesn't look that bad. You must be almost back to normal."

He laughed. A true laugh. "Am I? Almost 'back to normal?'"

Balim shook his head like she was completely blind. "The normal body type is Soren."

"Soren!" She refused to picture Kadir three times as wide. "No. I can't. It's just not you."

He laughed again, truly delighted, and drew her into his arms. "I am glad my body meets with my queen's approval."

"No, I mean, it's fine if you want to bulk up, but I just can't imagine you as *Soren*—"

A distant roar reached their hall.

Kadir's smile stilled. "That will be Soren."

"I meant to inform you. Soren is returning soon." Balim swam down the hall, calling over his shoulder. "And Adviser Creo wishes to speak with you."

"Of course he does." Kadir's eyes darkened again. In exhaustion. His shoulders sagged and he yawned.

She really had over-taxed him. "We could rest. Just a little bit."

His dark eyes glowed. "I do not wish to rest a little bit."

Her neither, but he was too busy. If resting was something she could give him, she would do it.

"You do give me energy, Elyssa," he said, responding to a thought she hadn't spoken. "More now than in a very long time."

Warmth glowed in her chest. She helped him. Her presence hadn't only made him tired. She took Kadir's hand. "I guess we should see what they want."

In the courtyard, the returning patrols all flushed and averted their eyes. It took her a minute to remember why. *They all knew*. Her, sex, the Life Tree.

Ugh.

Kadir kept her by his side and frowned with intensity. It eased the odd looks.

The warriors decided to eat dinner — which was good because she was *starving again* — and gave their reports.

Lotar described the increasing pattern of shark attacks, which might be used to find the raiders. "With three brave warriors, I could trace the patterns back and locate their camp."

"And then what?" Soren growled, looking up from his dinner and silencing the warriors who offered themselves bravely. "We cannot spare a unit to initiate an attack."

Lotar's gray eyes flicked to Kadir.

Kadir nodded, even though the tension in his body told Elyssa that he did not wish to agree. "Our priority now is Sea Opals. Soren?"

"The wreckage is dangerous. The cave guardian regularly stops our work with his aggression, and many sharks are driven in by raiders from the open ocean." Soren stabbed a thick fish steak and tore into the flesh. The raw sashimi steaks were delicious, but she felt like she needed sharper teeth. "Balim studied the ancient drawings. It is possible the mechanism to raise and lower the city is still intact. We target the main tower, where we are most likely to discover Sea Opals and the mechanism to accomplish our original goal."

"Good plan." Kadir rubbed Elyssa's knee absently. "It is thoughtful and careful."

The large warrior flinched with the compliment. He looked away and rubbed the back of his head. "You would do better."

"No, Soren. Your instincts are sharp and you motivate your warriors to work together well."

Soren glanced from the corner of his slitted eyes. "If your mood is improved this much, you should always join under the Life Tree."

She choked on her seaweed.

The warriors nearest Soren smiled. Most mer seemed vaguely amused. Not the adviser, of course. He hated everything she did.

No, that wasn't true. Adviser Creo worried about her. He wanted her to be like the old brides from the sacred islands. Her wishy-washy attitude worried him, and he was right to be worried because her doubts and misunderstandings caused Kadir real pain.

"You should not put brides on display," he said, to all nearby.

Well, he had a point. Since she had just publicly displayed herself.

And he was the one in charge of approving Atlantis.

Dear Aya. On my first day on the job, I insulted the adviser in charge of approving the city and I nearly caused a riot. On the second day, I had loud public sex under the Life Tree. Please don't let me screw up in front of Adviser Creo anymore.

Kadir nudged her gently. On his dagger was a thin slice of steak he had cut for her.

Aw. She chewed it and he rubbed her shoulders softly. His warriors required his attention, but he still sensed her anxiety.

She didn't want to make him worry.

Was she really doing any good here? She just needed a small sign. One that proved she was all right. That her presence was good, and would help Kadir, so Atlantis could thrive.

Zoan swam into the courtyard furiously, interrupting the gathered meal. "My king! My king, the Life Tree, it —"

"Is injured?" The adviser rose with fear. He was visibly sick at the alarm. "Damaged? Destroyed?"

"No." Zoan turned away from the adviser and focused on Kadir. Shock and hope lit his normally teasing face. "It has blossomed."

CHAPTER EIGHTEEN

The Life Tree has blossomed.

The adviser closed his eyes in relief. Everyone else remained frozen.

Elyssa lifted her fist to cheer. Hooray! Right? They needed blossom nectar to transform the next bride into a mermaid.

Shock silenced the courtyard. The mer warriors froze. No one knew what to say.

Oops. She froze her half-raised fist.

The adviser opened his eyes again and noted her unfinished gesture. His sour mouth pinched.

She released her fist and hid her hand behind her back. Whatever he felt about her — which couldn't be great, seeing as she was constantly accidentally flipping him off — he really, truly cared about approving the city and ensuring the health of Kadir's Life Tree.

"Blossom? Nonsense." Balim looked up from where he was studying fragmentary stone tablets etched with drawings of the ancient city. He squinted at Zoan, and behind him, swimming more slowly and correctly, Nilun. "Elyssa already drank the nectar and transformed into a bride. No other female is present. There must be some mistake."

Nilun reddened and slammed his fist against his chest. "I will fight anyone who denies what we saw!"

The courtyard erupted in rumbles.

"Silence!" Kadir rose, solemn and majestic. "We will see this blossom."

How exciting!

They all stormed across the water, bunched up to enter single-file between the granite-like petals, and zoomed down the corridor. Kadir swam hard and fast, Elyssa curled around him. Excitement hummed in the water, charged as electric eels.

"Zoan noticed changing tones of light," Nilun called, puffing to keep up. "We inspected the Life Tree. The blossom is there now."

At the inner sanctum, she uncurled from clinging to Kadir and grabbed his hand to cross onto the soft, white dais together.

The Life Tree glowed with radiant beauty. Its music sang in her soul. Where was the blossom? Oh, there. In the center of the trunk, where she had rested her forehead, a tiny bud unfurled into a teeny flower.

"I have never read about a blossom forming on the trunk," Ciran murmured to Balim behind them. "And it is so small. Can a bride use this to transform?"

"I doubt it. There cannot be more than a single drop of liquid."

"Then what is the meaning? This was not in my research. Will it develop into a seed instead?"

"If a seed, it will be the smallest seed ever created."

The warriors murmured behind them.

Elyssa let go of Kadir's hand and knelt before the twinkling blossom. It was like a water lily. Small, white petals curved around a sparkling center. The Life Tree glittered proudly.

Maybe that was the meaning. The Life Tree somehow knew she wanted to be a queen. This was its proof that she was right and belonged.

She stroked a soft petal. It felt like touching starlight. "This is where I—"

The flower released from the trunk and floated toward her.

The mermen gasped.

Her heart melted. The Life Tree really did gift her with the blossom. She captured the twinkling starlight, cupping it like a fragile butterfly. It winked in her hands and slowly faded to an ordinary white color, like a kiss drying on her skin. She cupped it in her hands in gratitude. *Thank you.*

The twinkling intensified.

"She broke it," someone cried behind her.

Oh.

Wait. What?

"Broke?" Adviser Creo pushed past the warriors blocking his way. His eyes widened. He thrust his finger at her. "You removed the blossom from the Life Tree?"

Elyssa held her cupped hands to her chest. The flower tickled her closed palms. "I barely touched it."

He turned his shocked eyes on Kadir. "She touched it!"

"You touched it?" Soren frowned from farther back. "Why would you do that?"

"I don't know. It's a flower. It called out to me, kind of. I touched the petal."

"She admits it! This is why brides must remain far from the Life Tree, separated by guards. This is why access to the Life Tree is restricted! Injuring the Life Tree is treason.

Kadir. What are you going to do?" The adviser turned his accusatory finger on Kadir.

Kadir was silent. His eyes were hard, dark, and sad.

What? She had screwed up?

The adviser detailed it. "She admits to damaging an irreplaceable flower. It is too small to provide nectar. It will never produce a seed. She has broken its stem and no more will grow to replace it."

Her belly crunched. "What do you mean, no more will grow?"

The mer warriors murmured amongst themselves. Adviser Creo threw up his hands and faced a solemn Kadir. "Where did you find this uneducated bride?"

Kadir's nostrils flared. "She is my queen."

His claim silenced the sanctuary. Quiet tinkling of the Life Tree calmed all.

Kadir's shoulders sagged. He rubbed his face.

Oh. She really had done wrong. "I'm sorry, Kadir."

He growled. "That word."

Oops. She shut her mouth.

Behind her, murmurs among the warriors boiled into loud dissent.

Soren snapped at them. "Form lines."

The warriors stiffly obeyed. Their dissent fell silent.

Kadir avoided her gaze. He faced his unsettled warriors. "The fault is mine. Modern brides do not have the knowledge. I will tell Elyssa now. Everyone else, resume our meal."

They filed out of the sanctuary.

"I told you this would happen," Adviser Creo told Kadir. "The more you twist what is natural, the more you injure your bride. Or cause her to injure herself! Restrict her to her castle now. Under guard!"

Kadir growled. "No more mistakes will be made."

"Forcing her to embrace a warrior's ways is the mistake. In this under-defended city, she will be caught by predators. Led astray by enemies. Hurt in an attack. Why can you not see this?"

His nostrils flared.

She wasn't a simple bride anymore. She was a queen.

Elyssa itched to say that aloud. But interrupting an argument with Chastity Angel never helped anything. And she hadn't proved herself by Adviser Creo. Not by a long shot.

"Judge our city," Kadir finally ground out. "We will judge our queen."

"You lack judgment." The adviser left, grumbling.

Then it was just her and Kadir again.

The flower brushed against her inner palms like a sad, desperate butterfly's caress.

He turned to her heavily.

She held her cupped hands to her chest. "I am really sorry. This is weird, but, I thought the Life Tree wanted me to have it."

"This tree is young. You do not know your strength."

"I swear, I barely touched it."

"Look here." He pointed out striations in the bark. "These are the strength lines of the tree. This nub is where the flower bloomed. Resin will build up at the injury and create a Sea Opal."

A teensy bead dotted the nub.

A dagger was sheathed in the ground near the tree. He pulled it out and touched the tip to the nub.

"After any injury, the tree swells and bleeds." He carved around the pearl gently. "Ordinary metal poisons the tree. That is why all ordinary tridents and daggers must be left outside the sanctuary, to avoid accidents. If the tree is cut for any reason, purify the injury with adamantium to cauterize it."

The Life Tree almost sounded human the way he described it.

But she did feel bad. "Can we save this flower?"

"No. Its life is over. It will blacken and wither."

Oh. No. "I'm sor—uh, I mean, that's awful."

He sheathed the adamantium blade in the ground beside the tree and rested his hands atop hers, closed over the blossom. "You understand how important it is we have a seed. It is our pride and our identity. And, it is a requirement of recognition from the All-Council."

Elyssa opened her hands to release the tiny blossom.

It fluttered up, glowing and sparkling, just as it had when it was alive.

Kadir made a noise. "It lives!"

Oh, and the stem was cut. It must need to be purified.

Elyssa pulled out the adamantium blade.

It was carved from a single piece of rock as long as her forearm and the smooth pommel was too big for her hand. Clearly, it was made for a mer warrior. It tapered to a wicked blade.

What kind of metal was adamantium, anyway?

Elyssa touched the blade to the thread-like stem of the flower. It danced on the tip, sliding along the metal as if it were a living creature.

She sheathed the blade in the same place she had pulled it out from and captured the blossom again in her open palm.

Kadir stared at her. "What did you do?"

Huh? Had she done it wrong? "I cauterized the poison."

"But I saw it die. How is it once more alive?"

She didn't know. "Does this mean I can reattach it to the Life Tree?"

"Reattach?"

"You know. Graft it back on so it grows into a bigger flower?"

He shook his head. "I have never heard this tried."

Oh. "Well, I don't want to cause any more—"

"I have never seen or heard of a plucked blossom returning to life." He scooped it up. The blossom danced across his index finger playfully, fluttering in the micro-currents like a tiny flower fairy. "I almost doubt my eyes."

"I was touching that spot earlier today and it felt like the Life Tree was giving me a gift. You know. Welcoming me."

His brow furrowed. The blossom hopped off and fluttered free. "The Life Tree does not put forth a blossom for new warriors. It also does not make those strange chimes. Maybe it is normal for modern brides."

She captured the blossom in her hand. "I guess you need more to come so we can find out."

His brow smoothed. "Yes."

She let out a sigh. Her mistake was forgiven. She was fine.

Now, she and Kadir could—

Iyen flew into the sanctuary. His tone was taut; his expression, deadly. "My king, my queen, you must leave immediately. Warriors from another city have been sensed in the city's currents."

Elyssa held the blossom to her chest.

Kadir leaped from the ground, his feet transforming to fins with a flick. "Where is my trident?"

"Soren has it. He requests you remain here."

"If he has my trident, he knows I will join him." Kadir shot out of the sanctuary, Iyen right behind him. His command echoed back into the chamber. "Escort Queen Elyssa to safety."

Queen Elyssa.

A thin warrior just outside the sanctuary puffed with importance. He gripped his banged up, old trident and shouted after the flying warriors. "Yes, my king!"

"Are we in danger?" Elyssa paddled with painful slowness toward the young warrior. "What do they want?"

"To cause us troubles." He waited patiently, alert. His dark evergreen tattoos shimmered.

They flew to the Life Tree. The castle seemed so close when Kadir swam her. Now that Elyssa was under her own power, it took forever for her to reach. And she was useless to help.

"Maybe they're friends," she huffed on her endless journey. "Maybe it's all a misunderstanding."

"The warriors are from my city. If I do not return willingly, they will kidnap me."

The young warrior moved with a surety and alertness that was much older than his skinny body and small face. His trident was ancient and bent at a funny angle. His dark green eyes were too large and luminous, like Elijah Wood when he played Frodo. He seemed unconcerned with the danger to himself and confident of defending her.

Her heart slowed. Okay. This would be okay.

"Your name is Tial, am I right?"

The warrior straightened. "Yes."

Thank god. There were too many tattooed chests and too few name badges. "Why would they kidnap you? You're here."

"My city is near a vent, like Atlantis, and the abyssal creatures that sometimes rise out of it are difficult to fight. More difficult now that a unit has left to recapture me." He gripped his trident. "But I will not go. When I tried to escape the first time, the elders gave me this."

He showed her his left hand. It was scarred and missing the ends of the last three fingers.

She shuddered. Barbarians. "That's awful."

"They told me the next time I tried to leave, the goliath grouper would bite off my male seed instead."

Male seed? Was that like...oh. "So they fed half your hand to a fish and threatened to do the same to your, uh..." Well, call it like it was. "...uh, testicles?"

He nodded.

The mer culture was too brutal. "I can see why you wouldn't want to go back."

"Even if they retracted their threat, I would not return. My father secretly helped me escape. I wish to repay him by making him a grandfather."

"You will."

He puffed his chest again. His bent trident almost looked noble. "Thank you, Queen Elyssa."

Well, she hadn't done anything to be thanked over. "You know, if your city really wanted to keep you home, they should have offered you a shot at fatherhood. Not threatened to cut your balls off."

"But they cannot offer me the shot." He led her down the long corridor into the castle and across the vast, empty inner courtyard. "I would have to wait until I am older than Faier to join with a bride according to the old way."

Right. These males had such simple wishes. Children. Wives. The chance to start a family.

They didn't care about the newest cell phone, the most scandalous celebrity gossip, or who saw the last blockbuster. They just wanted to meet a good woman and settle down.

Tial *would* get his wish. They all would. If Elyssa could

do one thing as queen, she would fill this city with women so they could find mermen to love.

He escorted her to the heart chamber. It opened to her hand print. She went in and sat.

A small, orange octopus darted in after her and swam around the room vigorously. Its noise sounded like a radio station turned to almost-static. It stopped in front of her and regarded her with curious eyes.

"How adorable!" Elyssa addressed the palm-sized cephalopod. "What are you doing in here?"

"She is the house guardian." Tial seemed visibly relieved. "She is small now, but she will grow and defend you and your castle with her life."

Elyssa tucked the tiny Life Tree flower behind her ear and coaxed the little octopus onto her hand. Tiny, curious suckers curled around her fingers, and the octopus walked up her wrist to her forearm. The little beak gnawed on her thumb. Not painful, but curious, like a puppy.

"Now, you are safe. The house guardian will protect you. Please wait here." He turned to leave.

And she was just supposed to sit in the room alone? Useless? "Hey. Isn't there anything I can do?"

"Perhaps once your fins are grown."

Nothing? She stroked the orange octopus. "Should I have a trident?"

"I will find you one for the next incident."

So, this happened often enough there would be a next time. A new thought occurred to her. "Tial, you should stay inside too. These warriors are hunting you."

"I must face my enemies honorably, even if they are my former friends."

"But wouldn't it be smarter to hide?"

"That is not possible." He paused in profile. His jaw was set. "I must stand with my king."

Right. This was about honor. "What if one sneaks into the castle? Who will make a last stand with your queen?"

His face blanked in surprise. "I had not considered this."

"You can't leave me unguarded."

He frowned deeply. "I will be right outside."

"But if they trap you, they can swim in and capture me."

The grooves in his forehead deepened. "Many Atlantis warriors are near the city. No raider would dare harm a bride."

"I'm not a bride, though."

"Yes, you—"

"I'm a queen."

There. She said it herself.

A *sching* sounded. Maybe only in her head. But loud enough that it reverberated in her heart.

His protests stopped. He stared into space. Conflicting emotions passed over his young features. Anger, disagreement, anxiety. She knew those feelings well.

"Kadir introduced me as a warrior," she said quietly, capturing his gaze. "Atlantis is a rebel city. No one knows what to do with a queen."

His brows lifted with sadness. "I would pledge my death before anyone harmed you."

"I know." She straightened her shoulders. "And that's why I'm ordering you to remain here and guard me."

His mouth twitched and flattened. Every muscle in his body tightened and his face closed. Fury seared his young brow. For a moment, she thought he was going to break down and scream.

His eyes closed and opened on resignation. He gripped his trident. "I will remain in the inner courtyard at the entrance to the heart chamber."

Yes! She had done it. Bossed someone around, even though it made him angry. She couldn't let Tial throw himself into danger. Aya would be proud. "Thank you, Tial."

He left without a word. The wall sealed up, enclosing her with the octopus.

Then, a whole lot of nothing happened.

But, of course, the instant she got up to check, the attack would come. She'd do something stupid, screw up. The adviser would yell at her, Kadir would get more serious while defending her, and everyone would join Soren in wondering why, oh why, had he chosen, of all people, *her* to be his queen.

So. She wouldn't move from this room, not even if she starved. Her stomach growled. Dinner had been inter-rupted, after all. They would find her in a hundred years, nothing but a skeleton, still waiting here.

How to be useful? Apparently, kidnappers showed up pretty often.

Perhaps once your fins are grown.

She flexed her foot one direction and the other. Actu-ally, they did feel different. Or did they? Had her feet always been heavily ridged? These creases could be seams. Her bones might separate and the skin stretch between them, turning solid feet into beta-like fins. Kind of like a flying squirrel. It looked mostly normal until it leaped off a branch and soared.

But her fins wouldn't go.

Elyssa must be extra unskilled. Her first hour as a

mermaid, Lucy could flex half her foot. Elyssa couldn't flex a darned thing.

Of course, Lucy had been a scuba diver and expedition leader long before she met Torun, so she probably had skills and qualifications Elyssa would never —

No. Now was not the time to be sad. Now was the time to support her people. Her city. Her husband. Her mer.

The little octopus played with Elyssa's hair. The blossom flew loose and spun in the water. The octopus batted it between tentacles while emitting a soft, tuneless gargle.

Abruptly the room darkened. A high-pitched keening shook the walls.

Uh oh.

The small octopus abandoned the floating flower and zoomed around the small room, furiously reacting to the sound outside.

Was the castle breached? Was Kadir okay? What about Tial and the others?

What could Elyssa do?

The Life Tree responded to queens. Lucy had summoned its power once to protect Torun. Elyssa had already brought a flower back to life — maybe. Kadir doubted his eyes. But maybe.

Perhaps Elyssa should stop getting frustrated by her fins and focus on something more productive.

How did one summon the power of the Life Tree?

Why hadn't she asked already? Talk about useless. She would have to ask Kadir.

Since there was nothing else to be done, she crossed her legs and rested her wrists on her knees, yoga-style. She closed her eyes and imagined the white light of the Life

Tree growing and flooding into her warriors, into her castle, into her.

Did it work?

She opened her eyes. Maybe the room was brighter.

Or maybe it was the same. How could she know? Was this even the right thing to do?

We all know you will never do anything important.

Who was she kidding, to think *she* could do something?

The blossom floated in the center of the room. It shone with magic.

Mermaid magic.

Right? She had brought it back to life by accident, without even trying. She *was* a full-blooded mermaid queen.

Elyssa closed her eyes again. *Focus.* Helplessness wasn't an option. If she did have a power, she had to use it now. Use it now and wait.

CHAPTER NINETEEN

K adir patrolled the crest between the ancient wreckage and his city. Soren kicked to his lower right and Iyen kicked to his upper left, patrolling.

A volcano opened in his chest and burned hot.

How dare these raiders attack with Elyssa in the city? Before, when there was no bride, an attack was understandable. The other cities wanted their warriors back, by force if necessary. But now a bride was present.

He would crush them into pulp. Where were they?

Soren and Iyen flew ahead of him. He kicked hard to catch up. They slowed and waited.

He couldn't order them to separate and he couldn't stupidly ignore his weakness. If he was felled, his Life Tree was too young to survive. And what of Elyssa? No, he accepted the assistance of the strong warriors as they passed the old city.

Across the ancient city, a tiger shark bugled a challenge. It should not be here. This was outside its regular hunting ground.

"Another tiger," Iyen noted aloud. He or Lotar would be tasked with driving it off later.

Soren grunted. "Keep looking. The raiders from Newas were heard here, between two hidden echo points, inside our border."

They kept swimming.

Tial's city, Newas, was far away. Near Elyssa's continent, north of Florida. This war party came to cause damage, to steal resources, and to shame or punish the one who had defected. They were not known for herding sharks, which meant they were likely not the only city's raiders camping out beyond his borders, waiting for a chance to attack.

He tightened on his trident.

Suddenly, in the city behind him, the Life Tree flashed.

His heart squeezed. Elyssa! He turned and swam for the castle. "Come!"

The others wheeled. Across the city boundaries, other patrols also turned and flew.

What had happened? Were they too late?

Surprised shouts and cries echoed across the water. He increased his kicks. Soren passed him, deadly intent setting his black brow. Kadir's limbs burned. He forced himself faster.

Foreign warriors had triggered the defenses of the castle by trying to enter it, even though they were not accepted by his Life Tree. The castle entrance made a high-pitched keening as it cinched closed. Newas raiders were trying to hold the tightening corridor open while their fellows dragged out a net. Someone struggled inside.

No. They would not take *his* mer. They would not violate his castle. They would not threaten his queen.

Kadir screamed his war cry.

The Newas raiders jumped at the sound.

Soren bellowed. Behind Kadir, Iyen joined the call. The other patrols, much farther out, screamed as the whole of the city converged on the castle.

It was enough.

The raiders dropped the net and shot out — into Ciran's patrol. Tridents clashed.

Bloodlust pumped in Kadir's veins. His trident stretched forth to meet his enemies.

But his enemies scrambled from their battles and fled. They flew furiously to outrun an enraged and terrifying Soren. The other patrols chased after them.

Freed of the foreigners, the castle entrance continued to seal, protecting its occupants. The net disappeared as the entrance closed it inside. What of Elyssa? Kadir stuck his hand in just before the hole completely closed, cutting off his view.

The castle squeezed his wrist like a vise. His hand tingled.

Where was she? Was she hidden? Was she safe?

Then, sensing his resonance, the entrance slowly released him and opened. He swam down the tunnel as it returned to its original shape. Who—

Tial struggled free of the net.

"Elyssa?" Kadir demanded.

"In safety with the house guardian."

The tightness in Kadir's chest eased. She was safe. That allowed room for the fury. "They penetrated my castle. You were inside."

The young evergreen-tattooed mer flushed with embarrassment. "Your queen ordered I stay."

"You endangered her!"

The blood drained from his face.

Kadir spat. They had too few warriors to finish the raiders' job and punish Tial with a coward's exile. "Go to Soren. Assist him in finding out how they invaded."

"Yes, my king."

Sudden pain seared Kadir's legs. He bent over and hissed. He had flown too hard after Balim ordered him to rest. He really was not recovered. Kadir grunted and gripped the cramping muscles in his calves and thighs. But he would not let pain stop him from confirming the health of his queen. "Hold, Tial. Help me to Elyssa."

The young warrior held out his forearm stiffly.

Kadir forced his cramping legs to function, gripped onto Tial's forearm, and limped into the corridor. Tial swam slowly and steadily, his face pale. Kadir's muscles twitched, threatening to cramp again.

The heart chamber was sealed tight.

His chest relaxed another notch. He placed his hand on the wall. It recognized his resonance and opened, revealing Elyssa.

She sat in the middle of the chamber. Her legs crossed over each other and her open palms rested on her knees. Her eyes were closed. The house guardian curled in her lap.

His thundering heart slowed and synced with her. How strange he should be out of control one moment, and then calm the next. He released Tial and floated into the room.

The small guardian uncurled and swam at him aggressively. He continued forward. She puffed her body sac, trying to make herself more intimidating. When he would not be intimidated, she looked at him more closely with her small eyes, seemed to recognize him as the king, and floated off with what seemed to be a disgruntled harrumph.

Elyssa slowly opened her eyes. She tucked the flower

behind her ear, pushed off the wall, and floated toward him. A gorgeous smile lit her face. "Kadir. You're okay."

Her feet unfurled in long, salmon-pink fins.

He opened his arms and accepted her, savoring her contact. She was whole. Soft and gentle, sweet and full. Everything was fine. "Your fins."

"Hmm?" She glanced behind her. Her eyes widened and she jackknifed. Her skull hit his chin and knocked his teeth with a clunk. "Oh my god!" She reached for her fins.

They reformed into her human feet.

"No," she whimpered. "Come back. They'll never do that again."

"Elyssa," he chided softly, rubbing his throbbing mouth. "They will do it many times."

"Yes. You're right. Sorry." She hugged him fiercely, and he was too grateful to chastise her for the forbidden word. "I'm so glad you're okay. Oh!" She released Kadir, swam to the corridor, and found the young warrior. "Tial! What happened?"

He looked away. "Raiders entered the castle as you foresaw, Queen Elyssa."

Kadir gritted his teeth on his growl. The raiders had only entered the castle because Tial had rejected his duty and cowardly hidden inside, endangering everyone.

She curled one arm around Kadir, easing his anger with her comfort. Her gaze was locked on Tial. "You're bleeding." She brushed Tial's hair away from a mild scratch.

He froze.

Her touch didn't bother Kadir. She resonated with him only. Tending for a warrior was a fit duty for a queen.

Tending to a coward who had betrayed them he could not allow.

Kadir pulled her hand away. "Come. We rejoin the other warriors and discuss fitting punishments for cowards."

Tial's face turned even whiter. He swallowed hard.

"Make sure Balim heals your injury." She hugged Kadir, resting her head on his shoulder and nuzzling tight into his arms. "How did the raiders get past everyone? Was there a whole army?"

"No. That is what we must find out." Kadir kept her at his side as they returned to the courtyard.

Adviser Creo swam up to them. Panic tightened his body to agony. "Raiders entered the castle! You are injured? Frightened? Hurt? Did they attack?"

"No," Elyssa said, hugging Kadir. "I never saw them. You all protected me."

Adviser Creo's whole body relaxed as the tension drained out. He rubbed his forehead and built up his fury.

"Never in all my years has a raiding party entered a bride's castle." He wheeled on Kadir. "It is your fault! I warned you. This city is not well defended. It is too dangerous to display your bride as you have done up to now. You will listen to me and guard her properly."

"I was guarded," Elyssa protested.

Kadir did not contradict her, but the adviser was right this time. "We will decide how to proceed now."

Adviser Creo nodded firmly, reading Kadir's agreement. He swam to his neutral observer location outside the gathering ring of warriors and waited to see his advice enacted.

Although restricting Elyssa to the castle and cutting off her contact with all other warriors went against his ultimate vision, she *must* be made safe. He had to do something different. Soon, Balim would confirm his health had returned enough to work at the wreckage. She would be left alone. Raiders could once more attack.

There could be no cowards inside her castle, endangering her.

Elyssa nestled against Kadir's side. "It's unfair. I was guarded."

He cupped her waist, keeping her tight where she belonged.

Once the chaos settled and all warriors were counted, Kadir called to Soren. "What have you found?"

"We tracked the raiders to the ruin. Lotar continues the pursuit." A new cut graced Soren's cheek, and his mood suggested he had not exacted his full revenge. "You, Iyen, and I were the fourth patrol to pass near the old city. They must have crossed before the second or third patrols."

"Why were they not seen?"

"They were."

The mer warriors all shifted and muttered. The second and third patrols gripped their tridents.

"I am loyal!" Nilun snarled, a warrior in the third patrol. "Any who doubt me will taste my blade."

The growls from the other warriors rose.

This chaos was normal. Mer of different cities did not trust each other. The tentative unity forged when Elyssa asked them all to claim Atlantis as their home crumbled under the threat of being blamed for dishonor.

Kadir raised his palm. They quieted. "You have risked much to be here. You have more honor than any warriors I have ever served with."

Everyone settled.

"But," his burning rage awoke once more, "if I am wrong and a betrayal can be proved, I will rip the betrayer in half with my bare hands."

Many of his warriors tightened on their weapons,

promising, like Nilun, that after Kadir finished with the betrayer, they would chop the remains into chum.

Tial remained white. He knew his status. He had betrayed Kadir and endangered Elyssa. Kadir would deal with his dishonor later.

"Now. These foreign warriors crossed into our territory. They snuck across it unseen. How?"

"They hugged the ground," Soren said. "The patrols can only protect the outer rim. If an enemy has help passing the outer patrols, he can move anywhere within our territory undetected."

"Not anywhere." Balim finished patching a slash on Zoan's arm and moved on to Pelan, who had a shallow gash down his side. "Entering our castle triggered its defense system."

"Because Tial is a coward," someone muttered.

Tial bowed his head. His trident crossed in front of him as though he were a prisoner of war.

"He will be punished," Kadir said.

Elyssa stiffened against him.

He continued. "Now—"

"Punished?" She released Kadir suddenly and stared at him wide-eyed. "Why? I asked him to stay inside."

Tial had said that too. But that did not matter. "All warriors must fight."

"He did fight. You saw his injury."

"That was an injury from the raiders' net."

"Are you saying he waited for them to net him? Without putting up a fight?"

Tial twitched. He kept his head bowed.

This was all beside the point. "It is a warrior's honor to face his enemy in open combat."

The others, from their continued mutters, agreed.

"He faced his enemy," she insisted.

Of course he could not expect a human to understand. Elyssa often grasped things readily. But this was outside her experience.

"I asked — no, I ordered him to stay inside," Elyssa said.

"All warriors must defend their city from a direct attack," Nilun shouted. The others rumbled in agreement. "The punishment for cowardice is exile!"

She reddened. Her heart thumped so loud Kadir could hear it from an arm's length away. She pressed her flat hand against her chest and raised her chin. "Don't all warriors also have to obey orders?"

"No commander would order a warrior to hide like a coward inside."

"I did." Her chin trembled. "Are you saying none of you would have stayed if I'd ordered you?"

Nilun shut his mouth. His flashing eyes told the truth.

She looked lost.

Kadir tugged her back into his arms. "You do not know our ways. An experienced warrior knows which orders will compromise his honor."

She remained distant. Lost in thought. Her mouth curved down in distress. "I caused him dishonor?"

"He is young." Kadir rubbed her stiff back to comfort her. "His punishment will be softened for his inexperience."

Tial gripped his trident harder. Kadir's words were meant to assure Elyssa that they would not permanently damage Tial, but they also did Tial greater dishonor. He had to endure the suggestion that he was too immature to deserve a full punishment.

Kadir was too angry. Tial should never have risked Elyssa.

She touched the shimmery blossom in her hair.

Now that this misunderstanding was resolved, Kadir turned to Soren to continue the—

"No," she said softly. "I gave Tial an order. Dishonorable or not, *he obeyed my order*." She snapped up to face Kadir. "I don't think there should be any punishment. Or, if there is one, then I should also endure it."

Tial looked up in surprise.

"No," Kadir ordered. Although it was good Elyssa regained her equilibrium, her new request made no sense. "You should not endure any punishment."

"Why not? I gave the order. You all made it obvious that no other warrior would have obeyed it. Tial knew it compromised his honor. He protected me, knowing it compromised his honor!"

"He did not protect you, Queen Elyssa." Faier spoke cautiously even though it was clear he should have been confident. He had seen much in peace and in war. "Warriors will not enter the castle. None would ever hurt a bride."

"Are you really so sure?" Elyssa raised her hands. "If warriors always leave, why did the raiders enter?"

"To capture Tial," Nilun said. "The coward."

Tial's lower lip trembled.

"But he was only inside because *I ordered him*. This isn't the first time these raiders attacked. Did they enter the castle last time?"

"Tial was not inside the castle last time."

"Right. So why would they think that *this time he was inside the castle*?"

The mer dropped silent.

"The raiders used their eyes and saw he was not

outside," Pelan tried, gripping his daggers as Balim sealed his gash.

"How did they see that? Did they cover every inch?"

"No," Ciran said, quickly calculating. "Our territory is too large. Making such a decision with their small party is logically impossible."

That led to a different rumbling. Someone must have seen Tial enter the castle with Elyssa and not come out. They must have remained behind and shared that information with the raiders. A traitor was within the city. The same one, perhaps, who assisted the raiders' entry.

They would uncover the traitors as soon as they finished punishing Tial.

Someone else muttered what they were all thinking. "We should give the coward back to his people if they still want him."

Tial flinched.

Elyssa made a frustrated noise. "Am I talking to myself right now?"

Kadir rested his hand on Elyssa's taut shoulder. "What is your meaning?"

"If all warriors are supposed to exit a castle at the first sign of battle, why would anyone try to break in?"

"To destroy a seed."

She gestured at the empty pedestal. "You don't have a seed."

This was true. But it seemed unrelated. Why was she wasting their time with these observations?

"Ah." Balim looked up from his patient. "Queen Elyssa. You believe Tial was not the target."

She closed her eyes. "Yes. Thank you. Finally."

What?

Even Tial looked shocked.

"Of course he was." Gailen voiced everyone's disbelief. "They were from his city. They tried to kidnap him before. Nilun and Zoan fought them off."

"Yes, but a raider should not enter a castle on a whim," Balim pointed out. "To risk activating the defense system, they should only enter to destroy a seed or capture someone they know will be inside. And who did the Newas raiders know would be inside?"

All warriors must exit to face their enemies. Only one person should remain inside a castle during an attack.

"You are saying..." Kadir's chest clenched. He forced the words. "Their target was *my queen?*"

"That is impossible!" Adviser Creo shouted. Others vehemently agreed.

"We all sensed the joining," Balim said. "They attacked the castle. The only sensible target is your queen."

The burning started again. He would find those Newas warriors beyond the old city and destroy them.

"Tial saved my life," Elyssa said firmly. "If he hadn't stayed, I might have died. Tial's not a coward. He's a hero."

Silence fell over the courtyard.

Tial finally lifted his chin. Wretched anguish filled his eyes and his lips trembled at the disgust of the other warriors. But he could face the dishonor now knowing that he had sacrificed himself for a worthy reason.

Kadir's error had been assuming, like Faier, that no warriors would dare to hurt a bride. His assumption put Elyssa at risk. Adviser Creo had warned him about this possibility. He would no longer be blinded by the very traditions he sought to destroy.

"My queen will always have a guard," he rumbled. "In peace and in battle. From now going forward."

His warriors silently recognized his order. Adviser Creo

puffed his chest. He had wanted Elyssa under guard from the beginning, and now Kadir recognized his wish.

"And my first guard will be Tial," Elyssa declared.

The others growled. Tial blanched in shock.

"No," Kadir said.

She rounded on Kadir. "Why not?"

"You will have a warrior who is honorable."

"Tial is honorable!"

Kadir shook his head. She did not understand. No other warriors could forgive Tial's dishonor even if his action had accidentally ended well.

She pressed both hands to her glowing chest. "Tial valued *me* above his honor. He knew the consequences just like everyone else. He valued me more."

The other warriors shifted uncomfortably.

Nilun growled. "Queen Elyssa, honor is—"

She blazed at him with magnificent fury. "Don't call me queen. You won't obey my orders. The title doesn't mean anything."

His eyes widened. Rage trembled his entire body. "You question my loyalty?"

Kadir moved in front of Nilun.

Elyssa glowed brighter. "Will you obey my orders? Or will you leave me unguarded in the middle of a battle to protect *your* honor?"

He did not dare answer.

"I want a guard who cares about me." She lifted her chin. "That guard is Tial."

The others shifted again. Agitation filled the castle.

Kadir raised his arms to quiet them. "Elyssa, this is not our way."

"I don't care." She huffed and crossed her arms. "Are you just going to stick me with whoever's convenient?

Everyone else said they'd ignore me. Only he, out of all these 'honorable' warriors, obeyed *my* command. The others can call me whatever they want, but it's obvious to me that he's the only one who treats me like a queen."

Nilun turned his anger on Kadir. "You cannot allow this obvious dishonor."

Yes. Tial's cowardice had endangered... No. That was not quite right.

Kadir's calves cramped painfully. He had been clenching the muscles during this discussion and now it cost him. He grunted, bent over, and massaged the taut muscles.

Elyssa dove beside him, realized what he was doing, and massaged his other calf. Her touch soothed him with healing.

His warriors waited for his judgment.

He took the time to organize his thoughts.

Was punishing Tial not the right response? Elyssa had ordered him to remain with her. Despite the dishonor, Tial had obeyed. Wasn't this situation the same as dismembering a male for saving another warrior's bride? It was such a radical shift that Kadir's thoughts turned as muddy as a war-churned muck cloud.

Elyssa glowed at him brightly. Warm, golden light flowed from her outward, shining over the rest of the mer.

There was only one answer that mattered.

His muscles relaxed.

Kadir rested his hands on hers. She smiled. Somehow, she knew what he would do. Together, they straightened.

"We are founding a new city," Kadir rumbled, Elyssa by his side. "The judgments made now will become our traditions going forward. We must honor the past. But we must also understand that we are living in a new era. An era of modern brides. An era of queens." He turned to the young warrior. "You are the first warrior to be tested by the new era. My queen made an unorthodox command. Few warriors would have the discipline to listen."

Tial gritted his teeth, his formerly pale face now flaming, as he awaited Kadir's judgment.

"You did well, Tial."

The young warrior's eyes widened. The other warriors rumbled with disagreement.

This city would be founded on new traditions. No matter how they surprised even its king.

Kadir boomed over the disruption. "You will be the queen's first guard. You will protect only her. And you will obey her above all other mer." He put his growl into it, over the others' shock. "Even me."

Elyssa glowed like the sun.

That, even more than his growls, quieted the mer.

She *was* different. She was more than a bride. Her glow proved it.

"Do you accept this honor?" Kadir asked Tial.

Tial swallowed hard several times. "My king."

"Rally to your queen, Tial."

Tial's eyes glimmered. His chin wrinkled and smoothed. He swallowed again, bowed to Elyssa, and straightened. "I await your orders, my queen."

CHAPTER TWENTY

I await your orders, my queen.

That...was official. Elyssa's chest swelled. Tial truly respected her.

So did Kadir.

He returned to his warriors. "Answer. How did these raiders enter our city? Third patrol."

Nilun jerked his enraged gaze from Tial and turned the full force on Kadir. "I will fight any who question my honor!"

"I do not question your honor," Kadir snapped. "I question your eyes. Explain."

The mer's hackles slightly lowered and he described the patterns his patrol had used to monitor the border.

Tial rested close to Elyssa. His color slowly returned to normal. His fingers remained clenched on the trident, ready at any moment to defend her — and himself — from the obvious unhappiness of the other warriors.

She hadn't meant to throw everything into chaos. She hadn't meant to fracture the loyalty of Kadir's warriors — and it was obvious that many of them silently protesting en masse were fractured. Her orders had been like demanding Tial tear down the flag and stomp on it and then get him promoted while the rest of them seethed.

But she also couldn't let him face a punishment for doing what she had asked. It just wasn't fair.

"We all saw the flash of the Life Tree," Kadir said finally when their debates had been exhausted. "It flashed as in ancient times. We all rallied to its defense. In that, we are united."

The tired warriors straightened again. Even Balim, the total skeptic, raised his chin. Elyssa raised hers as well. This was Atlantis.

"It should be easy to review who was nearest the Life Tree. That warrior should have also seen the raiders."

"I felt its flash," she said. "I should have gone out to see."

Kadir stroked her cheek. Intent emotion crossed his face. "No. It is too dangerous."

"I know I'm not a warrior, but I could still be useful."

Adviser Creo harrumphed. "A bride should never be near the battle. She will never be as powerful as a warrior."

Despite the fact that it was probably true, it wasn't very nice. Just like when Chastity Angel criticized her, Elyssa felt hot and cold and itchy, all at once.

Kadir darkened on the adviser. He clearly wanted to growl but did not want to anger the powerful representative.

Tial shook his trident at Adviser Creo. "Respect my queen!"

Everyone froze in shock. Tial took his guard duties more seriously than just protecting her body. He also defended her honor.

Adviser Creo's eyes narrowed. "Do not threaten a representative of the All-Council, young warrior."

"No matter who you are, you must respect my queen."

"Do not speak so recklessly."

"I am level-headed." He shook his trident again and thumped his evergreen-swirled chest with his closed fist. "If you continue to dishonor my queen, *I* challenge you to honorable combat."

Unlike Nilun, Tial was the last to take offense, and he never initiated a challenge. He was in good shape. He lacked experience, but the adviser might find himself outmatched.

The adviser clearly thought so too. He shifted uncomfortably. "I state only facts. She *is* a human who cannot transform."

That was patently untrue. "I can so," Elyssa said.

"Lies."

"You are incorrect, Adviser." Kadir stroked her back gently. "We observed her fins a short time ago."

"Do it now." He crossed his arms over his chest. "Prove it."

Okay. That should be easy. She just had to think ... and...go... She flexed her feet and concentrated until her arms shook and her face burned. Nothing happened. At all.

It wasn't fair.

Everyone stared at her.

The water felt hot. "Well, I can't do it on command, but I can do it."

The adviser shook his head.

"Enough." Kadir straightened. "Re-form patrols. This attack cannot unsettle our mission. Elyssa will be guarded. Sea Opals must be uncovered in the ruins. We must focus all our strength on excavating the old city."

The warriors began dispersing.

Pelan muttered to his friends. "And now we enter

another rotation of patrols-patrols-excavation-patrols. Did you hear what was missing? Sleep."

Nilun remained red with anger. He turned away from Pelan's complaint abruptly.

Zoan patted Pelan's cheek. "I will sleep with you, Pelan."

The black-and-red warrior rolled his eyes. "Forget it."

"You carry me to the excavation site and I will carry you back. We will sleep like brides in our warrior's embrace."

"Ugh. Zoan. Stop."

The trio headed for the castle exit.

There had to be something Elyssa could do. She swayed to Kadir. "I want to help."

Kadir rested his hand in the hollow of her soft waist. Some uncertain emotion flickered over his face and disappeared. "Remain here, where you are safe."

Being safe was important. But what was that tenseness beneath his gaze? She let it go for now. "How can I help you here?"

He softened and stroked her cheek. "Make your fins."

Fins. That was something she could do. Probably. Just how was it helpful? Even though he had assigned her a guard, he must not really think her capable.

His lips twisted to the side. He nuzzled her as though he could hear her thoughts. "Even young fry are confined until they can swim."

Accept your limitations. Give up.

No!

Kadir was *not* telling her to give up. He was saying she could grow and become strong. She had to exceed her limitations. Then, she could help out.

"I'll do it," she said.

His tension eased another notch.

The warriors dispersed. Soren and Balim both had more details about the ancient city to report to Kadir. She practiced flexing her fins to no avail. Kadir finished his conversations, acknowledged Tial watching over her, and gripped her hand.

"Come," he ordered, tugging her down the corridor.

Tial caught her eye. He would truly fight Kadir if she wanted him to intervene. Tial was taking his guard duties extremely seriously.

She let him know it was okay and swam with Kadir. They approached the heart chamber and his kicks grew more propulsive. He opened the chamber with their palms, dragged her in, shooed out the orange octopus, and sealed the chamber again.

Did it mean what she hoped it meant? Her feminine center tingled with promise.

He turned on her with intensity. His hard lips parted, his intense gaze fixed on her, and the water itself seemed to boil into flame.

He wasn't angry. He wasn't hurt from the attack. He wasn't tired.

Kadir backed her into the wall and crushed her in his kiss.

He wanted her. Just as she was, right now. His shining light. His queen.

Elyssa heard the words in her heart.

They lit her on fire.

She wrapped her legs around his taut waist. His lithe muscles bulged. He palmed her soft derriere and his hard cock pressed against her slick, throbbing center.

His cock slid into her channel like she was made to fit him. Pleasure exploded. His possession swept away all thoughts. All doubts burned. They connected as two souls locking into one.

It was too intense. Frighteningly beautiful. She writhed against him.

His hands tangled in her hair. He yanked her head back and nipped commanding kisses down her jaw to her earlobe. Hunger ravaged her. He contained her powerfully, branding her and marking her, as though she would never escape him.

She belonged here with him.

Elyssa relaxed into his total domination.

His cock rammed in and out of her pleasure-filled channel. She clenched around him. He carried her to the brink. Orgasm showered delicious wonder down on her. Because she trusted him. Because they belonged together.

He tensed and growled. His seed shot, hot and throbbing, into her womb. He collapsed, resting his forehead on her shoulder. His shuddered with feeling.

She stroked her warrior's broad back. Gentle. He carried so many burdens. She only wanted to help.

He lifted his head. His eyes were black with exhaustion and also vulnerable with hunger. Not hunger for her body, not after that. Hunger for something else.

She cupped his cheek.

He closed his eyes, regaining control, and kissed her palm. Then, he disentangled himself. "I must excavate the ruin. Practice well."

What? No! She tried to catch his cheek again. "Balim told you to rest."

"That time was taken by the raiders."

"So? Excavating the ruin doesn't have to be now."

"It does have to be now." He rubbed his eyes. "You must go to the surface soon."

Her stomach dropped.

He was getting rid of her? She had displeased him? The two-year contract was already over? Well, she *had* insulted all his warriors and demanded to be queen. She—

"Stop these thoughts." He pulled her into his arms, fixing her with him. "Your first-month check is nearly now."

Oh. She started laughing as she slumped against him. "Sorry! Sorry. I'm being dim, aren't I? In more ways than one."

He tightened his grip. "Do not speak the words that darken your soul. Do not go away from me like that."

Her heart melted a little. She hugged him back.

Their heartbeats synced. His chest felt so broad and warm and comforting. She had to work on these doubts. Get more confidence, or else her light was going to go out, and she was going to keep hurting him.

She patted his back and let him go, affirming with her posture and her smile that she was her normal cheery self. "If you hadn't explained things to me, I would have thought only five days passed since we tumbled off the dock in Miami. Although, they were the longest five days of my life."

His worry remained. He stroked her cheek with his thumb. "Many things happened."

"You can say that again." She grabbed her right foot and flexed it. "Have fun at the ruin. I'll join you as soon as I make my fins."

He opened the heart chamber and paused in the doorway.

She flexed her feet. Somewhere inside her skin was a whole lot of fin. Hey, even if she couldn't make it right away, it was a pretty good foot massage.

"Elyssa."

"Yes?" She looked up.

He was solemn. "Do not leave this chamber without a guard."

Because it was dangerous. Because the other warriors were angry. Because someone let in the raiders and wished her harm.

Her cheerful feelings evaporated. This wasn't fun and games. She had to make her fins so she could escape danger, support Kadir, and become the strong queen Atlantis needed.

Or else the whole city would be destroyed.

CHAPTER TWENTY-ONE

"I understand," Elyssa said. Boy, did she.

Kadir nodded once and then he was gone.

She remained in the heart chamber for the rest of the...what, afternoon? It was impossible to say now that she had been reminded of the strange passage of time. She joined Kadir and the other warriors for meals. Tension had increased in the waters. The easy camaraderie she'd experienced in the first few meals was gone. Her selection of Tial changed the tone permanently. The others treated her with more distance.

But also more respect.

She rubbed her elbows. Was this how Aya felt? Doing the right thing and standing firm against strong opposition was harder than getting along.

That wasn't the only reason for less boisterousness and dwindled laughter. Warriors went on triple patrols, returned exhausted, and barely shoveled in food before they collapse in the courtyard gardens, asleep. The mer who were not patrolling or sleeping worked feverishly to excavate the Sea Opals locked in the ancient city.

Once they paid the debt for Elyssa, then they could get another bride. More warriors would join their city. Life would become easier.

Something had to be done...

Elyssa focused on growing fins with all her might. Nothing happened. Actually, she got sweaty and irritated, and the tiny blossom in her hair wilted. Forcing her fins was a bust.

She'd been concentrating on the Life Tree when Kadir limped into the heart chamber. She'd seen him and her heart had swelled with joy. *He was alive!* Tears had come into her eyes. *Thank you.* She raced to him and her fins had unfurled.

Tears sparkled behind her eyes just remembering it.

Elyssa scrubbed her face, gathered up her rinds from the latest meal that she finished after Kadir led another group to excavate the ruins, and pushed off the green castle wall.

Gailen shouted from the gardens below. "Queen Elyssa! Your fins!"

She looked back. Long pink streamers trailed behind her toes.

There they were!

She kicked. Her fins swished, shooting her across the courtyard into the opposite wall. Oof. It was softer than the granite petals sheltering the Life Tree, but it still didn't have a lot of give. She rubbed her bruised nose.

The fins sucked back in and became human feet again.

No! *Come back.* She grabbed her foot and flexed every which way. Angry sweat leaked from her pores. They were gone.

But...wait a minute. What the heck was she doing? The

secret was to be calm, meditate, and fill with joy. She kicked and — yes, fins! — she flew.

"Very fine." Gailen popped up from gardening duty and floated alongside her. "You are no longer a confined young fry."

She had done it.

Elyssa kicked toward the entrance.

Gailen turned effortlessly. "Where are you going? The Life Tree?"

"The old ruin."

He darted in front of her. "You cannot."

"I made my fins."

"It is a long distance to the ruin."

"I don't mind."

"No?"

She tried to stop. But she couldn't. She flailed and braced for the crash.

Gailen floated effortlessly out of her path. Confusion made him tip his head as she sailed past. "What are you doing now?"

She bounced against the green wall. Near the exit, it was hard as marble. At least she wasn't going fast.

Elyssa pushed off again and kicked to the tunnel. She almost said, "Failing," but instead she took a moment to think harder. What was she really doing? "Practicing."

He accepted it without comment.

See? He didn't even question her. "Where's Tial?"

"Resting. I will awaken him." Gailen pivoted.

"Wait a minute." She brought up her knees and focused on slowing. The motion made her somersault gently. The castle rotated around her.

If anyone complained about pulling endless patrols with no sleep, it ought to be Tial. He had guarded her from

Kadir's appointment onward. He waited in the corridor while she was in the heart chamber. Kadir finally told him to rest for the first time during today's meal, and he had nearly collapsed from exhaustion.

"Tial should rest," she decided finally. "But I do need a guard outside. Would you mind?"

Gailen's face blanked. "Me? As your guard?"

"Tial can't guard me all alone. I need at least four or five warriors I can rely on so you can get in breaks. And you've always listened to what I say." For better or for worse, like during the wedding feast, when her tossed-off comments had fired him up and almost started a mass exodus to claim brides.

His shoulders went back and his pepper-orange chest puffed out. "I accept this great honor."

Great honor? She laughed softly. "I'm so glad to hear that. But I don't want to cause you problems. You have to tell me if I'm making impossible orders that are going to cause discord with the other warriors."

"The other warriors whine like tired young fry."

"You have to tell me," she emphasized. "I'm trusting you."

His chest puffed. "I will tell you anything you wish to know."

That was kind of reassuring, actually. "Is there any reason not to go outside and practice right now?"

"Some warriors will think it is untraditional," he said immediately. "If there are predators, you must return inside."

That sounded realistic. "Let's go."

Gailen told Balim about the change of guard and their destination. The healer looked up from the ancient city's diagrams and squinted his acknowledgment. If Elyssa wanted an excited cheerleader celebrating her fins, skeptical Balim was not her best choice.

Swimming with fins was fun and weird. It felt like she was learning to drive a stick shift for the first time. If she kicked too hard, she'd slam into the wall, but if she moved too cautiously, her fins would roll up into her feet and she'd be stuck with the doggy paddle.

Gailen trailed Elyssa out of the castle so she had more room to practice. In the open, she zoomed across the city, around the Life Tree, and down the stem column to the rocky ground where it anchored. Coral exploded in a thousand spiny colors. Small fish fluttered like butterflies and larger ones flapped like birds. She lost her fins and recovered them, practicing the transitions.

At her request, Gailen gave her pointers on how to move faster and control her direction.

"You never stop," he said, as she crashed again into the warm, black sand where the Life Tree root anchored. "That strange pose you make, with your arms and feet in front, will not stop your forward momentum. You must kick harder to change to the opposite direction."

She bounced on her human feet off the sandy bottom. "That's like saying 'I never fail, I only succeed in the wrong direction.'"

"Exactly." Gailen did not appear to understand why it tickled her funny bone.

She relaxed and rested her back against the thick cable that anchored the Life Tree. It was curved, but so thick it would take at least her and Kadir and Soren to wrap their arms around it, and they might not touch fingers. Long green streamers floated in the current. Her toes dug into the warm sand. The thick roots bulged close to the surface. It was as peaceful as the ocean shore near her parents' home.

She wanted to bring Kadir here.

Gailen picked up a sharp piece of chert from the sand, nicked the column, and began feeding the long, green streamers back into to the thick stem. The Life Tree glowed brighter as he did it.

That chert must be raw adamantium, or else the cut would have poisoned the stem. "What are you doing?"

"The Life Tree puts out feelers searching for stronger anchors. There are no boulders or cliffs nearby. The Life Tree is strongest. I am anchoring its feelers to itself."

What a strange and beautiful concept. Now that she looked, there were small loops all over the stem. Little knots where the streamers had sought for a more powerful external rock, and the mer redirected its strength inward.

"You have a green thumb," she said.

He looked at his thumbs. They were bent slightly crooked, as though he were double-jointed.

"It means you like to garden."

"Ah. Yes. Gardening makes it easier." His expression set into something less pleasant. He finished feeding the vine in and started another.

She pushed. "Easier?"

"To wait." He frowned. "I cannot resonate with the Life Tree. I cannot make it bring forth blossoms or seeds or castles to secure brides. Only you and King Kadir can do that. And I know you will. It takes time."

Her heart swelled. Like Tial — like all of them — Gailen only wanted the chance to meet the right person and fall in love. Start his family and thrive.

"It will happen," she promised.

"I know." He glanced at her from the side. "When I left my old city to come here, a raiding party caught me twice.

They broke my hands so I could not escape. They told me I would never see a bride."

He stared at his crooked thumbs for a long moment. Lost in thought.

It was suddenly hard for her to swallow. She got past the painful lump and focused. "But you did escape."

He glanced at her. His brows relaxed and he was young Chris O'Donnell again, sunny and grinning. "And I am also seeing, and speaking to, and honored as the personal guard of my king's bride."

She wasn't the only one trying so hard.

Making a good impression, trying not to cause disruptions, wanting to help Kadir — the other warriors felt the same way about her.

She was their queen.

Rather than a representative of Van Cartier Cosmetics who was supposed to secure a trade deal for Sea Opals so she and Aya and countless other would-be mermaids could live their dreams, Elyssa needed to be a representative of her warriors, securing the chance for them to live theirs.

"Right," she said, making a fist of encouragement. "We'll raise the old city, start a sushi restaurant, and meet a hundred brides."

He laughed, a genuine bubbling vibration in his wide, pepper-orange tattooed chest. "We will need more warriors for a hundred brides."

"They'll flock here once they see how great it is."

Behind her, the stem seemed to glow. The Life Tree, too, shared her vision.

Yapping up above caught her attention. Her small, orange octopus was flying down the stem toward her.

Gailen cocked his brow. "That is amusing. House guardians do not usually leave their castle."

It reminded Elyssa of one of her stepdad's terriers, small and fierce and bright. "Benji."

Quickly overtaking the orange octopus swam Lotar, Iyen, and Tial.

"Queen Elyssa." Tial spoke formally. The dark hollows beneath his eyes looked better; he had needed his rest. "It is time to go to the surface."

Time to see Aya, then.

Maybe they could avoid Chastity Angel. Elyssa couldn't wait to tell Aya all about her future life. She would be on their side for saving the mer race and finding her warriors brides.

CHAPTER TWENTY-TWO

K adir needed more time.

"Take that fulcrum," he ordered his warriors, lining up along the thick bar. The collapsed wall barred his entry into his last hope to enter the old Life Tree sanctuary of ancient Atlantis. "Heave."

They pushed, their human feet digging into the muck coating the derelict ruin. Even Soren's bulging muscles strained and shook. The bar moved a hands' width. The collapsed wall shifted...and settled deeper into the structure.

Curse it. "Release!"

They eased off with disgruntled moans, rubbing their legs and arms. Pelan stretched backward. His black-and-red vertebrae popped.

Everything ached and Kadir's head pounded with exhaustion. But he did not rest with the other warriors. Kadir scraped at the seam between broken walls. It had sealed even tighter. He forced the wedge free and searched for a new location to push it in.

Soren growled at him. "Rest."

"I will rest after we have found Sea Opals."

Soren's growl deepened. "Do not destroy yourself honoring an agreement forced by enemies with no honor."

"They are not enemies yet."

And even if they were, he did not like being delinquent. At the time he had agreed, it had been necessary to secure Elyssa, and they had had a month to search the ruin. Balim thought this central tower, jutting like a broken tooth above the rest of the ruined city, was the best location for a treasury.

Now Lotar was bringing Elyssa here to begin their first journey to the surface. Kadir's time was down to the last hour.

He forced the wedge against the seam. His hand slipped. The wedge fell. His wrist banged the rough wall and cracked painfully.

Soren growled and scooped up the wedge. "Do not injure yourself. You have a long journey. Rest now."

Another king might bristle at being addressed so forcefully by his first lieutenant, but Kadir knew Soren's orders came from a place of worry and kindness. He obeyed.

Anyway, Soren was right. Kadir did need his strength.

Soren called the others up and pushed the fulcrum at its new location. The wall didn't budge.

Kadir had to face the strong likelihood that in a short time, he would confront Aya with the news that they did not have the rest of the Sea Opals. And she would have to accept. Not steal Elyssa away from him.

He rose with a growl, the new thought energizing him.

No one would steal Elyssa away from him. Not away from his Life Tree or Atlantis. No one.

In the distance, a group approached. His warriors

released the fulcrum with a puff of dust and watched beside him. Lotar, Iyen, Tial, and Gailen encircled Elyssa.

She kicked steadily on long, pink fins. A beautiful color, like the rest of her, they fluttered delicately in the water, glowing lightly as though sprinkled with the same energy as her golden chest. She was tired from this short swim but saw him and lit up. It eased his chest and his tiredness, as every time. He pushed off, his own silver-streaked fins unfurling, and opened his arms.

She tumbled into them with a laugh. He caught her and they wheeled over. "I didn't stop. Sorry! I need more practice changing direction."

He tightened his grip. "Do not apologize."

"Oh, I know." Her heart pattered with excitement. The warriors ranged around her.

"You brought Gailen," he noted.

"He's my guard now."

The mer straightened. Those at the ruin craned to see what had touched Elyssa so especially about this young, enthusiastic, orange-tattooed warrior.

Kadir regarded Gailen over Elyssa's shoulder. "Guard her with your life."

He puffed his chest. "My king. Yes."

The others shifted uncertainly. A handful felt uncomfortable with assigning warriors the additional role of special guard to the queen. It had not been done since ancient times, of course. But many had looked as though they felt the longing in their chests when Elyssa had declared Tial *her* guard and not an exile. It was the ultimate act of mercy. Kindness and validation wrapped in an all new honor. Given time, even those who felt uncomfortable with it would change.

She pushed free. "Look, I can make my fins on command now."

Her human feet wiggled. She frowned and squeezed her eyes shut, her hands in tight little fists. Nothing happened. She abruptly opened her eyes. A wave of discouragement was followed immediately with realization. "Oh! Sorry. I'm doing it wrong."

He needed to convince her not to use that word.

She closed her eyes again more calmly. A moment later, her chest began to glow. She paddled her human feet...and they unfurled. She opened her eyes and smiled lazily. "There. I *can* do it."

"Good."

Instead of looking happy, she grew concerned and stroked his cheek. "You look tired."

He had no time for tiredness. "I am capable of the journey."

"That's not what...well, I mean, good." Her lips folded. His assurance did not comfort her. "Are we going to the surface now?"

Dishonoring the agreement irked him. He released her. "We will make one more attempt to open this room. Lotar, Iyen." He gestured for them to join him. Tial and Gailen floated forward.

"Can I help?" she asked, paddling after him.

"Remain here. The ruin is dangerous."

She linked her fingers with worry. Her guards closed around her.

Soren grimaced as Kadir organized the already tired warriors to push with the two rested ones. His grimace told Kadir he thought tiring his warriors was a bad way to start an already untimely surface journey.

He ignored it. "Ready? Push!"

They all strained together. The wall shifted. Dust puffed. Not quite enough. They released and rested. He would give this one more attempt before giving up for now.

Elyssa floated at a safe distance with her guards. Gailen pointed out the distant boundaries of the ancient ruin. Tial watched for danger.

"It's like a huge square," she murmured. "Like a whole city block. A Vegas strip size."

"The disagreeable noise is the cave guardian that lives below the tower," Gailen said. "He is sleeping."

She made an excited noise and her light glowed. "Sleeping? Aw. I've always wanted to see one."

"This one should not be disturbed. It is bad-tempered and frightening, like Soren."

Soren's gaze flicked to Kadir. Kadir suppressed his smile. In another city, casual comments like Gailen's would result in a terrible punishment—just like Soren's frequent outbursts and refusal to respect rank. Gailen's home city of Aiycaya had not punished its free-speaking citizens harshly — until they tried to leave.

In Atlantis, the bad-tempered and frightening first lieutenant would only give Gailen some hard tasks to increase his respect.

Kadir nodded for his warriors to take the fulcrum one last time. They rose and did so. He tensed for the final push.

"What's that?" Elyssa asked.

Her tone gave Kadir pause. He followed her gaze.

"It is your house guardian," Tial said quietly.

Gailen squinted. "Odd. The house guardian should not be so far from the castle."

"She followed us." Elyssa swam out to meet the small octopus. Her guards followed closely. "When I was a kid, my second step-dad had a Jack Russell Terrier that followed him everywhere. We had to leash Benji to the yard."

The house guardian yap-yap-yapped as she swam head-first to Elyssa.

At the base of the tower, the loud cave guardian squeal abruptly changed to a lower, more menacing pitch. A giant shadow rose.

Kadir's gut clenched.

Soren swore. The warriors dropped the fulcrum and scattered.

Elyssa studied the giant cave guardian rising from below.

Tial and Gailen urged her to the ruin. Tial called. "On your guard!"

"Take shelter," Gailen cried.

She raised her hands, stopping them. "Just a sec."

No! She had no idea what she was disturbing.

"Elyssa!" Kadir grabbed his trident from the wreckage and flew toward her.

Between them, the cave guardian's huge form cut her off from Kadir's vision and he continued to rise, tentacles flowing out like a wall. His body was old and scarred. His huge plus-shaped eyes focused on her. His tentacles curled.

Kadir swooped over top and dropped to her side.

"Hi," she said, placing one hand on Kadir's shoulder to keep him from dragging her to safety. "This is awesome."

His chest jumped. It was awesome in the wrong way. Like a sonic wave moving ahead of a tsunami.

He curled his hand into a fist. If he dragged her away now, the movements could aggravate the cave guardian to deadly rage. His warriors weren't armed or prepared to take on a mammoth of this size.

His anger sought Tial and Gailen. How dare they allow her to endanger herself?

Both waited where she had ordered them to remain. Exposed. Taut. Ready to do anything to rescue her.

Obeying her orders.

The giant cave guardian stared at her and she stared right back. Fearless. Her chest glowed like the sun and the cave guardian, who was usually violently bad-tempered, hesitated.

"He's kind of majestic," she whispered to Kadir. "Like a Clydesdale."

One wrecking-ball sized tentacle reached out. Cautious, curious. It stopped in front of her and waited.

Behind them, the house guardian's yap grew louder and angrier.

The mammoth turned a threatening green.

Kadir gripped her arm and kicked, pulling her back slowly.

The cave guardian growled.

"Okay. Everybody chill. Kadir, it's fine. Benji, here." Elyssa turned to the rapidly approaching little house guardian and opened her arms. "I've got you."

The house guardian swerved past Elyssa and flew at the huge octopus.

"Wait! No!"

The mammoth shrieked and withdrew his large tentacle. The house guardian did her duty to distract the mammoth. Benji followed the giant tentacle, yap-yap-yapping. The huge tentacle swiped and connected with the house guardian. She flew, turned, and flew at the mammoth again.

The mammoth puffed darkly.

Elyssa kicked forward, breaking out of Kadir's grasp, and swam directly into the arms of the monster. "Wait!"

"Elyssa, come!" Kadir raised his trident to attack.

The giant cave guardian unfurled its tentacles in a deadly rage.

"Stop!" she shrieked. "All of you. Stop!"

A light flashed next to her ear. The Life Tree flower flew from her hair and floated in front of her. It strobed the ocean.

The flash of light hit him like a physical smack in the center of his chest. Kadir pulled up short. Benji also quieted.

The giant cave guardian reached out a tentacle and touched the flower. It was like a glowing plankton on the tip of the tentacle. The glow faded. The flower returned to a dead, dull white.

She recaptured it, held it in her palms for a moment, and stuck the *now glowing, clearly alive* blossom once more behind her ear.

Elyssa had brought it back to life once more without even seeming to realize it.

The giant cave guardian kept reaching. His tentacle curled around the small of her back. He drew her forward.

Kadir's gut clenched again. He fought the instinctual panic. She had true power. The cave guardian recognized it. And Kadir would not begin a fight while she was wrapped in gigantic tentacles.

Soren would. He growled and led the other mer forward in attack.

Kadir barked in warning. "Hold!"

"Seriously, wait," Elyssa pleaded.

The warriors obeyed.

The cave guardian studied her with his big, plus-sign-shaped black eyes. Small suckers suctioned her skin gently. He turned her and looked at the flower in her hair.

"Hello," Elyssa said softly.

Benji yapped.

A minor tentacle thumped Benji.

The small orange octopus ducked under Elyssa's hair and yapped loudly, undeterred. The mammoth gargled. A tentacle thrashed. It missed the small house guardian and hit the wreckage.

The wreckage shuddered and pieces crumbled off.

The warriors jumped. Soren raised his trident in warning to resume the attack.

Kadir lifted his palm. It was too late to intervene. He had to trust in his queen. His warriors once more stopped.

The mammoth hit another chunk of wreckage. More pieces broke off.

The warriors tightened on their tridents.

"Please stop that," she told the mammoth. "We're trying to get the Sea Opals out safely."

The giant curled his tentacles around themselves.

"If you open that room, we'll take what we find inside and go away for awhile."

Abruptly, the giant cave guardian released her. He floated back. His song rose to calmer scratches.

Now. Kadir surged beneath the raging tentacles, grabbed her in his arms, and flew her to safety. Tial and Gailen flew around him. They reached Soren's warriors in defensive battle formation, tridents out.

Kadir held her tight. His arms were shaking. "Never again."

She looked dazed. Her cheeks were red and her eyes glowed. "Huh?"

"Never." One hand still clenched his wicked silver

trident. The other hand slid around the back of her neck and hauled her mouth to his. "Mine."

Their lips meshed. She opened her lips. He thoroughly possessed her. His tongue stroked hers. Heat pulsed in his cock. Their heartbeats synced, hers speeding up as his slowed down, to meet in a steady, unstoppable rhythm.

His kiss branded her.

She welcomed it.

He lifted his mouth. Her chest glowed with his possession. He lowered his arm to her waist and held her tight.

While they focused on each other, the giant cave guardian floated past them. His tentacle curled around the lever. He smashed like a giant fist into the ruin.

The walls collapsed inward with a terrifying groan. Mer, fish, guardians scattered. Dust poofed and debris swirled in a blinding cloud.

Kadir's throat closed. His guard formed a defensive perimeter around them.

The giant cave guardian suspended in front of them as though he was waiting for something.

"What do you want?" Kadir demanded.

"Oh. I think I know. He wants to be thanked. Um, thank you," she told the giant guardian. "That was very helpful."

He shimmered a satisfied red color and ebbed away.

She truly did have the power of communication.

The dust settled. They all crept close to the dark hole. Even the cave guardian peered in.

Kadir kept Elyssa close by him. He would not release her from his arms a second time. Never again.

"Did we find treasure?" she asked hopefully.

Soren and Lotar were closest. They squinted. Shadows

moved inside, and sudden awareness changed their expressions to horror. They shoved away. Out and down.

"Needlefish!" Soren shouted.

Kadir's heart kicked in his chest.

Hundreds of long, skinny fish with serrated beaks erupted from the hole.

Elyssa frowned and held out her hands in a warding gesture. She closed her eyes.

What was she doing? Kadir slammed into her. Tial and Gailen hit a moment later. She jostled and her eyes opened. "Wait. I'm trying to summon—"

Knives stabbed Kadir's body with piercing agony. He roared. Beside him, Tial and Gailen both jerked with impacts.

The needlefish dispersed. The giant guardian followed and scooped handfuls of the escaping fish into its beak.

Pain lanced his shoulders, back, and torso. Kadir checked her. "Are you injured?"

Elyssa looked troubled. "No, I'm fine."

"Good." Agony closed him in its fist. He collapsed.

CHAPTER TWENTY-THREE

The deep blue ocean wheeled overhead. His body was numb. He floated in and out of consciousness.

Soren's face was set. So serious. He was striving for some goal. Kadir floated helplessly in his arms. Why?

Ocean again...

Kadir struggled to open his eyes. His queen. Where was she? "Elyssa—" Sharp pain pierced Kadir's body. He spasmed.

Numbness. Flashes of light. Ocean again...

Elyssa's sweet voice, taut with nerves. "Stay with me."

Stay with me.

Yes. He would stay with his queen. Of course he would do this. She must stay with him. *Do not go to the shore. Do not disappear.* She was the reason he had flown so far...

He forced his eyes open once more. Now, he rested in the heart chamber. His body was numb again. No, he was not numb enough. A heavy weight crushed his torso. His chest and shoulders were bound tightly with sea cloth.

Elyssa's voice sounded.

Kadir turned his head.

Everything whited out. Pain so sharp it was ripping him in half...it eased. He focused.

Another mer. Dark red tattoos. Elyssa was talking with Balim.

"Are you sure this is okay? A hole in your heart doesn't just go away. He needs surgery."

"He will heal. And he was lucky. The needlefish only nicked his heart."

"If you say so." She moved to Kadir and softened. She brushed his hair from his forehead. "Hey. Welcome back."

"Where did I—"

White pain again. It stole his words and his thought. He stared at Elyssa's profile until she came into focus again.

She winced. "Don't talk. I mean, not more than you have to. I'll talk enough for both of us."

"Remain still." Balim appeared over her shoulder in the tiny room. "You took five strikes and are much injured."

"But he'll make a full recovery, right?"

Balim hesitated. "Of course, my queen."

Curse it all. Kadir stared at the ceiling. Even moving his eyeballs hurt. He closed his eyes. How long until he made the recovery?

He had never been full strength around Elyssa. They had barely tried to make young fry. She must leave for the surface. Her people. Would she return? Had this final accident frightened her beyond reason? Anyone would understand if she chose to stay away. He was a failed husband. He could not protect her or join with her. She had many reasons to wish not to return.

Elyssa caressed his brow. "I'm so sorry."

Even her kindness hurt.

"That is a bruise," Balim said.

"Ah!" Her hand withdrew. "Sorry. Sorry."

And she used the forbidden word. Her touch hurt, but he preferred her near him, touching him, than far away, alone.

"I'll just look," she said, seeming to hear his unspoken desire. "I'll be right here."

His chest eased.

His aches increased.

Soren's voice rumbled from the hall. "My king. I know you would want to know right away. We did not find Sea Opals. The room was empty."

All for nothing. His injury. The warriors' uncertainty. Kadir pressed his lips together.

"We will search again," Soren growled. "All the rooms. Until we have found them."

Yes. Good.

"But not before Elyssa has to go to the surface," Balim said, the dispassionate voice of reason. "Say your goodbyes."

He opened his eyes.

No. She must not leave him. Not when he was vulnerable like this. Not now.

Do not leave.

Elyssa floated above Kadir. She was as close as possible without actually touching him. Her liquid eyes shone so brightly. His pain eased. She would not leave—

"I'll go as fast as I can," she said, glowing eagerly. "I'll explain about the Sea Opals. Aya will understand."

She was escaping him. Eagerly escaping him. To go to the surface.

To return to her people.

And he had no choice. It was his duty as king to let her go.

Just like the old covenant.

CHAPTER TWENTY-FOUR

E lyssa was supposed to be in Kadir's arms, flying to the Van Cartier Cosmetics platform to see Aya.

Instead, she was forced to wear a harness that was dragged by four mer warriors and one surly Soren.

They were trying not to touch her. She got that. And she was still slow. She'd barely practiced with her new fins.

But if she had to hear one more time how badly she was to blame for Kadir's injury, she was going to strangle the beefy male with the harness cable like Princess Leia strangled Jabba the Hut in *Return of the Jedi*.

"You should not have wandered off, you should not have dismissed your guard, and you should not have ordered a cave guardian to attack the ruins," he told her, for the five hundredth time, when it was his turn to drag her.

She bit her lip. He was right. But she had already apologized. What else did he want?

"The old brides never left the city. Consider your shortcomings. You should have taken more care."

These mid-ocean currents were supposed to be the

fastest route to the surface platform, but from her perspective, they were not fast enough.

"You know you are not the brightest bride."

That was *it*.

"Fine, Soren, I shouldn't have done all those things. I'm very, very sorry. Are you happy now?"

"No. You do not mean your words."

She was going to strangle Soren with her bare hands. If only she could get her hands around his thick neck.

"I wish you were not here now," he said.

"You know what? I feel the same way about you."

He stiffened.

"I wish I was swimming with Kadir. I wanted to show him off and tell Aya all about our new life together. I wish you had gotten injured instead!"

Soren rounded on her, growling with fury. "He was injured because of you!"

She kicked forward, facing him head-on. "I know that!"

"And still you think you did nothing wrong?"

"I'm not saying that."

The other mer quickly formed a barricade between her and the enraged black-tattooed warrior.

Yes, she was to blame. She had seen the amazing giant octopus and all she'd thought about was meeting him up close. She hadn't meant to frighten everyone.

Then, when the needlefish flew out of the wreckage, she had tried to summon the Life Tree to form a protective barrier. Lucy could make one, so why not Elyssa? But just when she thought one might be forming, her warriors had slammed into her. She'd startled and lost her concentration. Everyone suffered.

She should have forgotten the barrier and just gotten out of the way.

"I wish I would have done everything differently." Tears pricked her eyes. She fought through them. "And if I'd known that 'Octopus Kong' would smash through the side of the tower, I would have chosen my words more carefully. So you know what? You can take a hike, you big hulk." She struggled with the harness. "I'll swim the rest of the way myself."

Iyen intervened. "We must make speed."

Even her desire to show up Soren was thwarted. She wasn't going to take it out on Iyen. She crossed her arms. "Fine."

Soren shoved free of the harness. Iyen shouldered it and pulled steady and hard. Soren floated back to growl at her.

"I do not know what this 'hike' is, but I have no desire to take it. I will do my duty here. Even if it is protecting a selfish woman who I do not like."

He swam ahead.

She shouted at his broad back. "I don't like you either!"

The ocean passed by really fast after that. Even though she couldn't get out of the harness, she kicked because she was enraged. The other warriors fell behind. Maybe they were afraid of her now and trying to give her space. Well, good! Soren might get lost. See how he liked that!

Too bad that didn't solve her real problem.

Because honestly, he was right. Aya wouldn't have been so stupid. Gailen and Tial had tried to keep Elyssa from exciting the cave guardian. Both were recovering with needlefish injuries in their arms and legs, but neither were hurt as severely as Kadir.

And he was already recovering. How much more hurt could he take?

Iyen reduced his speed to swim close to her. "Queen

Elyssa. Do not become so angry at Soren that you do not return to Atlantis."

What?

Iyen and Pelan were watching her with concern. Lotar was too far ahead.

She was going to leave because of a fight with Soren? Really? Was that what they thought?

"Don't worry," she assured them. "I'm not going to leave because of one jerk. I wouldn't give him the satisfaction."

And anyway, if she judged the whole of Atlantis by a few outliers, she'd have to kick that adviser guy in the tail fins too.

They were still regarding her cautiously.

"What's up?" she asked. "Am I 'swimming angry'? Or did I get 'dim' or something?"

They shook their heads.

"No." Iyen's maroon tattoos moved as he flexed. The cable between them remained slack as she kicked her fool fins off. "Your light brightened since your fight."

So, fighting brought out the bright lights in her. No shocker there. Her desk never got organized until after she'd had a good fight. This one with Soren probably built up a healthy glow.

"It is impressive," Ciran said, kicking hard behind her. "Most warriors find it easier to face down ten bull sharks than Soren. He is a powerful warrior. Yet, you only glowed brighter to match his. Do you not fear him?"

Soren's anger was like a flash-bang, only growlier.

"He feels bad about what happened. But he has to get used to it. I'm going to make stupid mistakes. If you wanted a queen who's smart all the time, you should have chosen Aya. Soren had better learn to cope after disaster's struck."

As she spoke, Soren changed from a tiny speck to a

dropping well within earshot. Could he sense her anger the way the other warriors did? Hopefully, it smarted.

"You also communicated with the cave guardian," Ciran continued. "We have never seen one respond to a command."

"Octopi are smart." They regularly escaped out of their tanks and feasted on unfortunate fish in nearby aquariums. They were the Houdinis of the marine world. "Octopus Kong probably picked up English at your weekly lessons."

The mer exchanged thoughtful glances.

"I'm just kidding," she said.

Although honestly, who knew the limit of octopus intelligence? She was no marine biologist.

She started mowing down Iyen. He glanced behind him and focused on his speed. His fins brushed the slack sling cables and threatened to tangle.

"I'm feeling pretty good about my fins. Please can I get out of the sling?" she asked.

Iyen and Ciran both looked at Soren.

"On the return journey," he finally growled. "Rest now."

Fine. She stopped kicking and slacked. But it seriously felt like Iyen must be dragging her like a wall through the water.

As they neared their destination, Soren allowed her out of the sling after all and then began issuing orders. "Iyen, point. Lotar, scout. Ciran, stay with me until Elyssa is on the platform. I will provide security from the humans."

Security? From Aya? "I don't need security."

"We are not bringing the second payment."

"I'll explain everything," Elyssa promised. "Aya's in charge. She'll understand."

Soren growled. "My promise is to Kadir."

"Didn't you say you don't honor any promises?"

He blackened. "I honor what I want."

She rolled her eyes. "Okay. Whatever. Secure me. But just out of curiosity, what are you so afraid my cousin's going to do? Last I checked, I'm still an American. It's the land of the free."

Ciran spoke up. "We are not going to American land. We are going to a platform on the sea."

"Which I can't exactly leave."

"Except by their underwater platform, helicopters to the mainland, and a submersible," Soren snapped.

"Except that," she said. "But I'm not going to. Wait. They have an underwater platform with a submersible? Since when?"

"A short time." His face brooked no disagreement. "I will secure you in the air."

What he was really saying was that he wanted to make sure she came back. They all did. And she was. So she shut up and stopped fighting.

They reached the surface platform. In the last hundred feet to the surface, the water changed texture. Looking up, the 3-D, holographic ocean flattened to a grainy photograph. Gravity lightened to moon-gravity. She could break right out of the ocean like a humpback whale and go flying off into the sky.

She surfaced with a mouthful of salt water. Ugh, not only her mouth but also her throat. The waves slapped and tossed her. Horizons tilted like crazy. She choked.

Descend!

She escaped to the cool, calm ocean.

Soren grabbed her wrist.

Right. No, she was supposed to surface. She had to ask

Aya to stop the demand for Sea Opals. Aya had to understand.

Elyssa kicked to the surface again. Chaos. Waves bounced her up and down, the worst ever water park ride. Soren and the others tried to help her to the stairs leading up to the platform.

It was bigger than she'd envisioned, like the deck of a large ferry boat, and its glassed-in shelter top bristled with antennae and satellite dishes. Was it a scientific platform, then? The stairs heaved up and down, making their own waves, and splashing her away. Finally, a small aluminum dinghy descended from the platform, and the warriors brought her to it.

She grabbed the lip and heaved herself onto the hard metal. The sky rotated. Seawater sloshed in her lungs. Ugh. She leaned over the side and puked her guts out.

A motor whirred above and the boat lifted from the water.

She gasped her first ragged breath of air in a month.

And coughed it out again. Air stabbed her throat in a hundred places. Each breath seared and she coughed raggedly like the water was full of broken glass.

Then, her nose clogged with mucus and her throat coated with it too, and she coughed like a normal person with asthma and bronchitis and pneumonia all at once.

The chaos of the surface eased into a soothing, gentle roll of the open ocean. Her little dingy reached the top and the winch stopped.

Aya stood on the platform. She held out a towel.

Had it already been a month? She made her red jump-suit and tennis shoes look businesswoman-sharp.

Her welcoming gaze passed over Elyssa and hit Soren. Her eyes widened and her mouth dropped open.

Elyssa stepped onto the corrugated metal and grabbed for the towel.

It dropped out of Aya's limp hand.

Elyssa continued to reach for it. Her legs felt weird and shaky like she wasn't used to walking. Her bare feet slipped. She slammed face-first into the metal mesh.

CHAPTER TWENTY-FIVE

Her cousin cried. "Elyssa!"

Elyssa's face throbbed like she'd been punched. God, how long had it been? It was impossible to trip underwater. She pushed up to her knees and touched her face. No nosebleed. "I'm fine."

"Come here." Aya helped her up, covered her with a huge towel, and squeezed her with a worried hug. "Welcome back. You're a day late."

"I'm slow." She released Aya and adjusted her blanket-sized towel more securely.

Soren hulked across the deck completely naked.

Aya's eyes followed his huge form. "What are *you* doing here? Where are the rest of the Sea Opals?"

He growled. "I do not answer to you."

Aya stiffened.

Elyssa defused the tension with a calming hand on Aya's arm. "I'll explain."

Aya glared at Soren and turned away. "Fine."

Funny how Elyssa had been naked for a month and felt

perfectly normal, and she'd been out of the water two seconds and felt all exposed. "How are you? Are you okay?"

"Of course I am. What about you? Come get dressed and let's talk."

Aya led her inside to a dining galley. Elyssa pulled on a matching jumpsuit and chowed down on the foods she had requested that last night at her parent's house — a peanut butter sandwich, jumbo Dr Pepper, and buttery, gooey squares of her step mom's rice crisp treats. Her dad had put in a postcard from their homeowner's association, in case she forgot what the gated community looked like, and scrawled, "The morning crossword seems quieter without you. Hope you're having a great time."

Tears sprang to her eyes. She swallowed hard and placed the card on top of the lovingly plastic-wrapped treats.

Aya had put on her reading glasses. She sat across from Elyssa in the private booth and arranged a mini satellite, recording equipment, and lights around her laptop.

"We're just about ready. Do a test. Tell me one interesting thing you saw yesterday."

"I saw Moby Dick," Elyssa said. "That was amazing. Oh, actually the same day, I saw a giant octopus. Kadir got hurt saving me from needlefish, which is why he's not here. Oh, tell Lucy I can make my fins go! But only when I stop thinking about them."

"Great." Aya adjusted some dials, totally focused on the screen. "Give me one more minute."

Heh. She was the same old Aya after all. Everything had to be scientific, in its place, and done properly. No last-minute interruptions, forgetting something at home, or unwelcome surprises.

"While we're waiting, fill out the questionnaire." Aya pushed a five-inch-thick stack of papers at her.

Elyssa flipped through the stack.

"We'll also take your vital signs and tissue samples. You said you could make your feet into fins? We'll get a sample of that tissue too."

Elyssa picked up the pen. "It's not going to hurt, is it?"

Aya stared at her blankly. "The sample?" Something flashed on her computer screen and she looked away. "I'll spike your Dr. Pepper."

"Aya!"

She snorted.

Oh. Ha ha, funny joke.

"No, it shouldn't hurt at all. We're taking a swab. I'm expecting dead skin cells from the top layer, or," she wiggled her brows, "scales."

"I don't have scales," Elyssa promised, tapping the pen against the paper stack, "but I'll do whatever I can to help you uncover the mysteries of the mer."

They spent until dark with Aya interviewing and recording. It was obvious when Soren hulked in the background. Aya's gaze wandered and she forgot her question.

They'd offered him and the other guards food while they were waiting, but Soren snapped that it wasn't necessary, and the other guards did not surface for Elyssa to ask herself.

By dark, Elyssa felt tired and wired. Probably it was the rice crisp-and-marshmallow sugar high after a month on the sushi-and-seaweed diet.

"Your transmitters went out," Aya told her when they were reaching the end. "We lost them at a thousand feet. Here are replacements that go deeper."

Elyssa took off the broken transmitter earrings and put

in the new ones, screwing on the backs to make sure they stayed in. "Do these make a high-pitched squeal too?"

"I don't hear anything."

Hmm. Elyssa didn't either. Maybe she sensed the whine with her mermaid powers. She'd find out in the water.

Aya picked up the old ones and studied them with her reading glasses. "Okay, let's drill deeper into this conundrum. If we know more about how the Life Trees grow, perhaps we can grow our own. How deep are you?"

"Forever deep."

"Are you in the Sunlit Zone or the Twilight Zone? Or is it the Midnight Zone?"

"I really don't know."

"Is it bright out, or does everything have bioluminescence and it's dark?"

"I don't know," Elyssa repeated patiently. Aya sometimes got so focused on a problem she didn't actually hear the answer. "Everything's bright underwater. It's like being in a football stadium, except you can see about a million miles in every direction, including down."

Aya raised a brow. "A million miles? Elyssa, this is for science."

"It's crazy. You can see forever. Way farther than on land."

A chime sounded on Aya's laptop.

She sucked in a breath, straightened, and tapped the keyboard. "That's time."

"Today went by so fast." And Elyssa still hadn't gotten the chance to ask Aya about the Sea Opals. She shifted on the hard plastic bench.

"Maybe we can move the platform." Aya hummed as

she studied the maps and reviewed Elyssa's directions. "Which direction is the current?"

"I can tell you when I'm in the water again."

"Oh, of course. We'll track it on your transmitter." She closed the laptop, removed her glasses, and smiled. "We need the Sea Opals by the next meeting. It's the last time I can put it off. Make sure King Kadir provides."

And that was it.

Aya took a deep breath and started to rise.

"Um." Wow, how to ask this? There was no way to sugar-coat Elyssa's counter-request. "I'm actually hoping for an advance on more brides."

Her smile flattened. "What?"

"Well, a lot of mermen really deserve a chance to start their own families. The earlier the better."

"Kadir hasn't even paid off you!"

"And I also don't think it's fair to ask for so many Sea Opals just for one person."

"Yes. It is."

"Van Cartier Cosmetics already owns the world market."

"Do you know how much it cost to put this together?" Aya gestured at the laptop, the platform, the rice treats. "Do you know how much these military-grade transmitters are worth? Two sets of them?"

"But it wouldn't cost much more to support a second or third bride."

"Impossible. The legal fees alone—"

"Don't you want to be a mermaid?" Elyssa pushed. "Wouldn't you do it for free?"

Aya stared over Elyssa's shoulder. The night was dark now and the windows only reflected their image inward. She looked back at Elyssa, made her lips into a flat line, and shook her head. "I could never be a bride. Not for all the Sea Opals in the world."

That was what Aya had said on the shore, on the dock the day Elyssa left. Even now, it sounded crazy. "I don't believe you."

"I've thought about this a lot since the bride pageant." Aya toyed with her manicured nails. When they were kids, she used to bite them down to the quick. Now, the acrylics were smooth and beautiful. "Why I wasn't chosen. The reason is that I don't have the ability to love."

What the heck? What had Chastity Angel been telling her while Elyssa was gone? "Yes, you do."

"I've never even had a pet. I couldn't give my love to a child. Especially when things went bad and I was forced to give my child up."

"You'd never have to give your child up!"

"Read your contract. If you can't remain in the relationship, you give up all rights to your baby. It's the same as their old covenant. You're no more than a merman's surrogate."

Elyssa sat back in the cold plastic seat. This was what Aya had wanted to tell her. She knew that Elyssa would have agreed anyway because Elyssa was born from a surrogate.

Elyssa's biological mom had viable eggs but no womb. Aya knew that in the worst case, if everything between her and Kadir was destroyed, she would never deny him their baby.

The thought made a dull pain in her heart.

If Kadir blamed her for the accident at the ruin like Soren, if she failed to earn the respect of the warriors, if she caused another problem with the Life Tree...

She rubbed her chest. "I still see Helen off and on."

"Your family isn't normal. When a relationship dies, there are usually no survivors."

She couldn't think this way. "It will work."

"How will you handle visitation? Do you really think you can cross two separate worlds? You'll be left with nothing but memories, just like all the other brides."

Her fear was natural. After Aya's parents split, her father wouldn't even cross Miami to see her. Elyssa never met him once, not at a single birthday or swim meet or graduation.

The mer were different.

"Kadir went every year to the surface to see his mother, even though he never went to the shore."

"Isn't that more evidence of how impossible it is to sustain a relationship? You're too different."

"Aya." Elyssa put her hands on Aya's cool fingers, stopping her stream of fears. "I love Kadir."

The feeling of love swelled in her chest. She did love Kadir. That was how she knew everything would be okay.

Aya's brows drew together. "But does he love you?"

Oh. Wow.

Aya had a point. It was one thing for Elyssa to love him. He was intense and honorable and loving. When he pressed her against a wall, she felt the power of his devotion. But was devotion the same as love? She wanted to say yes. But what if she was wrong?

She didn't know what to say. "It hasn't come up."

Aya nodded slowly, distractedly. The project notes spread out across their table. She pulled her hands free of Elyssa's and studied graphs, charts, tables. "I want this program to be successful. I knew the instant you came up without Kadir that there would be no Sea Opals today. I just don't see how we can support more participants."

Right. Back to things that she did know. "The brides of the past asked for only a single Sea Opal."

"And theirs are starting to show up on the market too." Aya tidied the files. "We're holding the interest of investors now, but we won't be able to start clinical trials for another six months. The regenerative properties are just amazing. We're talking 'cure cancer, regrow your dead liver' amazing. Sea Opals have the potential to be not just a pretty face cream, but an actual fountain of youth. If you have the right response. You know." She trailed off.

She still felt awkward about the incident the last time they'd worked together. The one where Elyssa's parents got bought off and Elyssa gave up all credit for the discovery because *she would never do anything important.*

"Resonance?" Elyssa supplied.

Aya pushed past the sudden awkwardness. "Yes. Resonance. People who are resonant...the sky's the limit."

So, maybe the Life Tree could heal Kadir's punctured heart without surgery.

"But we'll need the supply for mass production," Aya said. "The Life Tree of Sireno overflowed with Sea Opals the size of boulders. A hundred is nothing."

Okay. Time for a hard truth.

"That's because the Sireno Life Tree was much older. The Atlantis tree is a wee little baby. Its Sea Opals are like seed beads."

Aya frowned. "Kadir already supplied us with thirty reasonably sized Sea Opals."

"They came from the other cities, the older Life Trees. We don't have any more."

Aya's chin dropped. "What?"

"Kadir was injured trying to find more in the old city wreckage."

Aya rested her forehead in her hand. "You're kidding."

"No." But Aya was devastated. Elyssa touched her forearm. "What's wrong?"

Aya laughed painfully and rubbed her forehead. "Agh. I was supposed to ask if you could give us an advance on the next bride's allotment. Like, in addition to the rest of your own. I'm not kidding. We need these Sea Opals now to draw in big investors while the public interest is still hot."

Van Cartier Cosmetics was poised to explode past the competition and become the name brand Aya's grandmother, its founder, had always wanted it to be. Sea Opals were their big ticket, and Elyssa had just told her the treasure they thought they'd found was an empty chest.

But her loyalty lay with her warriors.

"You're talking about money," Elyssa said gently. "These are people's lives."

Aya frowned and picked at her acrylics. The paint was chipping off her ring finger. "But we need these now."

"Then you need to approach Sireno."

Aya snorted. "After what Blake pulled there? We can't get them to answer a single request and trust me, I've been broadcasting underwater all over the Gulf of Mexico for months."

Lucy and Torun should have been only the first of many mer-human couples after they met in the Gulf of Mexico. Unfortunately, Lucy's ex-husband Blake had desecrated the Sireno mermen's sacred cave of Sea Opals and tried to shoot the mer army that surfaced to recapture them. The whole thing was caught on Lucy's cell phone and posted to Facebook. Elyssa and Aya had flown in by helicopter to arrest him. He had been stopped (and fired), but the damage had been done. Even though their sacred brides had left them desperate for more than two decades, Torun's home city of Sireno refused to answer any human broadcasts.

Blake was currently rotting away in a Mexican prison.

And good riddance. Before all this, Elyssa had been pressured to invest in the official Van Cartier Cosmetics expedition with Blake at the helm. She heard him talking about how *he* found Lucy's first Sea Opal, the largest gem ever discovered. Elyssa had studied Lucy's discovery extensively and knew that was a lie. When she confronted him at a company party, he'd gotten this mean look in his eye. Like he wanted to cut her. Even though they were in the middle of a crowded room, it gave her the shivers.

She'd poured her money into Lucy's expedition so fast, her bank had to call to check for her authorization.

Yes, it was a good thing Blake was locked away.

"Try Dragao Azul, maybe," Elyssa said. "I think it's off Portugal. That's where Kadir and Soren are from."

Aya wrote it down. "Off Portugal? Can you be more specific?"

"Nope."

Aya sighed. "I'll see what I can do."

"You have a submarine so it shouldn't be too hard."

Aya looked up. "What?"

"I could hear it for miles. And man is it loud."

"That's not ours."

Weird. "Soren said it was. It's tethered to the underwater platform that's also connected to this ship."

Her gaze seemed to turn inward, and whatever she saw there only made her grim. "I'll look into that."

"Good luck."

Aya studiously made notes.

"Really, though, don't get your hopes up. Atlantis is the only city that's trying to find modern brides. Everyone else wants to wait and get them from their old sacred islands, which are mostly empty."

Aya chewed the end of her pen shrewdly. "How would they feel if I repopulated their 'sacred islands' with new colonies?"

See? Aya was so creative. Elyssa would never have thought of that. "You can try it. If Jolan is still king of Sireno, he's trying to challenge the Council to accept modern brides like Atlantis. Repopulating the sacred islands with modern brides might be the compromise they need. Torun would know the location of Sireno's sacred islands."

"They can't all have sunk into the sea," Aya muttered. "Second option: We can grow our own Sea Opal tree. Do you have any seeds?"

Ack. "Um, I kind of broke off the one flower that might have turned into a seed."

Aya looked up from her "solutions" document. Her brows drew together. "Elyssa...."

"I know!" Elyssa rubbed her forehead. "I felt so bad. I still don't know how it happened. I got in a ton of trouble for it. Oh! Here." She felt the wilted petals in her hair. "Oh god. Get me a glass of seawater!"

Aya raced to the galley and returned with a clear, glass mug full of liquid from the seawater tap.

Elyssa dropped in the fragile flower. It fell to the bottom. RIP.

"Oh no," Aya said.

Elyssa grabbed the clear mug, closed her eyes, and breathed. *Feel the power of the Life Tree flow through you.* The electric lights and the chilly breeze and the skritchy blanket and the hard booth chair disappeared. She meditated. *Breathe.*

"How?" Aya whispered.

Elyssa opened her eyes.

The petals had unfurled and the blossom floated in the middle of the glass, twirling gently, like a miniature water lily.

She gave the mug to Aya.

Aya didn't take her eyes off the flower. "Did you just bring this back to life with your mind?"

"It's the resonance," Elyssa said, *really* grateful for practicing, and also that it worked. God, if she'd killed the flower after all this time, she'd humble herself before Soren for the whole swim back to Atlantis and never leave her castle again. "I'm connected to Kadir's Life Tree now, and this is part of the Life Tree too, so it responds."

"Magic," Aya breathed.

"Yep."

Aya grinned at Elyssa. Her eyes sparkled just like when they were children, pulling on their swim tails and diving like little mermaids in the clear water.

Then, her smile faded. She looked down at the flower with sorrow. Her thoughts almost seemed to broadcast to Elyssa. *This will never be me.*

Elyssa reached out to her. "It will be you, too. Believe."

"I wish I could believe." Aya straightened, business-like again. "The Sea Opals are a serious problem. I will try these other avenues, but you have to convince Kadir to come up with the rest. Steal them if you have to."

"We can't steal them. We're barely able to keep others from stealing *us.*"

Aya double-checked the recording equipment was shut off. She glanced behind her, then leaned in and held Elyssa's gaze. Deadly serious.

"If you don't, all this," she gestured at the platform, "goes away. You get pulled out and sent home."

"But I don't want to go home!"

"I get fired. That's only the beginning." Her voice dropped. "We're not the only ones fishing in this ocean, Elyssa. The other fishermen are more deadly than you can possibly imagine."

CHAPTER TWENTY-SIX

While Elyssa was gone, Kadir remained still and isolated in the heart chamber.

The last time he had been in this curved room, it had glowed with his and Elyssa's love-making. Now, it was dull and empty. The difference cut like a blade.

The whole city felt strangely empty. Dimmer than before. As though not only five warriors had left, but his strength and faith left with them. He could not fight his fears, and without activity to distract him, those fears grew into monsters.

Elyssa had nearly died at the ruin. She had been crushed by a cave guardian and seen the horrors of a needle-fish attack. Her guards had failed to protect her. And before then, she had been shown the true atrocity of the raiders, who had chosen her to target in their attack. No more did a golden light dance in her chest. She'd faced the cold, hard reality of life with him in Atlantis. Her last act had been to leave it behind.

Eagerly.

Anxiety palpitated in the water like a living creature,

dark and toothed and hiding in shadows to assault him in the stillness.

Would she return?

The question was unendurable.

"Stop tensing," Balim ordered as he changed the dressings on Kadir's wounds. The pain was second to the anxiety jumping under his skin. "You slow your recovery."

"Patrols?" He fought through the white-hot pain to demand answers. "Danger?"

"You are the only danger," Balim muttered.

"Report."

Balim eyed him balefully. "Will you rest if I place you in the courtyard?"

Yes. He forced Balim to take him to the courtyard. The open currents forced him to make constant minor shifts, kicks he had never noticed, but which now sent fire through his muscles, excruciating.

It was better than drowning in Elyssa's absence in the heart chamber.

"We have driven off more tiger sharks," Faier reported. His hands bore new scars. He bowed from respect. "Zoan was injured but is recovering. He does not have Lotar's skill."

"Stay strong." Kadir's torso ached with the words. "Endure."

"Yes, my king." Faier's head remained bowed. His second city, Rusalka, had drilled in unquestioning respect. "Queen Elyssa is returning soon?"

It was an unnecessary question. They had all calculated the slowness of the sling travel, the time at the surface, and complications if she could not transform or had to be persuaded to descend.

"She will." Kadir gritted his teeth. "Soon."

Faier's head lifted. His gaze slipped to Kadir's bandages. He scratched the long scars raking his right leg.

He had received his injuries honorably while defending Rusalka from attack, but the elders had slammed him with dishonor. They declared him unfit, unable to protect a bride, and he had been passed over for another warrior.

In any other city, the same thing might happen to Kadir. If he were an ordinary warrior, this depth of injury might have caused his elders to take Elyssa from him and place her with another mer.

That would never happen in Atlantis. He would fight to the death.

She was *his*.

"Believe," Kadir growled. His chest vibrations lanced his injuries with agony.

Faier nodded and retreated a few strokes.

Nilun took his place.

"My king." Nilun stood stiffly, his gaze locked on a spot on Kadir's wall. Respect in Rusalka demanded a bowed head; in Djullanar, it demanded an unfocused gaze. "The Life Tree is in good health. Zoan's hand is injured but he continues his duties. He checks every hour for new growth. There are eight large branchings, six medium branchings, and twenty-two smaller branchings, but no flowers."

"Good. Diligent."

Nilun waited. His eyes remained focused on the wall.

"Question?"

"When will Queen Elyssa return?"

Again.

Kadir gestured behind Nilun. Someone had carried in a diurnal fish. The fish bumped against the top of the dome, meaning it was daylight on the surface. "Balim marks the days. Gailen listens at the echo point."

"She will immediately return without resting?"

Yes, that was what Soren had planned. Kadir nodded.

Nilun broke protocol and gazed directly at Kadir. His neck reddened. "She is a weak swimmer. She will tire."

"All warriors pull the sling."

Being pulled in a sling was only proper for injured warriors to be carried from a battlefield or the honored dead to be taken on their final swim. His question burst forth, hot and demanding. "How can you allow another male to carry your bride?"

Anger erupted like a fire. Kadir sucked in painful fury.

Only Kadir would taste her lips. Her soft body would only plaster to his chest. Her heartbeat would only sync to his rhythm. She was *his*.

His growl caused his chest to throb painfully. He cut it off. "She resonates with *me*."

Nilun snapped his gaze to the wall once more. He waited a long moment, as though he wished to speak more. Faier floated next to him. Both seemed to want something.

Balim passed the lingering warriors. His censure-filled gaze rested on Kadir. "You will re-injure yourself. Do not speak!"

Kadir lay back for the ministrations and immediately ignored Balim's orders. "Gailen? Tial?"

"They will soon be healed." Balim unwrapped his bandages and spread more healing paste. "Soren's group will not arrive for some time. If Elyssa returns, will you disband the queen's guards and restrict her to your castle?"

How dare he even ask this? "You listen to Adviser Creo."

"His questions are reasonable. Your bride's energy is easy and natural. The warriors find her presence enjoyable, but her mistakes nearly killed you."

"She learns."

"Not fast enough. And if you reject the All-Council's advice and Atlantis does not receive their recognition as an official city, the raiders who harass us will multiply. Our lives will become infinitely harder. Do not antagonize Adviser Creo for stating what we all believe."

What we all believe.

Did Kadir have to carry the faith for all of them? Did only he see the brighter future? Could no other warrior share his burden?

His voice alone floated on a sea of dissent. All the years in Dragao Azul. Then, when he toured the other cities. Now, he hit his limit. Exhaustion overwhelmed him.

Kadir stared at the fish swimming desperately at the top of the dome, searching for release from the dark pressure and escape into the light. His chest throbbed. A dull ache pounded in his head. "Where...is your faith? Balim?"

"It is in you." The warrior softened his tone. "You are king."

Kadir closed his eyes. *King?* He was Atlantis's greatest weakness.

Against all odds, he had discovered a city so ancient it had receded into myth. He had rallied others to join his dream. He had brought the first bride here to be queen.

If Elyssa did not return, the city would dissolve and everything he had ever done would be for nothing.

She had gone to the surface eagerly.

Adviser Creo intruded, pushing past Faier and Nilun. "Now, are you satisfied that treating a female like a warrior is an error?"

Kadir's gut clenched.

"Relax," Balim ordered, and Kadir forced himself to do so. He wrapped the new seaweed strip bandages efficiently. "Wait, Adviser Creo. You will have a private counsel."

"My feelings are known. My advice is public record." He focused on Kadir with heavy determination. As though he feared that speaking to Kadir would not help, but that he was determined to fulfill his duty. "Parading your bride around the ruin nearly ended in death. Hers."

The growl started in his chest. The ghostly twinge of his injury stopped him. Kadir wanted to argue but he could not.

"Stop tensing," Balim snapped.

Like Soren, Balim was fiercely protective of Kadir to the point of overstepping their roles — king and warrior — and demanding Kadir preserve his health. Unlike Soren, the reason for his attachment was less clear. They had not grown up together. Kadir had met Balim once in Undine, after his speech about modern brides and before the city rioted. The next time they met, Kadir had been wasting away in Soren's arms, barely clinging to life. Balim had used all his skill to strengthen that tenuous grip. And he continued to do so, injury after injury.

"You tense because you know my words are truth." Adviser Creo laid out his orders. "Treat your bride with more gentleness. Confine her to safe areas such as this castle and banish your warriors to the city. They will endure."

Faier and Nilun both straightened. Two different cities' military training marked their bearings. They would endure, without fright or complaint.

But they were also Elyssa's warriors. Kadir spoke. "My queen ordered—"

"That is your error!" The adviser reddened with anger. "How dare you make her give orders? I *cared* for my bride. I treasured her and kept her safe from all warriors! You make yours swim in this unguarded city with untried youths who can barely make their own fins. She might already be carrying your young fry. How can you be so reckless with your precious treasure?"

"Trust."

"You do not know these mer!" The adviser nearly shook with anger. "You do not know their fathers nor their grand-fathers. They are rejects. Rebels. Outlaws. Broken. Unfit. Unworthy!"

Balim finished tying Kadir's bandage with a sharper than necessary tug. Did that mean he agreed with Adviser Creo or was he angered by the adviser's insults? His taut expression was unreadable. He gathered his materials and kicked to the castle cabinet to store them.

Adviser Creo ranted. "Your first lieutenant is a disgrace who takes pride in refusing to follow rules. And if the other cities see how you torture your brides, no other warriors will join you. Atlantis will remain below the minimum popula-tion and destroy your only chance for All-Council recogni-tion. Now. Will you, or will you not, treasure your bride?"

His words rubbed Kadir raw. The growl burst, unstop-pable. "I trust my warriors *and* my queen."

The adviser's face blanched in shock.

Faier and Nilun hummed with his decree. Even Balim glowed with swift brightness before clamping down on his control and turning away.

Adviser Creo's lips pinched. "I came here, out of all the councilors, because I believed in your idea. A covenant with modern brides is necessary for our race to survive in this era. But never did I imagine you would hurt, frighten, and trau-matize your brides. I thought you made a bad bargain to allow her to visit the surface, but now it is clear that it was a mercy. She will not return."

His pronouncement punched Kadir in the soft gut.

Fears swirled. The adviser was right. She had never wanted to be a queen and yet Kadir had forced her. Over and over, he had pushed her beyond her wishes. She would leave.

And yet, she might already be carrying his young fry.

"She is coming!" Tial burst from the entrance, shouting his announcement. His left shoulder was bandaged from the needlefish strike. "Queen Elyssa has been spotted beyond the ruin!"

Adviser Creo straightened and looked at Kadir with raised brows. He was surprised she had returned. Then, his brows lowered and he glared. He was more determined Kadir take his advice, confine Elyssa to the castle, and keep her safely isolated.

But Kadir would not. His steely gaze took in Adviser Creo and everyone else who had doubted him.

"She is my queen," he growled at the adviser.

"If you continue with this treatment, I cannot approve your city." Adviser Creo snarled at Kadir. "You will not care for your bride properly. Do not be surprised when she injures herself or commits treason against the Life Tree. Again."

CHAPTER TWENTY-SEVEN

Tial's announcement that Elyssa had been sighted beyond the old ruin electrified Kadir's mer. Not only Adviser Creo. The rest of them reacted also.

Surprise and relief blanked Faier's face. Gailen straightened eagerly. Nilun swam to Tial and demanded to know her location and how certain he was it was Elyssa. As if more brides might be heading this direction instead.

Shouts outside preceded her arrival. Benji rushed to the entrance.

Soren entered first. He caught Kadir's penetrating gaze and turned aside. The sling he would have carried Elyssa with was wrapped in his hands as though it hadn't been used.

Where was she? And why was Soren appearing to be defensive, acting so odd?

Balim swam to Soren and they began conferencing. It was too far for their low words to cross, but from the gestures and Soren's flashing reaction, Balim was clearly relaying the reports of the last hours, including the pronouncement by Adviser Creo.

Then, Elyssa entered and all other thoughts fell away.

Silence swept over the inner courtyard.

Her fins unfurled and she kicked languidly. Her eyes sparkled. She greeted the small orange house guardian, and then she continued on, skimming over the gathered crowd to him. Their gazes locked. Her light intensified.

His chest squeezed.

She kicked for him, arms out. "Kadir."

He braced himself. She would hit hard, but he needed her contact, even if it was slamming into him. Her eagerness lifted his chest and his pain eased. She had returned willingly.

He opened his arms. "No sling?"

"They said I was keeping up enough, especially on the way to the surface." She abruptly stopped just before she reached him and kicked hard, puffing up sand in his face and hair. "Oh. Sorry. My bad. Sorry."

Why did she not embrace him? "Elyssa?"

"Ah! Sorry. That's the last time I'm apologizing. Sorry."

He grabbed her hand.

She did not return his touch. She did not look him in the eye.

Unease slid over the courtyard.

He tugged her close.

She refused the closeness but finally sat beside him carefully. Her fingers ghosted over the taut bandages. "You look awful. Are you okay? Should you be up and about already?"

"I am improved." He rested one hand on her back, stroking her shoulders.

She eased away. "Let me say hi to everybody."

His chest turned cold. She was upset with his treatment of her. Why else would she turn away? "As you wish."

She greeted everyone, one at a time. The warriors glowed with her attention, and Adviser Creo glowered in pointed warning. Kadir panged at her distance. He needed her for himself. And she kept looking at him in fear and confusion, as though she wished to ask him something privately.

Faier asked her an important question. "Queen Elyssa. Your journey. It was hard?"

"Not really. On the way up, I got into a fight with Soren. But don't worry. We worked it out."

Faier's brows almost slid off his face. "You *fought* against *Soren*?" He looked at her other guards. Iyen, Ciran, Lotar.

The warriors who had accompanied her nodded.

Kadir's chest tightened. How had Soren failed in his duties to protect her and instead sought her destruction? He gripped her shoulders. "Soren touched you?"

"Oh, no. Sorry. We argued." Elyssa held his gaze. Her cheeks reddened. "I yelled. He yelled. I yelled back. No biggie."

His jaw ached. From clenching. If Soren were closer, Kadir would have his own words.

The other warriors were equally shocked. No one threatened a bride. Not their own, and certainly not another male's.

"Seriously. Guys." Elyssa rubbed Kadir's bicep and tried to ease her shoulder free. He did not release her. "I should have started a fight on the way back. I'd have been home yesterday."

Faier rubbed his jaw. "You fought against Soren and you won."

"Not fought. Disagreed. And I don't think either of us won."

"Her light was infinitely brighter," Ciran confirmed, and Iyen and Lotar nodded again. "It remained so for most of the trip."

She held up her hands. Her heart thumped rapidly. Was she embarrassed? "Forget I said 'fight.' It wasn't my best moment, to be honest. Anyway. I'm supposed to ask you all how deep we are right now."

"Fifteen songs," Ciran said, looking surprised that she hadn't asked him on the journey down. "Depending on the strength of the current."

She bit her lip. "Do you know it in feet? Or miles? Or, uh, fathoms?"

No. Those measures were unrelated to their lives.

"Okay. Thanks." She tapped her ears. A dark chunk of dead metal was in each one. She squeezed her eyes shut, shifted abruptly away from Kadir, and then faced him head on. Her eyes opened on desperation. "I'm so sorry. You would never have been hurt except for me. I explained the Sea Opal problem to my cousin. The company is really desperate for more Sea Opals. Apparently, it can cure cancer!"

So.

Her people had changed her loyalty. She cared for the Sea Opals and no longer resonated for him.

His heart contracted into a cold, hard ball.

He rested his fist on his bruised thigh. "Atlantis honors the agreement. We will search the old city."

"I'll help."

"No." Perhaps he had been approaching her wrong all along. "You will remain here where it is safe."

Her brows folded. She looked down and brushed her cheek. "I understand."

Now he would no longer have to worry about her

injuring herself.

Her sadness seeped into his veins like poison.

"I'll try to think of a way to help you here." She rubbed her head. Her hair floated free.

Something was different. "Where is your flower?"

"Hmm?" Elyssa put her hand to her hair. The flower was not there. "Oh. I gave it to my cousin."

It took a minute for her words to register.

His warriors looked equally shocked.

Adviser Creo's chin lifted. "Betrayal. As I told you. Because you forced her to have so much freedom, she has committed another treason."

"What?" She turned to Kadir. Confusion was on her face. "Why? Because I gave the flower to Aya? But it was already removed from the Life Tree. Like a Sea Opal or the blossom in Florida, the one I drank the nectar from."

The warriors watched her desperation. Stone-faced. Silent.

"Is there a problem?" Elyssa looked up at Kadir with big eyes. "Was it wrong? Actually wrong?"

She had done it. She admitted it. She *still* didn't understand it.

"Yes," he said heavily. "Those other items were dead already. You gave a still-living blossom to your cousin When you injure a living piece of the Life Tree, it also injures me."

"But the blossom already died, actually. I had to bring it back to life again. Am I injuring you every time?"

That was an oddity. Kadir had seen the blossom die twice, and she had brought it back to life both times. He hadn't felt injured. Had he?

The rules in this strange case were all new to him. He checked with the other warriors, but none reacted as though bringing the blossom back to life was as extraordinary as he found it to be. So, the old ruling of treason by causing injury to the Life Tree must hold.

"You cousin cannot return it to life. When it dies the next and final time, a mark will appear as a bruise somewhere on my body."

"An actual bruise?" She covered her mouth. Concern and horror flashed. "Sireno's king survived."

Pelan answered. "The old king was already dead."

Everyone turned to him.

He stiffened, relying on nearby Nilun's impassive correctness to anchor him. "The new king was not yet chosen or else he would have died."

"The king bears the brunt of an injury," Ciran said, taking over the explanation. "The entire brunt, with no young fry sons or other relatives to share his burden."

"So if this Life Tree got chopped down..."

"I would die," Kadir confirmed.

She covered her mouth with both hands. "No. I didn't know."

"It is a blood tie."

She reached for Kadir and twined her hands in his, finally focusing on him with her whole glow. "Tell me how to fix this. How can I heal you and the Life Tree?"

"Stay away." Adviser Creo flared boldly, his deepest proclamations finally justified. "Do not display yourself or risk injury. Seek the protection inside this castle and force its king to act as is proper."

She unfocused, staring somewhere over Kadir's shoulder. "I can stay inside. Will it really help?"

"Dismiss your guards," Adviser Creo ordered. "Empty the castle of threats. Otherwise, your next visit to the surface may be your final journey."

Her brows folded. Her light dimmed. "If that's what you need, I can do it."

Would this really resolve the treason?

No. Her treason was accidental. He overlooked it. It was unpunished.

The adviser laid out basic safety mechanisms Kadir had long refused to implement. Perhaps now was the time. Elyssa would not fight him.

"You are sad," Kadir managed.

She shook her head, lying to his face, and rubbed her thumbs over his knuckles. Her sadness broke over him in aching waves. "I want this to work. I'll do whatever I have to. Give me another chance and I'm fine. "

She was fine?

Lies. All lies.

The adviser turned to the others and waved his arms. "Go now. Leave this castle to its rightful bride. Assume your duties elsewhere with true honor."

The mer shifted.

Soren emerged from the shadows and floated in front of the exit.

"I'm sorry! Don't be mad," Elyssa begged them. Her desperation sliced his heart. "I understand now. I swear. I'll make it up to you. I'll heal the Life Tree and Kadir."

The adviser was right. Kadir's single-minded focus on making her assume roles that he hadn't prepared her for caused her this grief and dimmed her light.

"Atlantis will be a proper city yet," the adviser said as he herded the warriors out. "Now, we will charter a city with proper rules."

Soren floated in front of the exit and laughed. "Rules? There are no rules in Atlantis. Right, Gailen?"

The orange-tattooed mer jerked.

Soren sneered at the adviser. "Just what kind of a city do you think we are?"

The warriors shifted uncertainly.

"Calm," the adviser growled. "Exit, first lieutenant."

"First lieutenant?" His great mouth curved in deadly amusement. He slammed his flat hand against his breastbone. "There is no first lieutenant here. I am the disgraced warrior of Dragao Azul. An outlaw. Rebel. Unfit. Unworthy!"

Each label was punctuated with a gut-level growl, hurling the insults through the air with such force Soren somehow twisted them into marks of honor. They penetrated the other warriors' chests. The warriors all glowed.

Except for Nilun.

"Stand aside, unworthy disgrace." Nilun flushed a deep red as he shouted. "Your queen demands we leave."

"I heard no orders. She swears to heal the Life Tree. And Kadir."

The other warriors milled in surprise.

Soren snapped at the group. "All of you, shut it. We have not heard how she will perform this healing."

CHAPTER TWENTY-EIGHT

A t Soren's pronouncement, the angry, confused, hurt mer warriors turned and looked at Elyssa.

Oh god.

How could she make up for her misunderstanding? All this time she'd been treating the Life Tree like a tree when instead she should have been thinking of it as part of Kadir. Like, his skin part, or his beating heart. Which could somehow beat outside his chest. And she had the power to bring it back to life?

The metaphor was as hard to wrap her mind around as the actual example of real life.

But she did understand that right now was her crossroads moment. Kadir was so injured he could barely stand her to touch him. He tensed whenever she came near and did not seek her gaze. He did not draw her into his arms. That was the cost of saving her from the needlefish.

If staying inside the castle would bring back his attention, she would give up the newfound freedom she'd enjoyed in the ocean.

But if she could do something else — something that actually seemed more useful than lying around the castle alone — she wanted to try.

"Um, I'll do anything. What can I do?"

Adviser Creo growled in hot frustration. "Stop forcing your wishes on a fragile bride!"

Soren growled. "That 'fragile bride' swam on her own power across the open ocean."

Adviser Creo's face turned white. His hands trembled. He snarled from a place deep within his chest. "How *dare* you force your king's female to swim at the pace of warriors—"

"She paced us fine." Soren ignored him and gestured for her to swim forward. "How will you heal the Life Tree?"

How? She was asking *him* how. If she said the wrong thing, wouldn't they kick her out forever?

But they were all staring.

She spoke her best ideas. "I'll tend to it. Zoan can show me. My houseplants always did well. Although I did once kill a rose bush, but that was an honest misunderstanding. Grafting went wrong."

No response.

Probably talking about what she killed wasn't the right plan.

"I could also, um, I could sing to it. Plants like songs. Oh, but so do people! Because the Life Tree is a person too. I'm sure there have been studies like that."

Actually, yeah, she could definitely tend to the Life Tree with Zoan and chant. She'd focus her mind powers and bring *it* back to life. Why not? She would do this.

Kadir lightened. He stroked her cheek, calm. "Very well. You will sing to the Life Tree."

Thank goodness. This whole disaster could become

another bullet point in Aya's report of crazy mistakes Elyssa survived.

"Singing?" The adviser harrumphed. "Absurd. The Life Tree requires silence. "

Kadir's lips curled. "How do you know this, Adviser?"

"Perhaps he sang badly to his," Zoan said quietly to the stone-faced Nilun.

"How dare you." The adviser shook his fist at Zoan. The mer's eyes gleamed. "The Life Tree is a temple. I do not profane it with noise."

"Good. Then you will give my queen no competition." Kadir forestalled the fight between adviser and injured warrior and gestured for all to swim to the Life Tree.

Elyssa's stomach dropped. "Right now?"

The warriors moved en masse for the exit.

Kadir stroked his knuckles across her cheek. "Your song will deepen your connection to the Life Tree."

And me.

The last part wasn't spoken aloud. She heard it inside her head, somehow.

Was she supposed to help Kadir? He struggled and winced to remain upright. Oh, no, Iyen and Balim helped Kadir to swim for the exit, after the rest of the warriors.

Gailen came to her with a smile. "Please swim on your hard-earned fins, Queen Elyssa."

He encouraged her. She kicked her fins and sped after Kadir.

Outside the castle, Tial saluted and fell into place beside Gailen as her special guards always by her side. Faier met her at the entrance to the Life Tree with a generous, calm expression. She kicked between the thick, granite petals sheltering the Life Tree.

At the inner sanctuary, she stood on the white loam dais

beside Kadir on her human feet. Even Soren's impatient order to the adviser to remain quiet seemed protective and kind.

So. Singing. In public. Wow.

High school choir was about three lifetimes ago. She'd never been a soloist, but she knew how to hit a note. And she used to do karaoke in college. After three drinks, the words on the screen started to blur, but she belted out whatever she could see with gusto.

The warriors formed a circle around her.

What had she done in choir?

Stand tall. Feet shoulder-width apart; don't lock your knees. If you faint, try not to hit your head on a riser on the way down. Take a deep breath and...

Uh...

Oh.

Hello! What the heck was she thinking? There was no air. She couldn't exactly launch into show tunes. Her words always vibrated in her chest. Could she even make notes?

Everyone was staring.

Kadir nodded to her. "Begin."

Her gut clenched. Her palms couldn't sweat because she was already completely soaked in the water. Her palms weren't wrinkly, though. Mysticism of being a mermaid - no more prune fingers.

They waited.

Benji suddenly arrived, yapping and warbling. Her tuneless octopus music drowned the whole sanctuary in discord. Some warriors moved to grab her. She dodged them and bee-lined for Elyssa.

Elyssa scooped up the small octopus. It was kind of comical. "Did you come to help me out?"

The octopus simply continued with its awful noise.

Right. She didn't need to breathe. She just had to vibrate, um, resonantly.

Well, with accompaniment like Benji, nobody could hear whatever she sang anyway. She kissed the top of the orange octopus's head and psyched herself up.

"Um...uh..." Okay, here went everything. Camp songs, activate! "Make new friends, but keep the old. One is silver and the other's gold."

The Life Tree glowed steadily and quietly, unchanged.

She sang the second verse of the Girl Scout friendship song, and then she switched to "Row, row, row your boat," and other classics of the campfire. Ones that she forgot she knew, but which were ingrained in her, a culture fingerprint of her past.

The more she sang, the easier it was to continue. Who cared about everyone listening in? Her vibrations weren't operatic or anything, and she was accompanied by an octopus set to permanent "yip." But the performance seemed to satisfy the mer warriors, so maybe she wouldn't get kicked out today.

Suddenly, Zoan shouted. "A seed!"

Oh, thank goodness. She was out of show tunes and didn't want to attempt fuzzily-remembered karaoke.

The others gasped and rushed past her. Kadir hovered over the branch. At its tip dangled a white, dumbell-shaped leaf. Oh, no, the leaf was wrapped around a seed. Got it.

"Twin seeds," Kadir breathed. "Twin seeds!"

Awe spread over the gathering.

"I do not believe it." The adviser bustled through. "Let me see."

Kadir guarded it.

The adviser peered over his shoulder. After a long, long pause, he shook his head. His voice was much softer. "I have not seen one in all my years. Truly your Life Tree is blessed."

"What does it mean?" Elyssa whispered to Gailen, who was nearest.

"Two seeds grow as one," he replied in a low rumble. "It symbolizes great power. Whoever receives it will certainly have twin young fry, like Zoan and his twin brother, instead of just one, like the rest of us."

"Zoan has a twin brother?"

"Roa. I did not meet him, but he is also full of teasing and smiles."

"This twin seed will go to our king," Ciran said correctly. "Queen Elyssa, you must not give it to anyone."

"No! I won't, I promise. That was just a misunderstanding."

"And do not remove it until it has matured."

She curled her hands into fists and placed them behind her back. "I won't touch it. Not even by accident."

The adviser backed away, turned, and left the Life Tree. His lips pursed. He looked deeply troubled.

Kadir sought her in the crowd. His back was held straighter and his face looked less pained. "You will continue to sing."

She had done it. He looked better. The Life Tree was connected to him, so if it thrived, then he did also.

He smiled as though she finally got it.

Her chest throbbed.

He was so beautiful. Intense, thoughtful, visionary. Even now, with all of his injuries, she wanted to be alone with him. Wrap her arms and legs around his silver-tattooed torso, kiss his hard face, throw back her head as he sank his length into her hot feminine core. Give over to the ecstasy of his embrace.

But they were surrounded by warriors, he *was* injured, and they were on a desperate timeline to find more Sea Opals. And then, more brides.

She would help him. No matter what.

CHAPTER TWENTY-NINE

The emergence of the twin seeds blew new hope into Kadir's warriors. Their astonishment and joy lightened the group meals and the patrols, and the reports Kadir received as he quickly healed were more joyous and less accusation-filled.

Even Adviser Creo could not say an ill word about it.

"I have never heard of this," he said the next time it was brought up. "No city has a twin seed."

"In ancient times, it was common." Kadir had learned it in the forbidden archives of the All-Council. He'd snuck in often when he had been an innocent youth assisting Dragao Azul's All-Council representative. Now twins were rare; of all his warriors, only Zoan was such a twin. "You will see it with the return of queens."

Adviser Creo pressed his lips together, but even he could not stop admiring the small, determined, bright little seed.

Just like his queen. Bright and small and determined Elyssa.

"I'm sorry about the misunderstanding. Again. I'll make

it up to you." In the privacy of their heart chamber, she floated at his side and trailed her fingers down the taut muscles of his abdomen, caressing his thighs. Her hunger warred with concern.

She wished to join with him.

Despite his injuries, despite his disfigurement, despite that he could not protect her well. He warred with himself to confess his weakness. "We cannot join. I am much better, but I must go to the ruin. I cannot risk reopening my injuries."

"Well, you don't have to do anything." She licked her lips. "I could just use my mouth on you."

Use her...mouth?

The image made his cock twitch. Did people do such things more than once? She had given him this pleasure after their wedding. He wanted her hot mouth around his hard cock. "Your mouth does not make a young fry."

"Not everything has to make a young fry."

What a strange idea. Joining for pleasure? Not for the end result of a young fry?

Danger twinged in his belly. Had his disfigurement changed her mind? Did she no longer wish to have a young fry with him?

"No." He covered his hardening cock. "We must make a young fry."

She wavered, then grew more determined. "You'll like it."

"My pleasure is not important."

She huffed. "Well, maybe mine is."

Oh. She was upset he could no longer provide her pleasure.

"Just let me do this." She pushed his hands away, nestling herself between his thighs. Her knees rested on the warm, clean floor of the heart chamber. "I can't believe I'm arguing with a guy about giving him a blow job."

She teased her fingers lower and stroked him from stem to tip.

Pleasure. His cock pulsed.

But his release, when it came, would clench his torso painfully.

No. He could not risk this pleasure again now. He would allow himself to enjoy her body, even though it would not bind her with a young fry. Actually, perhaps pleasure was better.

"I will use my mouth on you," he decided.

Her lips parted. "Me? But—"

"You wish pleasure. Come."

"Oh, but I only said that because—"

He grabbed her around the ribs and lifted her easily. While she scrambled, he clamped her thighs and drew her soft, feminine center to his mouth.

She wriggled. "But I'm the one who screwed up. Wait! I want to do something for you."

"Stop." This was the same argument as at the beach coffee shop when she had desired to provide him with food. She gave him great pleasure whenever they joined. Well, he desired to give her the pleasure. She would accept this from him.

He caressed her folds. They were already slick and pink, glistening with invitation.

His cock pulsed again with heat.

Everything about her enticed him. Why had he never considered using his mouth on her before? The other warlords had not spoken of such methods to pleasure their brides.

He licked the soft creases. What was this flavor? He

must taste her deeply. His strokes caused her to open with a moan, revealing herself fully to him. Her chest glowed as bright as the sun.

He latched onto her bud.

She jolted and moaned. "Kadir. Don't reward me for...mmm."

He thrummed, easily forming the words in his chest while his tongue remained busy. "This is mine."

She rocked her hips gently. He caressed her over and over until her back arched and she came, shuddering, in their private chamber.

In the stillness, there was still a distance he couldn't bridge. She lay beside him, her eyes open when she should be asleep. In conversation, she trailed off. In the middle of laughter, she suddenly sobered.

What made her eyes lose their sparkle?

"Tell me." He cupped her cheeks. Her face was cool in his large, hot hands. "What pain are you hiding?"

"Pain? You're the one with all the pain." She tugged at his hands. "I'm just benefiting."

He caught her fingers with his thumbs and held them tight. "Elyssa."

"Fine." She closed her eyes. "It's not that I don't want to have young fry."

"You want five," he reminded her.

"Yeah." She lightened and stroked his cheek. Her frown returned. "It's just that I don't want our relationship to only be about the young fry."

"This means?"

"I want us to be together because you love me," she said. "With or without young fry."

"Warriors do not love. That is a human word."

His mother had used it many times with his father, and

his father had passed on that she had loved Kadir also. But that love had taken her to the surface. She had never longed to cross the surf and meet the son she had left behind.

In contrast, Kadir bound his soul with Elyssa's. He would never relinquish her and never take another bride.

Elyssa frowned. "Right. I should have expected that." She pinched her eyes closed. "If we don't deliver Sea Opals on the next trip to the surface, the platform is going away. I'll have no way to contact my family."

He stroked her cheeks gently. She must be frightened. The journey to visit would be longer and require more guards. "You will return to Florida."

"Yeah." She sagged. "I guess you're right. There's no way this could work out. When it's over, it's over."

"When what is over?"

"If the project is canceled on the surface, it's canceled here too."

Cold lanced him.

She wished to return to Florida permanently if they did not provide the Sea Opals?

No. He refused. She was his now.

He clamped onto her. His back screamed. He held tighter.

She gasped. "Kadir! Don't hurt yourself. Please."

He hushed her. She was his. No matter how she tried to get away.

Were the warriors of the past this possessive? His need frightened him. But it would not be denied.

"Listen to me," she begged.

"I listen," he growled. "You speak. I listen."

She stopped pushing on his arms. They rotated quietly in the heart chamber. First, she was on top, then he was on top, and then she was again. "I don't know what to say. Um. What did you want to hear?"

Anything. Nothing. Her voice.

"Speak," he ordered.

"What, you mean like a story? Or—"

"Yes."

"Okay. I guess, um, do you know the Little Mermaid?"

"Who is a little mermaid?"

"No one. It's a story. A simple story with a bunch of versions."

He held her tight while she told him all about a sad mermaid who could not catch the attention of a human prince. The prince married another human, and the heartbroken mermaid turned into a green surface liquid called sea foam.

The rhythm of her story was calming, and he relaxed, even though the sad story caused her melancholy.

"That is a strange story." Kadir stroked her back. "How did she accomplish the transformation?"

"The sea witch. She can do magic."

"And this mermaid could not shift into human form without the assistance of a magic witch?"

"Well, the original Grimm brothers probably didn't know about Life Trees or elixir." She snuggled closer. The places she touched felt warm and no longer hurt. As though her touch, gentle as her story, did deeper healing. "The moral is how difficult it is to communicate with people of different worlds. The mermaid tries to tell the prince over and over that she loves him, and he can't hear her at all. He doesn't see her for what she is. It's sad."

Ah. The true meaning of her story struck Kadir now.

She had been hurt. He had not paid adequate attention

to her. They were from different worlds. She was the human and he was the merman prince.

"We will bridge our differences," he vowed. "Or you must go."

She stiffened.

No matter how much it hurt him, she must never darken so much her sunshine smile turned to surface foam.

CHAPTER THIRTY

K adir was going to make her leave.

She could just feel it.

Elyssa padded across the Life Tree dais, trying to find comfort in her daily singing routine. Zoan was making tiny cuts with the huge adamantium knife and feeding hair-sized streamers back into the stem so it glowed. Tial was outside, taking his turn to guard the entrance, and Kadir was finally well enough to patrol the borders and supervise at the old ruin. Her next surface visit was looming, all the warriors were exhausted from pulling quadruple shifts trying to excavate Sea Opals from the ruin, and raiders had been spotted inside the borders twice. Soren thought they would attack when the guards left to take Elyssa to the surface.

Kadir had rested his hand on her bent knee over their last breakfast. "Do not fear. We will protect you on your journey."

That wasn't what she was afraid of.

He frowned and removed his hand. "Have faith." And

then he was called away to go to the old city, and she was left to her daily routine.

What she was afraid of was that he would take her to the surface and leave her there. If she screwed up one more time, she was out. Her time here was hanging by a thread.

They had not "joined" for real since before the needle-fish attack. He devoted himself to pleasuring her. But he held back. He refused to allow her to pleasure him.

He didn't love her. He wouldn't join with her to make young fry. Had he changed his mind? Did he need her to prove something? Like they had "bridged their differences?"

She'd thought everything would be fixed after she could make her fins on command. But now she'd uncovered secret mermaid powers, and she felt farther than ever from becoming Kadir's true queen.

"Queen Elyssa."

Zoan called her to the far side of the Life Tree. Pelan was there, resting skeptically. Since she was here every day, some of the restrictions about who could visit when had been lifted, and there were now mer nearby almost all the time. It was extra guards in case of an attack, and she kind of thought they got more revitalized from sleeping close to the Life Tree rather than far away, in the castle, or worst, outside.

Zoan waved her close. "Show Pelan the five gestures."

She made the peace sign, the hang loose sign, the thumbs up, the I-Love-You sign, and the Kiss sign. To make the Kiss, she touched her thumb to her fingers on each hand and brought the two together, finger tips touching, like two lovers kissing

Pelan considered them carefully, his hands resting on his empty dagger sheaths.

One idea to bridge the distance was to make a salute for

the city. She'd noticed that all the warriors made different welcome and farewell gestures, and some seemed insolent to others. Iyen almost got into a fight with Nilun for looking him in the eye for too long. And Gailen told her Lotar's isolationist city of Syrenka thought bowing was a sign of weakness.

She tried to stay away from fist-based signs because she was pretty sure they all had meanings to the mermen already. Rude meanings.

"I can come up with more gestures," she said when Pelan was taking too long to decide. "We're just scratching the surface here."

"I have seen the last one," he said finally.

The Kiss sign was the most popular, and some warriors had already started using it to salute her. It was like the "more" sign in American Sign Language, which pretty accurately symbolized all of Atlantis. More women. More kissing. More chances.

"Alright, if you like it, then it's official," she said.

Pelan was surprised. "The king has decreed it?"

Well, no. "It wins by the popular vote."

He frowned. "That is not tradition."

"Believe in your power, Pelan." Zoan made the more-Kiss gesture at him several times, as though proving some point between them. "New traditions are bursting out all over this city. Queen Elyssa, sing your one song, *I Will Survive*."

She obliged, channeling Gloria Gaynor in all her glory. The Life Tree glowed. Before Pelan's amazed eyes, a bunch of tiny hairs grew out.

Yep. Singing turned the Life Tree into a radiant Chia Pet.

"Now you have twice as much work," Pelan noted,

eying Zoan's huge grin. "What is so special about this song?"

The peach warrior shrugged and got to work, strengthening the stem while it continued to glow. His hands were streaked with mean-looking scars. They were still healing from a shark attack during her last surface visit. "The raining of men is also good."

The Weather Girls had made an appearance in Elyssa's daily repertoire. It seemed appropriate, especially as she was constantly surrounded by the hard-bodied, kind, protective warriors.

She stroked the strength lines of the tree, willing it to grow stronger.

"See here, Pelan." Zoan leaned back. "Queen Elyssa. Show the other power."

Pelan waited patiently.

She demonstrated, vibrating with a sustained, high note. The Life Tree glowed. On the branch, the twin seed began to twinkle even more brightly through the thick, protective seed covering. Below, the tiny Sea Opals glittered.

Pelan's mouth dropped. "What is this response?"

"Resonance." Zoan dug his elbow into Pelan's ribs. "Now you wish her to go to the old city again. Right? She will find the hidden Sea Opals with no effort. Me too."

Pelan's mouth closed. "The wreck is dangerous. Octopus Kong has many bad days."

They had adopted her name for the giant octopus.

If she learned to control her powers better, then she could go meet the giant octopus again. She stopped singing. The light faded.

Faier entered and bowed to Elyssa, which meant patrols changed. Pelan rose with a groan. It was time for his round, and then he would go to the old city and continue the excavation without Elyssa's talent.

Faier honored the Life Tree with a long bow.

Elyssa was here not only to perform her daily singing but also because she was waiting for Gailen. He had returned exhausted from the excavations, and she had ordered him to rest before helping her pack a samples bag.

She pulled out one of the empty conch shells they had collected. It was gorgeous, iridescent as Kadir's tattoos, and sparkly in her hand. She rested it on her palm and closed her eyes.

Lucy was able to summon the Life Tree energy to form a protective barrier over her warriors. Elyssa had failed during the needlefish attacked. When everyone converged on her, she'd gotten flustered and lost her concentration. Her trusted guards had been severely injured. But it had to be something she was capable of too, right? She had to master this power.

Someone approached. She opened her eyes.

Zoan grinned cheerfully. His body was tanner than the others, and he was more slender but still well-muscled. She hadn't come up with a celebrity yet to match. But like Gailen, he seemed to pick up everything she said. "Deep thoughts?"

"Pretty shallow, unfortunately." She tried to focus, but she was too aware that he was watching. And so was Faier. She gave up with a sigh. "I'm sorry. I'll figure out how to get Sea Opals and bring more women to meet you in the future. I mean, brides."

He shrugged. "It is alright if you do not."

That was surprising. "You don't want a bride?"

"This was my brother's dream. I followed him. We are

twin seeds." His easy smile faded. "Roa was lost while storming the prison."

"Oh, I'm so sorry." His twin, Roa, had clearly meant the world to Zoan. "It must have been rough when he died."

"Died?" His eyes twinkled as though he had deliberately misled her, trickster that he was. "No, I said he was *lost*. Roa is alive. When I am peaceful, I feel him." Zoan pressed his right hand against his chest. The skin was torn in a serrated half-circle. His mirth faded. "Someday, he will come here and be found."

"I hope so too." It had never occurred to her that the warriors here might not want a bride. "Sorry for disturbing your peace and trying to play match-maker. You're a great guard."

He waved her apology away. "You are interesting. I enjoy guarding you inside the sanctuary, but it is best that I do not become one of your usual guards. Another could command my loyalty."

She appreciated his honesty. He was telling her to her face that if Roa showed up, he would take off and strand her. "Thanks for guarding me here."

"If you are still seeking a third, fourth, and fifth guard, you should know that Gailen and Tial's pride is more common. Most others feel the same."

Her heart melted a little. "Really?"

"Yes." His eyes twinkled.

Wait. Was he making fun of her? Somehow?

"Queen Elyssa." Gailen saluted using a sign that she would now always think of as "more kiss" from the exit. "I am ready for hunting."

She grabbed the partially filled samples bag, left Zoan with the Life Tree, and swam down to the ocean floor. Aya requested samples. Aya would get samples.

While they swam, Gailen pointed out their surround-ings. "That coral is painful. That one is also painful. Do not touch that one. That one is good eating after you remove the outer covering, which is painful. That one is very painful. You call it Fire Coral, and you can guess why. That one is painful."

Elyssa sensed a theme. "Is anything not painful?"

"Yes." He jerked his thumb over his shoulder. "We cultivate them in the castle. This area is almost a wilderness."

Huh.

He swam below her. "It is the same pain as to brush-whack."

"Bush-whack," she corrected. "Yeah, I guess if you're bush-whacking through blackberries and thistles, it's no walk in the park."

"Do not bush-whack through the coral."

"I won't."

Off in the distance, schools of fish shimmered in the water like colorful leaves. A Moby Dick sperm whale chased after the flocks, thin mouth open in its thick, wedge-shaped head.

Wasn't this amazing? Aya would love it. Or her parents, or her boss in HR. Who would ever think Elyssa could be here? So deep under the water, seeing sights that no other human had seen before?

Behind her, her fins swooshed like a beautiful, rainbow-pink sail.

She had never been so happy and satisfied in her life.

Her relationship with Kadir had to work out. She had to bridge the distance with the other mer, and with Kadir.

A dark shadow skirted the edge of the current. She felt

it like a slime. It made the hairs on her arms rise, and she scratched the uneasiness.

Gailen also raised his head. He scanned the landscape carefully and finally frowned. "Let us go back."

They returned to the Life Tree. Tension remained in the other mer also; most, but not all, returned Gailen's cheery more-kiss salute. Some, like Adviser Creo, merely frowned at him and then returned to staring out edgily at the hidden enemies making everyone nervous.

Inside the Life Tree, the shift had changed again. Gailen passed Tial, who handed him some of Elyssa's earlier samples, such as the conch shell. Gailen put them in the bag. Zoan was buffing the petals forming the curved interior walls, making them shine.

She was starting to get a sense of time passing, at least, and it felt like it was almost time to go to the surface. She rested at the base of the Life Tree. Gailen set the bag beside her. It was sealed tight.

"I will seek your other guards." He saluted — more kiss — and swam off.

She closed her eyes. The future swirled as a mass of fear and worry. Could Aya convince the board of directors to be satisfied with the samples? Had she found Sea Opals another way? Would the city be attacked in Elyssa's absence? Even if she were here, could she help?

It felt like the calm before the storm.

She rested her forehead against the trunk and channeled her inner peace. So she could summon it when she needed it. Zen calm in the middle of complete terror.

Zoan's scraping stopped. His voice rose. "Where is the seed?"

Elyssa lifted her head and opened her eyes.

He dropped the scraper from his lax hand and kicked to the upper branch. The seed's papery white husk fluttered from his strokes. It was empty.

He looked at her. Panicked. "You have it."

Her stomach dropped.

She held up her empty hands. He swam around her, staring like it was somehow hidden on her. How? It wasn't like she had pockets. She swallowed back her own fears. It had to be here. "I'll help you look."

They searched the bare branches, the base of the tree, and all around the dais.

"Queen Elyssa, King Kadir has been delayed by—" Gailen stopped as he floated into the sanctuary chamber. "What are you doing?"

"The seed is missing," she explained tersely, crawling on her knees and moving her hands across the ground in case it had turned invisible and she bumped into it.

"Missing!"

"Could it have fallen and rolled down the petals?" she asked Zoan.

"Impossible."

"A traitor has taken it," Gailen growled. "Remain here. I will inform Kadir." He zoomed out.

"Isn't he at the old ruin?" Elyssa called after him, but Gailen was already gone.

If so, it would be awhile before Kadir arrived. They were on their own.

"I was here the whole time," Zoan promised, his gaze glued to the bare white earth. "I will discover this traitor. The seed cannot have disappeared."

"Who else was here?"

He shook his head. Faier, Pelan, Gailen, Tial. Warriors

that had always seemed loyal. Now, the normally cheerful Zoan seethed as though he were going to tear a serrated shark's bite out of the traitor.

Okay. She had to narrow it down. "When was the last time you saw it?"

He straightened and blinked. "Your song!"

Of course! She straightened and sang one solid note.

He began to swim toward the exit in anticipation of catching the traitor red-handed.

Her sealed samples bag began to glow.

She swam to it. He was right behind her. She picked at Gailen's unfamiliar knots. Zoan pushed her out of the way and tugged the correct ends. The bag fell open. Inside were all the samples, bound in protective seaweed. She sang. One of them very suspiciously began to glow.

He started to reach out and then stopped.

Huh? She picked up the packet and struggled again with the tight binding. Gailen knew how to wrap things securely. She finally got through the top layer. The white glimmer of the seed made her tension ease.

This was the seed. Wrapped up protectively and put in her samples bag.

"How did it get in here?" she asked.

Zoan was already looking at her. Denial gave way to confusion and then hurt crossed his face.

Wait. He didn't think — no!

"I didn't do this," she said. "The bag was sealed the whole time."

He frowned down at the bag. "I was here the whole time."

"You were at the wall. Who was here while your back was turned?"

He stared at her.

So, it did look bad. She'd been resting against the Life Tree with her bag. "The bag was sealed!"

"Then how did the seed get inside?"

"I don't know." She stared at the precious white seed. "I opened it to practice with the conch shell." Had she ever put the conch shell back inside? She'd gotten it out but couldn't remember putting it away. "Gailen arrived. He carried the bag." He'd wrapped the samples. But the traitor couldn't be Gailen. "Other warriors also collected samples for us outside."

"Who?"

She shook her head. "Lotar, Nilun, you...Tial handed me some. Gailen sealed the bag. I was just resting."

"And then the seed went missing." A new hardness tensed his jaw.

"The seed is missing?" Adviser Creo barreled into the sanctuary. His panic narrowed on her. "Who would dare steal the seed?"

Crap.

The adviser had been gunning for her since day one. He thought she was dangerous. He would just love finding out that the seed had gone missing and turned up in her sample bag.

Zoan shoved her hand — and the seed — back into her samples bag. "Stolen? No, adviser, I said the seed was *missing*. It will soon be found in King Kadir's hand."

His tone was light, but his glare was deadly.

The adviser only seemed to hear his light tone. His brows smoothed. "That is why Gailen flew out screaming for Kadir?" His shoulders relaxed. Then, he growled at Zoan. "Speak directly. These word games only cause amusement for *you*."

Zoan's lips formed an unnatural grin. "My amusement is all *I* need."

The adviser huffed.

Zoan tied the bag tight and handed it to Elyssa. "Adviser Creo, will you remain here? I must escort Elyssa to her guard."

"If she stayed in her castle like a proper bride, my intervention would not be necessary," he grumbled.

"Intervention?" Zoan's voice began to twinkle like his mischievous eyes, even though his expression was a forced snarl. "Adviser, I did not say—"

Adviser Creo put up his flat palm in dismissal. He had no patience for Zoan's teasing. "Go."

Zoan almost pushed her out of the sanctuary. They flew down the tunnel silently and squeezed outside. Tial guarded the entrance. He gripped his old, bent trident worriedly.

At her appearance, he made the more-kiss salute. "Where are we headed?"

"To Kadir." Zoan kicked in the direction of the old city. "Do not follow us, Tial. A foreigner remains inside, alone with the Life Tree."

"Foreigner? Inside?" Tial's eyes widened. "But my duty is to Queen Elyssa."

"Stay with the tree until I return," Elyssa told him.

He obeyed, flying into the Life Tree sanctuary, trident clenched.

She and Zoan kicked toward the old ruin. Elyssa carried the samples bag. It was like a blood weight in her arms.

"Foreigner?" she repeated dryly.

"Adviser Creo is not from Atlantis. Besides, it will give us a fast start to meet Kadir and explain what has gone on."

So Zoan really was taking her all the way to the old ruin. Her guts twinged. "You don't trust Tial?"

Zoan fixed her with an unnaturally hard gaze. "There *is* a traitor here. I do not trust anyone at all."

CHAPTER THIRTY-ONE

Kadir inspected the hunting fields. He was supposed to be at the old city now, excavating, but a few hours ago, one of his patrols had chased away a raider scout.

Excavations were canceled immediately. The patrols drew tight around the city. His investigation focused on the scout's hiding place.

"There are forty raiders," Soren reported grimly, pointing out the patterns of weapon markings on the sharpening stones. "Perhaps twice as many as we are. And they will attack when we are weakest. Missing warriors."

"What do you advise?"

"Delay Elyssa's surface visit."

"For how long?"

"Until the threat subsides."

Kadir twisted his lips to the side. "I cannot delay forever."

Soren growled. "Losing her will destroy your city."

"It is your city, too."

"She is *your* bride."

How interesting that Soren should say that. Kadir also felt more fiercely possessive of Elyssa than he liked. When she told him that she could give him pleasure without any risk of creating a young fry, he had actually cracked inside. A crazy thought entered his head. It would not let him go from its iron fist.

The old covenant demanded a bride stay until she gave birth to a young fry. Some of his warriors, or elders like the adviser, held that traditional view. For them, Kadir could keep Elyssa forever so long as she had no young fry.

He could keep her forever... Like his mother, on the shore, always perfect. Always his.

"My king." Pelan made a strange gesture. Both hands made a flattened circle and he touched the tips together in front of his chest. "Zoan sights no enemies here."

"Zoan?" Soren growled. "When did Zoan arrive? He is supposed to be at the Life Tree. Who is guarding the Life Tree?"

Pelan shook his head. "I thought he was on patrols. He is returning to the city now. Should I chase after him?"

"No. We will return soon. Continue your report."

"Lotar leads the patrol you removed from the old ruin. Will you send them back to excavate?"

"No." Kadir would leave the ruin undefended. Enemies might already be there, waiting for their usual excavations. Aya would go another month without the final Sea Opals payment. "We fall back to defend the new city. No enemy will penetrate our lines."

Pelan made the looped-fingers-touching-over-his-chest gesture. Iyen, swimming beside Soren, made the salute back at him. Pelan swam away.

"What is that?" Kadir demanded.

"The salute?" Iyen made it again. "Nilun showed me.

The queen wanted a salute that was unique to Atlantis. She created several and the younger warriors chose this."

Pride lifted his chest. The city was finally coming together. At the center of it, giving hope and encouragement, glowed his queen.

He was wrong to deny her young fry. She would be a wonderful mother. His selfish possessiveness shamed him.

Kadir spoke the words aloud to break the spell over his heart. "Did you know, Iyen, that my queen desires to give Atlantis five young fry sons?"

Iyen blinked.

Soren canted his brow at Kadir skeptically. "Is five even possible?"

"I do not know. Elyssa seemed to think so."

Soren grunted. "That is a question for Balim, perhaps."

"What would a city be like with five young fry? From the same parents? That has not happened in a thousand years, I promise you."

"Not in a recognized city," Soren agreed.

Iyen simply stared out over the chert fields, the evidence of their enemies before him. He was a soldier. He did not have time for fantasies.

Well, now Kadir had the urge to return to Elyssa quickly and make the most of his new resolution before taking her to the surface for her second monthly check.

"King Kadir!" Gailen flew to him, panicked and trembling. His chest vibrated so hard he could barely speak. "The twin seed has been stolen."

His gut clenched. While he was outside the city, their enemies attacked.

Soren shouted for the other warriors. They formed into deadly units and flew behind Kadir.

"Where is Elyssa?" he demanded tightly, chasing Gailen back to the city. "Who is her guard?"

"Tial. She is in the Life Tree sanctuary with Zoan."

That was impossible. "Pelan reported Zoan was patrolling here with us until moments ago."

"My king, I left him at the Life Tree to come to you."

Someone made a mistake.

They reached Tial, flying at the outer edge of the city, and it appeared likely that the warrior who had erred was Gailen.

Tial saluted using the new gesture. "My king!"

The dark feeling in his belly grew. He nearly slammed into Tial, grabbing the mer's biceps so hard he went rigid. "Where is Elyssa?"

"You did not see her?" He looked over Kadir's shoulder and kicked, trying to squirm free. "She was going to meet you at the old city."

His belly dropped for his feet.

"Where is Zoan?" Soren growled.

"He is not with her, either? Then, she is all alone!"

Kadir threw Tial from him and wheeled. Cutting through his own warriors, he sped for the ruins.

Soren shouted. "Wait! Guards—"

"Secure the city!" Kadir flew hard and fast, burning with shaking fury.

Why had he left Elyssa alone? Why now, of all times, did he leave the old ruin unguarded? He could not have predicted she would go there. Her actions made no sense. But still. He should have left his guard!

A steady light glowed near the center of the tower. Tension in his chest eased. She was alive. He redoubled his efforts.

The gargle of the giant cave guardian soon drowned out the near ocean. It was out, acting as a second guard.

Elyssa and Zoan flew slowly over the city. She carried a woven bag, which was glowing, and she was making a single note of sound. Zoan flew below her, searching for something.

"No Sea Opals." Zoan's voice competed with the cave guardian's gargle. "We have reviewed the whole tower. *Now* can we return to the new city and find King Kadir?"

Her single note cut off. "Yes." She sounded resigned. "I was just thinking that as long as we're here, we might as well —" She saw him and lit up. "Kadir."

He crushed her in his arms.

She was soft and sweet and *alive* and unhurt. They tumbled through the water. He pressed kisses to her hair, her forehead, her nose, her lips. She kissed him back whole-heartedly. Her chest glowed.

His tension eased. The worst fears drained away, leaving only anger.

The cave guardian watched their tangle and slowly sank back to his cave below the tower.

Elyssa squeezed Kadir hard. He pulled back.

She reached for him. "You—"

He forced her to arm's length. "How dare you break your restriction and come here? Now? When the twin seed is missing and the city is under attack?"

She blazed. "That's why I am here. The city *is* under attack and we found a traitor. Where were you?"

"A scout was chased from the south fields. The enemy will attack."

"They already have." She fought with the tie of the bag she and Gailen had been carrying to fill with samples. He took over, opening it with one firm tug. "Somehow, when I was in the Life Tree sanctuary, a traitor hid the twin seed in my bag."

She hummed and pulled out the glowing bundle. The seaweed was loosened and white bark shone through the cracks. It was mature and undamaged, ready for placing on a pedestal to honor as a foundational requirement of being a new city.

"I did not ask about the seed," he snapped, grabbing it and stuffing it back into the bag. "You disobeyed my order and remained at this abandoned ruin after you knew I was not here. On the eve of battle."

Her mouth opened and closed. "Because I thought, as long as I was here, I could tell you where to focus your Sea Opal search. The answer is not this tower. There are no Sea Opals anywhere near the center of the ruin. That's what Zoan and I discovered. So you can stop excavating right now."

"Is that all you care about? This seed? Your Sea Opals? The contract?"

"No!" She glowed hot and threw her hand at him. "I care about you. I love you. I care about this contract and seed *and* everyone else. I care so much I can't stand it. *You* will never love me. Why would you? I've destroyed practically everything I've touched. You got injured because of me in this very ruin. I'll be your surrogate if I have to. But—"

"Surrogate?"

"That's what we call women who arrange to have someone else's baby. They give up all interest in the child." Her face contracted with pain. The blazing gold of her soul darkened. "I don't want that. Every single moment of every single day I'm focused on what I can do to help you. To be useful. I want to be your queen. I'm trying so hard." Her voice rose to begging. "You have to believe me."

He watched his Elyssa crumple in front of him. Angry tears reddened her eyes. She made fists of determination. Agony wracked her soul.

This was what his selection had done to her.

He darkened her soul. He caused her agony. She was willing to be a surrogate, which meant a modern version of the old bride covenant. His wish for her to be his queen was killing her inside.

Adviser Creo had warned him. Kadir had ignored his advice.

Now she fluctuated terribly. Her soul brightened and fell dark. Like at the dock. Then, he hadn't cared about her struggle. Only how soon she would transform so they could return to the city. Now, he saw her true, deep, bitter pain.

He had tried to force her across the shore. Every stroke felt like swimming through broken glass. He was the human prince who ignored her little mermaid tears, just like the story she had told him so recently. She was turning to sea foam in front of him.

He made her life infinitely worse by being in it.

"Elyssa." He spoke low and rough. "This stops now."

"Don't give up on me," she begged. The pain radiated off her in waves.

"You cannot adjust. It is an acceptable reason to dissolve the contract."

CHAPTER THIRTY-TWO

E lyssa had failed.

Kadir was breaking up with her.

"No." Her chest felt like it was open and exposing her heart to the stinging ocean. She almost couldn't get her breath. "Please."

"This is killing you."

"I don't mind."

"I do." His tenderness was immobile as iron. He tied the bag shut and gave it to the stunned silent Zoan. "Return the seed to the city. I will take Elyssa to the surface."

He was really doing it.

Zoan struggled to close his torn right hand around the bag neck and took it instead in his left. "My king. It is not safe to swim across the open ocean with less than five warriors."

"Our enemies focus on the city."

"You abandon us on the eve of battle?"

"No. I leave Soren in charge. Tell him to do whatever he must to hold the city until my return."

Zoan hesitated. He did not want to abandon her, even

though he had already rejected being her guard. And he didn't want to let Kadir abandon their city. His close friends, Pelan and Nilun, would be with Soren inside. Elyssa could see all those thoughts and more crossing his normally cheery face. He couldn't seem to make a joke about it. He could only hesitate and frown.

Kadir growled. "Where do your loyalties lie?"

Zoan flinched. He finally made the more-kiss salute and carried the bag heavily back toward the city.

Where she would never be allowed again.

Her eyes burned and her nose clogged. "I didn't mean to cause so many problems."

Kadir's jaw flexed. He held out his hand. "Come. Hold on. We will fly."

Her arguments were useless. Like arguing with Chastity Angel. Nothing she said made any difference.

She reluctantly moved into his arms. He kicked. She was a screw up from the very beginning. This was her final swim as a mer queen.

It wasn't fair. Her head rested against his broad, flexing shoulders that were no longer hers. Her ear tuned to his heartbeat, which would never again sync to her rhythm. His long length would never pinion her with pleasure. The vanilla-hickory flavor of his skin would never radiate across her tongue as she licked his silver tattoos.

She couldn't control her power. She couldn't help him swim. She was barely a mermaid at all.

All reasons to get rid of her and start over.

It was like Aya said. Just because you tried hard or wanted something badly didn't mean you'd succeed.

Kadir raised his voice. He sounded exhausted and labored. "Elyssa. Relax against me."

She tried. She did not wish to. But she tried.

They flew silently through the empty ocean. Kadir had exhausted all his words. She couldn't think of a single way to reach him.

He knew she wanted to stay. He knew she loved him. He knew she would become a surrogate if that was his wish.

He rejected her. Every offer. Completely.

She had no words either.

All too soon, they reached the surface. She hauled herself into the lowered dinghy and threw up sea water over the side.

Kadir bobbed in the large waves. Was he going to give her a goodbye kiss? A goodbye speech? A sorry-it-didn't-work-out memento?

His hand curled over the side of the boat.

She started to reach out for his hand.

The dinghy jerked and the motor started winching up the chains. She rose.

Kadir turned away and pushed off. He disappeared beneath the waves.

The total emptiness of the ocean was hard to describe. A vast, open horizon of choppy blue waves and a haze separating sky from sea. Her throat was raw from coughing.

The dinghy rose to the platform. No one was there to greet Elyssa. Who had operated the winch? The control mechanism was abandoned.

She scrambled off the dinghy and skidded naked across the rusty metal deck. There was no Aya to tell her it was alright, no care package to surround her with comfort, no wool blankets to warm her up, no towels to dry her off. Where was the crew? Who had winched up her dinghy? The platform seemed as empty as the horizon. She finally broke into the dining galley.

Aya's laptop was set up for a conference call.

Elyssa found a dish towel in the galley. She covered her important bits, which felt weirdly exposed in the air, and turned on the conference.

Chastity Angel stared back at her. "You're late."

Elyssa shrank in on herself. It was muscle memory. The woman's hardened, mask-like face triggered her to automatically say sorry.

Her lips closed without speaking the forbidden word. All that training with Kadir had done something after all.

"Where's Aya?" she demanded instead.

"That is what I want to know." It was the dark of the night wherever Chastity Angel was. "Tell me quickly. What have you done with her?"

What had Elyssa done with Aya? "I don't understand. Why isn't she here?"

Chastity Angel's mouth pinched. "I do not see any Sea Opals."

Okay. "The Life Tree of Atlantis is—"

"Because of your failure — and my daughter's full knowledge that you would fail — she has taken it upon herself to do something drastic. Now. You will tell me where she is and how to reach her immediately."

Aya could be near Portugal, begging Dragao Azul to answer their undersea phones. Or she could be repopulating Sireno's sacred islands in the Gulf of Mexico with hand-picked brides.

"I don't know if you know this, but I've been underwater for the past month."

She whitened. "Tell me!"

"I don't know!"

"I swear to you, Elyssa. My daughter's life was perfect before you arrived. Your schemes lead her astray. Every time she works with you, disaster is right behind."

The accusation stabbed deeply.

"As of now, the Merman Bride Project is shutting down."

"It doesn't even matter." She rubbed her face. Aya wasn't here to make things okay. There was nothing okay about this. "Kadir already returned me. It's over anyway."

Chastity Angel regarded Elyssa with glittering eyes like a white-haired viper. "You are a failure in every possible way. Do not come back to Van Cartier Cosmetics. You are hereby fired."

She was a failure. In every possible way.

Don't choose Elyssa for our group. She's not an A student.

Sweetheart, your mom and I love you, but that college is out of reach for you.

I'll tell you up front not to apply for that promotion. You can't handle the added responsibilities.

She was fired?

No returning to a comfy HR job that was mostly college recruitment fairs and filing. No more giggling over mermen with Aya and planning how they were both going to become super awesome mermaid queens. No more sweet, determined mermen, striving so hard to protect their city and stop their eventual extinction.

No more Kadir.

Aya needs this for her future. Everyone knows you will never do anything important.

Elyssa had nothing left to lose. Everything she'd tried so hard to hang onto had fallen through her fingers like water. Like sand. She scrambled to catch it and lost all.

And if she lost all, what was left?

Not Important Elyssa. Not Bride Elyssa. Not Queen Elyssa.

Just herself.

Just Elyssa.

A small nugget of her past life dropped into her mouth. "Abandoning an employee in a foreign country at the termination of a job is a violation of labor laws in the United States."

Chastity Angel's eyes narrowed. "Tell me which scheme you talked Aya into, and I will consider informing a container ship of your location."

"Get it through your head! I *don't* know."

"You must."

"We talked about a lot of schemes, alright?"

"No, it is not alright. Her disappearance is your fault."

"Did it ever occur to you that maybe it's yours? Because you're always so horrible to her? And you never loved her as an adult or as a child?"

Chastity Angel froze.

How funny. She'd yelled at Chastity Angel before, but it felt amazing to actually shut the woman up and speak her mind.

"There are more important things than love," Chastity Angel hissed. "Like success. And being worth something. You wouldn't know either of those."

Elyssa wouldn't because she'd always been so busy trying to please people. Trying to be there for them. Trying.

Trying wasn't good enough.

Kadir knew. The other warriors knew. They saw some flashing light in her soul that said, "This is Elyssa, trying hard." They saw her caring too much. They saw her slip and fall.

So it was time to stop trying and show *herself* what she was capable of.

Chastity Angel was still waiting for her reaction. The

insults she flung had always crippled Elyssa before. But now, lines rimmed the woman's bitter lips. A lifetime of pinches and frowns. Makeup could only disguise it so far.

"You're right. I guess I can't help you. Good luck." She reached forward to turn off the connection.

"Wait. We're not done. You must tell me where Aya is."

"I can't tell you what I don't know. And don't you remember? I'm fired. I don't have to tell you a darned thing."

"You need me to return home."

"I'm not going home." She flexed her knuckles. They didn't crack because she was actually pretty flexible in her fingers, but she felt like Chastity Angel didn't know that. "Now that the Sea Opal contract is off the table, I have a few things I'd like to say to the guy who told me I didn't belong."

Such as that he didn't get to decide that. Kadir had claimed her and loved her. He wanted adjustment? Bossing a bunch of warriors around felt super easy after shutting up Chastity Angel with a single phrase.

"Goodbye, Auntie." Elyssa enjoyed the revulsion crossing Chastity Angel's face — she'd always hated that name — and tapped to close the conversation. The screen went black.

She rose and stretched. Her spine popped. This surface visit was done in record time. She might even be able to catch Kadir on the way back to Atlantis.

Elyssa turned to leave the dining area.

A twitchy, sallow-skinned man blocked the doorway. She started.

Wait. She knew that mean look. Brutal, like he wanted to cut her. They were no longer in the middle of a crowded company party, or on a yacht in Mexico surrounded by a paramilitary team, and he was no longer in the Mexican jail she had left him in.

Uh oh.

Lucy wasn't here to save her. Aya wasn't here to save her. Nobody was here to save her.

She swallowed. "Blake?"

"So, you do remember me."

She was hoping he didn't remember her. But it didn't look like she would escape. He blocked the only exit. His waistband sagged with the weight of a cold, black gun.

CHAPTER THIRTY-THREE

K adir rested just below the surface. He could still make out Elyssa's face, pale and sad, as she leaned over the side of the dinghy.

But if he reached out, he would only cause her agony. Again.

A motor started on the platform. The dinghy rose from the ocean and she disappeared from view.

She was gone.

His chest hiccuped.

He had taken the correct action. Kadir wheeled and slowly descended to the marine current back to Atlantis. He needed to rush as quickly as possible. The city might already be under attack. But he could barely make his fins kick. He was suddenly so tired.

Losing Elyssa will destroy your city.

Soren was right. But Kadir would rather destroy his city than hurt Elyssa. She mattered more. Another warrior could found a new city and become king. So long as she was safe and unharmed — so long as no white flowers were cast upon the water because of his unworthy wish to break the rules — so long as she remained safely on the shore and he in the water, he would sacrifice anything.

Even his deepest held dream.

So his city would be destroyed. His warriors would disperse. Their home cities would be glad to have them. Only he would swim the ocean, an eternal exile.

But even that was better than continuing to cause her pain.

I love you.

She had said that. It made his heart swell. But what had his love caused her?

Flinching. Crying. Begging. Desperation.

Every moment he prolonged her stay with him, he deepened the lacerations on her soul. Soon, she would be as scarred and cautious as Faier. It was good he had forced her to the surface...

But wait.

Faier had served Rusalka honorably. They had rewarded his faithfulness by declaring him unfit and denying him a bride.

Elyssa had cried over and over that she was trying. She wished to stay. *She loved him.*

By forcing her to the surface simply because he couldn't stand to see her hurt, hadn't Kadir treated her with the same grave dishonor?

Shock reverberated through him. He stopped in the current and treaded water.

He was a king, but he was also a warrior. A mer.

Elyssa had asked to stay with him. To join with him. To bear his young fry.

She loved him.

And that was why she could never be injured! Kadir fought with himself, kicking first deeper, then shallower once more. Taking her back to Atlantis in the middle of a battle could be deadly. She must remain on the surface where it was safe. Where he could find her again. Where she would be...

Be what? Treasured?

Leaving her on the surface was actually the easier path. Even though separating hurt him, it kept her safe. This was the cautious path Adviser Creo always wanted him to take. *Do not treat your bride roughly. Do not allow her to swim alone or love freely or make mistakes.*

Be a bride, Adviser Creole always said. Not a full queen.

But Kadir declared that he wanted Elyssa for his queen.

Didn't that mean he had to take her back to Atlantis? That he had to brave the raiders and face her fears and become strong enough for the both of them? And wasn't the one who was fearful, the one who had lost his faith, the one who needed to harden himself to endure pain actually Kadir?

The truth blazed through him like a bright, shining light.

Leaving Elyssa was the cowardly path.

This dull ache in his chest was much easier than the terror of turning back. Of accepting her into his heart. Of saying, "I love you also and will keep you with me no matter the pain or danger, to either of us, for the rest of our lives."

Could he not cross to that final shore?

He needed Elyssa. Atlantis needed their queen. The mer needed a modern bride who succeeded.

This was his final opportunity to save his city. He had to be strong enough, no matter the consequences, to cross to that shore.

He kicked to the surface. The dinghy was still lifted. He

swam around the platform until he found steps and climbed the rocking path to the deck.

There, inside a glassed room, a black-souled male threatened his Elyssa. His yellow teeth flashed. "So. You must have spent a lot of time thinking about me."

"Well, um, uh, not really."

He flashed cold, calculating rage. "You're about to."

Another shock stung Kadir. While he thought to leave her to the safety of the surface, a hidden enemy had sprung a trap.

The lesson was clear.

Kadir would never leave her alone again.

She pressed a small rectangle of fabric to cover her front. "I thought you were in a Mexican jail."

"I got out for good behavior." He pulled out a black weapon and began pacing. He was shaky and clearly unwell. "Your aunt wants me to ask about Aya. But I don't actually care where the ice witch is. Tell me where to find Atlantis's Life Tree and I'll let you live."

He had left the door open. Kadir edged closer. The glass was dark.

"You can't get to it even if you know," Elyssa argued.

"The submersible's ready." Blake waved his barrel at the ceiling. "You lead me to the city. I'll take care of the rest."

"Don't you want Sea Opals, Blake? Atlantis doesn't have any. They're all in Sireno."

He lowered the weapon to point at her. "You expect me to believe—"

Kadir leaped through the open door and slammed into the dark-souled male.

"Kadir!" Elyssa shrieked.

The male smashed to the ground. The gun bounced from his hands. He scrambled after it.

Kadir forced him onto his back and squeezed his throat. Under Kadir's mass, this male was skinny as a bundle of twigs bound with a cable. Fury peeled back Kadir's lips from his teeth. How dare this male threaten his Elyssa?

The dark-souled Blake popped an elbow at Kadir's nose. He had apparently seen a lot of scrapping in his life. It smashed into Kadir's throat like the base of a trident. He lost his breath and coughed. His grip on Blake slipped.

Blake rolled. He landed on the gun and pushed to his feet.

Kadir rose and faced off against the male. Fight honorably and destroy—

Elyssa shoved him out the open door. "Go! Now!"

He stumbled back.

She dropped her towel and ran across the exposed deck for the dinghy.

Kadir leaped after her.

Bang!

Zing!

A super-heated chunk of metal burned the tip of his ear. A projectile weapon. Kadir shifted to cover Elyssa's exposed back.

She scrambled into the dinghy

Bull shark fins cut the water below.

She vaulted over the side. Kadir jumped right behind her.

He would fight the sharks while she—

Bang!

A sharp fist pounded him in the shoulder. Pain splattered up and down his spine. Kadir roared.

They landed in the middle of the sharks.

Kadir transformed and flew ahead of her. Blood tainted the water metallic. It spilled from his shoulder.

The sharks bellowed. They swerved after Elyssa.

Curse it.

He turned.

She paddled in the water helplessly. Her heart ran away with itself. Her eyes were wide and white.

"Dive!" he yelled at Elyssa.

She paddled down. One shark swerved close. Elyssa shrieked. Bubbles flew past her cheeks and excited the sharks even more. She was holding her breath.

The sharks flew into a classic prey-driving frenzy.

Empty hands. His trident had been left. Where? Atlantis?

Elyssa exhaled and dove under Kadir.

A shark thumped him and swerved away. The bullet's pain lanced his back. He roared again.

Another shark dove at Kadir. Its big teeth bent inward. It bugled a challenge.

Kadir rolled to face it. His back spasmed.

The shark's jagged mouth loomed.

He fought the pain and exhaustion to brace for the shark's impact. The shark's nose slammed into his chest. He caught it at the two classic shark-wrestling hand-holds: nostril and below the first line of teeth. It shook its head. He released it. It darted away.

Three more dove at Kadir.

He braced and grabbed. He was in the mouth! No, he was fighting, holding its jaws open. Barely avoiding its teeth.

Another swerved at his torso.

He let go.

The two sharks attacked each other. Kadir wrestled with a third, fourth, fifth shark.

Elyssa wheeled. Her heart rate climbed again. She closed her eyes and held out her hands.

What was she doing? "Dive." He shoved the third one off and gouged its eye. It thrashed away from him. "Now!"

She twisted her lips in frustration but obeyed.

Wounded or not, he had the expertise to protect her.

The sharks peeled away for easier prey. He wrestled free of the last, persistent shark and joined her.

Kadir reached her. He gripped her face in his ripped up, bloodied hands. "Are you okay?"

"Thanks to you."

She was okay. Of course she was.

The pain spiked. He collapsed in her arms.

She entwined him as he had often done to her, holding him close and twirling in the water. He was so much larger, he towered over her. Her fin tips barely brushed his ankles. "You came back."

"I also love you."

Her chest rose with hope. "Really?"

"Yes."

Soft, golden light fell on him like the warmth of the sky's sunlight.

He had finally crossed that shore.

And then he collapsed with a spasm.

CHAPTER THIRTY-FOUR

E lyssa dragged Kadir's massive body through the current. It was hard. Solitary. And she had to keep adjusting him.

But it was also like a dream.

Ping. Ping. Ping.

He loved her. *He loved her.* The more she thought of it, the faster their journey went.

"Might...already be...too late," Kadir said, over the metallic pings emanating from the tracking bullet buried deep in his back. "Abandoned city...raiders...destroy everything."

"If it's all destroyed, my parents have a five-bedroom in the suburbs. You're all invited."

Kadir smiled. "Hold you...to that."

She kicked straight to the Life Tree. The whole journey, the bullet Blake had shot at them in his modified gun — which had lodged in Kadir's back — made a pinging noise. She thought that meant it was a tracking bullet, but Kadir was barely hanging on, and she was not going to stand around digging it out with her bare hands.

Soren met her at the border. The distant sound of metal striking metal echoed across the city, although she did not see its source. Some were already fighting but the main force hadn't revealed itself.

Soren wrestled Kadir from her arms despite her protests. "I carried him this far."

"And that is why he is nearly dead. Slow human."

"Well, sorry for that. I thought we went fairly fast."

Kadir roused himself. "Elyssa. Do not say that word."

Gah. Had she apologized again? Well...wait. No. "You know what? Forget that rule. I'm going to apologize. It's part of who I am. You're not going to stop me. And you can just accept that."

He smiled faintly. "You may apologize so long as you glow as you are now."

"And I will." Probably. She didn't know. "Let's get you healed."

Soren agreed. "We are moving quickly to the heart chamber, my king."

"Heart chamber?" She didn't want him that far away. "Don't you mean the Life Tree?"

"The healing chamber is in the heart," he growled.

"The Life Tree *is* his heart," she snapped back.

Kadir closed his eyes. "Obey your queen."

Soren snarled. "I obey no one! My king." Soren jerked him roughly through the water.

He grunted and winced. "Elyssa is gentle."

"See?" She outpaced Soren during the short swim.

"I should feed both of you to the cave guardian. Why do you cross the open ocean without guards? How are you injured *again?*"

Elyssa filled Soren in. The Life Tree glowed brightly, calling them into its embrace. Soren navigated the protective petals to the inner sanctuary and laid Kadir against the Life Tree. He nestled into the healing loam. The wounds on his back and hands looked bad.

Ping, ping, ping.

"What is that pinging noise?" Soren demanded.

"You hear it too?" Elyssa touched Kadir's shoulder blades. "I think it's the bullet."

"Balim is patrolling the outer regions. I will call him immediately."

"Hurry. Blake is piloting a submersible. I think he's using this bullet to track our location."

"The submersible is so loud, it would disguise any other enemy." He darkened. "Something is wrong about this attack."

"You didn't find the traitor?"

He shook his head. "One of the warriors heard someone speaking into the echo point, broadcasting dangerous news about our patrol patterns, but the traitor disappeared before he could be identified. Remain here, Queen Elyssa, and tend to your king."

His approval, after so long of thinking her unworthy, made her heart swell. "You believe in me."

"I believe in nothing," he snarled. "Guard Kadir. With your life!" He kicked out of the sanctuary, leaving them with Zoan and Adviser Creo.

Adviser Creo remained on the far side of the chamber. He rested his head in his hands and didn't acknowledge them at all.

Elyssa closed her eyes. *Concentrate. Summon the Life Tree to make a protective barrier.* She opened her eyes.

Nothing happened.

Well, Kadir's eyes cracked. "Why are you disappointed?"

"Lucy could do all sorts of magic." Form barriers. Protect warriors from speeding bullets. Make sonic energy blasts underwater. "I can't do anything but bring back a blossom."

He huffed and winced. "You have a strong push."

"Thanks." But pushing wouldn't win the war. "I need more."

He shook his head. "No."

What? "No?"

"No." He twined her fingers with his, keeping his injured chest stiff. "You are enough. Just as you are."

She was enough? Just as she was?

It was okay if she couldn't form energy barriers or make a shelter from speeding bullets. It was okay if she couldn't make an inspiring speech or persuade boards of directors to launch new programs. It was okay if she wasn't the smartest or strongest or most beautiful.

She was enough.

Elyssa could only bring a blossom back to life? That was useful right now. She spread her hands over Kadir's chest, closed her eyes, and concentrated.

He let out a relaxed sigh. Her hands glowed with warmth.

Growl-growl-growl.

A strange rumbling noise sounded on the far edge of the old city. Faint as a whisper, but out of place as an eruption.

Blake's submersible.

The distraction stole her concentration, and the warmth faded. Kadir opened his eyes and rose. He was still careful, but he moved more easily. He must feel a little bit better.

Good.

Zoan came to stand behind them. He held the long,

curved adamantium knife tight in his smooth, undamaged hands.

Smooth? Undamaged?

His hands had been all ripped up only a few hours — or was it days?— ago when he had fled with her to the ruins. Mermen certainly were fast healers when they had a need. Zoan almost looked like he'd never been injured. She wished she could figure out a way to heal Kadir so swiftly. Or Faier. He worried his deep scars all the time, but he'd told her his useless right leg was improving.

"Are we safe in here?" she asked Kadir.

He looked up at the granite-hard petals enclosing the Life Tree in its sanctuary. Soren had stationed guards to block the single entrance. "Yes. No enemy will penetrate these walls."

Outside, someone screamed.

Soren's war cry bellowed.

Elyssa and the adviser both jumped.

Other war cries returned his. Soren had been right. The raiders lurking beyond the city had awaited the submersible's arrival to attack. She reached for Kadir's hand.

He jolted. His hand flexed, jerking free of hers, and his eyes bugged.

The tip of the adamantium knife emerged from his chest.

Behind him, a man with darker peach tattoos and glowing, almost yellow, eyes spoke into his ear loud enough for Elyssa to hear. "No enemy will penetrate these walls because they are already here."

CHAPTER THIRTY-FIVE

Elyssa screamed.

Kadir clutched at the sharp point. He was frozen. Confusion drew together his brows.

The man they thought was Zoan was not.

"Roa!" Elyssa cried.

He cut his yellow gaze to Elyssa. "My brother talked about me?"

She backed away. "You were the whole reason he came here. He's been waiting for you all this time."

"Our reunion at the old ruin lacked warmth." He removed the knife and shoved Kadir forward.

Elyssa dove and caught Kadir's shoulders. His eyes and mouth bugged. He couldn't catch his breath.

"Probably it was because he did not want to give me this." Roa held up the twin seed. He grinned with sharp teeth, and he raised the bloodied adamantium blade to the seam. "Let us part this unnatural growth."

He sawed on the seed.

Kadir arched and fell forward, writhing with every cut.

Roa frowned and tapped the blade on the seed seam. "Tough little nut."

She rolled Kadir onto his back and placed her hands over the blood seeping out of the cut. She focused. Her hands warmed and his chest glowed. It worked! She was summoning the Life Tree's power and healing—

"Oh." Roa pointed his knife tip at Elyssa and waved it for her to remove her hands and rise. "I cannot have you doing that. Back. Up."

Adviser Creo hunched away. He knew what was happening. He deliberately chose not to look.

This was more than being a neutral third party.

"Help us," she cried. "Please!"

He curled his back.

"He cannot help you." Roa grinned wide and bounced at Elyssa. She scrambled away. "After all, he is the one who freed me from prison to come here and end this foolish city."

The adviser flinched. The accusation was true.

Roa focused on Elyssa. "Now, you move away from your king while I end his life."

"Kill me first!"

Roa tilted his head, considering her demand.

Then, he shrugged. "As you wish." He started for her.

Kadir grabbed his ankle.

Roa tripped and flew. The adamantium knife and seed went flying. Kadir rolled into his attack, grappling Roa with a snarl. Roa dug his nails into the bullet hole in Kadir's shoulder. Kadir screamed.

The Life Tree shuddered.

Elyssa flew for the knife.

Roa shoved Kadir aside and scooped the knife up first. He met her with the blade side raised. His dirty-gold, sunken eyes gleamed like Zoan's. But where that mer warrior teased, his twin brother had tilted into crazy.

She scrambled to stop.

Do not stop. Only change direction.

She kicked harder and angled up, popping over the top of the Life Tree. Roa chased her around the other side. She darted the opposite direction. Roa had endless energy coiled up from his long months in prison and his laugh sounded almost like an animal's scream.

The adviser walked on human feet across the dais and picked up the Life Tree twin seed.

"Help!" Elyssa cried.

Adviser Creo ignored her and carried the seed to Kadir. "How dare you show me a twin seed and then rule so recklessly you force me to destroy it?"

Kadir tried to crawl away from him. To help Elyssa somehow.

"I warned you over and over again. Treat your bride well. Treasure her. And then what is the last thing I hear? You will force her to give you five young fry." Adviser Creo stomped Kadir's bullet-injured shoulder. Kadir collapsed with a growl. Adviser Creo rolled him over and placed his foot on Kadir's neck, crushing him into place. "I had already decided this could not go on. That was when I knew I had no choice but to end you."

Roa flew over the Life Tree toward her. She dove and scrambled beneath it, keeping ahead of him. "Adviser Creo! Five kids was my idea!"

The adviser frowned deeply. "No. That is not possible. But it does not matter. Soon, you will also die."

Elyssa landed in front of the burly adviser, keeping him as another shield from Roa. "I thought you worried about brides!"

"It pains me." He looked much older as he regarded Kadir. "I once thought this city could be saved. Balim understands how dangerous your actions are. Iyen could become a disciplined leader. But they will not rise up and assume command. They have this strange loyalty."

"True loyalty," Kadir vibrated. The adviser crushed his throat but did not silence his chest-based voice. "Not neutral."

"They do not realize this city is dangerous. It will cause upstarts. And what if the other cities decide to implement your same strategies, and torture *their* brides? Better one dead now than thousands. Roa, to me."

Roa abandoned his chase and landed beside Adviser Creo.

What could Elyssa do?

"Kill him," Adviser Creo said.

"No!"

Roa raised the knife.

Elyssa shrieked the first thing that came into her head. "If you destroy this city, your brother could be injured."

Roa paused and tilted his head. "Injured? Or dead? You are right."

Thank goodness.

His eyes glowed. Twinkling with a strange light. "He did not rescue me from prison for all this time. He enjoyed himself here. He deserves to die." Roa started to bring down the knife.

Grinding sounds suddenly shook the sanctuary, unbalancing all of them. Elyssa and Adviser Creo fell on their backs. Roa fell forward, burying his blade in the dais without touching Kadir.

The granite ceiling cracked and broke into pieces.

A Buick-sized submersible smashed into the holy sanctuary.

The adviser darted out of the way. "What is this madness?" The seed fell from his hand. It rolled across the dais.

Dirt formed a thick, impenetrable cloud. The submersible engine grated, horrendous and teeth-on-edge annoying. The cloud settled. Inside the window, the pilot was the evil, pasty man. Blake.

Madness was right. He had come for Sea Opals.

The adviser looked for the seed and found it at the same time Elyssa did. He roared. "Roa!"

Roa left the knife buried in the dais and kicked. He was faster than her but she had moved first. They both converged on the seed.

She grabbed it.

He changed the angle and closed on her throat.

She evaded and screamed. The seed in her hand vibrated hard. The Life Tree flashed hot and bright like a strobe. Roa stopped and pressed a startled hand to his chest.

Above, the submersible's arm cleared debris. Whirring sounded as it dropped the pieces outside the sanctuary. Blake maneuvered the submersible in to grab another chunk.

Kadir crawled for the adamantium knife.

The adviser reached it first. He yanked the knife free of the dais and turned to Kadir.

Kadir rolled over, ready.

Adviser Creo raised his arm to bury the knife in Kadir's heart.

No.

Elyssa flew to attack the adviser.

Roa darted in front and backhanded her.

Bright lights flashed in her eyes. Pain burst hot in her brain. It felt like she'd slammed her face into the wall. Like all those times she slipped and hit her head.

She'd been training her whole life for this moment.

Roa kicked forward, so quick, his hands brushed her closed fist holding the seed.

She flew backward, kicking quickly even though the world wavered and she struggled to make sense of it. He gained on her. She kicked up, through the new opening in the ceiling.

The submersible claw arm pushed the last chunk away. The Life Tree was laid bare to its pincers.

Beyond Blake, the city erupted in a battlefield. Mer fought mer. Chaos, screaming, and blood filled the city. No help would come.

Roa grabbed her throat. It hurt. He shook her hard. "Give up. It is over. You are all dead."

A scuba diver kicked over the top of the submersible.

Elyssa would know that tall, slender, fearless shape in a dry suit anywhere.

Her scream vibrated deep in her chest. "Aya!"

Gigantic air tanks were strapped to her back. Bubbles erupted from a package on the back of the suit. Inside the tight, full-body neoprene, Aya was bundled up in a thick wool that just barely showed her features. She held a spear gun in one gloved hand and a large flashlight in the other.

The flashlight strangely flattened the glow of the Life Tree.

The submersible maneuvered behind her.

"Aya, watch out!"

Roa lifted Elyssa by the throat like a trophy. "Yes, watch out, human. Watch out as your loved one is crushed."

Aya took in the whole situation in an instant. She lowered the gun and pulled the trigger.

The spear flew across the short distance and buried deep into Roa's shoulder.

He screamed and released Elyssa, gripped the arrowhead, and yanked at it painfully. The barb would not come out. He fell back, along the outside of the sanctuary, struggling with the spear.

Only Aya would be a crack shot on the bottom of the ocean in the middle of a blinding battlefield.

Elyssa kicked down into the sanctuary. Aya dropped the used spear gun and paddled after her. Even with her plastic fins, she struggled to keep up.

Kadir scrambled in a life-and-death struggle for the knife. The adviser pummeled him in the bullet-hole and yanked the knife free. While Kadir writhed, he climbed onto Kadir's back, rendering him immobile. He lifted the knife over his head.

Elyssa grabbed the adviser's wrist with both hands.

He startled badly. "Do not touch another male, you filthy bride!"

She threw him off Kadir. He tumbled over and over, down the corridor toward the petaled entrance. Elyssa helped Kadir rise. Safe into his hands she thrust the twin seed.

They had all survived. Roa and the adviser fled. It was over.

The submersible engine whirred. The submersible flew forward and shoved Aya into the trunk. She jerked, pained, and tried to push free of the pincers. They closed down, crushing her to the tree.

The Life Tree screamed. It felt like a hand grabbing onto Elyssa's aorta and yanking.

Aya struggled.

The pincer crushed the Life Tree against Aya's tanks. They burst and crumpled. She clawed at her mask. Cracked glass filled with water.

Outside, visible behind the submersible, Soren roared. He shoved aside the warriors he was fighting and kicked toward the sanctuary. Invaders pinned him. He fought helplessly.

The submersible reversed. Branches separated from the Life Tree stem with a heart-squeezing rip. The submersible backed out of the sanctuary carrying the struggling Aya and the upper branches of the Life Tree in its metal grip.

Black poison raced down the remaining stump of the Life Tree.

Kadir collapsed. His face and chest turned a matching black. He clawed at his chest. His skin cracked into pieces, his body shattering like blackening glass.

He was dying. Right in front of her.

She had to do something. Anything.

He clawed at his throat as though an invisible hand squeezed him.

He was the Life Tree.

She grabbed the adamantium knife from the loam beside his spasming hand. *An injury causes the Life Tree to get poisoned. Only the knife can purify the wound.* She traced the blackness down the trunk, spreading like gangrene.

She sliced the upper half of the trunk completely off.

The adamantium knife sliced through the wood like slicing through a thick apple. The upper chunk dropped away. It turned into a blackened char.

Half a trunk remained. The blackness stopped spreading.

Okay. She had stopped the poison—

Kadir screamed.

It slammed into her like a second backhand. She bucked as the world turned red. Pain surged through her body as though it had overflowed Kadir's and seared down their connection. On his chest, blackness receded, but his eyes bulged. It was not natural. Every muscle in his body tightened.

"Don't give up." She tried to gather him in her arms. "Fight!"

He stopped shaking and exhaled. His body deflated and lay still. The twin seed rolled out of his lax hands and heat leached to cold.

She rubbed his skin, his body, his cheeks. It was too late. In mere moments, his body grew pale and bloodless.

Balim appeared at the edge of the shattered ceiling. Long scars marred his torso and his face was bloodied from battling. He vaulted the rubble and fell into the broken sanctuary.

"You have to save Kadir," Elyssa cried through clenched teeth and tears.

"I cannot."

"You're a doctor!"

"His injury is too much. His Life Tree is too damaged. They cannot survive."

"Try."

He curled up in a ball.

No one would help her. Kadir was dying. The Life Tree was nearly dead.

"Try!" she screamed.

"There is nothing to try." Balim rocked. "It is over. The dream of Atlantis is dead."

"No." She refused to hear it. "No!"

The Life Tree glowed low in the trunk. There was still life in the trunk, and still in Kadir also.

"His heart cannot survive. The shock is too great."

She had faced down Chastity Angel. She had gained the respect of Soren. She had yelled at the adviser and unmasked the hidden traitor.

All for nothing?

Then this wouldn't matter.

She plunged the adamantium knife directly into the Life Tree trunk, stabbing deep into *its* heart.

Kadir elevated from the loam. Pain wrung his body like a wet rag.

She removed the knife and pushed the twin seed deep into the purified hole.

Nothing happened.

"What are you *doing*?" Balim shouted. He tried to support the thrashing, red-faced, mouth-gaping Kadir.

"I'm feeding the seed into the Life Tree to strengthen it."

"It cannot grow. This is unheard of. Impossible."

"It's not impossible!" The trunk glowed again with her conviction.

"The seed casings are too hard to crack using ordinary force. You put them in without even trying."

"They will so grow!" She placed her palms on the trunk and willed it. Just like back on the platform, when she willed the flower back to life.

A lot of times, she had wanted something really hard and it had not come true. She'd failed the college placement test, she'd been left behind while Aya progressed, she'd been passed over for promotion. But that was okay. Those failures were nothing. She had saved up her good fortune to right now.

The Life Tree *would* regrow. Kadir would be saved. She was a queen.

Have faith.

The trunk of the Life Tree glowed impossible bright. Inside it, the seeds cracked. New life glowed brilliantly within its trunk. The light shone in her, and in Kadir. It glowed from their chests.

Balim stopped struggling. His eyes widened.

"New life for new life," she said.

Kadir's eyes opened.

"My king," Balim whispered. His own chest glowed. His expression opened with faith and tears. He turned to Elyssa, made the more-kiss salute, and bowed so low his face kissed the dais. "My queen."

Kadir rose.

The tracking bullet from his back fell out and landed on the dais among the ruined petals. His wounds closed and his body pushed out the foreign matter. Like the Life Tree sprouting before their eyes, he emerged with his full strength.

He turned to Elyssa and held out his arms.

She rushed into them and hugged him.

Their hearts beat in tandem. The pulsing glowed with the same rhythm in the new Life Tree, and in the chests of the returning warriors. Faith, identity, unity. They had fought to defend their city. They had refused betrayal and tainted power offered by the adviser, and instead, banded together in great harmony.

They had won.

She counted the number of missing. At what cost?

CHAPTER THIRTY-SIX

Kadir held Elyssa close.

She was his savior. She was his heart.

Their warriors gathered in the broken sanctuary. Those most injured were moved to the foot of the Life Tree. Faier limped to the dais; his one healthy fin was badly sliced. Iyen's face had been split nearly in two and would leave a terrible scar. Balim tended them.

The submersible was long gone. Aya had disappeared with it. Roa, the adviser, Tial, and Soren were all missing. Zoan had been recovered from the old ruins, tied up and beaten down.

His remaining warriors greeted the new Life Tree with awe.

The new Life Tree was a thin sprout growing directly out of the trunk of the old. Its bark was no longer only his silvery tint. The color had changed. Silver combined with a bubbly pink. Despite its small size, it was bright and sparkling. Fearless.

Just like his Elyssa.

The warriors looked to Kadir to explain.

He stood tall. "Today, because of treachery, the Life Tree died. And today, because of determination, the Life Tree was reborn. Because of Elyssa—"

"And everyone," she said.

"—and all of you," he confirmed. "We won today because of faith. Faith in our vision. Faith in our city. Faith in each other. So long as we keep this faith burning bright, Atlantis will withstand any attack. Someday, all will flock to our city. We are the future and the hope of our race."

Their worn faces lightened. Their backs straightened and they lifted their chins. Their injuries were still raw, but together, the pain could be endured.

Kadir linked hands with Elyssa. Together they wove through the injured crowd, pausing to speak with each warrior. They reached Faier.

He bent over his sliced fin and did not look up.

Kadir placed his hand on Faier's shoulder. "Ciran tells me you fought like two warriors in this battle. You defended Iyen after his injury and you saved Pelan's life."

He mumbled. "Does it matter?"

"Your injuries were honorably received. Atlantis is lucky to call you a citizen."

His head remained bowed.

"You will be included in all future selections for brides. No matter your injury."

"Does it matter?" He looked up. "What bride will join with a warrior like me?"

Deep slashes crisscrossed his face and gashed his chest and back. The wounds were horrendous. Much worse, even, than the wounds he had sustained defending Rusalka.

Faier's face crumpled. He looked away again. His fin leaked blood into the dais.

Elyssa's light burned even brighter in her chest. She

knelt before him and touched his elbow. "Many women, Faier."

He lifted his head.

"What women want is a kind, loving, determined male who would go to the limit to protect them. That's you all over. Maybe your face won't grace the cover of *Merman Weekly*, but from this angle, you kind of look like a rugged George Clooney."

He blinked. "What is that?"

"The sexiest man alive. For, like, twenty years in a row."

Faier frowned. "You are kind. That comparison is too incredible."

"Fine. Don't believe me." Elyssa rose and rejoined Kadir. "Kadir says you're going to the next bride event. You'll just have to see for yourself."

Her confidence made Faier think hard. He studied his injuries and stroked the clear parts of his mauve tattoos. He always strove to be considerate, fair, and thoughtful but he did not extend those qualities to himself. It made him an easy warrior to fight beside, but a difficult warrior who could not accept a well-earned honor. As Elyssa prophesized, only meeting the right woman would ease those fears.

Just as Elyssa had eased Kadir's.

Kadir tugged Elyssa to the next warrior, leaving Faier with his thoughts.

"Will he be okay?" she asked.

"Yes." Kadir nuzzled her. "His mind wars with his heart."

"I get that." Elyssa leaned against him. "My mind tells me to worry about Aya. But my heart says not to worry. I feel in my chest she's okay. Isn't it crazy?"

"You are steeped in resonance." He stroked her shoulder. "I also feel Soren and Tial. They are okay."

Elyssa tightened her lips. Her eyes reflected her concern. "I hope so."

A shout of welcome rose. Tial appeared at the crumbled wall of the sanctuary. His body was beaten and his hands were empty.

"Tial." Kadir met him at the piled rubble. "You are a welcome sight."

"You too." He was changed by the battle. His young face reflected an adult's confidence and determination. "Adviser Creo tricked me into the hands of my old city warriors. But, I fought them off." He touched his chest. "I feel rested for the first time since leaving Newas."

"That is a reward of your faith," Kadir said. "The Life Tree has filled us all with energy for our resonance."

Tial nodded. "Queen Elyssa, what is your will?"

"I am safe with Kadir." She stroked Kadir's chest. "You may do as you wish."

"I will patrol *my* city." Tial found Ciran and reported for orders.

"My king! My queen!" Zoan smiled through a split lip and double black eyes that forced him to squint. "A new shoot has grown."

"Good." Elyssa smiled at him kindly. "Feed it back into the stem for strength."

His mouth dropped in shock. "I did not say it was an ordinary shoot! This one has a bulb. It grows from the seafloor."

That meant a new castle was growing.

And he had deliberately misled them. Elyssa twisted her lips and wagged a finger at Zoan. "I'm watching you."

His eyes twinkled. He made the salute. His right hand bore new scars around the old, slowly healing shark bites.

Zoan was a resilient warrior. He had not fully processed

his brother's betrayal — and his brother had gotten away, it seemed — but he rebounded more easily than some.

"A new castle. Wow. It will be nice to have ours to be alone, I guess." Elyssa sighed.

"We will not have it for long."

"I don't understand."

"The Life Tree responds to our resonance," he reminded her, swinging her gently in his arms. "A warrior has claimed his bride."

"So ours will remain open to our warriors? Good. I like having a big, full castle." She smiled and relaxed. "I hope we meet the new couple soon."

He expanded her smile with a wondrous glow. This free, easy kiss between king and queen was the promise they had tried to achieve. This, here now.

Her deepening kiss spoke all.

Lotar and Gailen returned with Adviser Creo. He alone was dark-hearted and quivering, well aware of the amazing transformation of the resonant mer.

"You should not exist!" he shouted. "You treat your brides badly. Your city will cause a thousand deaths."

The two warriors threw him down roughly. Although they were angry, they had not otherwise mistreated him. Lotar controlled himself as always. Impulsive Gailen looked older, aged by the fight, and harder than before. Lost illusions hurt.

But disillusionment was necessary to fight for right. Kadir had also grown from trusting the wrong authority. Gailen had taken one step closer to his final warrior form.

"Adviser Creo. Rise."

The adviser gaped at Kadir. "You are still alive." He looked beyond him at the Life Tree. "Impossible. I saw it cut down. How can it be regrown?"

"From the twin seed you conveniently made available." Elyssa smiled with all her teeth. "You were the one who stole it off the Life Tree when no one was looking, weren't you? And then you wrapped it in seaweed and tricked Tial into putting it in my samples bag, thinking it was the conch shell. What would that have gained you? My giving away the twin seed to Van Cartier Cosmetics by accident?"

He sagged.

Kadir knew his answer. "Loss of faith."

She swung to him. "Faith?"

"Atlantis is not bound by tradition. Nor pointless rules. We are bound by trust. Loyalty. Faith in each other." He basked in the warm glow of her chest light. "Faith in our brides."

She met his kiss.

Adviser Creo started to shake. "Do not publicly display yourself in front of these desperate, single warriors! This clingy female is the reason you will—"

Lotar knocked the adviser in the back of the knees. Adviser Creo folded in half. Lotar slammed him into the Life Tree dais.

Everyone stared at Lotar in surprise. He fought sharks without blinking an eye, but he lost his temper after one insult?

"She is our queen." Fury inflected his voice. He raised to a roar. "You will honor Atlantis's queen!"

The others roared their agreement.

Elyssa glowed.

Kadir stroked her gently. She had worked hard to earn their loyalty. She deserved their recognition.

Lothar returned to his implacable position. His eyes flashed.

"Thank you," she said.

Lotar merely looked away and nodded.

The adviser rubbed the back of his leg cautiously. "Er, I see. This was a misunderstanding. I will judge Atlantis fairly and return my answer to the All-Council."

Elyssa looked at Kadir. Her skepticism said, *Oh, really?*

He squeezed her shoulders. Of course they shared this opinion without needing to speak it.

"Adviser Creo." Kadir released Elyssa and set his feet. He crossed his arms over his powerful chest and stared down at the male whose good opinion he had tried to earn, but had had to bite his lips together so many times to seal in the fury he gave himself a blister. "We have a Life Tree. We have a castle. *We repelled all threats.*"

He licked his lips. "So far, yes. But—"

"So far?"

Adviser Creo's gaze flicked to the new growth emerging from the freshly scarred stump. "Yes, I will include this in my report, of course."

"We have no need of your report. We have no need of the All-Council's approval. We will tell them so when we return you. We approve *ourselves.*"

The shimmer of rightness echoed in his words. The newly regrown Life Tree glowed and swelled with their agreement. They approved of themselves.

The adviser frowned. "But you do not have enough warriors."

"More will come.

"You will never be safe until you are approved by the All-Council."

"We are safe," Kadir corrected. "Because we possess a most powerful warrior."

"Soren is missing and—"

"Our queen."

Her pleased glow warmed his back. Ah, yes. He needed to speak these words frequently. Bright as she was now, she could become brighter and brighter.

The adviser stuttered. "But I have to remain here to advise you. I have to do this. It is my right."

Balim, Adviser Creo's formerly sympathetic ear, spoke aloud. "I think the other cities would be interested to know how 'helpful' the All-Council's adviser to us has been."

The others murmured agreement.

"It might cause them to think hard about accepting *any* advice from the All-Council in future."

His face blanked as he finally realized the harm of his scheming.

The city-destroying scheming of the "impartial" representative would cause a ripple in the other cities. Also, Atlantis possessed a super-weapon of old: a powerful, healing queen. What other city could claim that? And which one might remember old arguments and worry they might be the All-Council's next target?

Yes, Adviser Creo had done enough to damage the All-Council's reputation. The attacks against Atlantis might be over.

"Adviser Creo. Gailen and Balim will escort you to the safety of the next All-Council recognized city. They will take responsibility for conveying you back to the All-Council."

He relaxed and harrumphed. "You will regret this, Kadir."

Kadir smiled. The escort formed around him, hardened. He would receive no sympathy this trip.

"Regret is your own."

Elyssa swam forward to see her warriors off. "Thank

you for your service. I'm proud and grateful to work with you. Come back soon."

Balim frowned. His emotions rippled deeply beneath the surface. "Thank you, my queen."

A hint of Gailen's former carefree smile shone. "Take care of our city, my queen."

"You bet." She hugged them, startling both badly, and waved goodbye.

Kadir swam lazily behind her. "Where is my hug?"

She turned and ran her gaze up and down his body like a caress. "You're healthy for the first time in forever. I hope you're up for more than a hug."

Sudden heat pulsed in his veins. He drew her into his arms. Her mouth formed a sweet "o" of surprise. He hovered over those lips. "Yes."

"Sure?"

"I am yours." His kiss crushed her doubts. He focused on his heady, gorgeous, undefeatable female. "Lead me."

CHAPTER THIRTY-SEVEN

Elyssa led Kadir to the heart chamber.

His kicks were powerful and hard. Revitalized, he was tall, broad and thick. Muscle bulged on his arms.

The castle entrance was closed up tight from the attack. He placed his hand on the entrance and pushed her onto it, melting into her as their bodies melted into the green walls. Reacting to their presence, the castle defenses relaxed and opened up to allow them in.

Benji leaped from the entrance and raced around them, yapping crazily. She headed for the Life Tree and disappeared inside.

"Aw, don't tell me," Elyssa said.

"She searches for the seed," Kadir confirmed. His hands entwined hers. "Do not worry. Another will grow for her to guard soon."

"I feel bad."

"Do not." Kadir enticed her into the courtyard. His gaze held heated promises. "Your light is brightest when you play."

"Play? Well, there goes my plan of becoming a serious queen."

"Atlantis is a city of love. The Life Tree thrives on joy."

He finished his declaration at the heart chamber.

His sweetness made her heart tremble. No wonder he rallied warriors to him. Although he was not the largest or strongest like Soren, or the calmest or wisest or most experienced like Lotar or Balim or Faier, he spoke the words they most needed to hear. He spoke the words of their soul.

She was worthy. Not a serious, correct queen like the adviser expected. She was a playful queen who forgave mistakes and warmed people's hearts.

She stroked Kadir's hard abs, following the silver tattoos down his long torso. "I feel like I should tease you."

He pressed her against the wall of the castle. "Do as you wish."

His promise burned in his eyes. He loved her, truly loved her.

What did she wish?

Not just her pleasure. Sex. Wild, passionate, crazy hot. That's what she wished.

Elyssa wrapped her arms around the small of his back and pressed his hard length against her soft belly. She slid one thigh up his iron leg and nestled it against his flexed buttocks.

"We can play later." She claimed his mouth for her own. "We have five children to start working on."

He smiled against her insistent kiss. Pleasure rumbled in his chest. "Yes, my queen."

Heat fired in her veins and pulsed to her needy center. She stroked his back. Scarred, hard muscle.

He nibbled her lips. Yum. His flavor. Smoke and vanilla. This was the flavor of her king.

Of her husband.

He trailed tasty kisses down her jaw to her neck. She relaxed as his grip rested there. Controlling her. Commanding her. Her heart thumped. She yielded to him.

He palmed her breast. Pleasure ached for him. Her skin heated and her nipples pearled. He teased the pearl between his thumb and forefinger while his tongue laved her peak.

Her feminine center throbbed. Hot, slick, and ready.

She wrapped her leg around him. His long, hard shaft stroked her entrance.

"Come in."

He groaned. His palms lifted her butt. He bent and captured her nipples in his hot mouth.

Pleasure pulsed.

She tangled her fingers in his hair. "Kadir."

He lifted her thighs on his shoulders and bared her feminine pink to his mouth.

She tensed.

He nuzzled her, warm and soft. "You taste good."

She could never deny him. She relaxed into his expert mastery.

He stroked her with long laps of his tongue. It bathed her in shining golden rainbows. She floated against the ceiling. Or was it the floor? Everything was Kadir. He caressed her to the far edge of desire. She gripped his hair again. Even though the orgasm would be incredible, like the other times, she wanted more. Deeper.

To lose control.

"Come inside me."

He looked up at her. His smile slowly deepened. He kissed her mons and up her trembling belly. The fire of his desire spread over her body, teasing and marking her as his.

He moved her legs around his waist. His engorged head pressed like a hard promise against her throbbing bud. She moaned and shifted to take him. He gripped her buttocks, holding her in place with his bulging biceps. His cock teased her entrance.

"Kadir," she urged.

He slid deep into her slick channel.

Yes. Finally. They connected. Hot the way she wanted. Sweet and delicious.

She arched her back.

He pushed into her. Slippery pleasure throbbed in her center. He thrust. She clawed him. "Kadir!"

He pounded her pleasure zone. Unstoppable and beautiful. His masculine virility slammed into her. The tingles grew unstoppable. She clung onto his anchor. He slammed her over the edge, into the eye of the storm. Golden rainbows shattered across her body. The orgasm shimmered sparkles through her veins.

He roared and released his passion. His warmth filled her with a second wave of sweet pleasure.

She rested in his arms. He kissed her cheek softly. Were they floating right side up or upside down? Nothing mattered but being entwined together.

If she was ever going to become pregnant, this was a great start.

"Come to the surface with me." His dark eyes gleamed with silver flecks. "I want to show you the beach where my mother used to sunbathe and read. Will you?"

"I want to." She stroked his hair. "It won't hurt to remember?"

He gripped her shoulders. "No, Elyssa. Fear was my mistake. It almost cost me this. We must turn to each other for healing."

He was talking about way more than flesh wounds. She would make mistakes, and they might be serious, but if everyone banded together like today, they would win.

"I totally want to help," she said. "Let's go up together."

"Good. And we will visit your parents. I promised they would not be frightened."

"And then we'll come back," she said cautiously.

"Yes. We need you. Here, growing our city, and at the ruin, raising it so we can meet brides without any more intervention."

They needed her. He needed her. Atlantis was her future.

She was a playful queen.

The light in the heart room changed subtly.

"What was that?" she asked.

"Someone new has come." He disentangled and tended to her, kissing her roughened skin. "We must greet them."

She stretched her trembling muscles. Yum.

"I hope Aya and Soren come back soon." She bounced on her human feet. "I hope they escaped Blake and can each find love. I hope Faier finds love too. I hope every one of your warriors finds the woman of his dreams. I want everyone who comes to Atlantis to find the missing parts of their souls and make themselves whole."

"They will." Kadir's steady gaze filled her with confidence. "We will provide this place of dreams."

"Then let's do this." She could welcome strangers and treat them with kindness. Easy peasy. "I want to get started right now!"

"Of course." He held out his hand. "Come, my queen."

She took his hand. Her fins unfurled behind her. Together, they flew to the courtyard where she truly ruled.

Dear reader,

Thanks so much for reading. If you enjoyed this story, please leave a review on Amazon. Nothing helps an author more, and your fellow readers appreciate your honesty.

Would you like more mer shifter goodness? Join my newsletter and receive super secret bonus epilogues full of yummy mer warriors + the women who tame them. It's like the happy ending to the happy ending. What happens when Elyssa decides to host a very merman Thanksgiving? Find out in "Thanksgiving at Elyssa's House," exclusive for newsletter subscribers!

Starla's Newsletter: http://smarturl.it/StarlaNewsletter

See you next time!

Sincerely,

Starla

ABOUT THE AUTHOR

USA Today bestselling author Starla Night was born on a hot July at midnight. She hikes, scuba dives, and swims naked in the ocean. She writes about smokin' hot dragons and tattooed mermen at StarlaNight.com.

starlanight.com

Made in the USA
Middletown, DE
30 June 2020